Little Exiles

Robert Dinsdale lives in London and is working on his next novel.

Praise for *Little Exiles*:

'A superb novel' *Daily Mail*

'A heartbreaking story, very powerfully dramatised' *The Times*

'This is an utterly moving tale, sweeping and epic in scale . . . a story of hope' *Courier Mail*

'Contemporary fiction doesn't get much better than this . . . an exquisitely crafted must-read' *InDaily, Adelaide Independent News*

'Robert Dinsdale takes the raw facts and creates a clear-eyed story that is deeply moving' *Saturday Age*

'Compelling and unforgettable, this is a modern classic of endurance, resilience and recovery on the long journey home' *Good Reading*

'An epic, heartbreaking novel' *Weekend Post*

Little Exiles

ROBERT DINSDALE

THE BOROUGH PRESS

The Borough Press
An imprint of HarperCollins*Publishers*
77–85 Fulham Palace Road,
Hammersmith, London W6 8JB

www.harpercollins.co.uk

This paperback edition 2014
1

First published in Great Britain by
HarperCollins*Publishers* 2013

A catalogue record for this book is
available from the British Library

ISBN: 978 0 00 748171 2

This novel is entirely a work of fiction. The names, characters and incidents portrayed in it, while at times based on historical events, are the work of the author's imagination.

MIX
Paper from
responsible sources
FSC™ C007454
FSC
www.fsc.org

FSC™ is a non-profit international organisation established to promote the responsible management of the world's forests. Products carrying the FSC label are independently certified to assure consumers that they come from forests that are managed to meet the social, economic and ecological needs of present and future generations.

Find out more about HarperCollins and the environment at
www.harpercollins.co.uk/green

It is proposed that the Commonwealth seek out in Britain, by whatever means necessary, at least 17,000 children a year suitable and available for immediate migration to Australia.

Arthur Calwell,
Australian Minister for Immigration, 1949

BOOK ONE

THE CHILDREN'S CRUSADE

I

The boy standing vigil at the end of the lane, a Christmas lantern in his hand, still believes his father is coming home. Christmas, he has been taught, is a time of family, when errant sisters might come back to the fold, when black-sheep brothers might go carolling with the mothers they say they despise. He is eight years old, proud to be nearly nine, and he still recalls last Christmas, how he stood at the end of the lane, tracking every approaching motor car until the snow drifts climbed above his boots. It had taken his mother to prise him away. She had hoisted him up and hauled him back to the terrace, where his sisters were ready to welcome him with hot mulled wine – which was terrible to taste, but at least made him feel warm and fuzzy inside. He had gone to bed that night in squalls of tears, but risen the next morning to presents under the tree – a book he had pined for, *The Secret of Grey Walls*, a cap gun he had been told, time and again, not to expect – and it was not until the evening that he realized he had not thought of his vigil all through the day. This year, he has resolved, he will not be so cowardly. He has his cap gun tucked into his belt, he has brought mulled wine in a flask, and he has wrapped up warm. Christmas is a time of family and a time of miracles. The logic will not be denied.

It is 1948 and, though he has never once seen his father, he knows that he is coming home.

He was born in the middle month of winter in the year of 1940. He has twin sisters older than him by eleven years, and they are the ones who attended his birth, straining with his mother in the backroom of the terrace where they live. Of his earliest years, he remembers little. His mother kneads dough in a bakery before dawn and cleans houses in the afternoon, and it is his sisters he remembers making him breakfast and dressing him every morning. He grows up, quickly, between one end of the street and another. A shop mistress smiles when he enters her shop, secretly palming barley sugars into his hands. A neighbour invites him to play with her daughter in a backyard on the other side of the road. So lost is he in this world of women that it is not until he sees two brothers tumbling over one another further down the terrace that he discovers it is cowboys and Indians he longs to be playing, not with dolls' houses and ponies chipped out of wood.

At night, there are sirens. If the sirens sing before dusk, they hurry together to a shelter buried in the grounds of a house at the end of the terrace. Outside, the world quakes. Through a speak-hole sliding back and forth, the boy can see cascading oranges and reds, great reefs of smoke. He hears whispers of factories on fire and great barrage balloons strung through the skies.

If the sirens do not sing until after dark, they remain in their house, crammed into a cubbyhole beneath the stairs. Sometimes the building shakes. At first, the boy does not understand the fear – but, in the tomb under the stairs, terror is a disease that spreads quickly. One night, crammed into that cubbyhole, his mother begins to sob. The boy believes he can hear his own name in the tears: Jon, Jon, Jon, the word swallowed by the song of the siren.

He is five years old when he begins to ask about his father. It is 1946 and there are suddenly strange men in the streets, great companies of them descending on the taprooms and alehouses. Jon watches them from his window at the top of the terrace. He notices, for the first time, that his mother stands alone at the end of their lane each evening, watching these strange intruders march back from the ruins of warehouses and factories they are rebuilding. He wonders if she too is bewildered at the invasion of their city, but his sisters smile oddly when he dares to ask the question. They tell him she is waiting. Nothing more, and nothing less. She is waiting for their father to return.

They bring out photographs. A man with wild black hair glowering into the camera. A man with two young girls, one sitting on either knee. His name, they tell him, is Jonah, though he too is always known as Jon. It thrills the little boy to think that he, one day, might be like the man in the pictures.

At the back end of summer, a man in uniform arrives at the house next door, and the little girl with whom Jon is sometimes invited to play is introduced, for the first time, to her father. Jon watches as the man pauses, the little girl framed in the doorway, and crouches to urge her forward. At first she freezes, her mother looming behind. Then the man vaults the brick wall, scooping up the child and embracing her mother in one swift movement. In some of the other doorways along the redbrick row, other women have appeared to witness the reunion. One of them, Jon notes, begins to applaud.

There are stories to be learned. His father was a hero fighting a crusade on the other side of the world. His father was in the jungle teaching the natives to fly Spitfires. There are other stories as well – his father once worked at a lathe; his father was arrested in a backroom brawl – but these are not the tales with which the boy obsesses. Though the boy has never once met the man, he wants to grow up and be just like him, out in the world on grand adventures, with friends and family at home thrilling for news of his exploits.

He begs his mother every evening to tell some other tale of his father's derring-do. Sometimes he is swooped away by his sisters – but, sometimes, he is wily enough to trap his mother in the question. One night, after his sisters have put him to bed, his mother returns from an evening sweeping some factory floor. He waits for her to climb, wearily, to her bed – and then he pounces. He tells her he has had a nightmare, that he dreamed of his father lost, somewhere at sea, fending off sharks with the butt of a broken oar.

It is nonsense, she tells him. His father cannot swim; he would never have got himself into such trouble in the first place.

The boy does not notice, at first, when the stories stop being told. He supposes it may have been earlier than he first thought, for he was surely telling himself the stories as well, lining up his lead soldiers and imagining them his father's company, or building matchstick planes and putting his father in the cockpit. In his games, his father makes his way home from the jungles on the other side of the world, but is forever sidetracked by helpless villagers, or orphaned children searching for someone to protect them. Each time he goes to sleep he constructs a new fantasy, some other adventure his father cannot resist as, kingdom by kingdom, he picks his way back to English shores.

In a journal he writes stories about his father. At first, they are only short passages, idle thoughts: his father parachuting from a plane; his father in a coracle, tumbling helplessly over a wild waterfall. He is beginning to compose a longer story – his father crossing Siberia by sled with Nazis on his trail – when his mother discovers him at work, hidden under the bedcovers. He does not understand why she starts crying. She takes the journal away and forbids him from writing such stories ever again.

He is not permitted, any longer, to mention his father.

The winter of 1949 lingers long into the following year, but lasts longer still for Jon's mother. She is at home more and more often, lying in bed until hours after dawn, so that soon it is Jon's sisters who cook breakfast and scrub his laundry and take the ration books out to gather the week's groceries. On Christmas Day, she does not get out of bed at all. They open presents gathered around her bed, and bring a small tree into the room that Jon has decorated with stray strands of tinsel. Early in the New Year, he finds one of his sisters sobbing quietly to the other in the scullery. He listens at the door, but they are well versed in his ways and shoo him away.

Three nights later, Jon piles his few belongings – clothes and bedspread and a bundle of treasured books – into a suitcase and follows his sisters to a neighbour's house. He spends the night on the floor of the living room, where the deep rug before the fire is a more comfortable bed than he has ever known. He wonders, absently, why their mother has not joined them in the adventure, but is promised he will see her again soon.

Three nights later, his mother arrives on the doorstep and takes dinner with them: a broth made of onions, thickened with potato. She has brought hard bread from her bakery, but its appearance on the table causes deep and troubled sighs. His mother has stolen it, Jon understands – but a little theft does not damage its taste.

She comes intermittently after that. One Sunday, she strolls with him along the canal. Another time, she and his sisters go for a long walk – and only his sisters return. Easter comes, and she brings him a new book, wrapped in brown paper and tied up with string. He has been waiting for *Mystery at Witchend* longer than he remembers, and is so eager to sink into its pages that he does not realize, until it is already dark, that his mother stayed only a few minutes that day.

By the break of December in the year of 1950, he has not seen his mother in four long months. Christmas approaches quickly, and he is determined it will not be like the last. He makes plans to go to the old spot, to keep his customary vigil – but, just as he is preparing to leave, a familiar voice rises in the hallway below. Thundering down the stairs, he sees his mother standing in the door.

He does not run to her, though he knows it is what she expects. At the command of his sister, an adult now, he approaches gingerly.

His mother crouches and tells him that she loves him. He accepts the words, because he has always accepted them, has never for a second doubted she does not think of him as often as he thinks of her. She tells him to put his best coat on, to polish up his boots and gather together the books she knows he loves. At last, the boy understands: Christmas is a time of family and a time of miracles.

They are going back home.

Through the redbricks, piled high in frost and ice, he trails after his mother. They wander the old street, but they do not go back to the old house. They march on, instead, into thoroughfares Jon has never known, strange, foreign streets where black men stand out in the snow. They come to a broad thoroughfare from where he can see the lands beyond the edge of the city. There has been snow on the dales for many days now, and they loom luminescent in the night. A silvery moon hangs above, shipwrecked in banks of white cloud.

Between two houses, their windows boarded up, a lane drops

onto a street below. Thorn trees grow wild along the verge and, to Jon, it appears like the entrance to some fairytale forest.

His mother stops and crouches down so that his face is only inches from hers. Her eyes are shimmering. She produces an envelope and presses it into his hands. Do not read it, she implores. A smile flourishes and dies on her face. She knows how Jon loves to read – but the letter is not for him. He is only to pass it on.

She turns him to the alley flanked with trees. At its end, lights are burning in the windows of a sprawling redbrick pile. It will not be forever, she tells him. But there is no place for Jon with his sisters any longer. They have carried him where she alone could not, and they can take him no further. Yet, his mother will be well soon. She will have money, she will have a home, she may even have a man of her own. She brushes the hair out of his eyes, and turns him on the spot to usher him on his way. She will come for him before the new year is two months old – but, for now, he must float on alone.

Jon stands alone as his mother returns to the terrace. At moments his feet compel him to follow, but he is strong enough – defiant as he knows his father must have been – to remain rooted to the spot. Only when she is gone from sight, wreathed in a sudden flurry of snowflakes, does he fail. He fumbles after her for one step, and then another – and then he stops. It is not what she wants. It is not what his father would have wanted.

He turns to the trail, tucking the letter into his coat. He can see, now, that the redbrick pile is not one building but three, two houses hunching on the shoulders of a hall with a spire like a church. He walks, slowly, between two pillars of red brick. Then, down the ledges he goes, head held high so that none of the midnight creatures watching him from the trees might see that he is afraid.

In front of the tall spire there lies an open yard, where a motor car sits on blocks of stone and a single bicycle is propped against the wall. Washing lines criss-cross above him, beaded with snow. He advances slowly. The building looms, a fairytale castle made out of bricks and mortar.

Above the door, the legend reads, in cursive script, *Chapeltown Boys' Home of the Children's Crusade.* Beneath that, a shield is mounted on a tall cross, and emblazoned with words Jon has to squint to make out.

We fight for the paupers and not for the princes.
We fight for the orphaned, the lost and the lonely, the forgotten children of famine and war, the desperate ones who deserve a new world.

Jon barely has time to finish the final words when the doors on the other side of the yard open. Beyond them, he sees children – short and tall, young and younger still, more children than he has seen in his life – and, above them, wrapped in long robes, a man in black.

The man gestures to him. 'Jon Heather,' he intones, his voice old and feathery. 'We are so very glad that you have found us.'

II

'That little one's still in bed,' a voice, full of mirth, whispers.

'Might be he froze in the night.'

The first voice pauses, as if weighing the idea up. 'He'd have a better chance of not freezing if you gave him back his blanket.'

Once the voices have faded, Jon Heather opens his eyes. In truth, he has been awake since long before the morning bell, just the same as every last one of the mornings he has been here. At night, long after lights out, he forces himself to stay awake for as long as he is able, just so that they might not take his sheets, but even so, he wakes every morning to discover that his sleepiness has betrayed him, that he's been sucked under, that now he's shivering on a bare mattress with only the ceiling tiles to shelter him.

Once he is certain the dormitory is empty, he squirms back into yesterday's clothes – they are two sizes too big, hand-me-downs he was given once he had worn out the clothes in which his mother sent him – and ventures out of the room. If you are careful, you can walk the length of the landing without your head once peeping above the banister rail. It is a long passage, and overlooks a broad hall below. Along the row, there are other dormitories and, at the end, the cell where the returned soldier who leads them in games sleeps. Jon Heather steals past each doorway, mindful of other stragglers, like him, trying to avoid the stampede.

At the top of the stair, he stops. Here, the stairs cut a switch-back to the entrance hall below. Standing at the top, he gets a strange sense of things out of proportion, of the downstairs world drawing him in. He pauses, fingering the banister for balance. Through a gap between the rails, he can see the big double doors through which he first came, holding up his mother's letter like a petition. He has stood here every morning, waiting for her face to appear at the glass, or else for his sisters to come, raining their fists at the door and demanding his return. So far: stillness and silence, more terrifying than any of the dreams that have started to taunt him.

The hall below is stark, with a counter at the front like an old hotel. At the doors stand two of the men in black, conversing in low whispers. The elder is the man who first welcomed Jon to the Home. Wizened like some fairytale grandfather, he wears little hair upon his head. Beside him, another man listens attentively. Somehow, his skin is tanned by the sun, a stark contrast to the pallid men who shuffle around this place.

Jon wants to wait until they have passed before descending the stairs, but presently the elder man turns, sunken eyes falling on him.

'The bell,' he says, 'was more than fifteen minutes ago.'

Jon, wordless, shrinks back, even though he is a whole staircase away from the man.

'Breakfast. No exceptions.'

The men in black leave the hall along one of the passages leading deeper into the building. These are hallways along which the boys are forbidden to go, and all the more mysterious for that. At the bottom of the stair, Jon listens to their footfalls fade, and wonders how far the sprawling building goes.

Now, however, he is alone.

He can hear the dull chatter of boys in the breakfasting hall, which joins the entrance hall behind the counter, but something pulls him away, draws him towards the big double doors. The glass windows on either side are opaque, barnacled in ice, so that the world beyond is obscured. He stands, tracing the pattern of an icy crystal with his index finger, before his eyes fall upon the door handle. Then, suddenly, his hands are around it. At first, that is enough – just to hold on to the promise of going back out. Yet, when he finds the courage to turn the handle, he finds it jammed, locked, wood and steel and glass all conspiring against him.

Jon Heather pads into the middle of the entrance hall and turns a pointless pirouette.

Breakfast is the same every morning: milk and oats. Sometimes there is sugar, but today is not one of those days; there will be no more sugar until the boy who wet his bed and secretly changed his sheets is discovered and punished. By the time Jon Heather arrives, most of the boys are already done eating – and, because they are not allowed to leave the hall until the second bell sounds, they are now contriving games out of bowls and spoons. They sit at long tables, skidding bowls up and down, crying out the names of famous battles of which they have heard. One boy, who has not been quick enough in wolfing down his oats, has found his bowl upended and perched on top of his head like a military cap. The oats look like brain matter seeping down his cheeks.

'Just get it off your head, George, before one of them old bastards sees.'

'It's *hot* . . .' the fat boy trembles.

'More than mine was,' says the lanky, red-haired boy beside him, shoving his bowl away. 'Look,' he whispers, out of the corner of his mouth, 'you can eat up what's left of mine if you like. Just don't make *me* have to take that thing off your head for you.'

'I wish you would, Peter. It's getting in my hair.'

The lanky redhead groans. His head drops to the table for only an instant, before he sits bolt upright, swivels and helps the younger boy lift off his new helmet. 'I'm never going to hear the end of this from the other boys . . .'

'It's in my ears, isn't it?'

The older boy digs a finger in and produces a big clot of porridge. 'You want me to wipe your arse as well, Georgie boy?'

Jon Heather must walk the length of the breakfasting hall to get his porridge from the table at the front. When he gets there, all that is left are the congealed hunks at the bottom of the pan – but this is good enough; it's a tradition for each boy to hawk up phlegm into the pot as he takes his portion, and most likely it didn't sink this far. Besides, Jon isn't hungry. He carries a metal bowl back to a spot at the end of the table and pretends to eat.

Two months. He is only staying a short two months. His father has surely endured much worse, locked up in some jungle camp for years on end.

'You're *new*,' a boy, tall with close hair and sad, sloping eyes, begins, flinging himself onto a stool opposite Jon.

Jon does not know how to reply. 'I am,' he says – but then the second bell tolls, and he is spared the onset of another inquisition.

During the day, there are sometimes lessons. The men in black sit them down in the chantry, which squats on the furthest side of the entrance hall, and give them instructions in morals. Mostly, this means how to be good, but sometimes how to do bad so that good might prosper. This, the men in black explain, is a *difficult decision*, and to shy away from it would be the

Devil's work. When there are not lessons, the boys are left to their own devices. Often, the men in black disappear into the recesses of the Home, those strange uncharted corridors in which they study and live, leaving only a single man to prowl among them, making certain that the boys have made the best of their lessons and are growing into straight, moral young men. Today it is the sun-tanned man in black. Periodically, he appears in the doorway to summon a boy and take him through long lists of questions – What is your age? How long have you been here? Are you an *adventurous* sort, or a *studious* sort? – before propelling him back to his games.

Jon is hunched up in the corner of the assembly hall, listening to bigger boys batter a ball back and forth, when the sun-tanned man appears. He seems to be counting, with little nods of his head, eyes lingering on each boy in turn. Every so often, his face scrunches and he has to start again, as the gangs the boys have formed come apart, scatter, and then reform. In the middle of the shifting mass, Jon Heather sits with his knees tucked into his chin. Come night-time, at least there will be order; at least there will be a place allotted for each boy; at least the day will be over. Even if he has to sleep in the biting cold without his blanket again, listening to the whispers of the boys around him, watching the shadow of footfalls outside the dormitory door, it won't matter. Every nightmare is another night gone, and every night gone is another few hours closer to the morning when his mother will return.

The man in black's eyes seem to have fallen on another boy, the lanky redhead from breakfast, but something compels Jon to stand up. Dodging a rampaging bigger boy, he scurries to the doorway. At first, the sun-tanned man does not even notice the boy standing at his feet. Jon reaches up to tug on a sleeve. His fingers are just dancing at the hem of the cloth when the man looks down: violent blue eyes set in a leathery mask.

'I have a question,' Jon pronounces.

'A question?' The accent is strange, English put through a mangling press and ejected the other side.

'I want to call my father. He's coming to fetch me.'

The man in black nods, as if he has known it all along.

'I didn't know who to ask,' Jon ventures.

'I *see*,' the man says, placing an odd stress on the final word. 'And when was the last time you saw your father? Was it, perhaps, the night he brought you here?'

'My *mother* brought me here,' says Jon, exasperated at the man's stupidity.

'And your father?'

Jon Heather says, 'Well, I haven't once seen my father.'

The man gives a slow, thoughtful nod. He crouches, a hand on Jon's shoulder, but even now he is some inches taller and has to look down, along the line of a broad, crooked nose. 'Then it seems to me, you hardly have a father at all.'

At once, the man climbs back to his feet, barks out for the red-haired boy and turns to lead him along the corridor.

Alone in the doorway, Jon Heather watches.

'If you keep letting them take it, they'll carry on taking it,' the boy with red hair snipes. Tearing Jon's blanket from the hands of a bigger boy, he marches across the dormitory and flings it back onto Jon's crib. 'What, were you raised as a little girl or something? Just tell them no.'

'Thank you.'

'Yeah, merry Christmas,' the redhead replies.

Christmas Day has been and gone. This year, no card from his mother, no parcels wrapped in string with his sisters' names on them. All of this he can bear – but he cannot stand the thought that, this Christmas, he kept no vigil for his father's return.

It is the small of the afternoon and outside fresh snow is falling. Ice is keeping them imprisoned. Jon tried to hole up in the dormitory today, but with the grounds of the Home closed, clots of bigger boys lounge around their beds, working on ever more inventive ways to stave off their boredom – and Jon knows, already, what this might mean. If you tell tales to the men in black, they give you a lecture on the spirit. If you tell tales to the soldier at the end of the hall, he bustles you to a different room and, by the time you look back, he is gone. It is better, Jon decides, to stay away. A man, he tells himself, can endure anything at all, just so long as he has his mother and father and sisters to go back to.

He bundles up his blanket and tucks it under one arm. Then, with furtive looks over each shoulder, he bends down and produces a clothbound book that has been jammed beneath his mattress. He could read *We Didn't Mean to Go to Sea* a hundred times – he'll read it a hundred more, if it makes these two months pass more quickly.

'Where're you creeping off to?'

It is only the red-haired boy again, suddenly rearing from a bottom bunk where he has been tossing the rook from a game of chess back and forth. On his elbows, he heaves himself forward.

'I'm going to find a corner,' Jon says.

'Down in the chantry?'

Jon shrugs. The Home is still a labyrinth of tunnels and dead chambers, and he has not given a thought to where he might retreat. There are passages along which the boys know not to go, but mostly these lead only to barren rooms, boarded-up or piled high with the things past generations of boys have left behind. A brave expedition once found a box of tin soldiers here which they brought heroically back and refused to share – but not even those brave boys have dared to sneak in and spend the night in that deep otherworld. Bravery is one thing, they countenance, but foolishness is something else. At night, those rooms are stalked by the ghosts of children who died there.

'Maybe I'll go to the dead rooms,' Jon says, for want of something better to say.

'Well,' the red-haired boy goes on, allowing himself a smirk at this new boy's ridiculous pluck, 'you see George, you tell him I'm looking for him. I said I'd come looking, but I aren't ready yet. You tell him that.'

'Which one is George?'

'The chubby one. Got no right carrying fat like that in a place like this.'

The one who wore a cap of milk and oats at breakfast, Jon remembers. He sleeps in the bunk beside the red-haired boy and wakes early every morning to hang out his sheets to dry. On his first morning in the Home, Jon saw the red-haired boy shepherding him out of the dormitory and returning with crisp sheets stolen from the laundry downstairs.

'I'll tell him,' says Jon.

In the end, Jon does not dare follow the long passage from the entrance hall and venture into the boarded-up rooms. Instead, head down so that he does not catch the eye of a man in black scolding two boys for playing with a wooden bat, he slopes across and finds a small hollow behind the chantry, where old furniture is piled up and blankets gather dust. It is cold in here, but Jon huddles up to leaf through the pages of his storybook. So engrossed is he that he does not, at first, register the portly figure who uncurls from a nest of dustsheets.

Suddenly, eyes are upon him. When he looks up, the chubby boy is standing in front of him, holding out a crumpled blanket as if it is both sword and shield. He is shorter than Jon remembers, with hair shorn to the scalp but now growing back in unruly clumps. His lips are red and full, and the bottom one trembles.

'I just want to . . .'

Jon scrambles up. 'I'm sorry,' he begins. 'I didn't know anybody came here.'

The fat boy shrugs.

'You're George.'

The boy squints. He seems to be testing the name out, turning it over and again on his tongue. Then, head cocked to one side, he nods.

'There's a boy up there, said he was looking for you . . .'

At that, the boy seems to brighten. 'That's Peter,' he says. 'He said he'd come soon.'

Jon shuffles against the stack of chairs, as if to let the boy past.

'You don't mind if I stay? Just a little while?'

Jon shrugs, sinks back into his blanket.

'I come here before stories sometimes.'

Jon falls into his book, but he has barely turned a page before he hears the boy strangle a bleat. When he looks up, torn out of some countryside adventure – Jon has never seen the countryside, and marvels that people might live in villages on hills, climbing trees and boating on lakes – the boy is too slow to hide his tears. There is a lingering silence, and Jon returns to his tale: two boys are scrambling to moor a boat as fog wreathes over the Fens.

Again, the boy chokes back a sob. This time, Jon looks up quickly. Their eyes meet. The boy strangles another sob, and then rushes to mask the fact that he has been crying. For a second, his eyes are downcast; then, by increments, he edges a look closer at Jon.

At last, Jon understands. The boy *wants* his crying to be heard. 'What's the matter?'

The boy shrugs oddly, his round shoulders lifting almost to his ears. 'What's your name?'

Perhaps he only wants to talk – but, if that is so, Jon cannot understand why he is cowering in this cranny at all. 'I'm Jon.'

George gives a little nod. 'There was a Jon when old Mister Matthews brought me here. He was one of the bigger boys. He wasn't here for long.'

'He went home?'

George shakes his head fiercely. 'I think the men sent him somewhere else.'

Jon considers this silently. There might be no more than six or seven men in black roaming these halls, but somehow it feels as if they are everywhere all at once. They are quiet men who speak only rarely, unless it is to lead the boys in prayers or summon them to chores – yet when a boy has done something wrong, been tardy in making his bed or been caught whispering after lights out, they have a way about them, a gentle nod that they give. Then, a boy must go to a corner and wait to be dealt with. He might find himself running laps of the building, or locked in the laundry. The other boys say that he might find himself in one of the dead rooms with his trousers around his ankles and red welts blooming on his bare backside. One night, a boy was caught chattering after dark and taken from the dormitory, only to come back an hour later with the most terrible punishment of all. 'They're writing to my mother,' he said, 'to tell her I'm happy and don't want to go home . . .'

Surely, Jon decides, it is these men in black who are keeping him here. They have cast an enchantment on his mother, another on his sisters, and have raised up walls of ice around him.

'What's in your book?'

Jon inches across the floor, thick with dust, and holds the cover up so that George might see.

'Peter used to read stories to me when they put me here . . .'

'How long have you been here?'

'It was before the summer. There was snow in May!'

Jon is about to start spinning the familiar story so that this fat boy might hear it as well, when somewhere a bell begins to toll.

There comes a sudden flurry of feet. Jon crams the book under a stack of chairs. At his side, George is infected by the panic and, knees tucked into his chin, rolls up into a ball.

The footsteps grow louder. Then, a short sharp burst: somebody calling George's name.

'George,' the red-haired boy says, loping into the hollow with the air of an exasperated schoolteacher, 'there you are . . .'

George unfurls from his bundle, throwing a sheepish glance at Jon. 'I'm always here, Peter.'

The red-haired boy follows George's eyes. 'This one been pestering you, has he?'

Jon shakes his head.

'He's bound to pester someone, aren't you, George?' says Peter.

George eagerly agrees.

'How are you doing, kid?'

The fat boy shuffles his head from side to side.

'They told him about his mother last night. He told you about his mother?' asked Peter.

'My mother's coming back for me,' Jon begins. He does not know why, but he proclaims it proudly, as if it is an award he has striven for and finally earned.

'Yeah,' Peter says, slapping George's shoulder so that the little boy stumbles. 'That's what George here thought as well. But they called him into the office last night and told him she wasn't ever coming back. She's dead, George. Isn't that right?'

George nods glumly. It occurs to Jon that, though tears shimmer in his eyes, he is thrilled to hear it announced so plainly by Peter.

'Me,' says Peter, 'I been here longer than George, longer than lots of these boys. My mother's been cold in the ground for almost forever. My sister's with the Crusade too, but they shipped her off to a girls' home in Stockport, so it's not like I'm ever seeing that one again.' He exhales, as if none of it matters. 'So the one thing you got to understand, kid, is that whatever's coming up for you, it isn't Sunday roasts and trips to the seaside.'

In the hallways outside, the bells toll again.

'Come on,' says Peter, 'you don't want to know what happens to boys who skip their stupid vespers . . .' Peter scrambles past, out into the hall.

Momentarily, Jon and George remain, sharing shy glances. Then, Jon moves to follow.

George reaches forward and tugs at Jon's sleeve.

'She's really coming back, is she? Your mother?'

Jon does not mean to say it so, but suddenly he is full of spite. He whips his arm free. 'I'm not an orphan,' he says. 'I have a mother and a father, and they're both coming back. I don't care what Peter thinks – two months and I'll be gone . . .'

They push across the hall. The straggling boys are hurrying now, down the stairs from the dormitories above.

'That's how it was for Peter,' George begins, drying his eyes so vigorously that they become more swollen and red. 'But it's just like he always says. The childsnatcher doesn't come in the dead of night. He doesn't creep up those stairs and stash you in his bag.' They follow a passage and go together through the chantry doors, where the other boys are gathering. 'He's just a normal man, in a smart black suit – but once he calls you by your name, you never see your family again.'

In the doorway, Jon hesitates. The boys are gathered around, sitting in cross-legged rows, little ones and bigger boys both – and there, standing in the wings, are the men who run this Home: normal men, in smart black robes; childsnatchers, every last one.

December is cold, but January is colder still. It snows only rarely, but when it does the city is draped in white and the frosts keep it that way, as if under a magic spell of sleep.

It is only in those deep lulls between snowfalls that the boys are permitted into the grounds of the Home. It is Peter who is most eager to venture out. Jon himself is plagued by a relentless daydream in which the Home has been severed from the terraces beyond. In the dream, the enchanted whiteness goes on and on, and he begins to wonder how his mother – not nearly so brave as his father – might ever find the courage to cross the tundra and find him. George, too, takes some coaxing. He has not been beyond the doors of the Home in long months and stands on the threshold, squinting at the sky. Peter assures him it is not going to cave in, but it does not sway George. It is only when Peter admits defeat and bounds outside, leaving him alone, that George finds the courage to follow. Watching Peter disappear into that whiteness, it seems, is the more terrifying prospect.

Some of the boys build forts; others attempt an igloo that promptly caves in and entombs a little one so that his fellows have to dig him out. The returned soldier leads a game of wars, in which each gang of boys must defend a corner of the grounds – but the game is deemed too invigorating by the elderly man in black, and must be stopped. Even so, the boys continue in secret. George, swaddled up so that he looks like a big ball of yarn, sits in a deep fox-hole dug into the snow, dutifully rolling balls for Peter to hurl, while Jon – a sergeant-at-arms – sneaks a little pebble into each one, to make sure it has an extra kick. In this way, they are able to hold their corner of the grounds, up near the gates by the fairytale forest, against the onslaught of a much bigger army. Peter declares it the most glorious last stand since Rorke's Drift – but when Jon looks up to declare it better than Dunkirk, he sees that Peter is gone.

George is too busy rolling an extra big snowball, one they can spike with a dozen stones – Peter calls it the atom bomb – to see what Jon has seen, so Jon leaves him to his task and follows the trail of Peter's prints. He has not gone far. He stands at the gates of the Home, with the stone inscription, now a glistening tablet of ice, arcing above. Icicles dangle from the ornate metalwork of the gate, and in places a perfect pane of ice has grown up.

Peter is simply standing there, squinting through the gate at the long track beyond.

'Peter?'

Peter is still – but only for a moment. Then, he whips a look around and the expression on his face has changed. No longer does he look lost in thought; now he has a face ready for a challenge.

'Do you dare me to do it?'

Jon's eyes widen. 'Dare you to do what?'

Peter tips his chin at the metalwork. Where the two gates meet there is a great latch, around which scales of ice have built up, like the hide of a winter dragon.

'Go on, Jon Heather. Just tell me you dare it . . .'

Suddenly, the idea has taken hold of Jon as well. 'OK,' he says. 'I dare you!'

Peter finds a stone under the trees and, taking it in his fist, hammers over and over at the ice. When the first shards splinter off, neither Peter nor Jon can stop themselves from beaming. A big chunk crashes to the ground, spraying them both full in the face, and they laugh, long and loud. Now, at last, the lock is free.

Peter stands back to admire his handiwork. He shakes his hand, trying to work some feeling back into his fingers.

'Well,' Jon says, 'go on! *That* wasn't the dare . . .'

With aplomb, Peter drops the rock, flexes his fingers, and takes hold of the latch. He moves to lift it, but the latch is still stuck. Still, not to be dissuaded, he tries again, each time straining harder, each time falling back.

'You try,' says Peter. 'I can't get a grip . . .'

But Jon Heather simply stands still and stares – and when Peter, nursing a frozen hand, asks him why, Jon just raises a finger and points. Unseen until now, above and below the latch there stand black panels with big keyholes set in each. Though they too are coated in ice, it is not the winter, Jon sees, that is keeping the boys entombed.

Something draws him to look over his shoulder. From a window high in the Home, surely in one of the barren rooms, the ghostly image of a man in black peers out. He has, Jon understands, been watching them all along, safe in the knowledge that they cannot escape. 'Peter,' he says, 'we'd better get in.'

Before Peter can reply, a sudden cry goes up. When they look back, the little fox-hole around which they had been camping has been overrun. In the middle of a platoon of six- and seven-year olds, George sits dusted with the prints of a hundred snowballs, their atom bomb lying in pieces on his lap.

Jon sticks with them in those first weeks. When Peter is with them, the bigger boys in the dormitories leave them alone, and he and George are free to sit and push draughts across a chequered board, or make up epic games with the flaking lead soldiers that they find.

On the final day in January, they have ranged lead soldiers up in two confronting armies, when George asks about Jon's mother once again. Jon does not want to hear it today. He has been counting down the days, and knows now that he is beyond halfway in this curious banishment.

'Did she have short hair?' George asks. 'Or was it long?'

A ball arcs across the assembly hall, skittering through their tin soldiers to decimate Jon's army and leave George victorious. From the other side of the hall, the hue and cry of the bigger boys goes up. Jon reaches out to pass back their ball, George scrutinizing it like it is some fallen meteorite, but he is too late. Out of nowhere, Peter lopes between them and scoops it up.

'He asking you about your mother again, is he?' Peter drops the ball and kicks it high. One of the other boys snatches it from the air and a ruckus begins. 'George, I told you before. Don't you make it any worse for him than it already is.'

'I just want to know what she's like.'

'He shouldn't be thinking about his mother. You remember how much time you spent thinking, and look where that got you.'

One of the other boys launches himself at the ball and sends it looping towards Peter – but Jon scrambles from the floor and punches it out of the air. 'My mother's nearly here,' he begins. 'Less than four weeks.'

'Jon,' Peter says, waving the other boys away, 'I'm not saying it to be cruel.' He turns, chases the ball, and disappears through the hall doors.

Sinking back to the ground, Jon gathers together the tin soldiers and begins to prop them back into their ranks. He is determinedly lining them up when George reaches out to pluck up a fallen comrade and stand him next to Jon's captain. 'If she does come back,' he whispers, 'I'd like to see her, just for a second.'

The snows subside as February trudges by, and the boys are released into the grounds on more and more occasions, so that soon it is simple for Jon to find some cranny where he can curl up and while the day away. Now, there is an eerie stillness in the Home, only the guardian men in black ghosting wordlessly around, sometimes hovering to watch their boys at play. The sun-tanned man in black is the worst, forever appearing in a doorway to prey on a boy with his eyes and then nodding sagely if a boy returns his gaze, as if, somehow, a secret pact has been arranged.

George has pestered Jon this morning for more games of lead soldiers, but Jon has concocted a plan. Peter may think he knows everything; he may think that, because he has lived for years among the men in black, he can never be wrong – but Jon knows his mother is returning. What's more, he can prove it. He remembers the letter she pressed into his palm, that night she left him behind. In that letter, there is surely the proof that his rescue is imminent. He will find it and he will make Peter read every word – and, in only one week's time, he will wave goodbye to Peter and George and never think of this Home ever again.

He waits at the head of the stairs as the men in black hustle a group of boys out into the pale winter sun. When all is still, he creeps down the stairs. The entrance hall is the centre of the Home, the chantry on one side, the dormitories circling above – with all of the other offices where the men in black live and work snaking off behind. It is along these forbidden passages, in that labyrinth of boarded and dead rooms, that he knows he will find the irrefutable truth that will be his sword and shield, words scribbled onto paper with a signature underneath.

He is about to set off when one of the men in black appears from the chantry. It is the man with leather skin, tanned by a sun that has barely shone since Jon was left here. His hair is piled high, his eyes deep and blue, and for a second they fix on Jon. Then, a voice hellos him from deep inside the chantry, and he turns. Jon seizes the opportunity and scuttles away.

He has never walked along this corridor before. It drops down unevenly and, on each side, there are chambers. He peers into the first and sees a stark room, as austere as the dormitories above. In the next, a black cowl hangs against a bare brick wall, bulging out so that, for a second, Jon believes a man might be hanging inside.

At the end of the corridor, a tall door looms, its panels carved with branches and vines. The door is heavy, but not locked. Inside, the chamber broadens from a narrow opening and winter light streams in. There are no beds here, only ornate chairs around a varnished table, and a thick burgundy rug covering the floor. Jon dares to step forward, his bare feet sinking into the shag.

He looks up. He marvels. Two of the walls are lined in books, but on the third wall, facing the windows so that its picture might be seen from the grounds outside, there hangs a great tapestry.

It is unlike anything he has seen. On the left, there stands the broadside of a ship, moored at a jetty with sailors hanging from the rigging, gangplanks thrown out – and there, on the deck, a single man in black with his arms open wide. Beneath him, the jetty is crowded with children, a cacophony of arms and legs all groping out to reach the ship. Among them, more men in black stand. They are not shepherding the children on, but each has his head thrown back, as if to send up a howl like a lonely, vagrant wolf.

As Jon looks right, the tapestry changes, its scale lurching from big to small. The children gathered on the jetty become a thin procession standing in the narrow streets of some cobbled city. Maidens in long white robes lounge over the rails of balconies above, their eyes streaming as they rain shredded flowers onto the heads below.

Further along, the tapestry reaches a strange apex, a trick of perspectives that makes Jon think he is looking at some terrible picture of hell. The procession of children seems to have changed direction, so that now they walk not towards the pier but away, along a steep mountain road. Through crags they come, descending the ledges to a wilderness of sand and stone. Men with dark skin and cloths wrapped around their heads peer at the procession. One, with a sword in each hand, lifts his weapons as if to shield himself from their glow.

Voices rise on the other side of the door.

Jon turns, but it is already too late. The door handle twitches, and the great oak panels shudder forward. Quickly, he tumbles towards the far side of the room. Nestled in the towering bookshelves there sits a hearth, but no flames flicker behind the grate. He forces himself into the fireplace. It is thick with soot, but he tucks his knees into his chin and braces himself against the chimneybreast. Then, as the door finally opens, he claws out to pull a fireguard in place. It is made of thin mesh, and he squints through so that he might see the men in black appear. At first, they are obscured by the table and chairs – but, finally, they move into the great bay window.

The older man moves forward with a cane in one hand, the other walking behind. Jon cannot be certain, but then the face appears in profile: it is the sun-tanned man. He reaches out to bring the old man a seat, passing the fireguard as he does so.

Jon stifles a splutter; he has dislodged soot, and it billows around him.

'It will be the last season you see me,' the old man begins.

'Father . . .'

The old man raises a hand only halfway. 'I will not last another winter. An old man knows when his time has come.' He pauses. 'I am proud,' he whispers, 'to have seen it this far.'

They talk of all manner of things: the wars that have risen and fallen; the desperate families who have slipped through the cracks between the new world and the old. The old man remembers how it was the last time there was war, the great plagues that came afterwards like some punishment from on high. And now, he says, that hour has come again. A war might have ended, but the world has to limp lamely on. Across the country, the Homes of the Children's Crusade swell – and throughout Britain's once great Empire, the fields cry out for new hands.

'Father,' the sun-tanned man begins, glaring through the window at the endless white. 'What will happen once you are gone?'

'Why, the world will carry on turning.'

Something howls in the chimney, and instinctively Jon squirms. As he shifts, soot billows out of some depression and blots out everything else. His body convulses. He kicks out to brace himself against cold stone, but he cannot quite conquer the cough in his chest. When he splutters, his whole body pitches. The fireguard rattles in the hearth.

The voices stop. Jon gulps for air and slowly calms down – but there is no other nook in which to hide. He listens for the footfalls, sees the legs as they approach the fine mesh. He shrinks as the guard is lifted. The sun-tanned man crouches – and suddenly they are face to face.

'Come out here, little thing.'

The man reaches out his hand. For a second, he holds the

pose. Then, as if unable to refuse, Jon folds his own hand inside the massive palm.

In the shadow of the great tapestry, the sun-tanned man hauls Jon to his feet.

'Is he one of them?' he asks, dangling Jon by the arm so that the older man might see.

The elderly man nods.

'Very well,' says the sun-tanned man, and barrels Jon out of the room.

Behind Jon, a door slams. He reels against the wall and turns back just in time to hear a key turning in the lock. It is one of the cells he passed on his way to the library hall. There is little here but a bedstead with blankets folded underneath – and, high above, a single window glaring down. The branches of a skeletal willow tap at the glass.

He tries to sit, but he cannot stay still. He feels the urge to bury himself beneath one of the blankets, but he dares not unfold it. Instead, he parades the walls like a dog in its kennel.

There is scratching in the lock again, and the door judders open. The sun-tanned man does not say a word until the door is firmly closed behind him.

'Jon,' he begins. 'You are fortunate it is me. Some of my brothers take less kindly to little boys busying themselves in places they should not go.'

In response, there is only Jon's silence.

'This,' the man in black begins, reaching into his robe and producing a piece of folded paper. 'Is this what you came for?'

Jon totters forward and takes hold of the letter. Once it is in his hands, he snatches it close to his chest and holds it there.

'You may read it, Jon,' the man says softly. 'She told you not to – but what she says hardly means a thing anymore.'

Jon does not move. He knows what the man wants, knows that he desperately wants it too – but he will not tear open the letter while he is being watched. He holds the man's glare until he can bear it no more.

Once he is alone, he crawls onto the naked bed. He turns the letter in his hands. It is almost time to read it – but he will savour it first.

Hours pass. He dreams of what he might find within: his mother's sorrow at having to leave him behind, the dreams she has of the day he and his sisters will be reunited and the old house restored.

Darkness comes. It will be lights out in the dormitories above, but tonight there is moon enough to illuminate the cell.

He sits down and unfolds the paper.

It is not a letter, as he had thought. Instead, it is a form, typewritten with only two words inked in, and two more scrawled at its bottom: his name and his mother's, the last time he will ever see her hand.

I, being the father, mother, guardian, person having the actual custody of the child named JON HEATHER hereby declare that I authorize the Society known as the Children's Crusade and its Officers to exercise all the functions of guardians, including the power to house, home, command and castigate, and have carried out such medical and surgical treatment as may be considered necessary for the child's welfare; including, thereafter, the right to license guardianship of the child to a third party proven in its dedication to the moral upbringing of young women and men.

There are words here that Jon does not understand, but he reads them over and over, as if by doing so he might drum their meaning into his head. He dwells even longer over her name scribbled below. It seems that by declaring her name she has performed some magic of her own; she is no longer his mother. He puts the paper down, retreats to the opposite corner of the room, goes back to it an hour later – but it always means the same thing.

His mother is never coming back; he is a son of the Children's Crusade now.

The sun-tanned man's name is Judah Reed. He brings Jon milk and bread for supper, and they sit in the silence of the chantry as Jon eats. On the side of the plate is a single apple, waxy and old but still sweet.

'You have been selected,' Judah Reed begins, 'for a great adventure.' He sets down a book and turns to the first page: black and white photographs inked in with bright colours, a group of young boys beaming out from the veranda of some wooden structure.

'These boys,' he begins, turning the book so that Jon can see the happy faces, 'are the boys who once slept in the very same beds as you and your friends. Like you, they had no mothers, no fathers, no place to call their own.'

Jon bristles at the assertion, but his mother's signature is scored onto the backs of his eyes.

'They came to the Children's Crusade desperate and destitute, but they left it with hope in their hearts.'

Judah Reed turns the page. There, two boys sit in the back of a wagon drawn by horses, grinning wildly as they careen through fields tall with grain. Behind them, herds of strange creatures gather on the prairie.

'Where are they?' Jon breathes.

'They're safe,' Judah Reed continues, 'and together, and loved. They work hard, but they have full plates every night – and, one day, every last one of these boys will own his own farm and have a family all of his own.'

Jon fixes him with wide, open eyes.

'Have you heard of a land called Australia?'

In all the books Jon has seen, Australia is endless desert and kangaroos, convicts and cavemen. Of all the four corners of the world, it is the only place he has never imagined his father.

'Those boys are in Australia . . .'

Jon reaches out and turns the page. A postcard of some sprawling red continent, surrounded by azure waters, is clipped into place. Judah Reed offers it to Jon. In the corner of the picture, a small grey bear holds up a placard that cries out a welcome. A little Union Jack ripples in the corner.

'That's where you've come from, isn't it?' Jon says, eyes darting. 'You came to take us away . . .'

The man's fingers dance on Jon's shoulder. 'You must understand, Jon, that this is what your mother wanted for you. Little boys grow up into wild, troubled men on these streets – men who lurk in the factories by day and torment the taprooms at night. There could be no other future for a boy like yourself, if you were to remain.' For a fleeting second, Jon thinks he looks sad. 'It does not have to be that way, Jon. There is a better life waiting for you. Your mother gifted you to the Children's Crusade so that you might have just such a chance.'

The other boys, he goes on, have already been instructed. While Jon was locked away, they gathered in the chantry and heard the tale told. England groans with its dead – but its Empire is desperate for good souls to come and till its land, fish its lakes, conquer its wastelands. Australia is the Eden to which the orphaned boys of war are being summoned. It is not always that little boys, so full of malice and sin, are permitted back into the Garden. This is a chance, he explains, for Jon to begin again.

'You don't understand,' Jon trembles. 'I'm not supposed to be here.'

Judah Reed stands. 'If you had not been locked away, Jon Heather, for trespassing against the very same men whose only purpose is to rescue you, you might have learnt about the noble traditions of the Children's Crusade. How, many centuries ago, it was children who were called to do the Lord's work in the Holy Lands. And how their time has come again – how children, brave and unsullied, are to crusade to the other end of the earth, where the Empire will surely die without us . . .'

Jon does not care about the British Empire; he cares only about *his* empire – his mother, his sisters, red bricks and grey slates and the terrace rolling on and on. 'But I want to stay,' he ventures.

'You will find that the new world welcomes you,' says Judah Reed, striding to the chantry doors and stepping beyond. 'I'm afraid, Jon Heather, that the old world doesn't want you anymore.'

'Jon!' George tumbles out of bed as Jon steals back into the dormitory. 'Jon, where have you been?'

It is dark in the dormitory, but moonlight glides across the room as, somewhere above, snow clouds shift and come apart.

'Get back into bed, George.' Peter swings out of his bunk, biting back at some snipe from one of the bigger boys lounging above. He goes to George's side and, an arm around his shoulder, ushers him back to his cot.

'But I just want to . . .'

'Jon doesn't want to hear it,' Peter whispers. 'Not now.'

As Peter is tucking the sheets in around George, batting back his every question, Jon trudges the length of the dormitory and finds his own crib. It is just as he had expected: the blankets are gone and only the pillow remains.

'Jon, what did they say?'

Peter lopes out of the shadows, rests his foot on the base of Jon's bed. Sitting at its head, Jon realizes he is still kneading the postcard. It is creased now, and the ink has smeared his fingers.

He offers it up. When Peter takes it, he cannot make it out – but, nevertheless, he seems to know.

'They took us in the chantry and sat us down. They say it's

a paradise, waiting for boys like us, fresh fruit for breakfast and crystal lakes full of fish – that we'll all grow up to have big ranches and families and everything boys could ever want.' He pauses. 'Jon, there's something else, isn't there? What did Judah Reed say?'

From down the row, someone barks at them to shut up. Peter lets loose with a volley of his own, and the silence resumes.

'He said we were being rescued,' Jon begins. 'But – but I don't need to be rescued, Peter.'

Peter relaxes, sits beside Jon.

'I know what you're going to say, Peter. But I saw her letter. He made me read it. And . . .' He takes the pillow into his lap and beats it. 'There's still my father. It will all be OK when my father finally comes home. But if I'm not here, he'll never find me. I'm not like you, Peter. I'm not like George. I've got . . .' He trembles before saying it, but he says it all the same. '. . . people who love me.'

Peter stands. 'There's every one of us in here just like you,' he says. 'Every one of us had a mother and a father who didn't come back.' He turns, kicks along the row to find his bunk. 'We're the same in this hole,' he mutters, 'and we'll be the same on the other side of the world.'

Peter slopes back into the shadows, but Jon is not ready to let him go. Leaping up, he screws up the postcard and hurls it after the retreating silhouette. 'You want to go!' he thunders. 'You're happy to be going!'

The silhouette hunches its shoulders and turns around.

'Peter?' comes a voice.

'You go to sleep, George,' Peter whispers. He stalks back up to Jon, lands a heavy hand on his shoulder. 'You upset him over this, and I'll throw you overboard the first chance I get. I'm not happy, Jon, and I'm not sad. This place or some other place – it just doesn't matter to me anymore.' There is fight left in Jon, but suddenly he softens; his shoulders sink and he tries to squirm back. 'There isn't any escaping from it. We were marked for it the second we came through those doors.'

Jon curls up on his bare mattress and reaches into the slats for his beloved book. It is too dark to make out any of the words, but it doesn't matter – he knows it by heart. In the story, a gang of friends drift out to sea aboard the old *Goblin* and land, at last, on some foreign shore. There, among the alien faces, is the one they clamour for: their errant father, who takes them safely back home. Jon flicks quickly to those pages – as if, even in this darkness, he might breathe it in.

Something shudders at the end of his bed, and he reaches out to see a blanket suddenly lying there. On the other side of the dormitory, Peter slumps onto his bed and pulls an overcoat around him with a grunt.

'Thank you,' Jon whispers – but there is no reply.

Jon does not sleep that night. He lies awake, listening to the fitful snores of the other boys. In the small hours, he suddenly remembers the great brick arch through which he first entered the home, the stone inscription that was hanging overhead. At last, he understands what it means.

It is as the boys of the Home have always understood: the childsnatcher does not come in the dead of the night. He does not creep upon the stairs. He does not lurk beneath the bed, clutching a sack in which to stash all the little boys he carries away. He comes, instead, in a smart black suit, with a briefcase at his side and papers in his pocket. He crouches down and calls you by your name – and, once you take his hand in your own, you will never see England again.

III

They set out from a dock in Liverpool. It is as far from home as Jon has ever been, but now even this foreign city dwindles on the horizon, lost in mist from the sea.

They call it the HMS *Othello*. It has ploughed through countless wars, but now it is bound to a different journey. Below deck, the boys sleep three to a cabin. After the dormitory, it is a luxury to which none of the boys are accustomed.

After lights out on the first night, there comes a gentle rat-a-tat at the cabin door. Peter swings out of bed and whips the portal open. Still clinging to the cardboard suitcase they have each been issued with, there stands George.

'Can I sleep in here, Peter?'

There are three bunks in the cabin, Jon curled up in one, no doubt pretending to sleep; some other boy in the other. Peter shakes him until he stirs. 'Hop it, Harry,' he says. 'We need the bed.'

Muttering some incomprehensible complaint, the boy trudges out of the room.

As he goes, George creeps through the door and finds the bunk warm and inviting. 'Thanks Peter.'

'Don't thank me,' Peter says. 'Just go to sleep.'

There is only a moment's silence. Between them, Jon hears George begin to speak. Then, thinking better of it, he holds his tongue. Two more times he tries to be still, but it will not last long.

'What is it, George?'

'I didn't like the way the ship was moving. It feels like we could tip right over.'

Jon hears Peter's sharp intake of breath, decides Peter is about to admonish George, and scrambles upright in bed. 'I don't like it either . . .'

'You can hardly walk,' George goes on. 'One minute you're in the middle of the hall, the next you're up against the wall. Nothing looks right.'

Peter rolls over, drawing the bedsheets over his head.

'It's only Judah Reed can walk without stumbling,' George says. 'Why can Judah Reed walk like that, Peter?'

There comes another rat-a-tat at the door. George instinctively shrinks into his covers, while Jon dives back into bed. Only when he hears Peter pulling the door back does he open an eye to watch.

There are two boys standing in the doorway. The smaller, Harry, is still trailing his blanket; a taller boy looms above.

'We don't want this one in our bunk, Peter. Some of us want to sleep. There's enough little ones down the way, without throwing this one in with us.'

Peter throws a look back at George, now nothing but a bundle beneath the bedclothes.

'If we let you sleep in here, you'll sleep on the floor?'

Harry nods, eager as a dog waiting for its bone.

'You can take a pillow,' Peter adds. 'But it'll take Judah Reed to stop me pounding on you if you piss everywhere tonight.'

Peter slumps back into his bunk, rucking up his blankets to make up for his missing pillow, and snuffs the light. Moments later, George bleats out. At first, Peter thinks he is being a scaredy-cat yet again – but, when he tugs at the cord, he sees George sitting up in bed with wide, apologetic eyes.

'It's no good, Peter,' he says. 'Just the mention of it makes me want to . . .'

'What the hell,' Peter mutters. 'I wasn't going to sleep tonight anyway . . .'

Jon follows them out of the cabin, leaving the fourth boy to crawl, eagerly, into one of their beds. The corridor outside is narrow, lit by buzzing electric lanterns. The ship is a labyrinth, but Peter seems to know his way better than most. Jon and George trail after him like rats behind some piper.

They are not the only boys on board. There are others, boys in prim school uniforms – and, so the whisperers would have it, girls in smart pinafore dresses too. Nor are Judah Reed and the other men in black the only adults travelling south. Jon has already seen a group of swarthy men, speaking in some guttural language of their own.

Peter leads George up a small flight of wooden stairs, and fumbles with a clasp to kick open the portal above. When the doors fly open, sea spray whips at George's face.

'Isn't there another way, Peter?'

'I don't know, George . . .'

'I don't think I can go overboard, Peter.'

They venture up. There are still adults milling about the deck, keeping windward of the great hall that sits there.

Jon closes the trapdoor and, hand in hand, they scuttle towards the great hall. Creeping downwind of it, they search for the way in. The boys have never seen luxury like this: waiters are pushing trolleys, men with skin as dark as those who came to live in Leeds, while a chandelier dangles above. At last, they find an unlocked door and push inside. From here, Peter remembers the route. He leaves George at the toilet doors, and tells him to hurry.

'He'll only be at pissing again by the time we get back,' Peter whispers. 'That boy could not drink a drop for three days and still find water to piss.'

When George reappears, he is shaking. As they go back on the deck, the ship rises up on a deep wave and then rolls. Hanging lanterns throw light onto George's face, and Jon sees that he has been sick.

'Wipe it off,' says Peter, slapping him on the back. 'You'll get used to it.'

'I'm feeling it too,' says Jon.

'Yeah, well, don't you two go turning it into a competition . . .'

Peter pauses. He has been denying it to himself, but even he can feel a sickly stirring in the pit of his stomach. He looks up. The half-moon, beached there in white cloud, is the only thing that doesn't seem to be trembling in the whole wide world. 'You see that?' he says, putting an arm around George's shoulder. 'Even the moon's closer than Leeds is now. At least we can still see the moon.'

'It's the same moon, though, isn't it, Peter?' George marvels, as if he has uncovered some unfathomable secret. 'And the stars – they're the same stars?'

Peter turns and strides towards the edge of the ship. The starlight sparkles in the water, so that it seems there are silvery orbs bobbing just beneath the surface.

'I wouldn't swear on it,' he says.

The seas are rough that night. In his bunk, Jon cannot sleep. When he scrunches up his eyes, he can almost pretend that the cabin is not rolling with the waves – but then the lump starts forming in the back of his throat, and then he has to curl up like a baby to stop himself from throwing up. In the bed beside him, George has retched himself into uneasy unconsciousness while, beyond that, Peter gives a fitful snore.

Some time in the smallest hours, there comes a lull, as if the sea has flattened out to allow him some rest – but, cruelly, Jon is no longer tired. Careful not to tread on the younger boy Harry, he stands up and creeps to the door. As he steps out, the corridor pitches and lanterns throw long, dancing shadows on the wall.

The belly of the boat moans, long and mournful, but when the sound dies down, he can hear something else: another whimpering, not of the boat, but of a boy. Steadying himself with a palm against each wall, he shuffles along the corridor, until he finds a cabin door left ajar. With each wave, the door opens inches and then closes again, allowing Jon to peep within. In one bed, a bigger boy has his head buried under a pillow while, on another, a much younger boy, perhaps only four years old, has his sheets pulled up around him.

Jon curls his fingers around the edge of the door, stopping it from swinging, and suddenly the boy's eyes shoot at him.

'What happened?' Jon whispers.

The little one will not answer, but suddenly the bigger boy rears from his pillow and lets loose an exasperated groan. 'Get it to shut up, would you? It's keeping me up with its wailing . . .'

'Is he hurt?'

'Judah Reed came round,' the bigger boy says. 'Told him his mother's kicked it.'

Jon opens his mouth but does not have any words.

'Don't know why he's making such a fuss. He got a piece of cooking chocolate out of it. More than I got when they broke it to me. I got a pat on the head.'

The little boy lets out another cry but, when Jon goes to him, he only buries himself in his sheets.

Sitting on the end of his bed, Jon hears footsteps outside, and looks up to see Judah Reed himself standing in the open door.

'I believe this is not your cabin,' he says. The ship suddenly lifts, but in the passageway Judah Reed does not even stagger. 'Well?'

Jon nods, swings down, and makes to leave. In the doorway, he has to squeeze past Judah Reed himself. He smells of honey and charcoal soap.

'What happened to his mother?' Jon asks, remembering his own, the way she held his hands as she passed him the letter and took off up the road.

Judah Reed's blue eyes look immeasurably sad. 'I believe she was . . . *consumptive*,' he says, and steers Jon on his way.

In the morning, the waters have changed, reflecting the pale blue vaults overhead. Around them, the ocean glitters. There are landmasses on the horizon, hulks of earth gliding in and out of view. As Peter leads George and Jon onto the highest deck, they dare not look out at the vast oceans that stretch into the west, gathering instead at the port side of the ship and pointing out proud headlands and outcrops of rock.

Jon tells them about the boy from last night. He was not, it seems, the only one. Last night, Judah Reed stalked the passageways below deck, leading boys off to some office deep in the belly of the boat, palming a hunk of chocolate or toffee into their hands and telling them: your mother is dead; your father is gone; you're our little one now, and we won't do you wrong. It was, one of Peter's friends tells them, like a nursery rhyme, one they then had to repeat: *my mother is dead; my father is gone; I'm your little one now, and you won't do me wrong*.

In a launch at the stern of the ship, they find lifeboats, each stacked on top of the other. Finding a way into the first is simple enough – all they have to do is crawl under a lip of wood and work their way beneath a stretch of tarpaulin – but it does not feel the same as Jon thought it would. Sitting in the prow of the boat, with an oar latched either side, it does not feel like escape. He hears George approaching, crawling on hands and knees, and Peter following after, straining to contort his bigger body through the gap. He only has to look at George's face, breaking into a beam, to understand: like everything else that they share, this is just make-believe. He could spin a story of stealing this lifeboat and rowing back to England to find his sisters and wait again for his father, but that is all it would be – a fairy story to delight the fat boy.

'What is it, Jon?'

George is trying to pluck one of the oars from its clasps.

'Do you think Judah Reed's finished telling boys their mothers have died?' he asks, looking over George's head to where Peter crouches.

'I don't know . . .'

'Only, why did he tell them when they got on board? Why not back in the Home, like he did for George?'

Suddenly, George remembers. His hands stop prying at the oar, and he shoves them in his pockets. 'I didn't even get a hunk of chocolate.'

'He'd have come for me last night, wouldn't he, Peter?' Jon's voice rises helplessly. 'If she really was . . .'

He does not have to finish the words. Peter nods, but it does not convince.

'What happened to *your* mother, Peter?'

Now even Peter has his hands shoved in his pockets. 'You don't want to hear that silly old story,' he says, shuffling from foot to foot. 'Does he, George? He doesn't want to hear that dreary old thing.'

'I *like* your stories, Peter.'

Now they look expectantly at Peter, as if waiting for a bedtime tale.

'My sister, Rebekkah, she reckoned it was a broken heart. On account of the fact my father didn't come back. Dead in India, they said, but he wasn't even fighting. He was on a motorbike and it flipped. He used to ride one even before the war, and my mother always hated it. She said I went on it once, but I don't remember. Then there's a letter in the post and it says he was killed in action, but it wasn't really action and it wasn't really *killed*. It was just an accident, and my mother wasn't the same after that.'

'So she kicked the bucket!' chirps George.

Peter doesn't mind; he simply nods. 'Sometimes that's all it is, I suppose. There one day, gone the next. So Rebekkah and me, we tried to muddle through, but there was a neighbour who kept coming round with bits from her rations, and eventually she cottoned on. Rebekkah begged and begged, but it didn't work. They sent a man with a briefcase, and then we had to put some things in a bag. I thought we were going to be together, but they sent Rebekkah to a place for girls, somewhere called Stockport.' Peter pauses. He is hanging his head, so that Jon can barely make out his face. 'So then that's it. Children's Crusade and . . .'

'How long?' whispers Jon.

Peter shrugs, but it is a pretend shrug, as if there is something he wants to hide. 'I can't remember. Four years, I suppose . . . five months. A few days.' He hesitates. 'Nine days. You want the minutes and hours as well?'

There is a gentle pattering on the tarpaulin, rain beginning to fall across the ocean. Soon, outside, Jon hears the scampering of feet as people head for shelter.

'Peter,' says George. 'I feel sick again.'

'The ship's hardly moving, George.'

'It's not the ship. It's my insides. They're turning somersaults.'

When they emerge, the decks are almost empty, every man, boy and girl heading for their cabins. The rain now comes in sporadic bursts. Jon looks up. He wonders: was it a storm like this that waylaid my father? Is that why they really put me to sea? Or is it something worse?

'What if my mother didn't come for me because . . .' His voice trails off – for, along the length of the ship, towards the prow, he has seen the spindly black figure of Judah Reed, crouching above a collection of little ones.

Jon reaches out, as if to take Peter's hand. He does not know he is doing it until it is too late. Peter shakes him off, gives him a furrowed look.

'Come on,' says Jon.

If Judah Reed cannot catch him, he cannot tell him his mother has died. If it is true, Jon does not want to know. Quickly, he takes off, lifting the door back into the bowels of the boat.

Peter and George hurry after.

'Where are we going?' George puffs.

Jon Heather thinks: somewhere they can't find me.

Soon, in the depths of the ship, they are hopelessly lost. Peter demands that they stop as he paces a passageway, trying to get his bearings. Jon swears that he could find the way back to deck simply by listening to the creaking of the ship, but the doubt in his voice is all too plain, and suddenly George starts to blubber. A sharp slap on the back quells him, but after that he waddles nervously in Peter's wake, complaining of being hungry and thirsty and afraid of the dark.

'Can you be shipwrecked if the ship isn't wrecked, Peter? What if we get shipwrecked down here?'

'It's not shipwrecked if the ship isn't wrecked, George.'

'We could still starve. It's worse than a desert island, Peter. We couldn't even find a coconut to drink.'

At last, a staircase presents itself, and they emerge into a new passageway, where bright lights shine and a thick red carpet covers the wooden boards. There is a new smell here, of collecting dust and paraffin lamps, and the air feels dry. Jon follows the smell to the end of the passage, and pushes at the doors there, so that they open just a crack. Pressing his eye to the hole, he takes a deep breath and looks over his shoulder.

'What is it, Jon?'

Jon turns and pushes the doors apart. In the room beyond, the walls are lined with books. Tables are heaped high with newspapers bound in string. A dozen lamps line the walls, and big pipes run between the bookcases, radiating heat.

'You'll have read all these books, will you?' asks Peter, punching Jon on the shoulder.

Jon peers right and left. Surely there is no man alive who might have read every one of these books. They stretch from ceiling to floor, long shelves protruding from every wall to form alcoves in which a boy might hide away. Some of them are bound in leather with embossed titles: *The Natural Laws of Navigation*, *Colonies of the Cape*, and many more. Others are ragged storybooks with crumpled or missing covers.

Peter starts ferreting in a box, while George waits dumbly at the door.

'Here,' Peter says, tossing him a comic with the silhouette of an American detective on front. 'You liked this one when we were at the Home.'

'Are you going to read it to me, Peter?'

'Later. You look at the pictures for now.'

Beaming, Jon disappears into the shelves. The books are older here, with names he recognizes but cannot pronounce. There is a little reading area, where two ornate chairs face each other across a low table. Stretched out between them, there sits an enormous clothbound book. On the front, in golden letters, are the words *An Atlas of the World*.

Jon pores through the pictures. There are always maps of villages and dales in the storybooks he loves to read, but never before has he seen a map so vast. He sees oceans with names he has never heard, the shores of the Americas and Africa, the endless expanses of white at the fringes of the world. He traces the names of countries with the tip of his forefinger, but no matter how hard he searches he cannot find England. His eyes are drawn inexorably down, and he sees the scorched yellow mass that is Australia, sitting so lonely and remote.

He wraps his arms around the book and staggers to the entrance of the library. Peter is sitting cross-legged on the ground, surrounded by comics.

'I've never seen these ones,' Peter says, holding one up with a flourish. 'Dustbowl comics. They've come all the way from America, I shouldn't wonder. I'm keeping these.'

'You can't keep them!' George gasps.

'Some other boy'll just keep them if we don't, George. Don't be such a stickler.' Peter looks up. 'What've you got there, Jon boy?'

Jon flops down beside them. 'It's an atlas. Maps of the world . . .'

'They had a big thing like that at the first Home I was in. Showed everywhere that was British, with little Union Jacks all over.'

'Peter,' Jon wavers. 'I don't know where we are.'

'Well, we'll soon fix that.' Peter snatches the book and tears it open. 'How dumb can you be, Jon Heather? A few days out of England, and you're lost already!'

Peter peers down at the great map of the world in the centre of the book. His finger hangs delicately over Africa, then circles its way through the Middle East.

'There we are, Jon Heather. England!'

Jon cranes to look down Peter's finger. 'It's tiny,' he says, eyes flitting back to the sprawling mass of Australia.

George, too, crawls over to Peter's side, and peers at the world in his lap. 'Will we be together,' he says, 'on the other side? Everyone from the Home, back in the same place?'

When Peter looks up, Jon catches the look of unease in his eyes.

'What do you care?' he grins, fighting down whatever he has felt. 'You hate all those boys. They're rotten to you.'

George whispers, 'But I still want them to be there . . .'

Peter considers it. 'Yeah,' he scoffs, snapping the map shut, 'we'll be together, all right. All us boys of the Children's Crusade. It's going to be a grand adventure.'

Jon Heather spends long hours trying to judge by his atlas which shores they are passing, imagining in which of these strange lands his father might be lost. When the rains come, he hides again in the lifeboat, still clinging to his maps. Oftentimes, George crawls in after him, to listen to stories, or puzzle over why Peter always wants to sit with the girls from the girls' home, or else to just sit in silence, watching Jon read.

Today, however, Jon has been alone, with only his thoughts and maps to keep him company. When the rain has passed over, he wriggles back onto deck. There might be land on the horizon, or it might only be a trick of the light. He holds tight to the atlas and scuttles back below deck.

In the cabin, Peter is reading one of the dustbowl comics for the hundredth time. On the front, two horsemen stand in front of a rampaging wall of dust in which the title, *Black Chaparral*, is picked out in dirt. In the bunk beside him, George is twisted in the blankets, naked to the waist. His skin is red, as if some unseen birthmark has spilled over and spread.

Jon stops. 'George, what . . .' His voice trails off, unable to find the words to describe this horror.

Over the top of his comic-book, Peter glares. Only a second later, Jon knows why – for, suddenly, George's eyes scrunch tight, his lips part, and his face is flushed with waves of slobbery tears.

'Jon Heather, for someone who doesn't stop thinking, you

don't ever think!' He flings the comic down, rolls out of bed, and goes to give George a sharp slap on the back. 'What did I say, George?'

'There, there . . .' George replies, between mouthfuls of air.

'Not that part,' Peter interjects. 'What did I say's wrong?'

George looks up at Jon, with eyes ruddy and red. 'It's only a heat rash.'

'A heat rash?' Jon gasps. 'Peter, you can't possibly . . . Georgie boy, get out of bed.'

The fat boy's eyes flicker. It is as if he's been told to leap off a cliff, and is finding the idea strangely tempting. 'Peter says I should have my rest.'

'Come on!'

First, George must wait for Peter's permission. Peter, eyes drifting back to his comic, slumps back into his sheets, refusing to even look up – so, taking his cue, Jon marches over and takes a pudgy hand in his own. The redness is here too, staining the backs of his fingers in wild, webbed patterns.

It takes a few tugs to get George out of bed, but when he understands that Peter isn't going to rebuke him, he duly follows Jon out of the cabin. Turning away from the stairs that would take them to deck, they follow a labyrinth of passages.

'It has to be somewhere,' Jon says.

'What does?'

'He'll have a cabin, just like ours. Just like those dead halls in the Home . . .'

At last, Jon knows he is near. The cries of the children are faded now, and in a doorway left ajar he sees a desk, a pot of pencils, a little calfskin Bible. At the end of the passage, a door is propped open and there, at a chair inside, sits Judah Reed.

Jon does not dare cross the threshold, so instead he reaches out with his free hand and knocks, softly, at the door. When Judah Reed does not turn around, he knocks again. He means it only to be a little louder, but judges it badly; now, he is hammering at the door. The sound startles George, whose hand tenses in his own.

Still, Judah Reed does not turn around. Instead, he lifts a hand, one finger stiff to indicate they must be patient, and concludes whatever he is writing. Then, at last, he looks over his shoulder.

'Mr Reed,' Jon says. 'I need your help.'

'Very well,' says Judah Reed.

Jon moves to take George into the room, but quickly Judah Reed stands and strides towards them.

'How can I help, Jon?'

Bemused, Jon shuffles back, so that George is in full view. When even this does not do the trick, he steps behind and pokes George in the small of the back, driving him forward like a particularly truculent ass.

Judah Reed looks George up and down. 'Put him to bed,' he says, and promptly turns back to his study.

'But . . .' Jon bolts forward, making George clatter against the wall. 'Isn't there medicine? What about a doctor?'

Judah Reed's lips begin to curl. 'I can't take *that* to the ship's doctor. Be sensible.'

'He's . . .'

'Causing a bother?'

For the first time, Judah Reed crouches down. Now he looks George in the face, his golden jowls pock-marked, his blue eyes cold. He lifts a brown hand and, turning it over, presses it against George's brow. George shudders, wants to reel back. He felt that hand once before. The man had stroked his head, just as he was telling him the news: *she's dead, little one. I'm afraid your mother loved you very much, but now that's gone.*

'He's burning, isn't he?'

'Bring him back if he starts raving. We can't have another mess like last time.' Turning to go back into the cabin, he looks over his shoulder. 'I mean *raving*. Speaking in tongues.

Thrashing around. Until then, young man, you'll have to belt up. Your mother and father aren't here now, so you have to be a big boy.'

'My mother's dead!' George suddenly pipes up. 'You told me so yourself!'

'You see,' Judah Reed says, 'you're not really so sick after all.'

When they get back to their cabin, Peter is still sprawling on his bed. He has been lingering over the last page of his comic – though, Jon notes, he's now holding the thing upside down, as if he has had to quickly snatch it up and pretend he's been reading it all along.

'Well?' says Peter.

Jon doesn't utter a word, just ushers George back into bed.

'Told you so,' Peter goes on, snapping the comic shut. 'Never take a poorly kid to one of those men in black, Jon. They'd just as soon put you to sleep like any old street dog.'

Swaddled up in his sheets, George gives a startled look and buries his head under his pillow.

Now there is nothing but long days of empty ocean, a week when the wind fails to fly, another when no boy can sleep for the lurching of the ship and the nightmares it creates – of boys tossed overboard, starving to death in the bellies of whales.

Soon, the boys begin to linger below deck throughout the long days, for in the open they must gaze into the endless blue, unable now to distinguish between backwards and forwards, the old world and the new. It is worse, they say, than the endless days locked in the Home. At least, then, there were walls through which they wanted to break. Out here, there is only the ocean, stretching in all directions, absolute and indefinite. Once upon a time, they sat in the chantry and learnt that they were being sent to Australia, for sunshine, oranges, milk and honey – but nobody told them how far they would travel. Nobody dared to tell them that the world was so vast.

Peter crashes into the cabin, breathless but beaming.

'You two best gather your things up,' he begins.

'What is it, Peter?'

'It's land, George.'

They scramble onto deck. The word has spread quickly, and from every portal the passengers pour. They squabble their way to the highest sun-deck, but even there they have to fight to reach the balustrade.

Out there, the endless azure expanse is broken by a thin red line.

'I don't like it, Peter.'

'Tough, little friend. This is it. We got there in the end.'

They linger on the sun-deck throughout the day – and, although the red line hardly thickens, by dawn the next morning they can clearly see different contours in the land. The next morning, the sun rises somewhere beyond the continent, spilling vivid colours: bloody reds and yellows, vermilion light bleeding into the ocean.

Fists rain at the cabin door. When Judah Reed barges in, only Jon is there; Peter and George have long since been awake, watching the terrible continent growing in size.

'Come now,' Judah Reed intones. 'We're going ashore before dusk. You're to dress smartly. Nobody will let the new world down like they did the old.'

Judah Reed disappears. Moments later, Jon can hear his fists raining at other cabin doors along the corridor.

He pulls his cardboard suitcase out from underneath his bunk. In the suitcase there is a smart set of clothes, short trousers and a shirt, a necktie – so that every boy might look diligent as he enters the new world. There is even a pair of black shoes.

As Jon wriggles into these unusual garments, he pauses. He struggles with the necktie, though Peter has repeatedly shown him how, and finishes by cramming it into his pocket. Then, feet uncomfortable in new shoes, he finds his copy of *We Didn't Mean to Go to Sea*, wraps it in a bundle of his old clothes and forces it into the empty suitcase. As he leaves the cabin, he catches his reflection in a looking glass. His brown hair is longer than he has seen it before. Even his own mother would barely recognize him.

Out on the main deck, the parties are gathering. Jon can see the first boats rowing out. They fill the water between the *Othello* and the port. Against the redness, there sits a low, sprawling township, whitewashed walls sitting around a single stone tower.

A bigger boy paws his way through the crowd and claps an oversized hand onto Peter's shoulder. 'Judah Reed's looking for you,' he says.

At Peter's feet, George looks up like a startled rabbit.

Peter grapples through a group of schoolgirls to look down on the fore-deck below. Down there, Judah Reed stands before the elder boys of the Children's Crusade. Behind him, a contraption winches another boat level with the deck, and a seaman barks out orders.

Peter shrugs, hoists George to his feet. 'Time's up, little fellow. We're shipping out.'

George is reluctantly rising when the bigger boy doffs him on the shoulder and presses him back down. 'Not you,' he says. 'It's only bigger boys in the first run.'

Peter looks back over the rail. As if drawn to him, Judah Reed looks up and makes a single commanding wave.

Peter turns to Jon. 'How old are you?' he asks.

'I'm ten,' Jon begins.

Peter kicks George until he gets his attention. 'You heard that, George? You tell them you're ten too.'

Peter begins to stride away, but Jon hurries after. 'Peter,' he says. 'You're going to be there, aren't you? When we get to the harbour . . .'

Peter shakes Jon away. 'How in hell do you think I'd know?' he snaps. 'You make sure he tells them he's ten, Jon Heather. And you look after the sorry little bastard if they're about to split us up. Promise it, Jon.'

Jon nods. 'OK,' he says, 'I promise.'

From the balcony, Jon watches the bigger boys being shepherded onto the boat. Slowly, they are winched out of sight. Moments later, the boats emerge from the shadow of the *Othello*. From on high, Jon fancies he can see Peter sitting in the prow of the boat, heroic as some proud Viking figurehead.

He does not notice at first, but suddenly George is standing beside him, his arms wrapped around two cardboard suitcases. 'Peter left his behind,' he whispers, clinging tightly to the second case.

They set it down and open it up. Inside, there are no old clothes, no trinkets carried over from the old world. There is only a single sheet of paper, torn raggedly out of some book. It is a page from one of the atlases, the empty continent with every city and river marked upon it. In the west, somewhere south of a little town named Dongara, Peter has scrawled a giant cross – but this is no treasure map for pirates.

'We'll give it to him on shore, won't we, Jon?'

Jon folds up the paper and stashes it in the pocket of his stiff jacket. 'I think he meant it for us, Georgie boy. So we can find our way back.'

A call goes up from the fore-deck, Judah Reed hollering out for the other boys of the Children's Crusade.

'All the way back, Jon?'

Jon nods. 'All the way home, George.' He looks at the sky. 'One day . . .'

IV

They are the last of the Crusade to go ashore, gathered around Judah Reed with the sea spraying wild about them.

On shore, Judah Reed manhandles each boy onto the jetty. They march along the pier, into wooden outhouses where other boys are already lined up. When Jon and George join the procession, there is no sign of Peter or the bigger boys with whom he sailed.

'You remember what he said,' Jon whispers. 'You're ten years old.'

'I'm eight.'

'You're ten,' Jon insists, 'and don't forget it . . .'

There are other men in black here. They greet Judah Reed at the head of the procession and meander up and down the column of boys. To some, they whisper hellos; to others, nothing but an indifferent glance. Behind them, there stands a trio of ladies older still.

The boy in front of Jon trembles. Jon recognizes the gesture well enough. A little ripple runs through his body, and then he begins to cry.

The boy is practised at disguising it – a life spent in the dormitories of the Children's Crusade is good for something – but he will not disguise it forever. Jon wonders what Peter would do, reaches forward and jabs the boy in the ribs.

'You ought to stop that,' Jon whispers.

'I don't know where on earth we are.'

At the front of the outhouse, the boys are being confronted by the women. One by one, they announce their names, and one by one they are led through doors, away from the coast and the disappearing *Othello*.

Jon cranes to look out of the outhouse windows. On tip-toes, he can just see the column of boys walking across a red dirt yard to a motorbus sitting beyond. The bus is yellow, like those that once patrolled the fiery streets of Leeds, and its driver lounges against the side. Some of the bigger boys are already on board.

'George,' he whispers. 'I think it's Peter . . .'

George bounds up, springing awkwardly to try and see. 'Where are they taking him?'

Before Jon can answer, one of the women is looming above them. He looks up, shuffles quickly back into place. The woman has a shrewd eye on him – but she seems willing to let the misdemeanour go. She takes a step back, so that she can consider George.

'What is your name, little one?' Her voice is throaty, the accent an English one that Jon has only ever heard on the wireless.

'He's called George,' Jon interjects.

She goes on. 'I would like to hear it from him.'

George tries to look at the woman, but instead he looks back at Jon. Jon's eyes flare. It is an unspoken command, the kind Peter might make, but George is silent still.

'I'm Jon!' Jon announces. 'Jon Heather . . .'

The woman breaks from George and ponders it casually. 'There was a Jon at the start of this row,' she begins. 'Jack is short for Jon, is it not?' She seems pleased with this deduction. 'Yes,' she goes on, 'I believe Jack would suit. How old are you?'

Jon answers almost before the question is finished. The word seems to have a magical effect on George, for suddenly he spins around.

'I'm ten too,' he pipes up.

'Very well,' the woman replies. 'Across the yard and bear left. Each boy must follow the boy in front.'

Jon ushers George forward. In front of them, the hall is already emptying. At the threshold, framed against red dirt, Judah Reed stands watchfully. The sky, once a rolling blue expanse, is paling as evening approaches.

Side by side, they step out. The boys ahead are banking left, away from the yellow motorbus. There is a sweet smell in the air, and birdsong in the branches of trees Jon has never before seen.

The engine of the motorbus fires, chokes out exhaust and draws away.

George freezes, eyes drawn after the bus. 'Are we going the same way?'

Jon pushes him on. Along the verge of the dirt track there sits a collection of other vehicles. A ramshackle wagon already has a gang of six boys piled into its open back, with a single dog standing proudly among them. Dark and sandy, with deep drooling jaws, it is not like any of the mongrel street dogs of Leeds. Behind that, another utility truck is being loaded.

'Stop that dallying, you pair of scuttlers!' a gruff voice bawls out. 'It's getting dark already . . .'

A burly man shoos them towards the rear wagon like a dog might herd sheep. George is the first to run. Jon holds his ground only momentarily longer, George's hand suddenly pressed into his own. Settling in the wagon, they are greeted by the snout of the sandy dog and silent hellos from the boys already on board.

'Here,' one of them finally begins, 'take this.' His fist is bunched around a small green apple, which he tosses to Jon. Jon takes a bite; the fruit is sour, and he passes it to George.

'See,' the boy says, 'we've reached the Promised Land.'

The wagon engine begins to hum. A final trio of boys push their way aboard, bustling others out of the way as they scrap for a seat.

'You'll have to do better than that, boys,' Judah Reed declares. Jon turns to see him striding out of the outhouse. His black robe billows behind him – but, for the first time, he is wearing heavy brown boots that reach almost to his knees. 'You wouldn't want to be walking all the way on those sea legs, would you?'

Judah Reed strides to the back of the wagon, plants one leg firmly on the platform and lifts his hands as if he is miming pushing at a wall. The boys try and make room, but there is little to be found. In the end, they pile on top of one another, like cattle in a truck ready for the abattoir. Judah Reed climbs aboard, drawing the gate shut behind him. On his haunches, he hammers a closed fist against the bumper and the wagon kicks into gear. At first it sluices on the uneven ground, but soon the driver has hit the road.

'Boys to be farmers,' he begins. Somewhere behind them, a cheer goes up. 'And girls to be farmers' wives,' he beams, looking back at Jon. 'Son, this is the beginning of something for you and your sorry sort.' The wagon leaves the last of the houses beyond, and as far as Jon can see there is only red earth and scrub. In the fading west, he can still hear the shrieking of seabirds. 'This earth will give up its bounty to you, if only you leave that old world behind. But let even a scrap of those streets stay in you, and it will eat you alive . . .'

Judah Reed spreads his arms wide, as if he might embrace every boy on board. 'Boys,' he says. 'Welcome home.'

It is difficult to judge distance, without houses and snickets to guide the way. To Jon, it is almost as if they are back at sea, sailing across an ocean of scrub. Some distance out of town, the wagons turn from the highway and branch away from the ocean – and, so Jon believes, away from England itself. The scrub thins, until they sail above pastures of sand where only outcrops of coarse grass grow. Soon the roads grow rutted and worn, until there is hardly any road there at all.

On occasion, one boy whispers something to another. They point out distant rises of red, a strange creature flattened by a tyre, a single tree, capped with a bulbous crown of thorns.

'Jon . . .' George whispers. He ferrets in Jon's pocket until his fingers find the map Peter left for them. He wants to draw it out, but Jon clenches George's wrist as tightly as he can.

'But how will we find our way back?'

Jon looks back along the trail. The other wagons are still rattling behind, but other than that there is no mark by which he might know if they are in one place or another.

'Peter will know . . .'

The road starts to slope, and they sail into what appears to be a shallow canyon. The scrub grows thicker again, nourished by cool shadows, and they see birds for the first time since the coast: chattering yellow parakeets, of the kind wealthy boys might once have been given as pets. Deeper into the canyon, they see a waterhole between two hummocks of land. Other birds flap in the shallows, scattering when the wagon rattles through.

They rise out of the canyon, and below them the scrub rolls on. High above, they can see the violet night on the eastern horizon. And, if ever there was a sign that they are no longer on the same earth, here it is: it is not night and it is not day and yet, up in the sky, the sun and moon hang together, two great orbs beached above reefs of cloud.

'George,' he whispers. 'George!'

His head jolts, and he follows Jon's gaze.

'It's the same moon, isn't it, George?'

George is dumb for only a moment. Then he nods. 'That's what Peter said,' he agrees. The words seem to soothe him – but, all the same, he closes his eyes so that he has to see no more.

Jon must have fallen asleep too, for a sudden lurching of the wagon jolts him awake. It is dark all around. He scrambles to sit upright, George hunched in a ball beside him. There are trees on either bank, but they are stumpy and only half in leaf, the canopy of a fragrant forest so low that Jon can see for miles around.

'We're nearly there, boy.'

Jon wheels around, crashes against the side of the wagon. 'Nearly where?'

The wagons bank left. There are shapes in the darkness, silhouetted creatures that bound away from the convoy.

'There,' says Judah Reed, a wistful tone in his voice. Carefully, still grasping the rim of the wagon, he kicks his way through the curled-up boys to reach the cab.

The wagon suddenly drops down a ledge in the track. The jolt stirs the boys around Jon. George scrambles around, uncertain in which strange world he has awoken.

'Jon,' George begins, forgetting to whisper. 'What is it?'

In front of Jon, Judah Reed hammers the roof of the cab and the driver barks out. Seconds later, the truck's horn blasts, three short sharp sounds. They thunder around a narrow bend in the track – and there, for the first time, Jon sees lights in the undergrowth.

There is a clearing coming, harrowed land with little cauldrons of fires stirred at its fringes, as if to keep the desert wilderness at bay. As they near, the boys around Jon become more alert.

The wagons slow, banking hard so that their headlights sweep across what appears to be a ruined village. On the other side of the barren expanse there sits a collection of shacks, raised on stilts above the desert floor. Between them, causeways have been carved in the scrub – and, beyond that, the first of a row of sandstone buildings sits.

The wagons stop, and Judah Reed vaults to the ground. At first, the boys are resistant to follow, so Judah Reed reaches in and palms the first boy onto the ground. He stumbles to his hands and knees in the sand, scrambling aside just in time to avoid the other boy who comes tumbling after.

'Don't fall on your knees,' whispers Jon. He does not know why it is important; it seems like something Peter might have said – and, for the moment, that is good enough.

'What?' George asks. He will be the next to go; Judah Reed is already barking his name.

'Just don't let him push you over,' says Jon. 'I'll be right behind.'

Jon slides from the back of the truck, reaching back just in time to whip his cardboard suitcase with him. He presses a hand into the small of George's back, and together they scurry away.

'What is this place?' whispers George.

A boy beside them grunts. 'End of the world, little George,' he says. 'You'll be wetting that bed forevermore now.'

The boys gather along the fires. Behind them, the desert writhes – but, ahead, it seems, worse things are stirring. Boys have spilled out of the tumbledown shacks. Some of them are carrying lanterns. There are girls, too – though, at first, Jon does not recognize them as such. They all wear short trousers and ragged shirts, the girls in dresses that stretch to their ankles. They all have bare feet, and hair that has grown into great matted tassels.

From the night, a man in black strides forward, clasping Judah Reed's hand in his own. Then, suddenly, the women who met them at the docks are crying out shrill orders. The new boys form a long rank in front of the fires and, one after another, are dispatched into the shacks.

'Your suitcase, young sir . . .'

Jon clings tightly to the suitcase, and does not breathe a word. In there: his English clothes, his precious book – the only things he has left from the other world.

The woman does not ask twice. She cuffs him around the ear, a blow that stings more than he had anticipated – and, as he is righting himself, prises the suitcase from him. George gives his up more easily. She slings them back into the ute, where a dozen others are piled.

The woman whistles out, and a clot of barefoot boys scamper between two of the shacks. Jon pauses, but one of the boys takes him by the wrist. He resists, but not for long. Soon, he is clattering after them, along a narrow lane with tall banks of scrub. One of the boys whispers something, but Jon does not hear. He looks back, finally gives up the fight when he sees George being swept along behind.

They go deeper into the compound, past a square where a well, heaped high with stones, is set into the ground. The shacks here are darker, but groups of boys lounge on their steps.

'How many?' one of the boys hunched on the step asks.

The boy beside Jon shrugs. 'I reckon thirty, all told. They had girls in one of the trucks.'

The other boy nods, as if this news pleases him.

'What have we got here, then? Two little ones?'

'I'm ten!' Jon pipes up. When he elbows George sharply in the chest, George repeats the words, just as he has been told.

'Yeah, settle your shit down,' the older boy grins. 'We don't much like new boys, but it's not you to blame for that. We're on the same side here, all of us except Ted over there. You just pick on him if you ever feel the need.'

One of the other boys mutters a string of curses.

'I'm only joking, Ted.'

'I'll joke you in a minute!'

The older boy tips Jon a wink. 'He always says things like that. We haven't yet worked out what he means.' He stops. 'Up you get, then. There's an empty bed in the bottom corner. You two might have to top and tail it. Village muster's at dawn, so you've got . . .' He looks up at the chart of stars. '. . . about four hours, I reckon.'

Jon is the first to venture past the boys, up the steps into the wooden shack.

They enter a bare cloakroom, where hooks line the walls but nothing hangs. The smell in the air is at once familiar and horribly unreal. If George has forgotten it, Jon has not; he can still remember the first night he walked into the dormitory of the Children's Crusade back home, the smell of damp and piss that permeated the place.

Beyond the cloakroom, the new dormitory stretches to the furthest walls. Something dark scurries across the boards – a rat, or whatever other little creatures live in this far flung world. Banks of beds line each wall, simple wire frames raised at the head like a hospital stretcher, so that there is no need for a pillow. There are boys in each, but few of them are sleeping. They grumble as Jon and George stumble on, finally finding a vacant bed in a corner where the floorboards squelch miserably underfoot.

George rolls onto the bed. There is only one sheet, but he wraps himself in it tightly, as if hopeful he will disappear.

'George,' Jon whispers, jumping on the bed alongside his friend.

George looks up, pudgy face drawn.

'Yes?'

Jon does not know why he thinks of it, but he cannot stop himself now. 'What was your mother like, George?'

'I don't remember,' says George lightly, as if it is the most terrible thing.

Jon squints at him.

'But I wish she was here.' He offers some of the sheet to Jon. 'Jon,' he whispers, wary of the wild boys shifting around them. 'Do you have it? Do you still have Peter's map?'

Jon reaches into his short trousers and pulls out the page of the atlas. It means nothing any longer, just a few scribbles on a part of the coast they could not find again, even if they spent their whole lives trying. All the same, he stretches it out and, in the preternatural gloom, he and George study its contours.

'That's where we'll find him,' says Jon. George's eyes widen. 'He'll be waiting for us there.'

Jon lies down in the bed, curled around George. The sounds of boys wheezing, the chatter of creatures in the scrubland, the endless desert where there is nothing to run to and no one to hear you cry – this, then, is his new world. He says his prayers to unknown stars and wakes, the following morning, to an alien sun.

V

'There once was a boy who ran away. He ran as far as he could run, and when he could run no more, he burrowed down into the baked red earth. When he could not burrow any further, he curled up and slept – and, when he woke, he found little droplets of moisture on the walls of his den. He stayed there through the day, and the following night as well, rooting up worms and grubs for his dinner, lapping at the water that seeped out of the earth. And, in that way, he decided, a little boy could *live*.'

George likes this story. He has heard it three times already, but there is something in it that troubles Jon. All the same, he stays at George's side while the boy continues. Breakfast is almost over – and though Jon cannot bear spooning the slop into his mouth, he knows he will be aching by the afternoon without it.

One of the cottage mothers drifts by, trailing rank perfume behind her. Some of the littlest boys, four or five years old, are bickering in the corner of the stark breakfasting hall, and she glides towards them. Moments later, one is lifted by his ear and taken to the front of the hall, where a corpulent man in black, his face full of jowls, receives him and carries him out of the hall. On the dirt outside, Judah Reed is waiting.

'The little boy spent every day and night in his den. He did not grow up like the boys who did not run away. He couldn't grow a single inch bigger, because his den wouldn't let him. The seasons came and went without him seeing another living soul but the grubs he ate – until, one day, he heard the song of a kookaburra chick, lost in the desert . . .'

It is always the sound of the kookaburra that brings the smile to George's face. Neither he nor Jon know what a kookaburra is, or what it looks like, but for George it is enough to imagine this otherworldly creature coming to the runaway's help. There might still be friends to be found in this red and arid land.

Jon's spoon clatters in his tin plate, but the sound is quickly drowned out. The corpulent man in black is back, clanging the hand-bell, and he parades up and down the long trestle table. The little one who was taken away is nowhere to be found.

'Eat up, George. You've got to get going.'

The story will have to be finished another day. Jon pats George on the back and scurries out of the hall. The sun is already up, but the heat is not yet fierce. The boys here say that this is winter – though Jon can remember winter well, so it must be just another of their tricks. He leaps over the soft earth where the kitchen sinks empty out and takes off at a run.

The dairy is at the other end of the compound, over fields that, come the spring, the boys here will be tilling. He is running barefoot, but it no longer hurts; it took less than a day before his shoes were wrestled off him. At the head of the sandstone buildings – where Judah Reed himself lives – he vaults a fence and takes off across the field. In the scrub that surrounds, the youngest boys of the Mission are out on village muster, collecting up the kindling that will be used to stoke the boilers tonight. Jon spies a little one he knows as Ernest on the very fringe of the field, where the fields back onto a low forest of thorns. Ernest waves at him; some of these younger boys can barely say a dozen words. Left alone on their daily forage, they grow languages of gestures and grunts.

'You're late, Jack . . .'

Jon careers into the dairy. The old herdsman, McAllister, who comes in from the cattle station to check over the goats, lurks at the back of the barn – but Jon manages to slip in unnoticed.

'I'm sorry,' Jon begins. 'I came as fast . . .'

'Ach,' the boy spits, wrapping his fists around the teats of the next she-goat in line. 'I couldn't care less, long as I don't have to squeeze your share of these udders.' He uncurls his fingers from a teat and, dripping with warm milk, reaches out to grasp Jon's hand. 'Name's Tommy Crowe,' he says. 'Pleased to meet you, Jack.'

'My name's Jon.'

The boy named Tommy Crowe smirks. 'You got a familiar voice on you,' he finally says. 'Where'd they ship you in from?'

'England,' Jon shrugs, kicking his bucket into place.

'I could've figured that one. There's some lads from Malta came once, but you can tell them a mile off.' He pauses, pinching out a squirt of milk as he ponders this problem. 'Isn't it . . . it's somewhere in Leeds?'

Jon nods.

'I knew it. Second I clapped eyes on you, I said to myself – Tommy, I said, that lad's got Leeds written all over him.' He tweaks a teat and shoots a warm spray of milk straight into Jon's face. 'I'm from the old place myself!' Tommy Crowe goes on. 'Well, never spent hardly a month there, if I'm to be truthful about it. They shipped me over almost as soon as they could. Just made sure there was none of them nasty U-boats still sharking around, and packed us all off. There was a bunch of us, got evacuated out into the dales, and when we come back – bang! Nothing to come back to. I must have been about seven. Had myself a giant family – brothers and sisters, half-brothers, cousins who were brothers, brothers who were sisters. Almost every kind of family. Then . . .' He shakes his head, grinning at the absurd tale. 'I thought some of them might wind up here too, but I haven't seen them since we were in that Home. Maybe they ended up somewhere worse – what do you reckon?'

Tommy Crowe must be thirteen years old, though he appears much older. He has a pointed chin like some comicbook hero, and sharp eyebrows that rise villainously, so that there is always something contrary about the way that he looks.

'You done with that bucket yet?' Tommy asks. 'You can't mess around in here, Jack the lad! McAllister's known to take a riding crop to a boy for a bit of spilt milk . . .'

Jon looks over his shoulder. The old man McAllister is kneeling now, pressing his forehead to the face of one of the billy goats in its stall.

'What's he up to?' Jon asks.

'He's eyeing up which ones are for the block,' Tommy Crowe grins. 'You won't know how to slit a throat yet, will you? Lad, you're going to *love* it. Nothing quite like it when that kicking stops!'

He flashes Jon a grin and, buckets dangling from shoulders, elbows and wrists, lumbers out of the door.

In the red dirt outside the barn, Tommy Crowe stops. When Jon hurries after, he sees him, leg raised on an upturned pail, surveying the untilled fields. The smallest boys are ferreting around in rabbit holes in the undergrowth beyond. The rabbits have long been driven from those warrens – even rabbits grow wise to the habits of hungry boys – but it is a ritual among the little ones to set traps, just in case. Rabbits, it is said, are *English* – and this is a magical thing to the boys of the Mission.

One of the boys has strayed further than the rest, has almost disappeared into the shadow of the eucalyptus trees that grow in strange clumps, their many trunks opening out like the petals of a flower. At last, he drops down a ridge between two low, sprawling trees, so that only the top of his head can still be seen.

'Here,' Tommy Crowe says, 'give me that bucket.' Jon does not know how to ladle another bucket into Tommy's arms, but somehow he slides it into the crook of an elbow. 'You'd best be after that boy,' he says. 'Have you seen what they do to boys they think might run away?' He pauses. 'I'll stall McAllister if he shows hisself . . .'

Scrambling between the rails of a fence strung with barbed wire, Jon scurries over untilled earth, finally reaching the bank of red earth where the little ones are camped out. The eldest and most brave dumps his collection of kindling at Jon's feet and smiles eagerly, like a dog that has brought back a pigeon to its master.

Jon clambers over the bank, kicking dirt into the mouth of one of the rabbit holes. Behind him, the boys suddenly shout out, chattering animatedly at this transgression. Over the bank, Jon can just see the silhouette of the boy skipping from one tangle of roots to another.

It is Ernest. Jon calls after him, and though he half-turns his head, he does not stop. When Jon has almost caught him, he slows, trots cautiously three steps behind. The little boy slows to a dawdle and they plod on together, coming to a spot where a pool of light spills through the trees.

'It just goes on and on,' says Ernest, his tone one of wonder. 'It doesn't end.'

Jon looks down. There is a look like fear on Ernest's face, but it is wrestling for space with a burgeoning grin.

'I thought there'd be a fence,' he begins, watching Jon turn in bewildered circles, trying to seek one out. 'Maybe there'd be a wall. A big old wall with spikes and locked gates.' He shakes his head in disbelief. 'But there isn't a wall,' he says, taking a seat between two huge roots. 'Isn't it the weirdest thing? You could just walk and walk forever.'

Jon reaches a barrier of tussocky grass and pushes through, feeling the jagged curtain fall shut behind him. He feels, for a moment, like a storybook knight, fighting through walls of thorns to rescue the princess trapped on the other side – but when he emerges he sees only the same shadow wood going on forever.

There is rustling behind him and he turns, expecting to see Ernest creeping through on hands and knees. The creature that emerges is something he has not seen before. It is only two feet tall, the bastard offspring of a kangaroo and hare. Tiny black eyes study him cautiously, and then it bounds away.

Jon pushes back through the thicket – but on the other side Ernest is nowhere to be seen. He starts, wonders if he has come back the same way at all, or whether the forest has, somehow, turned him around, stranding him only a short walk away from the Mission.

Then, he hears voices, shrill cries of delight. After long months of waiting, the boys of the Mission have finally trapped a rabbit.

Jon follows the voices back to the field. Some of the little boys are already kindling a secret fire; they will sleep well tonight, on bellies full of wild rabbit instead of the usual mutton and bread. Beyond them, Tommy Crowe is laden down with another yoke of pails, striding heroically out of the dairy.

Jon rushes to help him, remembering suddenly the threat of Mr McAllister – but all that day, and long into the night, he cannot forget the lesson of the scrub. It is a thought too terrifying to share with George or any of the other boys, something only he and Ernest might understand: in this prison, there are no walls.

That night, George is already tucked up in bed when Jon reaches the dormitory. Since the second night, they have slept in different beds, but George ordinarily sits at the foot of Jon's, listening to stories Jon can remember from books. Soon, he will have to start changing them, bit by bit, to keep them fresh. No matter how much George asks, he does not want to start telling the stories they hear from other boys in the Mission – kookaburras befriending boys hiding in holes, jackeroos and jolly swagmen. Jon does not want his head filling with Australian stories, not if it means losing some of his own.

Jon slinks past George's bed as softly as he can but the covers buck and a fat little head pops out, like a grub from its knot in the wood. Jon presses his finger to his mouth and George nods eagerly. It isn't rare for one of the cottage mothers to hear boys chattering after lights-out and turf every one of them into the night so that the cold might teach them some manners.

The floorboards around the bed are still acrid where George had his accident three nights before. It was the first time he slipped up since they came here, but at least the boys in the nearby beds were understanding. Some of the others would surely have told tales.

'You been to the latrine, George?'

'I hate it when you call it that,' George answers.

In truth, it's hardly a latrine. It's a shallow ditch the boys are meant to dig out, but rarely do.

'I've been,' George nods. He hates going there, but there's a special dormitory on the compound's edge where the bedwetters go, and he'd rather go to the latrine a hundred times a day than have to sleep there.

'I'm cold tonight, Jon.'

'This is winter, little George. It won't get much colder than this.'

'I miss the *proper* winter.'

Deep snow and howling wind and waking to icicles hanging from the inside of the window – yes, Jon misses the proper winter too.

Jon climbs into bed. The mattress is old and stubbornly refuses to bend to him, even when he kicks and punches. Like lots of the other boys, he has fashioned a pillow from old sacking that he has to hide every time the cottage mother makes an inspection. He beats it into shape and lays down his head.

'Jon . . .' a little voice ventures, 'are you awake?'

'I'm thinking,' Jon says.

'How come you're always thinking? You never used to be thinking . . . Even in the Home, we used to play games.'

'We don't have *things* to play games, George.'

George grumbles, too afraid of upsetting Jon to snap back. 'If Peter was here, he'd find them. He could make games out of windows or beds or pieces of brick.' For a moment: only the whisper of wind around the dormitory walls. 'Hey, Jon, *what* are you thinking?'

Before Jon can reply, the door opens at the end of the dormitory and, in the light of a lantern beyond, there appear two silhouettes: the first a boy, no older than Jon, and the second an imperious cottage mother who steers him on his way with a hand in the small of his back. The boy shuffles forward and behind him the door closes – yet there are no sounds of footsteps retreating. Every boy among them knows: the cottage mother is waiting to hear what happens next.

Jon and George watch the boy totter forward, moving between the banks of beds until he can find his own. All around them, the other boys turn away. Some bury their heads in their makeshift pillows. Others feign snoring, as if they have long been asleep. The only boys who watch are those who tumbled from the boats with George and Jon, but soon even some of those are turning away.

The latecomer climbs into bed and rolls onto his side. He has not undressed and, if the cottage mothers find him like that in the morning, he will be due a punishment, a naked lap around the dormitories or no breakfast and double chores.

George's bug eyes swivel from the latecomer to Jon, and then back again. It is only moments before the whimpering begins. In his bed, the latecomer crams sacking into his mouth to strangle the sounds.

'Jon,' George whispers, 'what happened?'

'Maybe Judah Reed had to tell him . . .' Jon's voice dies. '. . . that his mother died.'

Jon drops from his bed and, keeping his eyes fixed on the splinter of light under the dormitory door, crosses from one bank of beds to the other. When he reaches the latecomer's bed, the boy turns suddenly, so that he does not have to see Jon's approach. Undeterred, Jon gets very close and whispers, 'What happened?'

When the boy does not reply, Jon tries again. He reaches out, puts a hand on the boy's shoulder, as if he might force him to turn. Suddenly, the boy does just that, wheeling out with a clenched fist to catch Jon on the side of the face. Jon's ear burns, and he staggers back. The boy brings his fists up to his face, forming an impenetrable wall – but before the wall closes Jon has time to see eyes swollen and red. These are not the tears any boy might shed at bedtime. Here is a boy who has cried himself dry, summoned up strength, and sobbed himself senseless again. Tonight's whimpers are only the distant echoes of something else.

'Judah Reed just wouldn't believe,' he says. 'I told him everything, and he said I was making it up.'

Jon creeps back to his own bed, hauls himself up.

Beside him, George is feigning sleep, but one eye pops open. 'Well?' he asks. 'Is it his mother?'

'No,' says Jon absently, his mind somewhere else. 'He . . . had an accident. Out on morning muster. He fell and . . .'

'There isn't a doctor here, is there, Jon Heather?'

'No,' says Jon. 'Not for miles and miles around.'

Across the dormitory, the boy gives a great wet breath, and then he is silent.

Dawn. In the breakfasting hall, Judah Reed appears to have quiet words with some of the bigger boys, and then ghosts on, nodding at each gaggle of little ones in turn. When the bell tolls, Jon is the first out of the breakfasting hall, barrelling through the Mission until he spies the dairy buildings ahead. A shock of parakeets rise from the branches of the shadow wood, and he watches them cascade over. He wonders if they know what is lying on the other side. If he were a boy in one of those sorry Australian stories, he would probably stop and ask them.

In the dairy, Tommy Crowe is waiting, while McAllister shuffles in the recesses of the room, whispering sweet promises to the goats.

'There was a boy in my dormitory last night,' Jon says, sitting down to take a teat in hand. 'Came in long after lights' out, with one of the cottage mothers. He wouldn't say what was wrong.'

Tommy Crowe nods thoughtfully, rounding off a pail and shuffling another one into place.

'I heard there was *honoured guests* back at the Mission. Maybe it was that. They haven't been round for a while. If you ask me, they're rock spiders, every last one.'

Jon is struggling to produce any milk this morning, but at last a warm jet ricochets around the bottom of his pail. 'Are they poisonous?' he asks, picturing these savage monsters stalking the shadow wood.

'Jack the lad, wake up!' Tommy laughs. 'A rock spider isn't a spider. It's . . .' He pauses, not certain how to explain it. In truth, he is not certain where he heard the words. 'It's friends with Judah Reed and the rest. They come by sometimes, to take kids on outings, off to proper farms, show them how the Australians do it, or . . . Sometimes they get to go to a town. They have ice cream. They look in shops. That sort of thing.'

Jon tries to picture it. 'Do they . . . adopt us?' He does not say what he wants to say – I *can't* be adopted, Tommy; I still have a mother – because, suddenly, he knows it for nonsense.

'I think they took one or two lads once. One little lad called Luca. And a bigger one. I don't remember his name. They brought that Luca back, though. I don't think they liked him much.' Tommy Crowe pauses, mindful of McAllister prowling behind them. 'Look, Jack the lad, if there's one thing you should know, it's . . . keep your head down. Don't go with an *honoured guest*.'

'Why not?'

'I don't know, Jack, but isn't it funny? A day out with ice cream and big fat steaks and all the lemonade a boy could drink . . . but, once they've been, nobody *ever* wants to go out again. Some things just aren't what they promise.'

Jon Heather knows that well enough. Australia was supposed to be a land of milk and honey, kangaroos taking them to school and plates piled high with treats. Now, he looks up, out of the dairy doors, at nothing but flurries of dust and wild little boys picking up sticks.

'Come on, Jack the lad, I've got a special treat for you today! McAllister's done his numbering, and we've got ourselves a billy to slaughter.' Tommy Crowe grins at him sincerely, proud to be sharing this prize. 'You ever killed a goat before?'

The question is so absurd that Jon is lost for words. Until only a few days ago, he hadn't even seen a goat. He'd seen rats and cats and dogs, even a fox one night, ferreting through the dust-bins on the terrace – but, for Jon Heather, cows and sheep and horses and goats are as much a fairytale as unicorns and serpents.

'Is it . . . difficult?' Jon asks, desperate to fill the silence.

'It doesn't have to be. You can do it nicely, if you're good.'

At the back of the dairy, one billy goat has been separated from the rest. Tommy Crowe wanders over to the stall, and the goat approaches him tenderly. Crouching down, he cups its bearded jaw and strokes its brow.

The old man McAllister rears up from a neighbouring stall. Up close, Jon can see that he really isn't that old after all, no older, perhaps, than Judah Reed. A fat black moustache hangs over his top lip, and his eyes hunker below bushy brown slugs.

'He'll cook up nice,' McAllister says. 'You showing this little one how it's done, are you, Tommy?'

Tommy Crowe nods.

'Reckon he'll chuck up?'

Tommy laughs, secretly shooting Jon an apologetic look. 'Wouldn't be normal if he didn't.'

At once, McAllister's face darkens. 'Just make sure he doesn't chuck up all over that meat. It's what you bairns got to eat. It all goes in the pot, chuck-up and all.'

After McAllister wanders out of the dairy, Tommy Crowe turns to Jon. 'Let's get started,' he says. 'You get round the back. He's bound to kick if he gets a whiff of what we're doing, so just watch out. I saw a boy break his ribs that way, once. He couldn't go in his dormitory after that, so they had him locked up with one of those cottage mothers.' Tommy shakes his head. 'He'd have been better in the bush.'

It is Jon's job to get around the back of the goat and force it from the stall. This is easier said than done and, in the end, Tommy Crowe has to leash the billy with a rope and tug him out onto an expanse of bare earth.

Tommy hands Jon the rope and shoots back inside to collect the killing knife. Alone now, Jon Heather watches the goat. It does not try and run, but simply drops its head instead, chewing contentedly on a clump of coarse yellow grass.

Its eyes are tiny, lost behind tufts of grey and white, but Jon thinks he can see deeply into them. Once, he had dreamed of having a pet dog. He would tame it and train it and take it on walks in the terrace, and call it his very best friend. A goat, he thinks now, would have done just as well.

'Here you go, Jack the lad,' says Tommy, reappearing from the dairy. 'Take hold of this. I'll tell you when it's time.'

Jon finds the knife already in his hands. It is smaller than he had imagined, with a short handle and a longer blade that curves back against itself. Tommy has others stacked up – one with jagged teeth like a saw, one a huge cleaver sitting on a wooden shaft – and he circles the goat gently, cooing at it all the while.

'Give him a hug, Jon.'

Jon recoils. He thinks of Judah Reed, putting his arm around a boy just before telling him: *they're all dead; you're the only one left.*

'Go on, Jon. If you hold him properly, he'll roll right over.'

Tommy Crowe is right. Jon advances, strokes the back of the billy's head, and then drapes himself over its body. Bemused, the goat nevertheless relents, rolling onto its side like an obedient pup. It is then an easy thing for Tommy Crowe to take the rope and knot together its back legs and fore.

'Keep pressing down, Jon. He'll only try and get back up again.' Tommy bows low, rubs his forehead onto the goat's shoulder. 'Won't you, lad? You only want to get up!' Tommy looks up. 'Have a go, Jon. Bring his head back, see. The first cut's the hardest, but after that, it's plain sailing.'

Jon understands, too late, why the knife is in his hand. His eyes widen, he flicks a look at Tommy, another at the throat now exposed. Still, the goat is silent. Jon Heather thinks: it might at least cry.

'Take it in your hand like *this*,' Tommy says, snatching up a stick to show him how. 'Then . . .' He tugs the stick back. 'Don't be shy. If you're shy, you'll hurt him.'

'Tommy, I don't . . .'

'Of course you don't! Street boy like you . . . But, Jon, you *have* to. We *all* have to. If you don't, they'll know. Then they'll come and *make* you.' Tommy is silent. 'It's better they don't have to make you, Jon. The thing is, they enjoy making you. It's better not like that.'

Jon isn't certain that he understands, but he pictures Judah Reed standing here, pressing the knife into his hand.

'They're making me anyway, Tommy. *You're* making me . . .'

Tommy releases the goat's hind legs. The poor brute kicks out, and Tommy must tackle him again.

'I knew a boy who wouldn't,' he breathes. 'It was when we were building the sandstone huts.'

'Building them?'

'We built them our very own selves. There was hardly a building standing when I got dumped here. But this boy, he wouldn't mix bricks, and he wouldn't kill goats, wouldn't go out on muster or even pop the head off a chicken. Wasn't that he was a cry-baby. I don't think I ever once saw him cry. He just wouldn't do a thing he was told. So . . .'

'They *made* him.' The way Jon breathes the word, it might be a spell that they cast, a terrible enchantment. 'How did they make him, Tommy?'

'The same way they'll make you, if you don't cut this goat. With nights in Judah Reed's office and big old welts on your bare backside. With slop for breakfast and tea, so you'll be begging for a hunk of lovely goat. Going out for lessons with *honoured guests*.' Tommy Crowe pauses. 'Do you want to know why I'm the only lad in this whole Mission who's never had a strap across him?'

Meekly, Jon nods.

'It's because Judah Reed doesn't even know my name. I never gave him a reason to learn it. He might have put me on that boat and brought me here, but he doesn't even know I was born. And that, Jack the lad, is the only way to do it. So . . .' He pauses, tilting his head at the blade still in Jon's hands. '. . . are you going to cause a stink about this, or what?'

Jon strokes the top of the billy's head. The silly creature must love it for, willingly, he tips his head back. With one hand, Jon steadies the head against the earth; with the other, he plunges forward with the blade.

He must have done something wrong, stabbing like that, for a jet of red shoots out at him and Tommy Crowe winces.

'Don't skewer it, Jack the lad! Bring it up, like *this* . . .'

The second time is more difficult, for now the goat knows what these two turncoats are about, and now the goat resists. Even so, somehow, Jon gets the knife back in. He tries to draw it up, opening the neck, but over and again it slides back out. Now he is mindlessly hacking, hands covered in pumping red, the blade so slippery he can hardly keep hold.

Quickly, the goat relents. Its kicking stops, and Jon reels back.

'Up and away, Jack the lad! We've made a meal of this one!'

Tommy rushes around, grabs a broom handle from the dairy wall, and runs it between the goat's hind legs. With one mighty heave, he throws the billy on his back and staggers to a dead tree by the dairy doors. Here, he slides the broom handle into the crooks of two branches and steps back with a flourish, the goat hanging from the tree with its throat open to the ground.

'Damn it Jack, you're letting it spill!'

Jon looks down. Too late, he sees the puddle of blood spreading around him, his feet islands rapidly being submerged in a grisly typhoon. Too stunned to do anything, he simply stands there, imagines the tide getting higher and higher, subsuming his ankles, his knees, the whole of his body. At last, Tommy Crowe pushes him out of the way, kicking two milk pails into place so that the blood might be caught. 'It's for sausages, you dolt . . . Blood sausages, remember?'

Jon looks up. The goat dangles with two gaping smiles: the

first its lips, the second the great gash they have carved in its throat. Only minutes ago, it was a real, living thing; now it is a cruel mockery of everything it used to be.

'You want to help with the butchering too?'

Against his will, Jon nods.

'It's easy enough,' says Tommy. 'Just take a hold of this knife . . .'

Once the goat has bled out, they strain to carry the buckets of blood away, into the dairy where fewer flies can set to feasting. Now, Tommy Crowe explains, there comes a job any old boy can do, without even a hint of training.

'All you have to do is twist until it pops off. You ever get the cap off a bottle of milk?'

Jon nods, eyes fixed on the goat's gaping smile.

'Same thing, Jon. Go on, give it a go . . .'

Jon might keep still, then, were it not for the footsteps he hears behind him: McAllister knuckling around the corner of the dairy. With Tommy Crowe's eyes on him, he steps forward. The goat is strung high, so that the head dangles almost into his lap. Up close, the stench is severe, steamy and sour.

He places one hand on one side of the goat's head and, holding his body back as far as he can, the other hand on the opposite side. Eyes closed tight, he turns the head. It has moved only inches when it resists, and he lets go. Behind him, Tommy Crowe insists that he just has to try harder. When he tries again, something gives, and now the goat's head is back to front. He turns again, his hands now oily with blood, and at last there is a sound like a *pop*. Stumbling back, he crashes into the dirt.

When he opens his eyes, the goat is staring back, a disembodied head bouncing in his lap like a baby boy.

Next, the legs have to be broken. This, Tommy explains, will make it much easier to whip off his skin. Each leg needs a good old yank, but when Jon takes one of the forelegs, dangling close to the ground, he can barely get a good grip. There's a trick to this, Tommy Crowe explains. All you have to do is *twist* at the same time as you *snap*. In this way, the bone shatters inside. Legs, he explains, really aren't so difficult at all.

'You ever had a broken bone, Jack the lad?'

Jon shakes his head, hands still clasped around the two ragged ends of the leg he has ruined.

'You will,' mutters Tommy. 'It hurts like hell.'

Under Tommy's instruction, Jon is supposed to slice up the goat's tummy, from its star-shaped backside to the great gash in its neck, but the hide is thick and it is all he can do to force the blade in. If Tommy Crowe were doing it, he says, he could have the skin off a goat like this in ten seconds flat – but every time Jon tries to draw the blade up, it sticks on fat and flesh. First, he has the knife in too deep; then, not deep enough, so that it rips out and Jon staggers, catching his own arm with the tip of the knife. Now, his own blood mingles with the goat's, but Tommy tells him not to worry.

'It takes some practice, Jack the lad. Once you've killed a dozen of these bastards, you'll be able to skin anything. A cow, a kangaroo, Judah Reed himself . . .'

Even with Tommy Crowe's help, it takes an age to wrestle the skin off. Now, it is naked, glistening white and red. The first thing Jon must do is collect up the guts. This is easy enough, because they slide out straight away. All it takes is the right incision – but when Jon sinks the blade in, a smell like shit erupts, and he staggers back. Coarse brown muck pumps from the hole he has made, and Tommy Crowe rushes to finish the job.

'That'll happen if you're not careful,' he says, wiping his hands of the thick slurry. 'You put that knife straight in its shit sack.'

Jon tries to wipe his hands clean up and down his thighs, but all it does is make a dark brown mess, massaging it deeper into his palms.

'Look,' says Tommy. 'I'll cut you a deal. If I get this bladder out, you do the rest. If this goat pisses all over itself, he'll be ruined.' He stops. 'Shall I tell you what pissed-on goat tastes like, Jon Heather?'

Tommy is a deft hand, and Jon watches as the guts cascade out of the carcass and flop into another pail. Some of it, Tommy says, can be saved for offal, but some of it can be fed back to the other goats. As he sets to sorting out the delicacies from the rubbish, he throws out instructions at Jon. First, the goat can come down from its hook, onto a stone slab at the dairy wall. Once in place, Jon can start hacking up pieces of flesh. This, Tommy Crowe explains, is the *fun* part. Each leg comes off easily enough, but you can carve up the back and neck almost any way you can think of – 'use some *imagination*, Jon Heather!' – and grind it down for sausage and stew.

For the longest time, Jon stands over the splayed-out carcass, trying to imagine it the way it was: head and legs, fur and face. A few strokes of the knife, he realizes, and it isn't even a goat anymore. He stands frozen, willing the blood back from the bucket, willing the guts to writhe up like charmed snakes and dance back into the body.

'Here,' says Tommy Crowe. 'I'll finish it. Honestly, Jack the lad, I had you pegged for stronger stuff.'

'How many goats have you killed, Tommy?'

Tommy Crowe shrugs, severing a big haunch of meat and raising it aloft. 'They don't call me goat killer for nothing!'

'What about . . . back home?'

For the first time, Tommy Crowe blanches. 'Not back then, Jon. It was Judah Reed himself showed me to kill a goat.'

By the time they are finished, dusk is thickening. Tommy rinses his hands in one of the goat troughs and, wiping them dry on his legs, steps back. 'I'll take these slabs down for salting and stewing,' he says, hoisting up the wheelbarrow into which the remnants of the goat have been piled. 'You happy enough cleaning out here? Them flies get everywhere if you don't . . .'

Absently, Jon nods. As he watches Tommy go, he stands up.

Even if he does not look, he can see the gore in the corner of his eyes, all up his arms and splattered across his shirt. In places it is already dry, caked with coarse sand, and he hurries to the trough in which Tommy washed. The water in the stones is milky and red but, even so, he drops to his knees and plunges his arms in. In the swirling water, flecks of flesh start to bob to the surface so that, every time he draws his arms out, another shred of dead goat is clinging to him. Worse still, the redness has seeped into his skin. Now he looks like George did aboard the HMS *Othello*, his hands and arms marbled, as if by a birthmark, deep lines of red in the crevices of his knuckles and the folds of his palm.

Jon rips his shirt off, balls it up to hide the gore inside, and tries to use it as a washcloth – but it is no use; his skin has changed colour inches deep.

Jon is still sitting there, watching the shadows lengthen over the untilled field, the darkness solidifying in the shadow wood beyond, when gangs of little ones stream past, arms heaped high with kindling from their daily muster. At the end of the procession, dragging his bundle behind him on a length of orange twine, there comes Ernest.

Today, he has red sand caked up one side of his face, as if he has been lying in the dirt. Jon finds himself hiding his red hands underneath his bottom, but it only makes him more conspicuous.

When he is almost past, Ernest looks up and, leaving the other little ones to march on, wanders up. 'Jon?'

Jon Heather gives a little shake of his head.

'What are you doing here? It's almost time for the bell . . .'

'I want to find the fences,' Jon croaks. He had not known it, but he is close to tears.

'There were no fences . . .' Ernest whispers, throwing a look over each shoulder.

'There have to be,' Jon says. Anything else is too difficult to believe. There have to be walls. There have to be gates. There have to be locks and chains, just like at the Home in Leeds. If there aren't, he thinks, this isn't a prison at all. This is just real life. And you can't escape from real life – not until, like that billy goat gruff, you're stretched out on a stone with your insides taken out. 'We just didn't see. We didn't go far enough. There has to be something . . . somewhere . . .'

Ernest lets his length of twine fall through his fingers and slumps down, using his bundle as a seat. Yet, he does not have time to sit long. Suddenly, Jon Heather is standing. Then, he is over the fence and into the untilled field.

'There might be another rabbit,' he says. 'We can . . .' He is going to say *catch it*, but then he remembers the blood on his hands, and checks himself. '. . . *watch it*,' he finally says. 'To see where he lives.'

There are no men in black by the dairy tonight, and it is a simple thing to climb up, over the red bank, and disappear into upturned trees and walls of thorn. He wonders what it might be like under those branches, how far a boy might have to go until he is in the woodland and not in the Mission. There is, he knows, only one way to find out.

The first step, and he feels warm red sand in between his toes. The second, and he is between two trees. He realizes that he is creeping, as if sneaking up on the lodge of Judah Reed himself, and when he takes his next steps his chest swells out. They are only a stone's throw from the fringe of the scrub, but when he looks back half of the dairy is obscured by upturned Christmas trees.

He does not look back again until they reach the bushes where they last stumbled to a halt. He rests back, in the palm of one of the eucalyptus trees. It hardly seems to matter, anymore, whether they push further or not. They might be anywhere in the world.

'Do you want to go back?' he asks.

Ernest shrugs. 'Do you?'

Jon Heather says, 'I just want to see the fences. They'll be at the edge of the wood.'

He takes off. Bolder now, he begins to run. Behind him, Ernest is still – but, moments later, he too begins to fly, whooping as he dodges an outgrowth of low boughs.

The trees are sparse and, for a time, grow sparser, so that soon they can see the sky darkening above, stars beginning to twinkle in the endless expanse. Then, at once, the trees disappear. Ahead of them, nothing but undulating redness.

'No fence,' whispers Ernest. There is fear in his voice, but there is awe too. They are looking at something beautiful yet terrible, evil and alive.

Jon Heather stutters to a stop. The sun must have disappeared suddenly, while they were in the shadow wood, for not even its red fingers touch the horizon. 'It can't be far,' he trembles.

They bound across a world of low bushes and branches, unworldly things that seem to have been pruned into spidery shapes by a malevolent gardener. The sky is vast above them and the world is vast around.

Finally, a stitch in his side, he stops. Ernest catches him up, and then drifts on. 'Maybe we missed it.'

'We can't have,' says Jon.

'We might have come through a gate. One they left open . . .'

The stitch in Jon's side is severe. He presses his hands to it and crouches down. Ernest must be mistaken, either that or a fool. The men in black would never leave a gate wide open for any old boy to wander through. In Leeds, there were big black bars, with latches and locks and chains, all encased in ice.

'Maybe it's this way,' says Ernest. He wanders on a few steps, and then a few more.

As his footsteps fade, Jon looks behind. Though he can still see the border of the shadow wood, he cannot see beyond. Perhaps the wood itself is supposed to be the fence that should be keeping them in. In the summer, its walls will close and its traps will be sprung, but in the winter, the cracks appear and a boy might slip out.

His eyes are lingering on the shadow wood when he hears Ernest cry out. To his later shame, he freezes, cannot even turn around.

'Come on, boy,' begins a deep, throaty voice, one Jon does not know. 'You've come far enough.'

'I . . .'

It is Ernest, floundering for words. Jon Heather sinks into the dust, feels something scuttle over the tips of his fingers.

'Let's be having you, boy. It's almost dark.' The man's voice seems to soften. 'Don't worry. I'll tell him you were out *before* dark. It's worse if you're caught after.'

Now there are footsteps again. Jon scrabbles sideways, desperate not to be in their path.

'I'm sorry,' Ernest begins, somewhere in the gloom. 'I wanted to . . . see the fences.'

They are almost upon Jon now. He crouches, listens for a footfall, and darts forward. In that way, a few yards at the time, he tracks back towards the Mission. The shadow wood is fading in front of him, swallowed up by the gathering night.

'I promise I . . .'

Ernest, Jon hears, has started to cry.

'Save the tears, boy. It isn't so bad. I could have left you out here, after all. It'll be over soon, and then you can be a good boy again.' He stops, the footsteps suddenly still. 'But I can't listen to your blubbering, boy.' His voice hardens, yet it is barely a whisper. 'So stop your crying, or I'll give you something to cry about.'

Jon cannot bear to hear Ernest swallowing his tears, so he hurtles forward. He takes huge strides, desperate not to be heard, leaping over the plain until the scrub starts to thicken around him.

He is almost at the edge of the plain, the eucalypts ranged in their ragged frontier in front of him, when he feels crunching under his feet. He stumbles. At his feet, there is a little cairn of bones: scrub chicken, if he is not mistaken. They are, he sees, not very old at all. He crouches down to peel a wing bone from his heel, and sees that the ground is scuffed up around him, as if some animal has made this its nest. But animals, Jon Heather notes, even *Australian* animals, don't stop to build cairns out of their kills.

He might wonder about it further, but he hears them again: the man in black, and Ernest's little voice drowned out underneath. They might be anywhere behind him; the voices seem to curl from every direction, borne on flurries of desert sand. Perhaps, he begins to think, the men in black are their own kind of fence, watching out for boys slipping through to pick them up in the nothingness beyond.

He crashes back through the shadow wood. Things skitter in the trees, but he pays them no mind. He only scrambles on, overjoyed to see the orbs of the border fires burning in the Mission beyond.

The darkness is almost absolute when Jon Heather crashes back into the Mission. On the opposite side of the untilled field, the dairy sits empty but for the goats milling within. Further on, the first wave of boys is already emerging from the dining hall, bellies full of gristly goat. Jon hangs at a distance and sees George among them, hands shoved in pockets, head tucked into his chin. He wants to call out, run over and fling his arms around the fat boy, but instead he looks over his shoulder. Other figures have emerged from the shadow wood now: the man in black, with Ernest propelled in front of him. If Ernest has been crying, Jon cannot see. He waits until they pass, and then waits longer. He does not have to follow to know where they are going, but he follows all the same. Soon he is standing at the centre of the Mission, where the column of sandstone huts marks a big cross. The man in black takes Ernest through a door, and then they are gone.

'Jon Heather, you missed dinner!'

Jon turns to see George gambolling towards him.

'Well?'

'Well what?'

'Well, why did you miss your dinner?'

Jon wants to tell him. There's nothing out there, George. There's only more *nothing*, as far as the eye can see – nothing in the north and nothing in the south and nothing in the east and nothing in the west. That's why they brought us here – a nothing place for nothing people.

He wants to say all of this, but he cannot. He could never describe the yawning terror of standing there, knowing that, even if you ran and ran, you wouldn't get any further away. There isn't a boy who would believe it if he didn't see it for himself.

'What happened to your hands?' George suddenly asks.

Jon looks down. It still looks as if he is wearing scarlet gloves.

'It's nothing, Georgie. I was working.'

'It's nearly bedtime, you know . . .'

Jon feels his feet rooted to the spot. 'I'll be along, George. I'll catch you up.'

George folds his arms. 'What are you up to?'

'It's . . .' Jon turns, feigns a big smile. 'I didn't finish my work,' he lies. 'They say I can't go to bed until it's done, or I'll have to go for Judah Reed.'

George's lips curl. 'Rotten old Judah Reed,' he whispers, conspiratorially. 'Can't I help?'

Eventually, George is convinced and scurries for the shelter of their dormitory. It would not do, he knows, to be caught out after dark, not with cottage mothers and men in black drifting around, looking for lurkers.

Now that he is alone, Jon is suddenly afraid. He hears, dimly, one of the cottage mothers rounding up little ones as if they are stray chickens, clucking after them as she forces them up into their shacks. They will come for him soon enough, demanding to know why he has not also retired. If he was missed at dinner, somebody will know; somebody will ask questions, and he doesn't know what he'll say.

Once silence has settled over the Mission, he hears the faint sound for which his ears have been straining. He drops to his haunches, eyes fixed on the sandstone door, and tracks along the wall, trying to discern the exact spot from which the noises come.

Somewhere, in there, a boy is crying. It is, Jon Heather knows with a terrifying certainty, Ernest who is making those sounds.

The noise comes in fits and starts. Ernest bleats out, and then there is silence; Ernest screams that he is sorry, and then he is still. Every time Jon thinks it is over, it comes again, and soon he begins to notice a pattern in the sound, a rhythm, as if Judah Reed is a conductor and Ernest his orchestra.

Then, without warning, the sounds just stop. Jon listens out for them, realizes that he desperately wants to hear. As long as Ernest is crying, at least he knows Ernest is still alive. Yet now there is only silence: dull and absolute.

Suddenly, the door twitches and opens. Jon springs to his heels, ready to dart into the stretching shadows, but he is too late. Ernest appears before him, the man in black hovering above.

Judah Reed has a hand on each of the little boy's shoulders, and he ruffles his hair as he sends him on his way. 'You'll be a good boy,' he says, gently leading Ernest down the step and onto the bare earth. 'Good boys make good men.'

Ernest walks forward, stiff and deliberate. His head is down, but still he seems to see Jon staring. Now, his steps grow longer. He is, Jon understands, trying to run, but something is stopping him. Dumbly, Jon watches him go.

When Jon looks back, Judah Reed has come closer, to fix him with a curious gaze.

If you were clever, Jon Heather, you would run yourself. If you were as clever as you think you are, you might have hidden in the shadow wood while the man in black escorted Ernest back into the Mission – and then, safe in the knowledge that the lookout was gone, you could have carried on running into the big bleak nowhere.

Judah Reed looks down at him, along the line of his crooked nose. 'Let me see your hands,' he says.

Jon could not resist, even if he wanted to. A force he does not know compels him to stand up, and he finds his hands coming out of his pockets, his fists unfurling to reveal those blood-red palms.

Judah Reed crouches and takes Jon's hands, one at a time, in his own. It seems as if they are both wearing gloves: Judah Reed's, monstrous and leathery; Jon's, tiny and red.

'It was a very good goat,' says Judah Reed. A smile blossoms on his face. 'You did a very good job. You fed the whole Mission. I hope you are proud.' He pauses. 'Are you proud, boy?'

There is a look in Judah Reed's eyes like fire, a look that tells Jon: there is only one answer to this question. Being ashamed, he sees, is not an option. So he nods, because nodding is all he can do.

'Some of the boys in this Mission could learn a thing or two from you. Australia will be grateful that you came.'

'It won't come off,' blurts out Jon. His inside crawls, for surely he should be petrified, surely he should want to take flight – but, strangely, he finds that he *wants* to be here. It is the most peculiar sensation. There are a thousand things he wants to ask. It is, he realizes, only Judah Reed who really knows the way across the big bad nowhere and back to England. 'I scrubbed and scrubbed but it wouldn't come off.'

Judah Reed says, 'It never does,' and, smiling, returns through the sandstone door.

VI

Two days later, Judah Reed leads them in a Sunday service and, afterwards, they are permitted to write letters. In the assembly hall, Jon finds a seat at a long trestle table, and begins to dream of an opening sentence. At the far end, one of the cottage mothers looming on his shoulder, George wriggles onto his stool and stares, puzzled, at his paper.

Jon throws a look around the room and sees, for the first time, that none of the older boys of the Mission have come. He wonders why they do not care about writing to their mothers – and then he feels George's sticky hand on his shoulder.

The little boy is standing beside him, stubby pencil in his fist.

'You'll have to sit down, George. If one of them sees . . .'

'What can I write, Jon?'

Jon shuffles over, offering George half of his stool. Eagerly, George flops down, almost upending Jon.

'Will I write to the Home, do you think?' he wonders. 'Or Peter?' He stops. 'Where *would* I write to Peter, do you think?'

Jon looks into George's expectant eyes, recalls vividly that morning in the Home when George was crying behind the chantry.

'You can write to my mother, if you like.'

Jon lifts the pencil out of George's fingers and pushes it back in, the right way round.

'What will I say?'

'I don't know, George. It's your letter.'

'Can I have a look at yours?'

Quickly, Jon wraps his arm around the page. Isn't it enough that he's sharing his stool *and* his mother, without George having to share every single word?

Bewildered, George mirrors the action around his own page.

'I might tell her about being a sailor,' he decides, and promptly breaks the point of his pencil.

While George is scratching away, Jon ponders every word. This letter has to be perfect. The perfect line could send his sisters scurrying halfway across the world. He sketches sentences lightly, using only the very tip of his pencil, and when it does not sound right he starts again, pressing harder this time to disguise what went before. He wonders if he should tell her he is well. He *wants* to tell her – but perhaps she might think he is better where he is, and not come for him at all. He wonders if he should tell her how terribly they live, how there is no food but the food they forage and butcher, how Judah Reed might appear at any moment to take boys into his study for a beating – but he does not want to upset her; she does not deserve that.

At last, Jon decides that he will tell the truth, without any fancy. His mother will surely appreciate that.

He writes each letter perfectly, just the way she always liked.

Dear Mother,

There has been a dreadful mistake, and I am in Australia. I know you did not mean this for me, because you love me, but the men from the Children's Crusade say we have to be Australian boys. I promise, mother, I am forever your English son.

I know home is hard and there is not money until my father comes home. I promise I will help. I'll be eleven soon, and then I can find work, in a shop or on a bike. Or I can come and clean houses with you. I wouldn't be a nuisance. I don't need Christmases and I don't need birthdays and I don't even need a Sunday dinner. I'll have bread and gravy.

I'm sorry I made it so you had to give me away. But anything bad I've done or anything bad I've said, I haven't meant a thing. I want to be good for you. I love you and I love my sisters, and I'd love you wherever we lived, even if we never go back to the old house.

I'll be your best boy, if only you come and take me back. I'll get you anything you want – and, mother, if I haven't got it, why, I'll go for and get it.

I am your son who loves you,

Jon (Heather)

It fills one side of the paper and, rearing back, Jon is tremendously proud. He suddenly thinks of what Peter might have said if he had seen such a letter, and inwardly he cringes. This is nothing of Peter's business. Peter is gone, and Jon can think whatever he wants.

He glances at George, who has made a mess of one side of his paper and started again on the reverse. His letters are big and crude, but he has made more words than Jon thought possible.

You will be ever pleased to know Jonn looks after me like my one brother. Its not the same as peter but he is in deed a very good boy. He promises I can live with you when we are to get back in England

Jon wants to rip the paper away – and perhaps George senses it, for he shifts his body around and the words are gone from sight. It is better this way. Let him think whatever he wants – but there will not be room for him at the old house.

Some of the boys have finished their letters and, sealing them diligently, hand them to the cottage mother sitting at the front of the hall. On the other side of the hall, Jon spies Ernest, creasing his page and carefully lettering an address on front.

'I'll catch you up, Georgie . . .'

Jon sees Ernest almost at the cottage mother's desk, and scurries around the long table to catch up. Ernest seems eager to avoid him, for he is almost at the door by the time Jon's hand lands on his shoulder.

'I'm . . .' Jon does not know what to say. '. . . *sorry*,' he whispers. 'I didn't . . .' All his words have failed him. He does not know what to say sorry for, but for some reason he can picture himself with a stick in his hand, beating Ernest over and over. 'I just got scared.'

Ernest shrugs. 'I didn't tell, you know. They were sure they'd seen me with another boy, but I said I was on my own.'

Jon nods, dumbly. 'Did it . . . hurt?' he finds himself asking.

'He had a hockey stick.'

A curious sensation spreads, like warmth, across Jon's stomach, up his chest and down his arms, as if he has too much energy, as if he should jump up and sprint in circles. He remembers Judah Reed telling him he ought to be proud, and realizes what the feeling is: guilt, not for letting Ernest be beaten, but for something else.

They stand, neither one really looking at the other, complicit in some secret.

'You write to your mother too?' Jon begins.

'Every month, ever since I came.'

Jon cannot bear to ask how long that has been. Nor can he bear to ask the question that floats in the air between them, daring to be voiced. If Ernest has been here for years, if he has written a letter diligently each month, why, then, is he still here?

'What did you tell her?'

'I told her about the fences.' Ernest tucks his head down, shuffling away as if embarrassed by what he is about to say. 'I told her she can come and get me almost any time she wants – 'cause if there's nothing keeping us in, there's nothing keeping her out.'

They walk together out of the assembly hall. Sundays are supposed to be spare days, no work and no worry, but it doesn't feel that way to Jon. Boys are gathering with nothing to do and nowhere to go. Some of them, it seems, have already found a way to cause mischief, and a strident cottage mother is hauling them by their ears to a waiting man in black, a creature much older than Judah Reed, with hands wrinkled like oversized gloves and a deep stoop that makes him look like a tortoise.

Ernest comes close, breathing out words Jon cannot hear.

'What?' asks Jon, tilting his ear.

'I saw a road,' whispers Ernest. 'When he got hold of me to march me back, I looked up . . .' He pauses. This, it seems, is much more magical than a world without fences. 'It had a bank on both sides and . . . there it was. Like a river without any rain.' His face dares a smile. 'Tyre marks in the dust. There was a glass bottle on the edge, like someone just threw it there.'

'There's somebody out there . . .'

'I saw it. They can't stop me having seen it.'

Jon Heather stops. He looks at his hands, no longer bloody,

except where the blood has worked into the crevices around his nails. 'Where?'

'Into the sun,' says Ernest. 'We should have been running into the sun.'

That night, sleep will not come. Jon imagines his letter, winging its way to England. Over glittering oceans it goes, through tropical monsoons, around the cape of India, taking up with a flock of migrating birds who will keep it company all the way back to English shores. It is night when it arrives in the old town, but it roosts with those same birds in the gutters of one of the old terraces, diving down to find his mother as soon as morning comes.

She will hold that letter dear to her. Jon knows it. Perhaps she will write a letter of her own – but it will only be her emissary. She will be following soon after.

If he wasn't so certain of the fact, perhaps he might be dreaming differently tonight. He pictures coming through the scrub again, the lone wallaby skittering out of his path, and seeing nothing but the bush rolling on. The world had never seemed so huge as it did then. His mind's eye rolls on, and he sees Ernest, dangling from the arm of a man in black, the pair of them silhouettes against the dying light. Beyond them, Jon can see nothing but the undulating red plain – but Ernest can see more.

Somewhere, out there, there is a road.

He closes his eyes, ignores George's pleas for a story, and pictures it snaking back to the sea. A road can lead you anywhere. A road can even lead you back home.

'Jon Heather, you lazy sack! We're going to be in trouble!'

Jon wakes, to feel fingers grappling with his foot, trying to haul him out of bed. There is a moment in which he might be anywhere in the world, but then he *remembers*. Fear grips him and he rolls over – and it is only then that he realizes it is George, not some haughty cottage mother, urging him to rise.

'You were talking in your sleep,' George says, indignant.

'What did I say?'

'I don't know.'

'You must have heard something.'

'We're going to be late!'

Jon blinks the sleep out of his eyes, bewildered that he might have slept so soundly, and looks around the dormitory. All of the other boys are gone.

'You shouldn't have waited for me, George. Now you'll be for it too . . .'

'I can't go out on my own, Jon Heather, you know I can't.'

They are fortunate, this morning, that their cottage mother is not feeling particularly vicious. When they emerge, blinking into the sun, she is drinking tea from a dainty cup, and simply waves them on with a withering gaze. All the same, Jon knows, she won't forget it. They'll have to be doubly careful for the next few days.

In the breakfast hall, Judah Reed is taking a register. He does not have a roll call of names, so instead barks out ages, and every boy of that age must then go to a certain corner of the room. Then he begins to count.

'Remember,' George whispers. 'I'm ten too.'

'Is there,' Judah Reed proclaims, 'a boy named Peter here?'

George's eyes light up. His head swivels, like an owl's, to find Jon's.

Across the room, nobody raises their hand.

'Does he mean *our* Peter?'

Judah Reed must hear, for his gaze falls on George and hovers like a hawk.

'Shut up, George.'

'David?' Judah Reed calls.

This time, a little one raises his hand, but Judah Reed quickly dismisses him as too young.

'Must have gone to the stations,' Jon hears Judah Reed mutter. 'Do we have the right number?' The cottage mother beside him nods. 'Very well.'

Once the head-count is complete, Judah Reed rings a hand bell and breakfast begins. Jon watches as he shares whispered words with two other men in black, and a particularly serpentine cottage mother. They sit together at the head of the hall, and two girls from somewhere else in the Mission bring them a tin tray piled high with bacon, eggs, and a jug filled with orange juice.

'I was number one,' says George, considering the bowl of dry hash he has collected.

'Don't you think . . .' Jon's thoughts are too fast for his words to keep up. 'There isn't even a list.'

'So?'

'The boy in the dairy, he reckoned Judah Reed doesn't even know his name . . .'

'I don't think he knows mine.'

Jon Heather thinks: better keep it that way, George.

'Eat up,' he says, remembering, dimly, that first morning in the Home, the fat boy with porridge pumping out of his ears.

George pokes some of the food into his gullet, but the taste is horrific; it must be the scrapings from the bottom of a pot. After a few attempts, he perfects a way of poking it to the back of his throat, so that he barely tastes a thing, but by that point the hand bell is clanging.

'Dairy for me today,' says George. 'I'm going to sneak a suck of milk.'

Jon should have thought of that. 'Tell Tommy I said . . .' Jon falters. 'Hey, George,' he says, as they traipse after the other boys into the morning light. 'You do what Tommy tells you, OK?'

'You don't need to badger me, Jon Heather. You're not Peter, you know.'

After they have parted ways, Jon joins a rag of other boys outside the sandstone huts. There are boys of all ages here, only the very youngest spared and sent off for village muster, and Jon finds a spot to stand among them, not too close to the front and not too close to the back.

'What is it today?' asks a little one next to him.

Jon Heather only shrugs.

They seem to stand there, in a useless clot, for an age. The coolness of morning evaporates, to be replaced with a dull, insistent heat. Finally, Judah Reed and another man in black appear from the dormitory shacks. They have, Jon knows, been carrying out inspections, making mental notes of which boys have failed to make their beds, or which boys have sneaked banned treats and trinkets under their mattresses. Once, a boy was found to have been saving chunks from his evening stew to have as a midnight supper. He had to make a trip to Judah Reed's office and wasn't allowed dinner for five nights straight, in order to teach him a lesson.

Judah Reed approaches and the boys part to let him through. Without looking back, he makes a simple gesture and, snatching a shovel from its prop against the wall, begins to march. As one, the boys follow. Jon tries to catch the eyes of a bigger boy beside him, giving him a questioning look – does *anybody* know where we're going? – but nobody cares to reply.

They walk the length of the sandstone huts, navigating around the bedwetters' dorm and the deep latrines at its rear, until they come to the very edge of the Mission, as far from the dairy as a boy could get. The scrub grows unruly here, with walls of thorn so thick a boy could not even creep through on hands and knees.

Judah Reed stops and turns on the spot. On his right, another man in black slowly comes to a halt. Judah Reed thrusts the shovel, hard, into the ground. The blade slices into the crust, and then the shovel just stands there, vibrating.

He looks up, at the gathered boys. 'A proud day,' he begins. 'The start of something new. When the Children's Crusade first came to this blasted land, there was nothing. No buildings. No roads. No . . .'

Fences, thinks Jon Heather. He catches himself dreaming, and reins his focus back to Judah Reed.

'It is time,' Judah Reed goes on, 'to make something new, to rebuild the land, just as you are rebuilding yourselves.' He pauses, lifts an arm. 'You have seen, of course, the sandstone homes in the heart of our Mission.'

The bravest boys look over their shoulders, back the way they have come. Jon Heather does not.

'Well,' smiles Judah Reed, 'they did not grow, like scrub trees, straight out of the rock. They were planned and crafted and built by . . .' He lifts his hands and turns out his palms, as if to prove he is not carrying anything. 'We can do the same here.' His eyes fall upon a little one, six years old, sitting cross-legged at the front of the throng. 'Perhaps you might like to make the first cut?'

Jon Heather cannot see the expression on the boy's face but, from the way he sinks back into the boys around him, he can picture it well enough. Even so, as Judah Reed extends his hand and steps forward, the boy gets to his bare feet. Judah Reed puts an enormous hand in the small of his back and steers him forward.

They reach the shovel, and the boy is instructed to lift it from its rest. The tool is almost as tall as him, and when he tries to draw it free, like Excalibur from its stone, he fails. Judah Reed whispers a word in his ear and the boy tries again. He rocks back until the shovel comes loose – and then, dangling all of his weight from the handle, he staggers back, the blade spraying clots of hard dust as it works itself free.

'You will always remember this day,' Judah Reed smiles.

The boy lifts the shovel and clangs it down. When it hardly breaks the surface he has to try again – and then again after that, and again, each time a wave shooting up the handle and jarring along his arms.

'Stand on it!' a boy cries out.

Judah Reed's eyes lift. 'Yes,' he says, his gaze drifting back to the little one. 'Stand on it. Give it some *fire*.'

The boy pushes the shovel as deeply as he can and then leaps on the blade. His weight hardly makes a difference, but he rocks from side to side, working the blade deeper into the crust. When, at last, it is embedded, he must haul back, chipping out clods until a tiny hole has been excavated.

The boy steps back, dripping with sweat, holding his left arm with his right.

'The first cut!' Judah Reed beams. 'Now,' he says, his hand dancing on the little one's head. 'Do it again.'

After that, they must all join in. Once Judah Reed is satisfied that work is underway, he convenes with the other man in black and sweeps off, deeper into the Mission, to look over some other rag of boys. Soon, the man in black is delivered a jug of fresh water by one of the Mission girls, and a bowl of oranges to peck at during the day. There is a trough of water in which the boys are permitted to dunk their heads, but soon it is thick with sand and not fit for drinking.

There are picks and shovels, and some boys are set to digging a big square, deep as a little one's head, into which foundations will be laid. Others are given scythes and books of matches, and duly dispatched into the scrub. It is their job to clear the land of trees and thorn so that more digging might follow. Jon Heather, meanwhile, joins a group of boys collecting up the excavated dirt and shovelling it into wheelbarrows that might then be ferried into another corner of the scrub. Some little ones are tasked with sifting stone from sand, and in the afternoon they will mix it with choking concrete powder from a mountain of big sacks. From these, Jon learns, blocks will be made.

Not an hour has gone by when he comes out of the scrub with an empty wheelbarrow and stops to catch his breath. Sweat and sand have dribbled into his eyes and he scrunches them tight to blink it away. When he opens them again, a bigger boy is looming near.

'Keep an eye out,' he says, pushing past Jon and tipping his chin towards a canvas chair set in the shade.

There, the man in black sits, fingers picking at the peel of an orange as his gaze settles on Jon.

'Thank you,' whispers Jon.

Ignoring the rumbling of his tummy, he heaves the barrow back to the excavations. Through the midday heat haze, he peers into the heart of the Mission. There, Judah Reed is standing by the sandstone shacks, drinking from a canteen – but it is not this that catches Jon's eye. He focuses instead on the walls behind him, the line of the stones, the pitch of the roof, the way the whole thing must have grown up, piece by piece, coated in the sweat of little hands.

George plods along the length of the sandstone shacks, reaching the edge of the untilled field long after the little ones there have started village muster. On the other side of the field, there sits a big spidery wood, but he cannot look at it for long. There was a different kind of wood surrounding the Home back in Leeds, but both make him feel the same way. His skin crawls. Anything can come out of woodland, and this Australia land has already thrown up too many monsters to want to contemplate any more. And so, with his head tucked down and his hands shoved in the waistband of his short trousers, he barrels up to the dairy steps.

Inside, there is a mean old man, whose face is dominated

by three moustaches – one on top of his lip, and the others growing wild where his eyebrows ought to be – but the man doesn't even notice as George clambers up the steps. Sitting on a pail, with his fingers tickling the underside of some scraggly goats, there sits a bigger boy. He is thin and wiry, with a chin like one of the heroes out of Peter's comic books, and when George approaches, he turns around with a broad beam.

'Jack the lad!' he exclaims. 'You're late!'

George turns an awkward little dance, looking behind him. 'I'm not Jack,' he says.

'Of course you're not,' the bigger boy beams. 'It's a name I call lads. Well, go on, pull up a pail! I'll show you how to get started. It's a big day, little thing. We can churn up some butter and then . . . I'm going to show you how to make a string of sausages!'

A string of sausages does not sound bad, not after the muck George ate this morning.

'Can I have some milk?'

The bigger boy flicks a look over his shoulder, to where the mean old man is playing with the billy goats in their stalls. 'Got to be some perks of working in this dairy, don't there?' he grins. 'Just wait until old man McAllister is out the way . . .'

This bigger boy does not seem as beastly as the rest – but with bigger boys, just like men in black, you never can tell. George won't admit it to anybody else, but there was a time, long ago, when he was even frightened of Peter.

'My name's George.'

'Tommy,' the bigger boy says, offering up a creamy hand. 'Now, let's get going . . .'

George's first attempts to get milk out of the goat result in the goat screaming and kicking out. In the end, the bigger boy has to put his hands over George's own and show him how to knead and nip gently, so that a squirt comes out and makes a rattle at the bottom of the pail. After a few minutes working like this, George can go it alone. The milk has a funny smell, but that does nothing to dampen his enthusiasm. As he watches the bucket fill, he begins to smile. This, he admits, is actually fun.

George fills two buckets in the time it takes Tommy Crowe to fill the remaining ten, a procession of goats moving past them and then out into the scrub to graze. Once they are done, George helps Tommy carry the buckets to an outhouse a little deeper into the Mission. Here, some girls take the buckets with shy smiles, and George has to wait outside while Tommy is chattering within. He hears precious little of what they are saying, but it seems to George that it is Tommy Crowe doing all of the talking, the girls just punctuating his stories with occasional bursts of laughter.

George is peeking around the corner, into the outhouse, when Tommy Crowe says his goodbyes and turns on the spot.

'Come on, little thing. We've got to get back to work before one of those men in black starts sniffing round . . .'

George stares wide-eyed at the girls pouring their milk into churning pots and does not turn to follow.

'I thought we got to churn up butter,' he says, wishing he was one of those girls.

'We could have helped if we'd been faster with the milking. We'll have to buck up next time . . .'

George knows what that bigger boy means; it was George being the slowcoach, not Tommy. With his hands clenched in tiny fists, he plods back to the dairy.

Just outside, that old man McAllister has separated one billy goat from the rest, leading him out of his stall and tethering him to a stake.

'This one?' says Tommy, approaching the unsuspecting billy.

Old McAllister hovers above, excavating his ear with a dirty finger. 'He'll be stringier than the last, but it's best he goes now. Most of it's for salting, so make sure the others know.'

George can barely interpret this strange conversation, so sits on the edge of a stone trough and watches. When McAllister catches him slumping down, his eyes flare. Tommy Crowe gives George a secret nod; he can, at least, interpret this and quickly gets up. Without knowing it, he has got his short trousers wet, and looks down to see that the water in the trough is a funny shade of pink, with deep black and red silt sitting at its bottom.

'Come on,' says Tommy, after McAllister has trudged away. 'I'll show you how it's done.'

It does not dawn on George what Tommy Crowe means, even when they have rolled the goat over. George's job is to hold him like that while Tommy Crowe disappears inside. Alone with the animal, George pets its head softly and tickles under its chin. The goat doesn't seem to mind, so George pets it again. He wonders if it might let him give its tummy a quick pat, but as he is separating the legs to sneak his hand in, Tommy reappears, carrying with him a rack of knives and two lengths of rope.

'He's been a good one, this,' says Tommy, getting to his knees. 'Seems a shame to tie his legs up at all.'

'Why do we need to tie his legs?'

'He'll kick out otherwise,' says Tommy, looping the rope around the billy's back legs. 'I saw a boy get kicked like that. It wasn't pretty. Though . . .' He studies George's girth. 'I dare say you've got some extra protection, eh?'

Puzzled, George tickles the billy's scruff again. He seems to like this, so it's a terrible shame when Tommy passes him a length of rope and instructs him to tie up the forelegs. Getting the knot right is difficult, but under Tommy's instruction he manages it. Tommy tells him, well done. George smiles, because this isn't a thing he's often heard.

'Well, now we get to it.' Tommy reaches out for the rack of knives, selects one, and offers it, handle first, to George.

George takes it limply in his hands. Then, suddenly, he looks into Tommy Crowe's expectant eyes and understands.

'But . . . why?'

'Look, just bring his head back and try and make it clean. You can do it in one cut, if you're careful. They don't expect you to do it right first time, though. Boys always make a mess of it. Just try your best, and they won't be able to do a thing.'

'Who won't?'

'Why, Judah Reed, of course. The rest of them. You've got to start off on a good foot, see, or else they'll number you for trouble. Then they'll keep on watching you just to see if you slip up, and you don't want that, George!'

Tommy Crowe is laughing, yet his words are washing over George. George isn't a troublemaker. He's never been in trouble in his life. Even when he had a mother she didn't get cross. The thought, now, of all those men in black knowing him for a bad lad is enough to bring tears to his eyes. He might be able to swallow them back, but then he looks at the goat. Its eyes roll towards him. He wants his scruff tickling again, his tummy patted. George can see that, plain as day. How can it be making trouble just to leave this dumb old thing alone?

George scrabbles back, sits in the red dirt. His short trousers, still wet from the trough, get sticky with sand.

'George, I'm going to tell you what I told your boy Jon.' Tommy puts a finger on George's chin and forces him to look up. Two big blubbery eyes meet his own. 'If you don't do it on your own, they're going to *make* you do it.'

'How?' sobs George.

Tommy Crowe says, 'Don't find out, George. Please don't find that out.'

'I don't see why I have to.' George folds his arms, but quickly they slide apart and he is, suddenly, hugging himself. 'It's just a poor old goat. I don't even want to eat him. I'll just have potatoes.'

'They cook those potatoes in goat fat, George.'

'I'll clean it off. I don't even like skins. I'll just have the insides.'

Tommy Crowe steps back. 'You *have* to do it, George. If you don't do it, it means I have to tell . . . But I'm not going to tell, see? Which means they'll have me strung up.'

'You wouldn't tell on me . . .'

'I just said I wouldn't, didn't I? But when they find out I didn't tell, they'll come for me and . . .' Tommy kicks out, launching a stone straight at the billy. '. . . they'll make me take my medicine. I've never taken my medicine before. Don't you get it?' He relents, shuffling up to the goat's head and gently pulling it back so that the throat is all George can see. 'Do you want me to go in Judah Reed's office?'

There are tears in George's eyes.

'Do you know what happens in Judah Reed's office, George?'

George straightens, finds the knife in his pudgy fist. 'What if it won't go in?' he says, trembling at the goat's exposed neck.

'You just have to push it.'

'He's going to be upset.'

Tommy Crowe strokes the billy's scruff. 'Not for long.'

George gets on his hands and knees and crawls over to the silly old goat. He can hardly hold the knife any longer; it only wobbles in his fingers. When he tries to press it on the goat, neither brute nor boy can even feel it.

'It's easy, George. Look, I'm holding him still. It's just like cutting your dinner.'

'A tough old dinner.'

Tommy allows himself a smile. 'Like that leathery stew they serve up here. It's like eating old boots.'

At this, George snorts, drawing strings of thick phlegm back into his nose.

'Go on!'

The knife is steadier now. George looks down, takes a deep breath. Perhaps, if he closes his eyes, it doesn't have to be so bad.

His body bucks, his stomach tightens and thrusts out. He drops the knife, but he is too late to turn. Jets of this morning's breakfast thunder out of his nostrils and lips, showering the goat in orange and green.

With the sick still smeared up and down his face, George jumps up and runs.

Jon Heather cannot see the blood on his hands any longer, for he is wearing new gloves of cracked concrete and sand. The day has passed, his face is streaked with sweat and trails of hardening grey, and he can feel the skin of his soles shredded and sore. The site has almost been cleared now, the bigger boys hacking the worst away with scythes and setting fire to the rest, while, on the outskirts of the site, the younger boys have taken their picks to the earth and dug down until they hit rock. This, it seems, is not nearly deep enough, for they will have to dig deeper tomorrow.

On the edge of the excavations, the man in black has been brought more fresh juice. He has a camping chair, against which his half hockey stick is propped. There was a moment, in the midday heat, when he looked to have fallen asleep – but all it took to bring him back into wakefulness was one of the smaller boys to crawl away for rest in the shade. That boy, now, could not crawl away for rest, even if he wanted. Judah Reed had to be called. He carried the boy away in his arms, telling him he would have to do better if he was to be a big strong man, not some pathetic little English girl.

Jon is loading a new wheelbarrow with stones, ferrying them off to slag heaps in the scrub, when he sees a blurry ball hurtle across the Mission and up towards the dormitory shacks. He turns back to his wheelbarrow, mindful of working too slowly, but he cannot ignore it for long. The blurry ball – that was George.

He looks up. Another boy is following close behind, straining against another barrow of stones, so he cannot stop for long. Over his shoulder, the man in black is deep in conversation with a cottage mother. He lifts the barrow high, hurrying the last few yards into the scrub.

The slag heaps have climbed high today, mountains breaking out of the bedrock. Jon upends his barrow, scraping the last rubble out with hands rubbed raw, and then turns, awkwardly, to let the next boy in. By the time he comes back out of the scrub, the man in black has drifted away, and boys across the site are standing idly back, propped on picks and pitchforks, waiting for the evening bell to ring.

By the time it does, some of the boys have already taken the chance and disappeared. Jon, remembering Tommy Crowe's words, forces himself to remain – but, as soon as he can, he ditches his wheelbarrow and makes haste for the dormitory shack. Inside, it is dank and dark. The only movement is that of a scrub rat, scuttling about the floorboards at the back of the room.

In his cot, George lies with his knees hunched up. He looks up only when Jon calls his name.

'Did you know?' he demands.

Jon approaches, unsure of his own feet. 'Know what?'

'What they do down at the dairy.'

There is no point in lying; George is waiting for it.

'Of course I knew, Georgie. They had me do the same.'

'But I'm only eight.'

'I don't think it matters . . .'

'It's because we told them I'm ten.'

This explanation seems to soothe George, but Jon cannot follow the logic. He nods, sits on the end of George's cot.

'It isn't fair, George, but it's done now. Don't think about it. It doesn't help.'

'I didn't do it at all!' George protests. 'It's only a poor old goat. How's it going to feel if I stick it with a knife?'

Some other boys begin to file back into the dorm. One casts Jon and George a questioning look, but soon moves on. It will not be long, Jon knows, before the bells go for dinner. By then, it will be too late.

'You didn't do it?'

George shakes his head.

'George, they're going to *make* you do it.'

'They can't make me,' George utters. 'It's my fingers. It's my hands. They can't make them work, Jon Heather. *I* can't even make them work, not with that old knife.'

There is something in these words that cuts Jon, just like his knife cut the goat. It's my fingers, he thinks. It's my hands. George doesn't know what he's saying, but he's right.

All the same, he remembers Judah Reed's office: Ernest keening; the latecomer's eyes in the dormitory at night . . . If he was brave enough, Jon might be able to imagine the ways in which men in black make boys grow up. Instead, he shakes the thought away, focuses on George. 'Georgie boy, you *have* to, before they find out. I did it. You can do it too.'

George rolls over. 'Would you do it again?'

'If I had to . . .'

'I mean for me, Jon Heather.' George chews his lips. 'I mean right now. Do it so I don't have to, Jon. It's what Peter would do . . .'

Jon can still feel the way the gristle resisted as he tried to draw the knife up. He hears the pop again, as the goat's head came loose and flopped into his lap.

'You'll have to do it sooner or later, George.'

Sensing an opening, George sits up and kneads his watery eyes. 'But not this time?'

'If they catch me, I'm for the . . .'

'They won't catch.'

'You don't know they won't.'

'I promise, Jon. I promise they won't. You've got to trust me . . .'

There is nothing more to say.

'Well, you have to come and help,' Jon insists.

Sensing some sort of triumph, George uncurls and flops off the bed. 'I can hold his legs, to stop him kicking.'

They make haste across the Mission. Little ones are coming back in from village muster, older boys sweeping up in the woodworking sheds. Along the way, George stops to show Jon the place where the Mission girls make butter, but there is no time for dallying; Jon grabs him by the wrist and drags him along.

At the dairy, Tommy Crowe is waiting. 'Jack the lad,' he says. 'You're back.'

In unison, Jon and George say, 'Yes!' Then Jon circles around the prostrate goat, George hanging back by the edge of the water trough.

'I see they got you building today. Learning about bricks . . .' Tommy shakes his head. 'I wouldn't mind learning about bricks, if we got to build *ourselves* a nice new house.' He stops. 'What are you doing here, Jack?'

'I came to do it for him.'

Tommy Crowe exhales. 'You can't do it for him. He's got to do it himself. It's not just him. It's all of us. It's . . . a lesson. He can't take the easy way out. He's got to . . .'

Jon looks back at George. 'Not this time,' he says.

'You're serious, aren't you?'

Jon finds the rack of knives on the dirt and picks up the one he judges best. On his knees now, he rubs the goat's brow, gently lifting back its head. He presses one of his thighs against its back, so that he might steady his cut.

'Jon, you'll go to Judah Reed's office if they find out. *I'll* go to Judah Reed's office.'

Jon looks up, eyes empty, not breathing a word.

'I can't help with this,' Tommy mutters. 'It'll only be worse, the more I help . . .'

Jon watches him hurry into the growing dark and throws a look at George. 'You said you'd hold the legs.'

'I'm not sure if I can . . .'

For the first time, Jon snaps, 'I can't do it if you don't!'

George totters forward, getting onto his knees to hold the goat's rump fast.

'Harder,' Jon says.

'But he knows what we're up to . . .'

Jon feels the goat tense, and senses his chance. This time, the blade goes in much more smoothly. The goat bucks, but he works fast, straining to keep the knife in as he saws up. He has not quite opened the full throat when he knows it is dead. The blood is pooling around his knees, but it is not this that has killed the goat; it has died of fear, moments before it died of anything else.

'Is that it?'

That's it, Jon thinks. It was easier this time. Next time, it will be easier still. He is not sure how far he can follow that train of thought, but he knows it is what the men in black mean for him. Just like building houses and mixing concrete and breaking ground; killing goats will make him grow up.

'Come on Georgie, we've got to get it in that tree.'

'What for?'

'To take off his skin.'

He remembers only in snatches what Tommy Crowe taught him, so that this time the pelt comes off in three big pieces instead of one, and this time – though he manages not to puncture the shit sack again – he has to slop the guts out in stages, and doesn't know how to separate the good offal from the bad. Up on the stone slab, he hacks away haunches, loading up neck and shoulders into the wheelbarrow, but the remains look uglier than they did the last time, and the head still dangles from the tip of the spine. Now, the goat is a grotesque millipede, glaring accusingly at them from a spine of glistening red and white.

'Is it finished?' asks George, looking dumbly at the meat piled up in the wheelbarrow.

'It goes down to the salting sheds. Or it goes in tomorrow's stew.'

Jon takes off his bloody smock to use as a wash rag and sinks his hands deep in the trough. He has been quick enough this time, that the stain cannot work its way deep into his flesh – but, all the same, his hands will never be clean again.

'Get your hands in here, George. Judah Reed saw my hands all bloody and told me I'd done good. Maybe he'll see yours too . . .'

The thought of Judah Reed telling him well done instead of taking him in his office propels George over, and quickly he is splashing the bloody water up and down his arms.

When he is done, he stands up, looking proud. Jon has drifted to the fences overlooking the untilled field. On the other side, a breeze moves in the branches of the shadow wood, setting them swaying.

'Thank you, Jon Heather.'

Jon isn't listening, so George has to say it again.

'I'll do better next time,' he whispers.

'Don't worry about it, George. Only . . .' Jon's eyes are drawn back to the dancing branches of the shadow wood. 'You ever think about what's out there?' he asks.

'Outside the Mission? You mean the sea – and England?'

'No, George,' Jon whispers. 'I don't mean that at all. I mean – there are trees, and there's desert, and then – well, there's McAllister. He doesn't live here. He's got to come from *somewhere*. And there's got to be schools and towns, just like the one we saw. And, George . . .'

'Jon, don't . . .' George begins. 'I know what you're meaning, so please don't . . .'

'There's got to be Peter, doesn't there? Somewhere out there. He has to be *somewhere*, doesn't he, George?'

Jon wriggles back into his sodden Crusade smock and nods at the wheelbarrow. 'It's best you wheel it in, Georgie. So they don't suspect.'

George nods, taking up the handles. 'You don't think we'll get found out, do you?'

Jon shakes his head. 'Not this time.'

The barrow is heavy, but George pushes it alone, huffing and puffing deeper into the Mission. There is a chance, Jon knows, that Tommy Crowe might already have told – but something tells him that he hasn't. Telling a tale would mean Judah Reed finally learns Tommy's name, and there isn't a thing in the Mission more terrifying than that.

In the doorway of the dairy shed, Jon waits until George has disappeared. There is a half moon tonight; it is beginning to shine in the preternatural gloom. He dawdles into the dairy, takes up a broom and begins to sweep at the earth, collecting up globules of sand and blood, shreds of viscera. All of this, he has learned, can go back into the goat's feed. Goat eating goat and boy eating boy; that's the Children's Crusade.

He has made only three sweeps when he hears parakeets shrieking from their roosts. Seconds later, another bird makes a long, looping sound. He props the broom against the wall and ventures into the dusk. Before he knows what he is doing, he has clambered to sit on top of the fence. He stares at the shadow wood and dreams.

Before long, as if sleepwalking, he has toppled from the fence and taken three strides across the untilled earth. It isn't just McAllister and it isn't just towns and shorelines and oceans.

All of that, he knows, is out there somewhere, across endless scrub. It's the road. Ernest saw it, curving away into the night. A road, Jon Heather knows, must lead somewhere. It must come from somewhere too. All a wily boy would have to do is follow that road, and he might end up . . .

He stops, realizes he is already at the edge of the shadow wood, one foot poised atop the sandstone bank where the little ones staked out their rabbit.

. . . *anywhere*, he thinks. A boy might end up anywhere but here.

By the time he has finished that thought, he is already deep into the woodland. Night falls quickly over the Mission and, when he looks back, he can hardly see the outline of the dairy through gaps in the trees. If he means to go further at all, it is only because here, with the fragrance of the scrub strong all around, he does not breathe in the stink of concrete dust and ash, cannot see the billy goat blood in which he has been bathing. Here, he might be anything or anybody – Jon Heather might still be a clean, loving little boy.

He reaches the edge of the shadow wood and creeps out, through a curtain of coarse grass, to blink over the endless expanse. Charts of unknown stars are plastered above and by their light he can see . . . nothing. No trees. No hilltops. No men in black, lurking out there to trap runaway boys.

All he wants to do is see that road – so he takes off, one step at a time. After a few paces, he looks back. He has come further than he thought; the shadow wood now squats some distance away. It does not beckon him back. He sets out again, his steps growing longer. Now he is bounding, taking great leaps like a deer, his arms spread wide to feel the rush of air and dust against his chest.

Ernest said that the road wound its way into the sunset. He tries to figure the route, recalling the way the evening redness bleeds over the dairy and untilled fields. When he is certain he is going in the right direction, he keeps careful watch for some loitering man in black or some old bastard like McAllister there to do their bidding. Yet all he can see is a lone cow, standing dumbly there in the light of the moon. Jon watches it for a while, intrigued that there are cows, too, at the ends of the earth. Poor brute – it too must have been shanghaied onto a ship and sent across the sea.

When he finds the road, it is almost by accident. The earth gives way underneath him, and he topples forward, catching himself on scrub that clings to a shallow bank. Really, it is not a road at all, certainly not like an English road with black tar and white paint. It is only a different kind of earth, packed hard and cleared of coarse grass. All the same, Jon marvels at it, dancing out into the middle and then back again, dodging imaginary buses and trucks. He knows, without a doubt now, that he has come further than he and Ernest came, that tonight nobody saw him slipping over the imaginary line.

He begins to sing. He does not know the words, only the tune, something his sisters used to warble when they sat him on their knees. If he can keep that song in his heart, then his sisters will not be able to disappear. He begins to march, bellowing out the song, absolute in his conviction that nobody in the world can hear.

He has never been more alone in all of his life. He has never felt so elated.

He wheels on the spot, turning back in the direction he believes the Children's Crusade must lie. 'Judah Reed!' he bellows. 'I'm gone! I'm going home!'

He finds a chunk of dry bread in the pocket of his overalls, something he had stuffed there at breakfast. He rests, for a moment, on a bulb of springy branches and chews on it. Shapes flitter in the darkness on the banks of the road, and he watches them go.

Through the night he runs, in fits and starts, halfway between the scrub and the stars. So featureless is the night that, though he can see spidery shapes in the starlight, he cannot tell how far he has come. He begins to think that he is running on the spot, play-acting. If he has gone anywhere at all, it is only because the world is turning underneath.

And suddenly the dream is a nightmare. He is running, running, running – but he is getting nowhere at all. Judah Reed has him by the collar. Judah Reed has him dangling in the air. His legs are kicking like a dervish, but he cannot tear himself away.

A lump forms in his throat – he wants to be sick. He stops dead, pirouettes. After he has turned three times, he no longer knows which way is running away and which way is running back. On his haunches, he looks up at the sky, remembering how, in *We Didn't Mean to Go to Sea*, the boys and girls could tell where they were by the constellations above. Yet these stars are treacherous; even if Jon Heather knew things like that, these stars are different from the ones with which he grew up. When they twinkle, they are mocking him, telling him, this is not your home; without the men in black, you cannot survive.

He tries to pick a direction, but whenever he steps out, something stops him. He cannot bear the thought that, like last time, he might be running back to the Mission. At last, he begins to feel the cold. It is not like the winter that had England in its grip when they left the Home, but he is aware, for the first time, that he is wearing nothing but his Crusade clothes, still damp from when he plunged them into the trough. He picks a direction and runs again, idling between bursts, but finds that it doesn't warm him up.

He shivers. Up ahead, where the road banks – who knows in which direction – there is a cavity in the ground. It is, perhaps, the only thing Jon has truly seen all night, a deep depression where the scrub hangs down and the starlight shadows are dark. Jon stops and stares. Then, he remembers . . .

There once was a boy who ran away. He ran as far as he could run, and when he could run no more, he burrowed down into the baked red earth . . .

Jon's legs carry him there without having to be commanded. The earth will look after him now. He sinks into the den, and finds that it fits his body perfectly. He will rest here for a while. He is not giving up. He will rest and then, refreshed, be on his way.

Jon is asleep almost instantly, too soon to see the morning redness rising in the east.

VII

Cold, spreading like disease, wakes him. He does not want to admit what has happened, so he lies there, very still, until he begins to shiver. Then, popping open one eye at a time, he risks a look at the bed alongside his own. It is still empty, and the very sight fills him with horror. He counts slowly – one, two, three – and peers again. The sack pillows are still crammed under the sheets, so that any curious cottage mother might be tricked, but there is no denying it any longer: the fat little boy is all alone.

He will have to sort this mess out himself.

He drops, very quietly, onto the floorboards. His nightshirt is sodden but, curiously, there are patches of his pants that remain dry. He pats down his mattress, feels for the damp patch, and whips off the sheet. Bundling it at his feet, he heaves until the mattress is turned over and pauses to catch his breath.

It's been so long since this happened. Probably even weeks. He didn't wake up like this once on the *Othello*, not when there was Peter in the cabin, telling him not to be such a big girl with that old grin on his face. Last night, though, all he could think about was petting that billy goat gruff, lugging bits of its body up to the salting shed and breathing in the tangy moistness that came up off its pieces. Maybe, he reasons, that's why he's slipped up – but no man in black here could ever understand.

He turns. Low sun is shining over the compound, and soon the dawn bells will ring. He will have to work fast.

If he is lucky, the cottage mother will not be awake. He rips off his nightshirt, crams it in with the bundle, and finds another shirt from the stash under his bed. By some strange mercy, they are all bone dry. Once he is dressed, he hurries through the beds and ducks out of the dormitory. There is no light on in the neighbouring sandstone building where the cottage mother lives, but, all the same, he crouches low as he scuttles to the laundry house beyond.

Inside, all is still. It is a stone outhouse, lined with great barrels and racks, with a pit sitting in the centre from which a deep channel rises to a water pump. The girls from the other side of the compound will be arriving after breakfast – but dawn has barely broken, so there must be time yet. He finds the barrels where the soiled sheets go – but, when he peers inside, they are empty. If he leaves his sheets here, somebody will know.

He stops, turns in circles, his mouth working like a fish as he realizes that, for the first time in his life, there is nobody who might tell him what to do. There is nothing else for it. He will bury them in the woods today, when he is out on village muster, an eight-year-old left to wander with the toddlers. If ever they're found, nobody will be able to tell if the wicked culprit is even still part of the Children's Crusade. It will be a perfect crime.

By the time he creeps back out of the laundry, the compound is starting to wake. Through two of the sandstone rows he sees a man in black flitter by. Floundering back into shadow, he bites down hard on his tongue and has to stop from squealing out. It is not Judah Reed himself, only one of his acolytes.

He has lingered too long already. There is a back way out of the laundry, and he plods towards it, suddenly out of breath. The coast, at last, is clear. Hitching the sheets up, he thunders across the earth as fast as his stubby legs will carry him.

By the time he reaches his dormitory he is puffing hard – but at least he has not been seen.

He has gone only two steps through the door, blinking into the gloom, when he sees the face in front of him: not the cottage mother, not Judah Reed, but a bigger boy, thirteen years old. He looms ahead like a solid stone wall, a barbarian in short trousers with scabs on his arms.

The bigger boy looks down, casts a quick glance back to see the bed stripped bare. 'George,' he begins, with a carefully crafted grin. 'Don't tell me you've been *bad* again?'

*

Jon is dimly aware of a steady rolling, as if he is still at sea and all of the Mission has been a bad dream. He can feel the sun beating down, baking the grit smeared across his face.

Beneath him, an engine hums.

He opens his eyes to see the desert rushing in all directions. Somewhere, something yaps, but Jon cannot see a thing. He has been wrapped in a blanket – and suddenly it seems to be smothering him. He kicks and punches until it flies away, landing in a heap at his side.

He peers around. He is in the back of a wagon, exactly the same as took them from the boats all those weeks ago. He cannot see any real road along which they are rushing, just a snake of earth as barren and red as everything else.

He reels to the edge of the ute. The wheels kick up clouds

of dust that he can track for miles behind. They jolt over a patch of uneven ground, and the dust rushes up to make him gag. Eyes streaming, he sinks back down.

From the blanket, a tiny yellow dog watches him curiously. Then, as uncertain of its own footing as Jon, it nudges forward, pushes him with a snout smeared in sand.

Slumped against the back of the wagon, Jon can see two people in the cab. The driver is an old man with wrinkled red skin, in a singlet and canvas hat. The other, one arm dangling out of the window, is the blackest man Jon has ever seen. He, too, is wearing only a singlet, with thick hair that hangs in heavy coils.

Suddenly, he is immeasurably afraid. He reaches out, thinking he might wrap himself back in the blanket and shut out the baking world, but instead the yellow pup waddles into his hands. At least with its heart beating in his lap, he can bottle up the fear.

When they have driven for what feels like forever, the desert's lonely silence is broken by shrieking birds, and Jon opens his eyes to see the lush greenery of a watering hole. The scrub is taller here – real trees, just like the ones back home! – and there is even colour, reds and yellows in the branches that, he realizes, are the birds who mock the passing truck. On the other side of the watering hole, they slow and turn left, following another trail. On their right, there is no desert: there is grass.

Jon throws off the blanket and the pup and peeps over the edge of the ute. He has not seen grass like it in what feels like a lifetime. He has seen coarse reeds and tussocks of plants that clearly *think* they are grass – but this is as lush as the parks he used to know. The world is opening up. He sees three men on horseback cantering over the grassland, a little shack with tents arranged around – and, at last, a farmhouse, built like some grand English manor, sitting at the end of the trail.

The truck wobbles through a gap in the fence, turns a tight arc, and judders to a halt. Off-balance, Jon crashes to his knees. When he gets back up, he hears the cab doors slamming and the tread of boots as the men clamber out.

The sun is still low, and when he squints up he cannot see the face peering, curiously, into his own. When he cups his hand to his eyes, he sees that it is the black man from the cab, shaking his head and hawing.

Jon feels certain he ought to understand, but there is hardly a word that he recognizes. The man grins, seemingly pleased, and throws Jon a gesture that even he can understand, ordering him to get off the truck. It is the last thing Jon wants to do – but he is so relieved at finally understanding that he has clambered to the ground before it even crosses his mind to protest.

The black man reaches over his head, whips the dog up, and plants it on the earth at Jon's feet.

'You're all up and awake then, are you now?'

Jon turns. The wagon's driver is sidling up to him from the other side of the truck, a belt laden with hammers and wrenches slung around his waist. He is wearing jeans and heavy boots and sweat shimmers all over his skin.

'Aw,' he says, 'don't look at me like that, cobber. If we hadn't 've been driving down that road, you could've been carrion by high noon.' He pauses. 'Look, you'd best tell us your name. We won't go misusing it. You've got my honour.'

Jon remains silent.

'Suit yourself,' the man replies. 'I seen more meat on a dead heifer in the Dry than on you, boy. We'll get you cleaned up, get you some tucker. Booty back there's gone to see if he can rouse up Cormac. He's got history handling your lot.' He pauses, but Jon just stands there. 'Well, what're you waiting for? Go on – hop it!'

The man lifts a mountainous tool, slings it nonchalantly over his shoulder and ambles towards the veranda. Halfway there, he looks over his shoulder. 'Do I have to sling you over me shoulder as well?'

This time, there is enough menace in the voice for Jon to follow.

Inside, there is a large kitchen, with two big ovens and huge pans, big as cauldrons, hanging above. Along one side, there sits a row of pantries; on the other, a window looks out of the back of the house, where three horses are drinking from a trough. Above them, there looms a tall tower, a giant water tank sitting on stilts.

The man leads Jon through the kitchen, and into a yard over which the roof extends. Jon can see the black man again, saddling one of the horses. Swiftly, he swings onto its back and pulls it around.

'Here,' the other man begins, dumping a bucket at Jon's side and opening a pump against the wall. The faucet sputters, before a jet of water erupts and rattles around the bucket like gunfire. 'You clean some of that muck off you. Booty'll be back before you know it. Then we'll get this whole mess righted out.'

The water is icy cold and, instead of soaking himself in it, Jon drops and drinks greedily. When he looks up, the little dog is again at his side. It rises on hind paws to take a drink, but can't reach. Accepting defeat, it looks at Jon with big, wet eyes.

'Here you go,' Jon says, cupping his hands together. 'It isn't your fault, is it?'

When they have drunk their fill, Jon curls up in the shade. It gets hot quickly. Every now and again, he ventures beyond the shade – but the sun beats him back, like some relentless marauder. On occasion, when he threatens to run straight into the furnace, the man reappears from the house and calls him back. Once, he brings him a plate with strange meats on it, tough things that Jon has to turn over and over in his mouth before he can swallow, and a mug of tea thick with sugar. The man says his name is Richardson, but still Jon won't give up his own. He says please and thank you, but that is all. His mother would be proud that he has not forgotten his manners.

A little while later, he hears another engine, and creeps around the edge of the house. Scrub chickens run wild along the fence, and they scatter at his approach, squawking in a pantomime of panic.

Another ute has pulled up, an older vehicle reamed in red dirt. There is a black man sitting in the back, but Jon cannot be certain if it is the same man who rode out on his horse. As he watches, the driver swings out of the cab, wearing a grubby white shirt and wide-brimmed hat.

The man named Richardson welcomes the driver, shaking him by the hand. Jon can see their jaws working, but he can't hear a word. He supposes they are talking about him, and suddenly the man named Richardson guffaws. It is like a knife in Jon's side.

He turns on his heel, scurries back to the shade at the rear of the ranch. Splashing water over his face, he manages to get rid of some of the concrete dust that has worked itself into his skin. Then, he snatches up a pebble – heavy, perfectly round – and secretes it in his palm. The pup noses forward to sniff at his closed fist, but he harries it away. 'Don't you go telling!'

The man named Richardson rounds the corner; then, only a yard behind, comes the stranger. He is tall, with big round shoulders and, though he is not old, he has thick white whiskers.

'Here the feller is,' Richardson grins. 'Spritely little thing, when he's not dozing in some fox hole . . .'

Foxes, Jon notes. They have rabbits *and* foxes on this side of the world.

'This here's Cormac Tate,' Richardson begins. 'He's gonna get this straightened out good and proper – and then we'll be shot of you forever!'

This is obviously a great joke, for both Cormac Tate and

Richardson slap each other on the back. Then Richardson turns. 'Make sure he ain't here when the foreman comes back, Tate. I don't care what you do with it, just get rid . . .'

As Richardson departs, the man named Cormac Tate circles Jon at a distance, picks up an empty bucket, turns it upside down and takes a seat. He is just on the edge of the shade; the sun shines brilliantly behind him and Jon has to squint to look into his eyes.

'I'm not gonna hurt you, lad,' Cormac Tate begins.

His voice is light and – Jon's heart soars! – it is *English*. Perhaps it has a strange twang to it – but it is at least as English as those haughty cottage mothers back at the Mission.

'You run away from the farm school, right? The Children's Crusade?'

Jon's fingers stroke the pebble in his palm.

'You can tell me, lad. There's no love lost between me and that lot in there.' He pauses. 'Why don't we start by shaking hands? That seems a good old English way to start . . .'

Cormac Tate extends a hand as big as Jon's head. Tentatively, Jon shuffles forward and puts out his own. As he takes hold of the giant fingers, the pebble drops to the ground and rolls away, set upon by the pup. Cormac's eyes are drawn that way, but if he knows Jon was harbouring a weapon he doesn't let it show.

'There,' Cormac begins, 'that wasn't so hard, was it?' He strokes his whiskers, pretending to ponder. 'What's next?' he muses. 'Shall we try a name?'

Jon doesn't want to give it up, tries hard to keep it down, but the word seems to come up of its own accord.

'I'm Jon.'

'It's a good name. Hello Jon.'

Jon does not know if he's meant to reply. 'Hello,' he ventures.

'They're a rotten ol' lot, aren't they? The Children's Crusade?'

It might be a trap. Jon vaguely shrugs. He was ensnared once this morning, and he doesn't want to be ensnared again.

'You wouldn't be the first to start off running. But there's boys been lost in that bush before, just like yourself, not even knowing the way back to those men in black.' He stops. 'So you shouldn't have run,' he says, more firmly now.

He stands, kicks the bucket away, and sits cross-legged on the dirt. Jon is taller than him now – and, somehow, that feels wrong. He idles from side to side before deciding he too should sit on the ground. The pup waddles between them, curious at this new game.

'You want to tell an old man why you had to run off, Jon?'

Jon teases the pup's ears. 'There weren't any fences,' he says.

It sounds stupid. He might have talked about the cottage mothers, listening to Ernest cry, what happens when boys have done something wrong and need teaching a lesson in manners. In truth, though, he could stomach all of that and more; it was only the idea of fences that wouldn't leave him alone.

'Did you think you could run home?'

'We were at sea for six whole weeks!'

Cormac Tate nods. 'So were we all, Jon, everyone who came out here. There's no running home – least, not for a young'n like yourself.' He pauses. 'Don't you have any friends in there, lad?'

Jon has not thought about George all morning. Today was going to be George's day for village muster. He will surely have been missed.

Cormac Tate stands. He lifts the hat from his head and twirls it high, so that it lands, spinning, on top of Jon's own. The hat is so big that it drops down in front of his eyes.

Grinning, Jon nudges the hat up.

'Richardson's had you eating his damn jerky,' Cormac says, kicking at the tin plate on the ground. 'That stuff isn't fit for the dogs. We'll get you a good feed and then think about sneaking you back . . .'

Jon does not quite understand what Cormac Tate means – but

follows him, all the same, into the ranch house. There are other men milling about now, some much older than Cormac Tate, some many years younger. To a man, they are dirty and unshaven. In a room alongside the kitchen, a gang are gathered around a breakfasting table, bickering over tin plates and dainty china cups.

'Don't mind them, Jon. They've been out mustering the cattle for God knows how long . . .'

'You found yourself another young'n, Cormac?' a voice calls through the doorway. 'Oi, kidder, what're they up to in that school? Teaching you ways of the flesh, is that it?'

There is an eruption of laughter at the table, but some of the younger men keep their heads bowed, as if embarrassed.

Cormac puts a hand on Jon's shoulder and shepherds him away from the door. 'You wait out front. Our lad's getting the wagon all oiled up. I'll be back in a jiffy.'

The man tramps up a back stair, and Jon ventures, with the little pup gambolling behind, onto the veranda. One of the utes has its hood open, and a figure much younger than the other men is ferreting about inside. All that Jon can see is an arm flashing out to grab a spanner, fingers black with oil.

It is scorching, even in the shade. He sits down, marvelling at how the greenery erupts from the red.

'You!' the voice from under the hood calls out. 'You there, get yourself up and over here!'

It takes Jon a moment to realize it is him being shouted at.

'Yeah, you!' the voice cries. 'I need your fingers in here, can't hold it myself . . . Are you listening, or just lazin' around!?'

Jon teeters down the steps and crosses the yard slowly. Under the bonnet of the ute, the boy is huffing and puffing like some big bad wolf about to blow his house down. It is an English voice, perhaps even more English than Cormac Tate.

'I need you to get your hand in,' the boy begins. 'I reckon it's a fan belt thing. Truth is, I don't properly know. But I'll be damned if that old foreman's going to come down on old Cormac for this like he did the last time.' The boy contorts himself out of the engine. Still obscured by the hood, he draws a grubby hand across his brow, no doubt leaving black sweaty trails behind. 'What, were you born a little girl or something? Ain't you going to help?'

The jibe is familiar, but Jon cannot recall where he has heard it before. He shuffles forward, ready to dip his hand deep into the engine, and then the boy rears from the hood. His face, as Jon expected, is smeared in black – and, camouflaged like that, it is a moment before Jon understands.

'Jon Heather!' cries Peter. 'Well, there's an ugly little face I never thought I'd see again!'

*

George comes out of the scrub, sheets safely buried, with a bundle of twigs under each arm – enough so that, if any cottage mother or likely bigger boy is watching, they might think he has just been being diligent with his muster. When he emerges, some of the little ones are sitting cross-legged in the field. They have formed a big circle to play one of their games. George would dearly love to be part of that game – but he's too old for the little ones to ever admit him. Instead, he sets his bundle down, uses it as a seat, and watches from a distance. He's seen this game before, and thinks he understands the rules. Each boy balances a stone on his head, and nudges the boy to his right. If the stone falls off, the boy loses and has to leave the circle, go back to work and collect twice as many pieces of stick. George is certain he'd be excellent at this game, and duly picks up a rock of his own so that he might practise.

Jon wasn't there when he went to bed last night, and he wasn't there when he woke up in the morning. Jon Heather is certainly a very bad boy, but George isn't going to tell. Maybe some of the other boys in the dormitory might go ratting on him – maybe even that mean old boy who caught George out this morning and wrapped him up in those dirty sheets until he could hardly move – but mostly they're a good bunch. It was their idea to stuff Jon's bed with sacks, in case the cottage mother came knocking.

George unbalances and the stone falls off his head. He knows it's only a silly game, but for some reason he's all choked up. Stupid Jon Heather. All that talk about fences and big wide worlds. They're not in England anymore. That's all there is.

'Hey, little man!'

Tommy Crowe appears out of the dairy building. He waves at George, hops the fence like a blasted kangaroo, and jogs across the untilled field.

'George boy, you got that goat done in, right?'

George shrugs. 'I carted it off.'

'I'm sorry I was . . .' Tommy pauses, senses that something is wrong. 'Hey, what is it? Look, you've done your first one, for all Judah Reed and the rest know. You won't have another one for weeks and weeks. Maybe then you'll be . . .'

George feels the wracking in his chest that means he is going to cry, and works hard to gulp it back down. When it's back in his belly, he shrugs again.

'What is it?'

'It's Jon Heather.'

There is a look like fear on Tommy's face. 'What about him?'

George hesitates. He's probably being tricked. The whole Mission must know Jon's gone already – and this bigger boy has been sent to catch him out in a lie. Then he'll be numbered with Jon, and have to pay a visit to Judah Reed.

'They saw him do it, didn't they? Chop up that goat for you . . .'

George shakes his head fiercely.

'Then what?'

If Peter was here, he'd be clever. He'd have some smart answer for the bigger boy, twist him up in riddles like a fox with a rabbit, and then it would be Tommy Crowe being picked on, not George.

George, though, is not Peter. If he tells another fib, he knows he won't be able to gulp down his crying.

'I don't know where he is.'

'You . . .'

'I think he ran off. He got cross when I couldn't do the goat, and then he didn't come to bed, and then he wasn't even there for breakfast.'

Tommy Crowe moves in an urgent circle, kicking a clod of earth. 'Why'd he go and do a thing like that?' he breathes. 'Doesn't he know what happens to boys like that?' Tommy launches the clod of earth as far as it will go, smashing it into the trunks in the shadow wood. 'Hey, you told anyone, Georgie?'

George stands up suddenly, swells to his full height. He barely reaches the bigger boy's shoulder, so he scrabbles back and jumps on a big mound of earth. 'I haven't told a single tale!'

'All right, all right!' Tommy says, stifling an obvious laugh. 'No need to be so plucky. Gosh, Georgie! Let's just hope he gets hungry real quick, eh?' He turns, gazes into the shadow wood. 'And let's hope he still knows the way back . . .'

George gets down from the mound, embarrassed to have raised the attention of the little ones further down the field. They have broken from their circle now and are scampering back into the fringes of the forest to pick up their bundles. To George, they look like rabbits scattering in the shadow of a hawk.

Tommy Crowe whistles softly. 'Looks like something's up, Georgie . . .'

When George follows his gaze, he can see three figures marching his way – their cottage mother, the boy who caught him out this morning, and a man in black – Judah Reed himself.

'You reckon it's Jon?' Tommy Crowe asks, suddenly grave.

But George cannot bring himself to say the thought that jumps into his head. He hopes to hell they're coming because of Jon – but, secretly, he knows they aren't.

His eyes flitter back to that patch in the trees where he buried his sheets – and then, unable to hold it in any longer, he cries, long and loud, for all the world to see.

In the shadows of the wood, the little ones look back. They've seen this before and they know what's coming next.

*

'You look silly as hell in those clothes, Jon Heather. That's what they're making you wear, is it? You'd look better running around naked.'

Jon has seen some of the little ones running around like that, so it doesn't seem as big a joke to him as it does to Peter. He stays stock still, can't quite believe Peter is standing there, wearing the same jeans as Cormac Tate, the same wide-brimmed hat. His fair skin is almost completely freckled and burnt, but, apart from that, he looks the same as Jon remembers.

'I never in a million years reckoned you was the runaway, Jon Heather!' He hoots it out – but Jon cannot tell what he's laughing at. 'Cormac's seen his share of boys bolting from that Children's Crusade, but I never in a thousand years thought *you'd* come this way . . .'

'A million,' says Jon.

'What?'

'You said a million. Then you said a thousand.'

Peter ponders it. 'I see they been teaching you how to count,' he surmises. 'But there's only one thing I got to ask you.' He stops, hands squarely on his hips. It is an attitude Jon has never noticed in Peter before. 'Where's George?'

Before Jon can answer, Cormac Tate appears out of the farm

building. 'They been in my things again, Pete. You seen which one of them it was?'

Peter – he has never been called *Pete* – shrugs. 'I had my head under this hood.'

Cormac Tate lumbers over to meet them. 'That's the third time them farmhands been in my packs,' he says, cuffing Jon around the shoulder. 'The sooner we're shot of this station, Pete, the better.'

'I do believe you're right,' Peter says, adding a little mock bow that brings a smile to Cormac's face.

'You two been getting acquainted, then?'

Cormac Tate stands between them, looking from one to the other. Jon wants to speak out, but something stays his tongue. Perhaps Peter doesn't want the old man to know they used to be friends. Perhaps he always wanted rid of Jon and George and all the other boys of the Children's Crusade. He's dressed up differently – that's for sure. Maybe he wants everything different, now they're not in England.

If that's so, Jon doesn't want to let him down. He keeps his lips sealed.

'Ach, we came over on the same boat, Cormac,' Peter finally admits. 'This here's my comrade, Jon Heather. Jon, this is Cormac Tate. He's not so different from us, so you can stop feeling frightened or whatever's going on in that little head of yours.' Peter squints up at Cormac Tate. 'Jon's a thinker. Got a head full of stories, so you never can tell what he's thinking on next.'

'Nothing wrong with that, kid,' says Cormac Tate.

When they took the bigger boys off the boat, Peter explains, there were men waiting, ranchers just like Jon's already seen – and, if they took a shine to a boy, he was sent off with them, to earn his board at a cattle outpost or a wheat farm, or sometimes even a telegraph station or railway. Jon wonders if these are like the honoured guests he has heard about, but doesn't think it right to ask. Once a month, one of the men in black is supposed to come and find out how Peter's doing, whether he might make a rancher himself when he grows up – but Peter hasn't seen hide nor hair of them, and he couldn't be happier. He's going to stick with old Cormac Tate now, follow him from station to station, wherever there's work.

Cormac drifts away from them, to inspect Peter's work with the engine. For a moment, Peter seems anxious to know that he's done well – but, as soon as Cormac Tate's head dips underneath the hood, he rounds on Jon. 'So?' he snaps. 'Where is he?'

Jon flounders for an answer.

'I mean, you're the one I put on looking after him – so it just stands to reason that, if you were gonna run, you'd be taking George with you. What did you do, stash him away somewhere when you found out the ranchers were onto you?'

He can't possibly tell Peter that it wasn't like that, that he just started running, that he curled up in some burrow and woke up already ensnared.

'You left him behind, didn't you? Jon Heather, you goddamn selfish bastard.'

Peter has obviously been spending his time with his head in a thesaurus, because he never knew words like this before.

'I didn't think . . .'

'No, you didn't think, did you, Jon Heather? And now little George is all alone, back in that silly little farm with Judah Reed and who knows what else!'

'It's a Mission . . .'

'What's that supposed to mean?'

'They call it the Mission.'

Peter almost grins. 'You know better than that. That's *their* word for it. You don't have to use *their* word for anything.' He stops. 'It's not the only one, you know. There's another farm school for the Children's Crusade in New South Wales. *New*

South Wales – can you believe it, Jon? They came to the other side of the world, and named it *New South Wales* . . .'

'Who did?'

Peter breathes, exasperated. Jon has heard this tone before – it is the way he would sometimes speak to George, back in the Home.

'The first settlers, Jon. The first Australians.'

'If they came from Wales, weren't they Welsh?'

'Jon Heather, you don't know nothing . . . They were Welsh when they left, and Australian when they arrived.'

It is a bewildering thing. Jon wonders what might have happened, somewhere over the Indian Ocean, that suddenly changed those settlers.

'Does that mean *we're* Australian, Peter?' His lip trembles when he thinks of his letter. He had *promised* his mother he was still her English son.

'That's too much thinking, Jon Heather. We've got things to be getting on with. Got to sneak you back under the noses of the Children's Crusade, for one thing . . .'

'I can't go back, Peter. Judah Reed . . .'

'You got to go back, Jon. You're not leaving George with those dirty old bastards. Someone's got to look out for him.'

Jon burns. Why can't George look after himself? He's barely a year younger than Jon. He ought to be able to get his own clothes on in the morning. He ought to be able to clean up his own mess.

Cormac comes up from under the hood. 'Pete's right, young'n,' he says, wiping his brow. 'I'd have you here if I could, but, well . . .' A fleeting sadness crosses his face. '. . . I tried to help out you runaways once before.'

Peter nods sharply. 'There was a lad, long before we came, used to visit all the farms and take away scraps. Then he just wasn't there anymore.'

'I reckon that boy went bush,' Cormac says sadly. 'I thought he might be out there with the bush blacks, but we never heard a thing. Even asked Booty to make some investigatings, but . . .'

The old man lumbers over, drops to his knee and strokes a stray curl out of Jon's eyes. 'The thing is, lad, they're your guardians now. That's the law. Only way to avoid them is to go feral, and you don't want to do that.'

'*In loco parentis*,' Peter interjects. 'That's English words.'

'It's Latin,' interjects Cormac, reaching through the window to test the ignition.

'Yep,' Peter nods, 'and it means they're your parents now, Jon Heather.'

'They're *not* my parents.'

Cormac slams down the hood of the ute, swings into the driver's seat and kicks the engine into gear. It rattles ominously, but then it purrs. Cormac throws Peter a look, nods sharply, and Peter salutes in return. It's obviously another Australian trick.

'It's time,' he says. 'We don't get you back in before you're missed, you'll cop it, Jon. They'll make you . . .' Cormac's eyes mist over, as if he is lost in a memory. '. . . take your medicine,' he finishes, voice trailing off.

Peter scrambles into the back of the ute and reaches out to help haul Jon up. As they round the first bend, Peter lifts a shoulder and gently barges Jon's own.

'I wish you was coming too,' says Jon.

The sun is climbing. Today he was meant to be back in the dairy. Probably McAllister is there already.

'Breaking *into* prison,' says Peter. 'Now, there's an idea.'

They pass the watering hole and follow another dirt track down, through scrub as tall as the wagon. There are gates here, at the end of a long drive, with the same old inscription that Jon first saw in Leeds. *We fight for the orphaned, the lost and the lonely* . . .

They do not stop here, but cut a circle around the back of the Mission. Over a plain of tiny bulbous bushes, a row of eucalyptus trees mark the beginning of what must be the shadow wood.

Cormac kills the engine and climbs out. At the back of the ute, he reaches out with big hands and lifts Jon aloft. Plopping him down, he puts a rough hand to his face and whispers, 'You'll be all right, lad. I can tell. You're a fighter. Same as I used to be.' When he hears Peter vaulting out of the ute, he turns. 'Pete, stick here, mate. I don't want you . . .'

'Come on, Cormac, if Jon's going in, I got to . . .'

Cormac's eyes fall. 'It's Jon knows the way back. It's Jon who's *got* to go. You don't have to set foot in that place.'

Between them, Jon Heather freezes, trying to work out on what battleground the argument is being fought.

'I know how it goes, Cormac.' When Peter next speaks, he seems to be parroting an old saying Jon does not know. 'You'll set foot in the Children's Crusade when there's snow on the Nullarbor Plain . . . but I can't hardly let Jon go on hisself. Just take a look at him!' He turns to Jon. 'Come on, let's find out how much bother you're in . . .' Then, after he has taken a few steps, he throws a look back at the dwindling figure that is Cormac Tate. 'I'm coming back, Cormac. I just want to . . . *see*.'

Jon and Peter trudge off through the scrub. As they go, Peter keeps asking questions – but Jon barely answers a single one. It is about George that Peter keeps asking. He hasn't once asked how things are for Jon.

'What was wrong with Cormac?'

'It's your little play school through these trees. He . . .' Peter doesn't know how to say it. In truth, he hardly knows. 'He's got stuff he doesn't like,' is all he can muster.

They reach the edge of the shadow wood and push within. It is new territory for Peter, and he keeps stopping to marvel at the alien trees, the creatures that dart hither and thither.

Before they have got even halfway, it is Jon urging Peter to hurry. The higher the sun climbs, the more certain he is he's already been found out.

At last, they drop through the last of the trees and can see, over the untilled fields, the dairy buildings beyond. The little ones are nowhere to be seen, and neither is Tommy Crowe.

'We keep goats in there,' Jon says, pointing for Peter. 'For milking and . . . eating.'

'Is that why you got blood on your shirt?'

Jon stops.

'I noticed it just now, but thought you was just being grubby.'

Peter pushes forward, careful not to break the final line of trees. 'I had no idea this is what the old men in black were up to when we were back at the Home.' He stops, cocks a look at Jon. Something, it seems, does not feel right. 'Hey, Jon – where is everybody?'

Jon does not know. He comes to Peter's side, still obscured by a low eucalyptus. It is not midday yet; he is almost certain of it. Now he's in Australia, he doesn't need a clock on the wall to tell the time. The little ones should be all over this stretch of the compound. He should hear the hue and cry of boys further inside the Mission, in the woodworking shacks or the sheds where the ploughs are wintered.

Peter pulls Jon back into the cover of the trees.

'They're onto you, aren't they?'

Jon shakes him off. If they're onto him, it's his problem; Peter can go back to running free with Cormac Tate. Jon isn't like George. Jon can handle it himself.

'Jon Heather, what are you doing?'

Jon scurries down the bank, almost losing his footing as he cartwheels onto the untilled earth. 'Get out of here, Peter. You don't have to worry about me.'

'Jon!' Peter cries. He pushes onto the top of the bank himself, but something stops him from dropping down. 'Jon, stop!'

Jon stops dead in the middle of the field, looks back.

'What do you even want, Peter?' he demands. 'You brought me back, didn't you? You got rid of me!'

'Stop being such a baby! It's . . .' He stops, lowers his voice to such a whisper that, from the field, Jon can barely hear. 'It's just that – well, I know where you are now, don't I?'

The words untwist the horrible knots in Jon's tummy.

'And, Jon . . . they ship us around, all us boys they farmed out. But – I've kept that atlas, and . . .' He hesitates. The words don't sound right. 'I'll be coming back this way when winter's out.'

'*This* winter?' Jon asks, squinting at the sun almost directly overhead.

'The *English* winter,' Peter grins back. 'Christmas, Jon. Make sure you've got me a present!'

With that, Peter is gone.

Jon hurries over the field and creeps up on the dairy house with his back pressed carefully to the wall. It is certainly not Tommy Crowe inside, for he can see the figure moving back and forth in the window: definitely old McAllister.

He only has one chance, then. He'll lie. Tell McAllister he's been running errands for Judah Reed – or, better still, one of the lesser men in black, the ones not deserving of names. Even if McAllister suspects, he won't dare question one of them. He's as cowardly as the little ones in that regard.

Jon takes a deep breath and leaps into the open doorway. McAllister is bent over one of the stalls, cooing at the goats, but when Jon lands, he turns suddenly around, his beak craning forward like a storybook stepfather. He seems puzzled by Jon's appearance, but this is not as it should be. He should be raging, demanding to know why the muck hasn't been shovelled from his precious goats.

'Shouldn't you be in the assembly hall, boy?'

Jon darts looks into the corners of the dairy. Some of the

goats have been milked this morning – but others are standing there with teats red and swollen.

'Answer me when you're spoken to!' McAllister barks. 'Why aren't you up there with the others?'

In three quick strides, McAllister falls upon Jon, hoisting him up by his collar and heaving him around. Half-dangling and half-scurrying to keep up with McAllister, he leaves the dairy with the old man and follows the track into the centre of the compound.

The assembly hall sits between the sandstone buildings, a great wooden construction that the first boys of the Children's Crusade had to build themselves. McAllister kicks the door with the flat of his foot, hoists Jon across the threshold and propels him forward. Jon lands on the floorboards, bloodies his face against the heavy grain.

'A straggler,' McAllister rasps. 'Didn't want him missing out.'

Jon gets up, kneading at watery eyes, and sees that the assembly hall is full. Tables have been shifted and stacked along its side, and chairs lined up to face the front, where a big ledge of earth acts as a stage. There must be every boy from the Children's Crusade in here.

Judah Reed is on the earthen stage. Jon's own cottage mother is at his side, along with another of the men in black.

Again, Jon is harried forward, until he is almost at the stage itself. From on high, the cottage mother looks imperiously down. This must be it, thinks Jon. Somebody has spied him sneaking back into the Mission. This is his welcoming party.

He decides he will not scream. He will not beg them to stop.

'Put him with the rest,' says Judah Reed.

A man in black has a hand on each of Jon's shoulders, and shepherds him to the very bottom of the stage. At last, Jon sees faces he knows from his dormitory. They are all lined up, in chairs facing the assembled boys. Jon looks out, tries to see why they are here. He catches sight of Tommy Crowe, sitting slumped in the crowd with his eyes downcast.

There is a seat at the end of the row, and Jon is forced down into it.

'What's happening?' Jon whispers.

Before the boy beside him can reply, a cane catches Jon on the side of the head.

Judah Reed stands, parades the edge of the stage. When he is satisfied, he nods. The cottage mother drifts off, out of sight for only a second – and when she returns, she is pushing a boy before her. He is rigid, his feet hardly moving, but still he finds himself propelled forward.

It is George.

Up there, his eyes are closed, but Jon wills them to open. He wants him to know. He came back. He's found Peter. They can be together again.

Judah Reed is making a speech, but Jon can hardly focus. George stands at the foot of the stage, and as the cottage mother delivers an order, all the boys of the dormitory stand up. Judah Reed counts down and, in turn, each of the boys leaves the column and approaches George. He is shaking now – but at last his eyes are open. Jon rises on his tip-toes, tries to see down the line, but the cottage mother bawls at him to get down.

There is a yelp, and the line moves forward. Another, and it shuffles forward again. By the time Jon has advanced halfway, he knows what each of those cries are. George must have suffered a dozen blows by now, but not one of them has been at the hands of Judah Reed; they have come from his brothers in the dormitory.

Some of them are pulling their punches – but Jon can tell by the pitch of George's cries which boys are doing exactly as they have been told, and thumping with all of their strength. He starts counting: one, two, three, four . . .

At last, he comes near the head of the column. George's face is streaked in tears, but he is crying out no longer. He is only whispering, the same apology over and again. Jon is not sure what he is apologizing for; perhaps simply for being George.

The boy in front of him throws a blow that catches George on the shoulder. It is a soft blow, thrown with the flat of the hand.

Jon steps forward. George peers at him. Whether he can see through his red, swollen eyes, Jon can only guess.

'I came back,' Jon whispers.

Judah Reed barks out, and Jon can say nothing more. George hangs his head, shaking swiftly from side to side.

Jon steps forward. His fist is clenched, but he keeps it loose. He has never hit a boy before, never brawled in a park or playground. He brings it back, desperately trying to think which part would hurt George the least. He still has puppy fat, even after all these weeks – perhaps if he feigns a punch to the stomach, George will understand.

He brings his fist back, just the same as he has seen the other boys do. He lunges forward.

He stops.

Judah Reed's eyes are on him – but that doesn't matter now; it's *Jon's* eyes that are on Judah Reed. It's Judah Reed who should be afraid. He lets the silence stretch. Then, just as the man in black is about to speak, he cuts him off. It isn't his turn to speak yet. Even if he is Jon's mother and Jon's father all rolled together, it just isn't his right.

He remembers George's words: it's *my* fingers; it's *my* hands.

'I won't,' Jon says. He says it softly – but then he says it again, bold as he can. He is shaking, and he holds himself so that he might stop. 'I'm not going to.'

George looks up. Even if he can't see through those bleary eyes, certainly he can hear.

'You can't make me,' says Jon.

Judah Reed turns on his heel, purpling with rage. He whispers something in the cottage mother's ear and she nods, sagely. Marching along the line of boys who have already struck George, she harries them until they turn on the spot.

A new column has been formed. Jon feels Judah Reed's hands on his shoulders, angling him so that the watching boys might see. His body is tight, but then it is suddenly loose; his arms and his feet tingle, and, absurdly, he is acutely aware of how much he needs the toilet.

'Back of the line,' says Judah Reed, crouching low and putting a consoling hand on George's shoulder. More than anything else, it is the softness of that touch that stiffens Jon again. He will not be afraid.

George shuffles to the end of the line. Even before he has reached it, the hazing has started all over again. The first boy pulls his punch, catching Jon softly on the shoulder – but the second has no such inhibitions. Jon doubles over, and before he has drawn himself upright the next boy has already approached.

When it comes to George's turn, he lets fly with both fists. Jon hardly feels it, but they rain at his chest, over and over again, until Judah Reed himself has to lift the fat little boy away.

Later, in the dormitory, the boys are silent. The tell-tale does not come in until late, his belly filled with whatever treats Judah Reed and the cottage mother have concocted for him.

George has no mattress tonight; he must sleep on the wire frame until his mattress is properly dry. He'll have to beat it with sticks in the morning, to give it air and get rid of the smell. Jon has promised to help him, but George isn't allowed any help.

Jon kicks the sheets off his own mattress and makes space for George to sit. Reluctant at first, he burrows down, bringing the sheet to his chin, desperate to cover every inch of him up. They sit in silence for the longest time.

George's voice breaks. 'You left me all alone,' he finally says.

'I know.'

'Where did you go?'

Jon tells him everything, not missing out a single detail. George sits, rapt, listening as if it is one of the stories Jon used to spin. Every time Jon mentions Peter, his eyes widen fractionally. It is enough to know that Peter is out there, running free. He'll shake off the Children's Crusade in no time. And, one day, Peter will come back for them. George is certain.

Jon could stop there – but something compels him to go on. It isn't enough to tell George about the plains and the ranch and the black man in the wagon. The story isn't complete until he confesses.

'I didn't want to come back, Georgie. I would've gone bush, just like that old Cormac said, if only they'd let me.'

George's face crumples, he opens his mouth to bawl out – but he is choked of all breath. Jon shuffles over, puts an arm around him – and, suddenly, George's arms are around him, hugging tight, the fat little boy dangling from his neck and refusing to let go.

'Don't run away, Jon,' he sobs. 'Please don't run away.'

The boys in the neighbouring beds avert their eyes. One of them sniggers.

'I promise, George.'

George hardly lets go all night. He has to return to his wire bed for the cottage mother's inspection, but after lights out Jon feels him crawling into the sheets alongside him. He shuffles over and makes space; there's not quite room for two, but there's room enough. Yet, as far as he shuffles, George shuffles further still. At last they sleep, each wrapped around the other, George still holding on with arms, legs, fingers and toes.

Jon wakes in the dead of night, strangely chill. He is sodden. He rolls George over, shakes him softly until he too wakes.

It takes George a moment to come round. When realization dawns, he gulps down a cry. Jon pushes a finger to his mouth and whispers for him to be quiet.

'I'm sorry, Jon. I didn't mean . . .'

Jon eases himself quietly out of bed. The boys around them are all sleeping. There is still some luck in the world, he thinks.

Over his shoulder, the dormitory door is closed. He helps George down from the bed and, with furtive glances to make sure nobody is watching, strips off the sheets.

'Come on, Georgie boy,' he whispers. 'We've still got two hours before dawn . . .'

VIII

They keep it up for a while. Jon barters with the tell-tales in the dorm, buying their silence by promising to write letters back home on their behalf. Jon is a good letter-writer and some of them, who can hardly hold a pencil, are changed when he helps them, as if the thing making them rotten has simply fluttered away. He makes friends with a girl from the laundry too, and she proves herself invaluable in hiding evidence. She is called Laura, from a foster family in Stockport, and she and Jon spend secret hours devising more and more elaborate plans to hide George's shame.

For a while, it works – but, for all their best efforts, by the end of the winter, George is living in the bedwetters' dorm. Jon goes to see him every night and every morning. He finds time to play games. There's one they've made up together, where they throw stones in the air and catch them on the backs of their hands, and Jon lets George win. He lets him win so often that any other boy might suspect foul play – but George just thrills, every time.

He wets the bed almost every night now, but so do the boys he bunks with, so it's never remarked upon. He smells funny to Jon, but that must only be the horrible, foetid dorm. The men in black make them wash their mouths out with soap. Jon thinks it a silly waste – the boys in his dorm don't even have soap with which to bathe.

In the middle month of summer, in the year of 1951, Jon Heather turns eleven years old. He remembers the date vividly, but this year there will be no celebrations. Lots of the other boys, Tommy Crowe tells him, don't have a birthday at all. Most of them only know the month by the turning of the seasons and, if they came here as little ones, they don't even know the date of their birthday at all.

When he finds out that George can't remember his birthday, Jon says they can share the same one. They get up early that day, and play an extra special game of stones at the back of the dairy shed. George wins, but Jon gives him a good challenge. Some of the little ones see what's going on and gravitate towards them. George says it is the best birthday party he's ever had.

That same month, Christmas comes to the Children's Crusade. The boys assemble in the main hall and there is a bird to share, something that tastes a little like turkey but the bigger boys call 'scrub fowl'. Jon does not sit at the same table as George, but they catch each other's eyes across the crowd. George has a present for him, a toy train he has whittled from a scrap in the woodworking shed; Jon, too, has one for George, a jar filled with honey the boys of his dorm have stolen from a wild nest in the shadow wood.

Soon after, the New Year dawns. There is no scrub fowl for dinner, just more of McAllister's mutton, and in the assembly hall Judah Reed does not make an appearance. The dinner is hosted by one of his acolytes instead, the gawky man in black who oversees the bedwetters' dorm, and Jon realizes he has not seen Judah Reed in days.

Rumour is rampant – Reed is no longer in the Mission. To the newest boys of the Children's Crusade, this is a glorious thing, something to be celebrated more wildly than Christmas, New Year, and a dozen fake birthdays combined. The child-snatcher has gone! For a little while, working hard to chew the piece of gristle on his plate, Jon is swept up in the excitement. Then, slowly, he understands.

It is almost exactly a year ago that he himself first saw Judah Reed. It is nearly exactly a year since he read that piece of paper with his mother's name signed at the bottom. Judah Reed might not be in the Mission just now, but he'll certainly be back – and he'll be bringing a ship's load of new boys with him.

There is a lighter air in the compound now that Judah Reed has gone. Boys no longer fear punishment – or, if they still fear it, they are certain it will not be as severe. They joke in the fields, make a mockery of old McAllister behind his back – and, late one night, stage skits for each other, pretending to be men in black and cottage mothers, and big, proud Australian boys.

It is lights out in the dormitory, and Jon Heather lies awake, listening to the chatter of boys all around him. Such a thing was unthinkable mere weeks ago, but without Judah Reed something seems to have slackened in the cottage mothers too. Tonight, she has made a cursory inspection, harangued a boy for not having tucked in the corners of his sheet, but taken no boy away for quiet words and lessons. Some of the boys are playing a game of pick-up sticks; another has found a rat with which to torment his friends. From the huddle between the beds, a boy calls out for Jon to join them. Jon, who has been absently dreaming of Peter and Cormac Tate, is about to drop off his bed and join them when a sudden thought strikes him: they never invited me to play games when George was here.

He settles among them and takes his turn teasing out a stick for several rounds, but eventually the thought weighs too heavily: he is almost *glad* that George isn't here.

Once he has thought it, it will not go away. He waits until his turn has passed and wriggles out of the huddle, creeping across the dormitory without a word.

With Judah Reed gone, Jon Heather is not the only boy stealing out of his dormitory at night. There are lights on in the homes of the cottage mothers, but he hears china cups clinking and knows they will not bother him tonight. All the same, he keeps low and scurries past, conjuring up excuses just in case he is caught.

In the gloom before full dark, Jon steals across the compound. At the border furthest from the dairy sheds, the bedwetters' dorm is surrounded by scrub left to grow like a thorny, green moat.

Jon tentatively pushes at the dormitory door. Here it comes: that familiar foetid smell. There are coats on hooks and rugs hanging on racks, smelling strongly of soap. White powder has been sprinkled on them and little footprints trail through the dust.

Beyond the entrance room, the beds stretch out. The few boys here are all little ones, not one of them older than five or six. At the end of the row, George lies in bed. Before Jon can cross the room, three of the little ones leap into his path. One of them yaps out in that unintelligible language of theirs, but an even littler boy pushes him back. He must be five years old, and he swells to block Jon's path. 'This isn't your dorm!'

A little one can be as fierce as a dingo. They have been known to bite a chunk out of a bigger boy's arm. All the same, Jon shoulders past.

'George,' he says, softly shaking his sleeping friend.

George rolls over. 'Jon! You're not supposed to be here!'

'Told you!' stamps one of the little ones.

Jon swings around and they dart for the cover of their beds. 'I wanted to make sure you were OK.'

George shrugs.

'Well, you're still here.'

George nods.

'Did you want to play stones?'

'You'll get in trouble Jon, if you . . .' George's voice trails off, his eyes revolving to watch one of the little ones creeping underneath his bed. There, Jon sees a biscuit tin, seemingly spirited out of the kitchens. The little one sees Jon's eyes light on it, and pounces, like a cat trying to protect its kill.

In the tin, Jon spies hunks of mutton, fished out of today's broth. It was, Jon remembers, a remarkably good broth today. There is always something that tastes better about it on the days when Laura is toiling in the kitchens. Perhaps it is only that she scrubs the tins clean between helpings, scouring up all the ants and other creepy-crawlies from the bottom of the mulch.

'They let you eat in here?'

'Oh no!' George gasps. 'They'd teach us a lesson if they found out, so we have to keep it a secret . . .'

'We take it to the wild boy!' a voice pipes up.

The boy on the bed, Martin, scampers after the little one who cried out. After delivering a short, sharp thump, he returns to his vigil.

'Who?' asks Jon.

George suppresses a beam. This time, it is his turn to tell Jon a story. It's nice to be able to pay back your friends.

'The boys in here talk about him all the time. They see him down by the latrines at night. Not every night. Sometimes he isn't there for weeks and weeks. But then, there he is! Ferreting around in the heaps . . .'

On the other side of the latrines, there is a patch of land where the girls from the kitchen pile their scraps. If it isn't fed to the animals, the piles are left to rot and are spread on the land when it comes time for sowing. It is commonly held that there's more of the boys' muck in that slurry than there are peelings and apple cores. As every boy will take glee in telling you, not a jot is wasted when you're part of the Children's Crusade; Mission boys practically eat their own shit.

'I saw him, Jon. I thought he was just a story, like the Mystery at Witchend, but there he was! He looked me right in the eye and scampered off.' George is suddenly still. 'I think I frightened him, Jon, but I only wanted him as my friend.'

It is a custom for the bedwetting boys to pay late-night visits to the latrines at the rear of their dorm, where the Mission ends and the wild emptiness begins. Sometimes the man in black looks over them as they go, but often they sneak out alone; a boy being watched cannot always make himself go, and then there are bound to be sodden sheets in the morning.

George was there one dusk, with a rag of little ones – and it was then that he saw the wild boy. He was tall and dark – not the same as the blacks but still dark enough – and his hair was wild and woolly like Peter Pan before Wendy. Rags hung from his waist, tied there with a thick piece of string, and he had a tucker bag open on the ground, into which he was piling pieces of peel.

Since then, the boys have been putting out scraps so that the wild boy might take them away.

'Maybe he's the boy who ran away,' says George.

Jon shoots him a look. George doesn't like to talk about running away, not since that night Jon disappeared.

'The one who lived in the hole,' he goes on eagerly, sickness seemingly gone. 'Maybe he climbed out of his hole and started growing up properly. What's that boy called, Jon, who lived in the jungle with tigers and bears?'

'He's called Mowgli,' says Jon.

'I'm going to call *him* Mowgli,' says George. 'We're going to keep him if we can.'

Jon recalls, starkly, the chicken bones, piled up in a little pyramid, in the shadow wood at night, the scuffed marks like footprints all around them.

'George, buck up,' he says severely, though even he could not say why. 'You can't go throwing food out like that. There's rats and dingoes and . . .' He flounders. '. . . probably devils, for all you know. That's what's taking your food. You oughtn't to go hungry for a . . .'

George trembles. 'But I've *seen* him, Jon . . .'

'You haven't,' says Jon, his teeth grinding together. 'It's not a game, George. I've . . .' He does not want to say it, for he still remembers that night after he came back, George grappling him as they lay together in bed. '. . . been out there. There isn't anything. There isn't even a fence.' He holds back; it feels, somehow, not only as if he is punching George, but punching himself as well. 'There aren't any little wild boys. There's just *nothing*.'

Indignant, the little ones gather around. The one named Martin pushes from his bed, elbows past Jon, and hands George his own pillow, a threadbare thing made from string and sack. When George accepts it, clinging onto it in the face of Jon's fire, another of the little ones crawls over and offers the same. This time, George – suddenly embarrassed – says no, and the little one skulks back to his own bed, holding the pillow like a boy back in England might his teddy bear.

'I saw him, Jon Heather,' he whispers.

Jon narrows his eyes. It isn't like baby George to fight back. Then, he sees the little ones arranged around, and something starts to make sense.

George has friends in here, that much is true – but Jon cannot help thinking he would be better off being bullied, back in his old dorm.

*

The ute swings wildly. Peter has never been able to gauge the dust on the road properly, and Cormac Tate reaches out to steady the steering wheel. He's just about tall enough now that his feet can reach the pedals at the same time as he peers through the windscreen. Peter can fix wagons, and that's to be applauded – but Cormac Tate says he really ought to be able to drive one as well.

There is a hump in the road, where red dust has hardened over a roadkill. The wagon crashes over it, jarring Cormac Tate's back.

'Pete, if you ruin the chassis, not even those deft fingers of yours are gonna fix her up. The foreman'll knock it out of your pay, and then you'll be a bonded slave for the rest of your days . . .'

'I'm already a slave, Cormac. They brought me over on a boat and everything.'

Cormac Tate grins. 'Boys to be farmers, and girls to be farmers' wives,' he says. 'You play it right, you could have a perfect life, just like me . . .'

They've shared this joke before, but that doesn't stop Peter from laughing. There are moments when Peter thinks Cormac's life might be perfect – out on the plains, sleeping under the stars, with no one in the whole world breathing down his neck – but the old man obviously thinks differently. Peter's happy enough to go along with the joke for now; Cormac Tate's life is a bank vault, and eventually he'll find the key.

At Cormac's command, he pulls over into a patch of scrub and they swap seats. They are near the old farm, the first one to which Peter was posted, and it wouldn't do for the foreman to see Peter driving the wagon. That sort of thing could get reported back to the Children's Crusade, and if there are too many black marks, Peter might be parted from Cormac Tate forever. Neither one will admit it, but that would make both of them sick.

Once they have arrived, Peter helps Cormac into the station house. They have been nine nights out on the range without a bed to sleep in, and Cormac says he's getting too crook to keep it up. Upstairs, Peter dumps the packs. Steak sizzles downstairs – the housemaid, one of Booty's daughters, cooks it up the best in the territory – and Cormac heads off to dunk his head in the water trough.

Peter sniffs his shirt, decides it will do for another few days. He has started to sweat more in the last six months, but that's probably just this cruel Australian summer. He isn't sure how he'd react, these days, if there was some old man in black or housemaid telling him when to wash and eat and take a shit. Cormac spends all his time grumbling, talking about the good life – apparently this means a pretty little house, a dog, and time to potter around in a garden – but Peter doesn't want to hear it. The good life is already here; Cormac Tate doesn't know he's born.

He begins to rest his eyes, but stirs quickly when he feels a dry snout against his face. When he opens them, the yellow pup jumps up and snaps, playfully, at his nose. He's bigger than when Peter last saw him, grown broad shoulders and giant paws.

'Dog,' he says. 'You ought to go stick your head in that water trough with Cormac Tate.'

He wrestles Dog down, lets him gnaw happily on his fingers. Perhaps he hasn't learnt to play properly, because suddenly he takes it too far, chomps down and tears the skin. Peter whips his hand back, and Dog sprawls backwards. When he looks pensively up, Peter can't bring himself to scold him. He remembers too well what it was like to be a little boy and have nobody to play with. It can turn you a little wild if you let it. Just look at Jon Heather, trying to turn himself into a boy of the bush.

Dog goes off, sniffing around the edges of the room, while Peter bandages up his fingers with an old sock, just the way

Florence Nightingale would have done it. When he's done, he looks down – but he's too late; Dog is already ferreting in one of Cormac's packs. He grabs the curious critter by his rear legs. Dog resists, but at last Peter wins out. He is glad nobody was here to see him wrestling, and almost losing, with such a mangy little puppy – but now there are bigger things to worry about: Dog's got a dirty shirt wrapped around him, and he's slobbering all over a pile of papers and a little book bound in leather.

Peter has never known Cormac to read or write. Sometimes, he brings Peter comics from stores he happens to pass, but he never even asks what's in them. All the same, something tells him that Dog's discovered something here. He feels suddenly guilty and hustles Dog away. Dog obviously thinks it's a game, and throws his front paws down on the ground, yapping out a challenge. Peter mimics the gesture, and Dog scuttles for cover underneath one of the beds.

Peter hurries to cram the papers back into Cormac's pack. There are photographs, envelopes, a tiny boot of brown leather. He sees a woman and two children – daughters – standing beneath giant karri trees. Then, a picture much older still, a blur of black and white: rows of children lined up in smocks horribly familiar to one he has seen before.

At the bottom of the photograph, a wooden board reads:

Farm Boys of the Children's Crusade, February 1923

Peter scans the faces. He can't be certain, but some of them seem hauntingly familiar. All of them are beaming, but he has seen boys smiling like that before. He smiled that way himself, when they had him back at the Home. In the middle of them, a tall, spindly man in black stands.

'It's you who goes through my packs, is it, Pete?'

In the doorway, white whiskers still dripping wet, stands Cormac Tate. He flushes a deep, dirty red. 'I never had a thought it would be you. I thought I'd been good to you.'

Cormac snatches the tucker bag away, starts cramming the papers and pictures back inside. 'Didn't those bastard priests beat any manners into you?' he snarls. 'Don't you know to respect an old man's property?'

Peter knows he ought to say something but, for the first time he can remember, the words evaporate before he can say them out loud.

'Damn it, Pete, I *liked* you.'

Cormac hoists the pack onto his back, the tucker bag over his shoulder, and makes for the door.

Peter dodges a flying hoof, crashes onto the bare red earth. He isn't as good with horses as he is with wagons – but, still, fixing a simple shoe shouldn't be taxing him like this. He throws a look like daggers at the horse, but it just snorts derisively. That's another reason wagons are superior; Peter hasn't once been mocked by a motor car.

He tries three times, each time wishing the horse a graver ill. In the house, the farmhands are feasting. Booty appears from the shade, a scrub chicken squawking helplessly in his hand, dangling by its feet. Throwing Peter a cheery grin, he passes out of sight.

He stares at the house for a long time. Damn Cormac Tate isn't going to get any pleasure out of this. He turns square to the horse and marches right back up to it, ordering it to lift its leg and let him get on with his work. It was bad enough having men in black order him around for four years; he isn't going to be bossed by a creature that can't even talk.

'I'll nail this shoe to your head if I have to,' he says. 'One over each eye. How does that sound?'

'Sounds about all she deserves.'

Cormac Tate's shadow has reached him by the time he turns, but the old man himself is still halfway across the yard. There, he stops. He has a tin plate in his hand, and he sets it down on the ground.

'I ain't no dog,' Peter says.

At the mention of his name, Dog rises from his blanket on the porch and noses forward.

Cormac comes forward, hands the plate personally to Peter. On it, there sit chicken wings and a hunk of cold steak, garnished with a mountain of sauerkraut.

'This is yesterday's steak,' Peter says, prodding it about the plate.

'Yeah,' Cormac replies. 'And it's *my* yesterday's steak, so just you eat it up.'

They sit, cross-legged, eating the steak in silence. On occasion, the horse looks back to see what they're doing. As if embittered that she's no longer causing such consternation, she shuffles back so that her tail swats Peter.

'Eating steak in the shadow of a horse's backside, Cormac. We know how to live.'

'Living like kings,' says Cormac.

The silence returns. When at last the plate is clean, and not a fleck more meat or shred of sauerkraut can be found to punctuate the silence, Peter looks up.

'Why have you got a picture of little boys from the Children's Crusade, Cormac?' He says it so quietly that it might be he's hedging his bets; if Cormac explodes, he can deny he ever breathed a word.

'That isn't a picture of any old little boys,' says Cormac. 'Pete, that's a picture of me.'

He brings the yellowing photograph out of his back pocket.

'I keep meaning to get rid of these things but, damn it, I just never do. I ought to have burnt it all years ago, every last thing.' He pauses. 'There,' he says, prodding it over the dust, 'take a look for yourself.'

The same faces peer at Peter. 'You?' he asks, finger dangling over some soul starving beneath his smock. 'Hardly,' Cormac replies. His thumb lands, leaving a thick smear, on one of the bigger boys, standing at the right hand of the man in black. 'I was a stroppy little bastard, but I kept my head down, got on and got out. That picture's taken three years before I left. In those days, they made you stick on until you were seventeen. We'd get given dormitories to look over. They called us Head Boys, like it was any old English boarding school.'

Peter looks at the younger Cormac. They must be about the same age. A thought spears him: would he and Cormac have been friends, if they had both been part of the same Crusade?

'You was in a Home back in England?'

It is the same old story. A son waits for his father, fighting in some foreign field – and when his father stays there forever, there is suddenly no place for him in England any more. They sailed in 1919, Cormac and a hundred others from the devastated English towns.

'I didn't know the Children's Crusade was that old . . .' Peter says. The boys here must all be men now. Real Australian men, mustering cattle and raising boys of their own.

'It's older,' says Cormac. 'They said we were the Second Children's Crusade. The first was thirty years before. Street boys from London, proper orphans and urchins . . . That's why it killed me, letting your pal Jon Heather go back like that.'

'Jon Heather's all right,' Peter says, without any real conviction.

'Look, I'm an old fool. And every fool's got a reason for feeling sorry for himself. Here's mine.' He picks the photograph back up. 'I'm sure as hell sorry I snapped at you like I did. Even if you were snooping, I shouldn't have snapped. You got a questing mind, Pete. That's one of the reasons I like you.'

'I always knew you was English.'

Cormac shrugs. 'There's only one sort of fella you can really count as an Aussie.' He pauses. 'Booty and the rest of the blacks – and even they must have come from somewhere, once upon a while. Can't have just sprung out of the sand, no matter what they reckon. Thing is, Pete, you give it a little bit of time, and you stop asking the question. You're just a mongrel, like Dog over there. Maybe you wasn't born that way, but you end up like it, a bit from here, a bit from there. I haven't thought about England in twenty years – but, damn it, I still keep these old things.'

Peter's never thought about being English before. He's just been Peter, little brother to a sister he'll never see again, shuffled from Home to Home until he strikes lucky and ends up with the wastrels of the Children's Crusade. He remembers the first time he saw George, shivering in his blankets with a look like confusion all over his face. Here's a boy, he remembers thinking, who needs *instruction*. Here's a boy who might make this place all right. It's not about needing anybody else, Peter concluded that day; it's about being needed yourself.

'There's something else I want you to see,' Cormac begins.

This picture is different from the last. It might be of England, because there's snow everywhere, deep drifts and trees blanketed in white. In the picture, there is a house of timber and boys in fur and mittens. They are gathered, grinning, around a big wooden cart with what looks like a giant, shaggy cow reined to it. In the back of the cart, there are little ones piled high – and, among them, another man in black.

'Where is this, Cormac?'

'Farm School of the Children's Crusade,' Cormac Tate recites. 'March, 1924.'

It isn't Australia. Peter's about to blurt out as much, but manages to stop himself; he doesn't want Cormac thinking he's stupid.

'Some place called Ontario,' Cormac says, as if reading Peter's thoughts. 'Canada. That little one up front of the wagon – that's my brother.'

Men in black in the terraces of Leeds is one thing; men in black in Missions in this arid scrubland he can just about contemplate; but to think that there are men in black up there, in the snowy north, sets the dominoes toppling in Peter's mind. Peering into the picture, he doesn't just see the boys of a Canadian Crusade – he sees a flotilla of galleons, piled high with lost children, leaving England under the cover of darkness, each one of them bound for some distant frontier. North, south, east and west they go, finding uninhabited shores where kidnapped boys might fell timbers and raise houses and start again.

'We were together in the Home,' Cormac Tate begins, kneading his hat in his hands. 'Three of us. Me, Finbar there, and Thom. He was the youngest. They said our old Dad died fighting for a mountainside in Italy but, to be honest, I was the only one who remembered him. I didn't think a thing of it when they put us in those motorbuses and took us to the docks. I just thought they'd be there. But I searched every cabin – and nothing. I never saw them again.'

'But . . .'

'It was Finbar tracked me down, Pete. Left to my own devices, I'd have died without ever hearing from them again. We wrote a bit. Never did come to nothing.'

All at once, Peter is back on the HMS *Othello*, watching the girls with pinafore dresses mill about the quarter deck. Jon and George bicker over atlases and charts, but Peter's thoughts are elsewhere. Because Peter used to have a sister – and, if she was sent to the Children's Crusade too, perhaps his sister is out there, even now, stitching furs in a shack squatting on the endless tundra, playing mother to a horde of little ones who shiver and freeze at night.

He cannot think about it. Rebekkah is gone. He has managed

not to cry in five years, and he won't cry now. Leave the crying to Jon Heather and George; all of this, it's water off a duck's back to Peter. He can weather any storm.

'You ever go home, Cormac?' he suddenly asks.

'Pete,' he says, 'it never seemed worth it. I never even tried . . .'

He steers Peter from the fence and back towards the house; the sun is already setting, gold and red, over the roof.

*

Jon Heather pauses, breathing in the stink of the latrines. Night flies buzz mercilessly. There are other boys flitting about the compound tonight, sneaking out of the dorms long after lights out. The cottage mothers will flap and the younger men in black will deliver punishments, but nobody cares. These months of late summer are the only ones the boys might enjoy without the shadow of Judah Reed.

With so many other boys on the prowl, it was an easy thing for Jon to jimmy open the dormitory boards, drop onto the hard-packed earth, and follow the harrowed land around the Mission's edge until he reached the bedwetters' dorm. He has been thinking on George's fairytale for long nights now, not knowing if he wants it to be true or not; thrilling as it is, if there was a wild boy, that would make Jon Heather a coward – because Jon himself turned right back round and came back to the Mission. No, what George and the little ones saw can only have been one thing. It's Peter, sneaking into the Mission to see his old friends, just like he promised.

There is a vantage point he searched out two days before, a crook between a sudden outburst of scrub and the remains of a stone outhouse, and Jon fashions a seat out of branches so that he might sit there unnoticed. At midnight, a trio of little ones sneak out of the bedwetters' dorm and descend to take their last piss before morning. They are all holding hands and, in the middle of them, stands George. The little ones worship him, their very own bigger boy, but the idea has never irritated Jon more.

Only minutes after the midnight piss, the wild boy appears. He is slight, a boy of bones, and he drops awkwardly out of the boughs of a low eucalyptus. When he skirts the latrines to find the can the little ones have left, he drags his left leg behind him, leaning heavily on the right. At the can, he crouches, sniffs and promptly upturns the contents into his mouth.

Jon is certain, now: this is not Peter. The boy stands there, head craned forward, keen to every rustle. He scuttles forward – but, when a light flares on the other side of the compound, he hurtles for the cover of the undergrowth.

Jon waits until he is gone, then creeps out of his hiding place. In his haste to disappear, the wild boy has left footprints running through the soft earth around the latrines. Finding the shovel the little ones use to dig the trenches, Jon flattens away the trail.

This runaway might not be Peter, but any boy who mocks the men in black is a friend of Jon's.

In the dairy the next day, he wants to tell Tommy Crowe all he has seen. Tommy Crowe has a way about him that makes you want to spill everything. But still, Jon gulps it back down. He's been careful not to share anything ever since the day he got hazed, and he doesn't want to lapse now. Once you make one exception, you'll make another. You have to have rules for yourself in a place like this. Build those rules like big brick walls and the men in black can't touch you.

Today is butchering day. By afternoon, they've got through two goats, a sheep and half a dozen scrub chickens. The little ones have to be shooed away from the chickens during summer – otherwise, they'll pilfer all the eggs and there'll be no chickens with necks to wring later in the month. Tommy is kind enough to let Jon do the chickens while he deals with the bigger fare.

At the back of the dairy sheds, the carcasses mounting at his feet, Jon corners a seventh chicken and, expertly, pops its head off. It is a stringy little thing that won't be missed, so he pushes it behind one of the milk crates and gets on with the day's work. The boys in the Mission will be joyous tonight; chicken is prized almost as highly as an illicit rabbit.

As soon as the lights are out that night, he levers open the loose floorboard again, and makes haste for the dairy shed. Once he has collected the chicken, he slopes around the harrowed land, reaching the bedwetters' dorm by the longest route. By the time he gets there, George and the little ones have already been on their rounds, leaving another tin can full of scraps set down in the earth.

Tonight, though, Jon Heather has a better treat.

He bolts across the harrowed land. The first tree is low and sprawling – and, in any case, too near the border to be safe from tell-tales. The next tree, however, is perfect, just tall enough so that the chicken might be safe from rodents. He takes a piece of twine, ties it like a noose around what's left of the chicken's neck, and dangles it from a branch.

He keeps watch for almost three hours before the wild boy appears. Stars cartwheel across the sky. The moon rises over the shadow wood. And there, moving towards the dangling chicken like a cat stalking one still clucking, is the wild boy.

Jon supposes he has been there for a long time already, lying in wait to see what ambush is being sprung. If he were a wild boy, that's exactly what he would do.

Tonight, however, there is no ambush. The boy jumps up, yanks the chicken down and whirls around, expecting to fend off some would-be assassin. When there are only shadows to confront him, he stalls. He looks perplexed. He limps forward, until he's as close to the border fires as Jon has ever seen. He is twelve or thirteen, and his face is tiny and soft-featured. His skin is dark, but he's certainly not like Booty or any of the black men back home. Only when he is certain there is no trap does he turn and disappear.

The next morning, George and the little ones are outraged. Nobody emptied their tin can last night.

Jon performs the same trick two days later, this time bundling up a loaf of bread and wedge of cheese that Laura smuggles out of the larder. She calls him her greedy pig, but Jon doesn't let on what he really wants the food for. That's another rule: keep your intentions to yourself; don't ask for advice, and don't let on.

The wild boy takes the bread and cheese and disappears into the scrub, only to reappear minutes later to sit on the bank beyond the harrowed land and eat it furtively, peering into the Mission. In his hideaway, Jon feels a pang of guilt, like he's a snatcher of stray dogs, luring them to a cage with pieces of bacon rind. Wild boys, he tells himself, are not for taming. They've got to stay wild. Otherwise, they're just any old boy from the Mission – and that way the men in black win.

Worried that he might be luring the wild boy into the Mission, Jon doesn't go the next night, nor the night after that. Yet, when he goes to play stones with George after work the following day, there is uproar in the bedwetters' dorm. The wild boy, it seems, has left them a present.

Jon follows the little ones. It is laid out on George's bed, slit from neck to tail with its innards taken out and a cross of sticks pushed through the flesh, ready to be toasted over an open fire.

'What is it?' Jon asks, peering close.

'A lizard!' George proudly announces. 'Like a baby dragon. What do you think, Jon? Maybe the wild boy slays dragons . . .'

That dusk, the little ones abscond with the lizard down to the banks of the shadow wood, and cook it like they would a rabbit. George reports that it tastes too salty, but Jon doesn't join in. Alone among them, only he knows what the lizard means: the wild boy wants to talk.

The next day, he risks wringing an extra chicken's neck – only, when he strings it up on the other side of the harrowed land, he doesn't take up his usual vantage point, but burrows down in some scrub beyond the chicken instead. He does not have to wait long. Tonight, the wild boy is less wary. An hour after the dormitory lights die, he creeps between the stunted trees.

He must scent that something is wrong. He yanks the chicken down and clings to it like any other boy might his favourite blanket.

In the scrub, Jon's heart starts to thud. His fingertips tingling, he reaches out and parts the branches.

That is all it takes – a flicker of movement. The wild boy whirls around, fending off some invisible shade by swinging the chicken. Loose feathers fly, dusting Jon Heather's face.

'Please don't run,' Jon begins, faltering when he recalls George begging him with those exact words. 'I only want to . . .'

Suddenly, Jon realizes his mistake: he is blocking the wild boy's route.

The boy drops the chicken and lunges to bowl Jon out of the way. He is scrawny, shorter as well, but he catches Jon off guard, driving him back into the thorns. Jon crumples, flailing to grab hold of the boy. Sprawled in the dust, the wild boy's foot rises and catches him in the jaw as he runs. And there, Jon sees black and red flesh, swollen and shining even in this dull light.

Jon gathers himself quickly, snatches up the chicken. There is only one thought in his head now: if the wild boy gets away, he gets away for good. He gives chase. This isn't like the last time he ran beyond the bounds of the Mission. This time, he isn't floating, alive on an idea; this time, his feet find every root and mound of uneven earth, catch and twist against every rock.

The branches of a low eucalyptus flay him, the burrow of some scrubland rat jars through his whole body.

Yet, as hampered as he is, the wild boy is hampered more, heaving his lame leg behind him. On the plain where the scrub has thinned, Jon grapples to catch him.

The wild boy turns, smashing Jon with the flat of his hand – and now they are on the earth, rolling together, locked in a preposterous playground embrace, a dead chicken pressed between. By some quirk of fate – for he is certainly the weaker of the two – Jon pins the wild boy down.

The dirty face opens its eyes, lets loose a volley of spittle and phlegm. 'Get off me!'

Jon is surprised to hear that the voice is not English. It is that, more than anything else – more, even, than the wild boy's stench, rank even to a boy longer than a year with the Children's Crusade – that makes him loosen his grip. It is enough for the wild boy to kick his way to freedom. He skitters to the end of the boulders. Somehow, he has regained the chicken.

'She'll still eat up,' the wild boy chatters, petting the broken bird, now devoid of any feathers.

Jon is perplexed. 'Why did you run?' he asks, finally able to breathe.

The wild boy scrunches his eyes tight. 'Because you chased! Come on,' he says. 'I got a camp.'

Somewhere sunrise of the Mission, there is a little thicket, and it is here that the wild boy has made his camp. He promises Jon there's water under the rocks, if you look closely enough, but to Jon it all seems the same dry emptiness. There isn't a fire, but that isn't going to stop the wild boy from toasting up the chicken he's still petting. You can't light fires after dark, he chatters, because then somebody might come looking, thinking you're a jackeroo or a swagman or a thieving bush black.

Jon doesn't know how he means to cook the chicken, but

he doesn't let on. He waits as the boy ferrets under the ashes of a dead bonfire and sees, buried underneath, huge rocks, still glowing with heat. The wild boy strains to tear the chicken apart and drops it, guts and all, into the rocks. Once he's kicked sand over the top, and flattened it down with yet another stone, he looks at Jon, grinning with a mouth full of gaps.

'I felt right better after I got that other chicken in my belly,' he says, rubbing a gut that seems curiously swollen. 'Even though I sicked some of it up.' He mimes it, like a pantomime. 'You like that goanna?'

'The lizard?'

'It takes a few of 'em, but you like 'em in the end.'

Jon doesn't have the heart to say he didn't taste it. 'What's your name?' he asks, because it seems a good place to start.

The wild boy darts him a look. 'What's yours?'

'Jon.'

The boy tips his head towards the Mission. 'You like it in there, don't you?' It is almost an accusation.

Jon shakes his head fiercely.

'I'm Luca,' he says, after considering it for some time. 'I used to be in there too.'

'With the Children's Crusade?'

Luca throws his chin upwards in reproach. 'Three years,' he says, 'but I been gone two now, so it's almost wiped out. I don't recognize you, Jonny Jonny *Jonny*. That's why I had to make sure.'

Jon tells him he's only been in the Mission a year, and the wild boy says he reckoned as much; there's hardly a scar on Jon Heather that wouldn't wash off in a good thunderstorm. Jon says there are precious few thunderstorms here, but the wild boy says that isn't true of all the places he's been.

'They still talk about me, do they?'

Jon isn't sure whether he ought to say yes or not. Perhaps

it's a matter of pride. 'I sort of keep myself to myself,' he says. 'You've got to have rules.'

Luca slumps, dramatically, onto a stone. When he lands, a pain ricochets up his bad leg, and his face contorts. 'I hate rules.'

'I mean rules for yourself,' says Jon. 'Not rules Judah Reed forces on you.'

'Like what?'

'Like – if you're angry at them, don't let them know you're angry. I did that once and they lined all the boys up to beat me. Or – if you steal something, don't brag about it. There'll be a tell-tale waiting to drop you in it. You've got to keep it inside.'

'What else?'

Jon thinks. He hasn't quite put this one into words. 'Rule two . . .' he says. 'What you thought the first time, that's the thing to think the rest of the time. Otherwise you'll start to think it's OK to be beaten, if it's just a *little* beating. Then you'll think it's OK to have a bigger beating, just so long as it's not a *really* big beating. Then you'll . . .'

Luca's face scrunches. 'Those *seem* like good rules.'

Jon shrugs. 'It's just things I've been thinking.'

'I wish *I'd* had those rules. Then maybe . . .' Luca stops. 'They got you yet?'

'They got me after I ran away, when I wouldn't hit George.'

'They got George, then?'

'He wets the bed.'

'So they tied him to the tree?

It is the beginning of a story Jon has never heard. He has seen boys taken into Judah Reed's office to meet the end of a stock whip but he has never seen them taken into the shadow wood and tied to a tree.

'I . . .'

'There was a boy, when I was in the Mission. Kept getting

the shits. He'd be in the fields or rolling up grain and he'd get the ache and want to go off to the long drop. But they'd be waiting for him when he got back and clout him round the ear for skipping out.' Luca wears a strange expression, as if he is almost wistful. 'It got that he was too scared to go to the shitter at all, so one day he just let it all fly. We were cutting grass and suddenly it was all down his legs and out of his short trousers . . . That's when the cottage mother saw him. She made one of the other boys wipe him down like he was a baby, but then he still had to go to Judah Reed. Well, Judah Reed'll swing his hockey stick at you all day long, 'til you promise you'll be a strong old Aussie, but there's some times he doesn't like getting his hands filthy. So, instead of beating this boy, he led him up into the shadow wood and just . . .'

'Tied him to a tree?'

'It's what happens if you're so bad a beating doesn't make it better. There's some boys get to like beatings, 'cause if you like them it means Judah Reed can't bother you anymore. But a couple of nights tied to a tree, with nothing to eat and no one to help you, and you soon learn.'

Jon does not want to know the answer, but tentatively he asks, 'What happened to that boy?'

'Well, that's just the thing. We all knew he was tied up in the wood. First night, I could even hear him crying. He cried a bit the next night too and one of the men in black, this old sort who was headmaster before Judah Reed, got so angry hearing him cry he said he was going to give him something to cry about. The Mission isn't for little cowards, see. But when he went up to give that boy his medicine, he wasn't even there.'

Jon Heather feels an unseasonal chill. 'Not there?'

'Not even in the wood.'

Emboldened, Jon pitches forward. 'He got out, didn't he? Just like you?'

'Not a chance,' Luca snorts. 'That boy wasn't for running. He was just for crying and shitting.'

'But if he didn't get out, what happened to . . .'

'No one went looking. There was one boy went to ask Judah Reed, but he had a bleeding backside that night, and he never went to ask again.'

'Somebody has to . . .'

'I can tell you what I reckon, for what it's worth.'

Jon's eyes beg it, but his lips will not ask the question.

'Somebody came in those woods and got him. Snatched him from right under the nose of Judah Reed and the rest. Some rock spider got in those woods and whisked him away.'

There it is again: rock spider, the same words Tommy Crowe used.

'Probably one of the honoured guests, needed a boy on his own farm.'

'Why do you call them rock spiders?' Jon Heather whispers.

'Well,' Luca says, 'a rock spider, see, he likes to get himself into little cracks as well.'

The smell of the chicken is strong now, and the night flies have descended.

'Don't you ever let them give you your medicine, Jonny. Stock whips or hockey sticks, take it like you have to. But don't go into those woods with them. There's worse things than Judah Reed, and them woods are being watched.'

The chicken is almost ready. Luca digs it up, prising up hot stones with a stick, and pulls out hunks of blackened flesh. He eats it ravenously, yowling from the heat, and licking blood and grease from his fingers. The insides of the hunks are barely cooked, but Jon eats them all the same; it's still better than Mission broth.

There are a hundred more questions Jon Heather needs to ask. Things he needs to know. There are five more years until he is old enough to leave the Mission. A boy cannot hunker down and barrel on for five years, not like he could for two months at the Home in Leeds. If it was hazings and hard work, perhaps it could be all right, even without a mother and a father and two sisters who love him; if it is more, Jon Heather needs to know.

'Did you . . .' he hesitates, unsure if he should ask, '. . . ever go out with an honoured guest?'

Luca is gnawing on a leg bone but drops it from his lips. 'Did *you*?'

Jon Heather shakes his head.

'The trick is not to look them in the eye. They'll hardly see you, when they come round, if you don't look them in the eye. There's some boys think it'll be a treat to go with an honoured guest, get out of the Mission even for a day . . . but they're the boys who'll end up going missing in the woods, you mark it down.'

For a moment, Luca returns to his chicken leg.

'You didn't answer my question.'

'I didn't want to.'

Jon sits in silence.

'Yeah,' Luca finally whispers. 'I had to go with an honoured guest once. Is that what you wanted to know?'

'No . . .'

'They'd come round, looking for boys to help on their farms. They even pay Judah Reed for it. I know, 'cause I had to carry the envelope, stuffed with shillings. There was a farm not far from here. A man called Richardson and a bunch of blacks.'

Jon's mind whirrs. Images flash through his mind. 'A man named Cormac Tate? Big white whiskers . . .'

Luca shakes his head. 'Not there. They had me in the fields. They had a man in black coming to check up . . . and . . .'

The chicken bone snaps in Luca's hand, drawing blood on its jagged ends. With a guttural snort, he tosses it into the scrub.

'I tried my best, Jonny. Honest I did. I did it all like they wanted, 'cause by then I knew all about honoured guests. But . . .' He cocks his head to one side, revealing his ragged, misshapen ear. 'See this? That was the first time I ran. I made it back to the Mission, went up to those sandstone shacks.' His voice breaks. 'I told Judah Reed every damn thing they'd done, and do you know what he did?'

Jon can only mouth the word 'no'.

'He put me on his knee and gave me six more for good measure. Those men on that farm were helping me, he said. Didn't matter what they did to me, every time I looked at them. If they were beating me, it was for my own good. I had to learn.' Luca's eyes are wide but there are no tears in them. He wrenches off another handful of the chicken and suckles on blackened flesh. 'Well, I learned, Jonny. I learned what happens when you ask Judah Reed for help.'

'I'm sorry, Luca . . .'

'Pah!' Luca snorts. 'Sorry doesn't cut it, not if you haven't even been *got*.' He pauses, seems to calm down. His whole body slouches. 'It's me who's sorry, Jonny. I don't want you to get got.'

Jon looks at the stars, trying to gauge the time. When Luca sees what he's doing, he starts nodding, like a demented clockwork toy. He remembers only too well what risks Jon is taking, creeping out after dark.

'You got to go,' he whispers, dragging his leg around the edge of the camp.

'Did you . . .' Jon doesn't know how to phrase it; it might almost be an insult. 'Did you want to come in?'

Luca reels back and spits out a tiny wing bone he's been sucking. He turns around, bends over, shoves his shoulder in Jon's face. Rising from the skin is a cross-hatch of welts, as if a stock whip had once been taken to him with an artist's precision. 'Ask it again,' he says.

Suddenly, Jon doesn't want to.

'Haven't you been listening? I didn't come back to the *Mission*,' he insists. 'I came back once and I won't do it again. And if those dirty old men get me again, I'll know who sent them.' Luca slumps, folds his arms tight across his chest. 'I brought you a *goanna*!' he blurts out, as if it is some kind of blood oath.

'I just thought, if you'd been running so long, why would you . . .'

Luca's eyes brighten, like an owl at the sound of a mouse.

'That's the thing, Jonny Jonny *Jonny.* I been wandering forever, and scrapping from stations and sleeping in holes, like that boy in the story they all tell. And . . .' He stalls. 'I never wanted to, but I been drifting back this way ever since it happened . . .' He lifts his leg. In the fading glow of the stones, it has an unearthly pallor. Jon sees, for the first time, that there are scars higher up too, where the boy's underpants are fraying.

'You been in the wars out there?' he begins. It is an old saying, one of his mother's, and he is surprised to hear it come from his own tongue.

'Oh no,' chitters Luca. 'I got *them* long before I ever ran away. I was one of the baddest boys ever sent to the Mission. But this . . .' His body doubles over and he sniffs at the leg. As far as Jon can tell, the wound isn't open; just a myriad of different colours, not one of them right. 'Something's wrong,' he says. 'Jonny Jonny *Jonny*, I think I need help.'

IX

'You see that?' says Tommy Crowe, squinting into the dust. He and a gang of boys have been ferrying a pile of tall karri trunks across the breadth of the Mission, a full day sweating under the interminable sun. In the woodworking sheds, boys are measuring them up and cutting them down to size, while another crew hauls them further, over to the sandstone construction. The foundations are laid now, and a skeleton is growing up, ready to be filled with the piles of bricks the little ones are crafting. If you are clever, you can see the pattern of the rooms within, like an archaeological dig: here, the new offices for Judah Reed; here, a little room where bad boys can be kept until they have learnt their lesson.

'What is it?' asks Jon Heather. He peers, with a hand cupped to his eyes, into the distance. Out there, a dust cloud is stirring. It seems to be circling the Mission, growing closer like the tightening of a noose. Jon Heather narrows his eyes, can almost make out the angular shape of the wagon, a raggedy cargo heaped up in back.

'Jon Heather,' Tommy Crowe says. 'This can't be good.'

Indeed it cannot; the dust cloud heralds Judah Reed's return.

This year, there are twenty-three new boys and girls to join the Mission. Last year, there were seventeen. Six lost children might not sound much, but to Jon it means everything: the Children's Crusade is growing bigger, like a colony of ants getting more aggressive and intelligent as their numbers swell.

Jon watches as the boys and girls are hauled out of the utes, stripped of their cardboard suitcases, and sent off to their new dormitories. Watching them go, Judah Reed stands high on one of the flatbeds, gazing over the Mission.

When he steps down, a little one rushes to help him with his knapsack. Judah Reed reaches down and ruffles the boy's hair. When his fingers hover over the scalp, Jon turns away, cannot bear to see. It will only, he thinks, be a few short weeks before that same boy is in the sandstone hut, begging to go home.

'It feels good to be back,' says Judah Reed, marching into the Mission. 'Breathe it in, boys! The smell of home.'

Jon looks up, feels the same fluttering in his chest that he felt that day he got hazed. He could march up to Judah Reed right now, spit in his eye, pile all the little ones back into the ute and drive straight back into the desert. But – you've got to have rules. He breathes it in, calms down. Let it fester inside. There is a bigger problem, now, than whether he wants to lash out at Judah Reed or not. Luca is depending on him – and, suddenly, sneaking food out at night is going to be a very different game.

George reaches down and grabs hold of another stick in his pudgy fist. Something black and horrid scuttles out of the sand,

and instinctively he throws the stick down. He's never seen a spider quite that big before. Suddenly ashamed that he's so afraid, he picks the stick back up and prods at where the spider stands. Too late, he realizes how fiercely he has poked. He lifts the stick up to the light and marvels at a spider skewered, just like a dragon with a spear.

He is standing that way when the little one, Martin, jumps up to tug on his sleeve.

Martin has a mop of dirty ginger hair, and a nose permanently encrusted with all kinds of grime. 'I've got a message,' he proudly whispers.

George flings the spidery stick down, as if caught with his hand in a contraband biscuit tin. 'For me?'

The little one presses a finger to his lips. From this, George deduces, it must be a secret.

'We're meant to be on muster,' he whispers. Ever since they watched Judah Reed roll in with the new boys, George has been careful to get on with his work and not look anyone in the eye. In truth, there was something reassuring about seeing the new boys arrive; it's never good to be the newest, wherever you are.

'He says it's *urgent*,' the little one answers.

George can't resist. He takes Martin's hand and finds himself dragged along, down to where Jon Heather's at work in the dairy. At first he thinks it must be Jon who wants to see him – perhaps there's an epic game of stones going on – but Martin leads him on, down to the furthest fringe of shadow wood.

George stops dead. The little one tugs at his hand, but he won't be moved. He begins to tremble.

Then suddenly, he takes off. Feet flying high, he barrels over the field, tumbling more than once but scrambling right back to his feet. The little one rushes to keep up – but nothing could be faster than George today.

At last, he cannonballs into the boy standing at the edge of the shadow wood. The boy is strong, but still has to strain not to fall over. He starts laughing, wild and free, great whoops that have never before been heard in the Mission. George strains at his shirt, smothering him in the embrace.

'Georgie boy,' Peter says, kneading a watery eye. 'It's good to see you too.'

'I thought you was dead!'

Peter's face wrinkles. 'Dead?'

'Maybe not dead.'

'You never thought I was dead.'

George releases his hold, shrugs his chubby shoulders. 'I didn't think I'd see you again.'

'Well, you have. Chin up, Georgie! It's Australia – it isn't hell.' He looks down at the little one. 'Go on, hop it!'

'You promised!' the little one squeaks.

Peter fishes in a pocket and produces something that glistens like the treasure at the heart of an Incan tomb: a hunk of toffee. He throws it up in the air twice, and then pats it towards the little one. It falls in the dirt, but that doesn't matter; he's up and away with it almost instantly, hollering for his brothers.

'Come on, Georgie,' says Peter, hunching so that he is George's height. 'I don't want to be seen . . .'

He inches towards the shadow wood, but George tugs him back. He shakes his head, fierce in a way Peter has never seen before. It strikes Peter, then, how much George has grown. Somehow he's stayed chubby, but he's taller now, his hair entangled in great, grubby knots.

'Is there a place we can go?'

'A place?'

A strange look has ghosted over Peter's face. 'I don't want them catching me. Cormac Tate says . . .'

George's face has crumpled, as if to reflect Peter's own.

'Don't bother, Georgie. It's just . . .' For the first time, Peter has the terrible feeling of being in a place of which he knows nothing. It is worse, he decides, than those first days after they came ashore. At least, then, *everything* was new: the sun, the sand, the sky. The world out there, on the other side of the shadow wood, he understands; in here, it is different – and he didn't even have to break down a wall, or scramble through a fence.

'Where's Jon Heather?'

George suddenly lets go of Peter's hand. 'You came to see Jon?'

'Not on your life, George. I came to see *you*. It's been a whole year, Georgie. You're getting all growed up. But, if Jon Heather's here, there's something I need to ask him.'

'You can ask me!' George beams.

'That I could. But this is going to get someone in a lot of trouble. And . . .' He winks, conspiratorially. '. . . I'd rather that person was Jon Heather.'

It is not far to go, but every step deeper in is another step he will have to travel back. Every time his foot falls, he hears Cormac Tate imploring him. His voice intones: *there'll be snow on the Nullarbor Plain* . . . His eyes dart back and forth. In the distance, he sees the sketchy silhouette of one of the men in black. He feels himself tugged after George. It has been an aeon since he was afraid of a man in black, but the old chill returns to him now.

George leads him boldly and, for the first time in his life, he realizes that George might just be the braver of the two. To his relief, they do not have far to go, only across the untilled field and up and over an ill-hewn stile. On the other side they find Jon in a dairy, with his hands elbow-deep in the belly of a billy goat.

When he sees Peter, he is not taken aback. His face sets in a deep scowl and he whips his hands out, splattering gore across the earth. 'What on earth are you doing, George!? McAllister's kicking around here!'

George's face flits between Peter and Jon.

Jon wipes the thick gore off his hands with a dirty apron. 'Here,' he says, scrunching it up and hurling it at Peter. 'Get this on. With any luck, he might think you're one of the new boys.' He looks Peter from top to bottom, can't quite believe his eyes. 'And Peter, you've got to get those boots off! They give you away a mile off!'

Peter sits on an upturned bucket, squirming into the apron, while George gleefully yanks his boots off.

'What are you doing here?' Jon demands.

'Shit, Jon Heather, king of the Crusade!'

At Peter's feet, George erupts in laughter.

'This isn't a game, Peter. You can't just waltz in here . . .'

Peter nudges George. 'He's getting real bossy, George. Don't tell me he's pushing you around like this?'

'Yeah,' Jon snaps, 'well, it isn't you who'll get the beating if you're found, is it? You'll just hurry off home. Back to Cormac Tate.'

It is a more vicious accusation than Peter realizes. Jon said *home* with as much of a curse in his voice as he could summon up.

The silence stretches. Then, slowly, the corners of Jon's lips start to twitch. As soon as he sees it, Peter bounces back into life. He ruffles George's hair and leaps from the bucket. 'There it is!' he says, watching Jon's smile finally break. 'Jon Heather, it's good to see you.'

'You too, Peter.'

On the ground, George beams.

'Jon, there's something I've got to ask you . . .'

Still on edge, Jon pokes his head out of the dairy doors.

'Jon, it's about my sister.'

'Your sister?'

'You remember I told you about my sister.'

Jon shrugs. He remembers he tried to tell Peter about the sisters of his own, but Peter wasn't interested.

'The thing is, Jon, I've been talking to Cormac Tate and . . .'

He produces the photograph, the Children's Crusade from the late summer of 1923. If it stirs anything in Jon, that the childsnatchers have been at work for generations, he hides it well. There seems something curious about Jon Heather today; it's as if there is a glass pane between him and everybody else.

'You think she might have been here,' Jon breathes.

'I haven't seen her in five years. But Jon, if she *was* here . . .'

'Then she's still in Australia,' Jon concludes. 'Boys to be farmers and girls to be farmers' wives.'

'She'd be nineteen now.'

'Too old for the Children's Crusade.'

'But they must *know* . . .' Peter insists, his voice suddenly hushed. 'Jon, Cormac Tate thinks there'll be records. Registers. Going all the way back, even to when he was here.'

It dawns on Jon, what Peter's asking. He turns a pirouette in disbelief. It is more believable that that dead goat will rise again than that Peter's really asking him to do this.

'There are pictures!' George pipes up.

They both look at him.

'In Judah Reed's office,' he ventures. 'All up on the wall, big and black and white. Old pictures, Peter. There's pictures of boys building the dormitories. Maybe Rebekkah's in one of those?'

Momentarily, Peter is touched that George remembers his sister's name. Then, a deeper thought strikes. 'You've seen these pictures, Georgie?'

George looks, suddenly flushed red, at Jon.

'It's OK, George. It isn't a secret,' Jon says.

'What's not?' demands Peter.

When George shrugs, Jon knows it's down to him. Damn George, but it's always down to him. 'George was in Judah Reed's office when . . . when I ran away, Peter. It was while he was . . . waiting for a beating.'

George might be about to start crying again, but a look from Jon forces him to hold back. 'I'm sorry, Peter . . . *It* just keeps happening. They moved me in with other boys like me . . .'

Peter's look says it all. He'd hated sending Jon back here, but now he *knows* he was right. It's positively flowering on his face. Jon boils. It's been a whole year, he's been doing his best, playing stones and telling stories and . . . He knows it's not good enough – but when could it ever be? As if it's Jon's fault George can't cross his legs at night! That's just like Peter. Don't blame George because George is just a baby – oh, but don't call him a baby, Jon, or then the baby will cry.

'You've done it before, Jon. When you went looking for your mother's letter . . .'

Jon wants to kick the dead billy goat, send its insides splattering out of the hole in its chest. Already, he knows he can't say no. And it isn't just that Peter's asking. It isn't just that Peter's his friend. It's that the men in black won't want him to do it. *That's* the real reason he'll say yes.

He sits on a crate, then stands back up again. He wishes he had a rule for this – but he hasn't got rules for how to deal with his friends. Not yet.

Then it strikes him: there's something he wants too.

There's a wild boy. He escaped from the Mission, but now he's back . . . Every night, Jon has left food out for Luca. Sometimes, when the moment arises, he has even sneaked just over the Mission's edge, to listen to his stories in the scrub. And he's started to notice those horrible, vivid colours on his leg – they're not disappearing; they're spreading, bleeding out like drops of ink in a pool of water. He eats everything Jon brings, and more – but the only part of him getting any fatter is that pot-belly, rock solid and tender to touch. Once, Jon saw him in the waning daylight – and he had no whites in his eyes, just a kaleidoscope of bloodshot yellow.

Bit by bit, Jon has been able to piece together Luca's story. He comes from Malta, was shipped out with a glut of English boys from Acton and Coventry, places Jon doesn't know. Back home he had been in an orphanage – but it wasn't until he boarded the HMS *Othello* that they told him his mother was truly dead. Yet there was something in Luca that didn't believe a word these new men in black said. At the Mission, he held to that, hoping against all hope that his mother had survived. He ran and got caught at a ranch. He ran and was brought in by black trackers. He ran, and he ran, and he took his beatings every time, his whole body wearing the history of the times he tried to get home. And when, at last, they threatened to send him south, to a place called Bindoon, where more men in black held sway, he ran away and never came back.

At first, it was difficult being a wild boy – but he learnt tricks wherever he could, from farmhands who took pity on him, from bush blacks bonded to a station at which he begged. Roaming far and wide, he came to the coast. Here, there were easy pickings to be had. You could plunge your hands into a tide pool and come out with enough fish to last a week's worth of dinners.

Then, high up on some rocks, stealing eggs from the giant terns he so admired, he fell.

He was one moon and more, holed up in a seaside cove, dragging himself out to find crabs and shells and seaweed – but, even when he could walk again, it was never the same. Something stirred inside him. He began to roam – and soon he could see familiar stations, familiar rocks and patches of scrub. He knew it was the Mission calling out for him, but though he skirted its boundaries, nothing – no man nor boy nor insidious thought – would make him ask for their help.

In truth, Jon doesn't want him to come in. Late at night, it is not the thought of Luca dying that fills him with anger;

it is the thought of him walking, meekly, into Judah Reed's office, pouring out his apologies and begging to be saved.

'I want to get him to a doctor,' Jon begins. 'A hospital. Somebody who can help. Maybe you and Cormac . . .'

Peter nods. 'I hear you, Jon Heather. That sounds fair dinkum.'

Jon shoots him a look. 'What?'

'It's something Cormac says.'

'Well . . .' Jon feels he might explode. 'It shouldn't be.'

'Look,' says Peter. 'Are you going to help me or not?'

George interjects, 'I'll do it, Peter!'

Jon steps out of the dairy. There's still no sign of McAllister, but the hairs are prickling all up and down his neck.

'Yeah,' he says, looking back. 'If you'll help me.' He reaches out his hand, still black and red, to shake Peter's. This very moment might be the birth of another rule: never risk yourself for nothing; always exact something in return, even if it's from the people you love.

'A bloody handshake,' says Peter, taking hold. 'Now, *that's* something we didn't get back home.'

In bed that night, Jon Heather lies awake, listening to the ferreting of scrub rats underneath the dormitory floor.

It has been two nights since he was able to bury scraps in the scrubland for Luca to find. He has been leaving them at the slag heaps, where refuse from the construction site now forms a range of miniature mountains – and though, every morning, the scraps have been taken, he is less and less certain that the wild boy is to blame. This morning, there was spoor all around the spot, the trails of some scavenger come to take the wild boy's food away. Tonight, the images will not leave him alone: Luca, growing weaker and weaker in his bush camp, his skin mottling further, long hours of the day lost to fitful sleep.

In the dairy the next day, he is scrubbing pails when a man in black ghosts through and takes Tommy Crowe aside. Jon knows not to watch openly, but slows in his scrubbing and squints out of the corner of his eye. The man in black whispers into Tommy's ear, and then drifts on.

'What is it?' asks Jon.

Tommy mutters darkly. 'See for yourself.'

They stand in the dairy doors and look deep into the Mission. Up there, the spindly figure of a cottage mother is leading a boy, by twisted ear, across the dusty expanse. She is approaching the sandstone huts, but before she has got halfway, Judah Reed himself emerges and strides towards her. It seems, to Jon, that he takes one mighty stride for every three of hers.

In the middle of the earth, they meet, the boy dangling between them. They begin to talk, animatedly, as if the creature is not suspended between them, already bawling out.

'He pissed hisself,' Tommy Crowe says. 'They'd been helping him hide it in the dorm, but that cottage mother was staking them out. She was going to give him a hiding but . . .' At this, Tommy Crowe's face breaks into a wild, unbidden smile. 'See the way she's holding her wrist?'

Jon nods. A smile is creeping onto his face too.

'That's right!' Tommy says. 'That little lad went and sunk his teeth in.'

'Do you think he drew blood?'

'I'd say so, Jon.' He pauses. 'See, there's going to be a hazing . . .'

Tommy leaves the dairy door to go back to the goats but, for the longest time, Jon lingers. Out there, Judah Reed takes hold of the boy's other ear and, like that, he is marched back to his dormitory: the scene of his shame, the scene of his crime.

'Tommy,' Jon says. 'I've got another job to do.'

Tommy Crowe nods. 'But I'm not carrying these pails for you.'

Jon hurries. He could approach the sandstone buildings from any angle, but he does so brazenly, crossing paths with Judah Reed as he marches to see sodden sheets and drops of the cottage mother's blood. He risks a look back, sees other men in black flocking the same way, as if eager to know what their leader might do.

There will never be a chance so opportune. He approaches the sandstone building, waits outside like an errant boy being made to brood before his beating – and then pushes through the door.

Inside, he stands in a little cloakroom, the same as at the front of all the dormitories. A big bright poster hangs on the wall, behind a sheet of glass riveted to the stone: *Build Your Children's Future!* it cries out, bold letters painted across a map of the continent made up in red brick and mortar. *£10 Can Take Them to Australia!*

There is only one hallway leading out of here. It seems to run the length of the long, oblong building, with chambers on either side. He keeps low, out of sight of the windows, scuttling past open doors and pressing his eye to the keyhole of every locked one. Somehow, he knows he is alone.

The hallway comes to an end – and, he feels certain, he is at Judah Reed's own chamber. Outside the door there sits a wooden bench, big enough for three boys to sit together, heads bowed, waiting to be lashed. He knows Judah Reed is not here, but still he presses his eye to the keyhole. Then, he puts both hands around the enormous doorknob and turns.

The same tapestry that he saw in the Home in Leeds hangs against the wall – but, on the other walls, above a big, plain desk, where countless boys have been exposed and taught lessons, it is just as George said: photographs of each generation of the Children's Crusade. Here is the Mission in its earliest days, with boys piled into the back of a horse and trap; boys draped over, of all things, a camel, with the sun beating down. And, underneath the pictures, legends: the names of the men in black, the names of the boys they have brought here.

Jon rushes over, toppling a vase of dried flowers. He rushes to put it back into place, treading dead petals into the ground. If Peter's sister was here at all, she was here four or five years ago. Jon knows nothing of her: a red-haired girl, tall and thin, prone to sticking out her tongue. His eyes rove over the pictures, but it is too tempting to drop further back in time. 1911. 1920. 1922. The Children's Crusade have learnt their profession well: there must be a thousand boys who have been dragged, kicking and screaming, through this Mission; a thousand Englishmen arrive, and a thousand Australians depart.

There, on the wall, is a picture Jon Heather knows – the very same one that Peter brought to show him, Cormac Tate as a little boy, pining for England but doomed never to return. Jon scans the names written below in cursive script. Cormac Tate is listed as *Cormac* only, as if, like all of these other boys, he has had to shed something in coming here.

Jon realizes, for the first time, that he has never asked George his surname. He has never asked Peter. They don't have surnames now – but Jon will always be Jon Heather. He'll have it carved into his arm with a penknife and a pot of ink.

Jon is about to look away, when another name catches his eye. He flits between the picture and the register, singling out the boy. He is standing only two boys removed from the young Cormac Tate, his smile as forced as all those around him.

His name is Judah, and his eyes glower, betraying his upturned lips.

Jon stands there for a long time. Too long. He is still standing there, trying to convince himself that this cannot be Judah Reed, that it makes no sense, when a shadow falls over the room.

He turns around – but he is still alone. A whisper of black moves away from the window, a man moving past and blotting out the sun.

He freezes. He does not know if he's been seen. But now there is a door slamming, somewhere in the sandstone building, and footsteps reverberating along the hall. He was trapped like this once before, but he won't be trapped again. He runs to the window, heaves and heaves to lift it up. When it won't move, he panics. Skitters around, desperate for another route. As he turns, he sees the clasp at the top of the window, holding it in place. He scrambles up, leaping the last few inches, and knocks the clasp free. Seconds later, feet kicking wildly behind, he is through the window, landing in a heap on the earth outside.

He does not wait to find out if, indeed, he was seen. If it was so, they'll come looking for him soon enough; no sense in walking to them, hands clasped, begging for forgiveness.

Scratch it into your arm, Jon Heather. Another rule in how to live your life.

At first, he runs for the dairy, but something draws him round, towards the opposite end of the Mission. George will be there, somewhere; today, the bedwetters are shovelling the latrines. He has to tell somebody. He hasn't found Rebekkah; he's found something immeasurably worse: once upon a time, in this faraway world, Judah Reed was one of us.

By the time he reaches the bedwetters' dorm, he is out of breath, with a stitch in his side. He rounds the back of the dormitory – but the latrines are the same as they've been for weeks. They haven't been worked today. He spins around, searches the avenues between the shacks in search of little ones out on muster.

By degrees, Jon's eyes are drawn to the dormitory shack. There shouldn't be anybody inside during the day, not when there's work to be done – but, if he cocks his head, he is certain he can hear voices within. It isn't just one voice, but a dozen and more, the little ones singing a song. If they're shirking their duties, they're bound to join the hazing this afternoon. Jon steals around the shack, treading softly along the latrines and approaching the doorway so that he cannot be seen.

At the door, he hears another voice among the little ones, and the soft strumming of a guitar. He peeps in, and the first thing he sees are glass bottles, lined up in a milk crate at the door. Except, they're not the same shape as milk bottles; they are thinner, with long necks, and black writing on the side. Somebody has been bringing the bedwetters Coca-Cola.

In the dormitory, the beds have all been pushed against the walls and the little ones gather around a younger man in black. In the middle of the circle, he sits on a wooden stool, a battered guitar in his hands. Perhaps he is leading the song, but the boys certainly know it off by heart; this can't be the first time they've gathered for a little singalong. It isn't a tune Jon knows, but they're warbling something about swagmen and billabongs and jumbucks, things he doesn't want to know anything about.

He is about to retreat, when the man in black shifts – and he sees, on the far side of the circle, George sitting among the others, fat hands clapping just like every other boy. Jon freezes. There is a smile on George's face that he has never seen before. His whole face is creased with it, like he couldn't keep it down even if he wanted. He sits cross-legged and, in between his legs, one of the glass bottles stands, still frothing at the top.

The song reaches its chorus, and Jon pulls away. If he listens carefully, he can hear George's voice, singing as loudly and proudly as every boy around him

Even when the song ends, Jon can hear his friend's laughter, cutting through all the rest.

In the afternoon, the bell rings and the whole of the Children's Crusade ditch their tools to flock to the assembly hall. By the time Jon and Tommy Crowe arrive, the hall is already full. Hoping to snatch the seat directly behind George, Jon kicks his way along one of the lines. When he is almost there, one of the bigger boys from his own dormitory drops onto the bench before him. Jon burns, tells the bigger boy to budge. The boy just stares at him, offering a stupid shrug.

'You give me that seat, or next time I do you a letter, I'll write to your mother that you hate her and wish she was dead.'

It is not the threat that drives the bigger boy away, only the idea that Jon Heather himself could spout something so vicious.

Jon drops into the seat and leans forward. 'George,' he whispers.

George has his chin tucked into his neck, but he won't be allowed to stay like that for long. If he isn't watching when the punishments begin, some cottage mother will clatter him with a cane.

'Don't, Jon,' he replies, not turning around. 'We'll get done.'

He wasn't so miserable only a few short hours ago, Jon thinks. A day off work for songs and Coca-Cola. Next, they'll be going on daytrips to the seaside.

'I got into Judah Reed's office,' Jon whispers. 'I saw the pictures.'

George looks over his shoulder, his eyes wide.

'It was just like you said, Georgie boy. Rows and rows of photographs, going back for . . .'

'Did you find Peter's sister?'

Jon shakes his head. 'I don't know what I'm going to tell him.'

'He'll be cross.'

He has no right to be. Jon might have been lashed for even thinking about doing what he did. Yet, George doesn't care. George just doesn't want Peter upset.

'I don't want you to go, Jon.'

'I've got to go.'

'Why do you got to go? You don't even know about Peter's sister.' He pauses. 'It's because of the wild boy, isn't it? He's your friend now. You want to be a wild boy.'

'Georgie . . .'

'Stop calling me Georgie. It's a baby's name. My name's George.'

Jon has never heard George snap so viciously.

'I'm sorry, Jon,' George finally whispers. 'You're my friend. But . . . you promised, Jon Heather. You promised you wouldn't run away.'

On stage, Judah Reed appears. It will be a simple, procedural thing. He says a few words, and then invites the boy onto the stage. The cottage mother whose hand he so savagely sunk his teeth into has a front row seat.

He can be no more than seven years old, and he has no idea what is coming. The boys from his dormitory stand, and one by one they approach.

After it is finished, Judah Reed leads the boys in prayers, and dismisses them. In their eagerness to dissipate, pews are toppled and boys pushed over. As George stands, Jon leans forward, whispers in his ear – but the hubbub in the hall is too much. He calls out, louder, afraid he is going to be overheard.

'What if you came with me, George?' He might need help, getting Luca to the rendezvous. George won't be much help, but there's nobody else to ask.

George stands, elbows past the little ones at his side. 'Why can't you just be like everybody else, Jon Heather?'

Then he is gone, clattering into little ones as he goes.

'George!' Jon calls after him, grappling out to try and catch his arm. 'George, please!'

George stampedes into the dormitory, flings himself onto his mattress. He buries his face in the sacking, starts chewing to keep the sobs at bay. When he rises for air, the first one bubbles up. His fists – useless, fat, *baby* fists – are clenched. He hits the mattress over and over.

Suddenly there are little ones at his side. Martin pats him, like a dog. At first George hates it, but slowly his crying ebbs away. He looks up. Martin looks like he might cry himself.

'Did Judah Reed *get* you too?' he whispers.

George shakes his head. He's never hated himself more. He doesn't want to be a cry-baby – he knows Jon Heather hates it. But Jon's a bully, just like the rest of them. It's only in *here* that they aren't.

He looks at Martin. Other little ones are ranged around, but Martin shoos them away.

'It's Jon Heather,' George trembles. He wants to say it out loud: Jon Heather's running away again. He's got the wild boy and he doesn't need me, and he's going to find Peter and they'll run away and, this time, they won't come back.

Jon Heather and Peter only pretend to like you, George. Like when a boy wants to read your books or have a go on your toy train. They'll take it and run it up and down the path and then throw it on the ground – and they won't even come in your house and have tea, because then people would *know*.

But all he says is, 'I don't want Jon Heather to go.'

Before he can go on, little ones on the other side of the dormitory start cheering. Through the window, George can see the younger man in black coming back towards the dorm, guitar in his hands. There'll be more songs tonight. They dare not hope for more Coca-Cola – but it won't be long before the little ones start chattering about it.

George dries his eyes and starts kneading his hands.

Up and over the latrines, through the thicket – Jon hurtles across the harrowed land. He doesn't stop when he hits the scrub, but scurries on until it is thick enough to hide him. A pair of scrub turkeys rise, horrified, from their nest in a flurry of wings. Jon keeps his head down, cursing the stupid birds. When he dares to look up, he doesn't see any men in black approaching. There's a flicker in one of the dormitory windows, but that's all. He's got two hours until his cottage mother will declare lights out and do her nightly march around the beds. Enough time to get out, make the rendezvous, and get back in – but only if he hurries.

His feet know the way. He bounces off roots, taking the shortcut through the branches of a sprawling eucalypt. Around him, the trees start to spread out, red land rising in hummocks between them. By now, the stars are coming out. He peers up, gets his bearings on the one that shines the brightest.

Luca's camp is sunrise of the compound. Ten minutes and he'll be there. He has already been out of the compound another ten. That leaves more than an hour and a half to get Luca to the meeting spot, help him into Cormac Tate's ute, and get back to the dormitory. Jon's legs pound against the hard red earth. He'll have to make up time now – when Luca's draped over his shoulder, they'll have to stop, take rests, hobbling forward like a three-legged race.

A shadow moves on the plain. Jon whips his head around, his vision blurred. When he can see clearly, he shakes off the chill – it is only an errant kangaroo, as sickly as Luca, plodding along. It senses him and dips behind a big red boulder.

Keeping the Mission on his right, he fixes his position by a toppled tree and sets out across the plain. Suddenly, it seems that the desert is writhing. He stops, tells himself he's being a coward; there's nothing out here that can hurt him. The things that can hurt him are all back *there*.

It dawns on him: he's scared. It isn't the same as standing on stage, glaring at Judah Reed. At least, then, he knew what was coming. Now, he hears a scuttling, a slithering, and every story he ever read is living in his head. There are monsters out here. Demons and diabolical things. He wants to flee, but he's already running. He leaps up, feet scrabbling as he flies.

'Where did you think you were going, Jon?'

The voice makes him stop dead in his tracks. He whirls around, searching for a figure in the darkness – but everywhere it is just the same textureless black. Without thinking, he takes off again, head down as if he might fly into some unseen barrier.

'Jon,' the voice repeats, calm and even, without even an ounce of anger. 'You mustn't think we are cruel. But you can't play these games of yours anymore.'

He has taken only two strides when something strikes him. The darkness explodes in front of his eyes. The ground rushes up. Suddenly, he's flat on the ground, heaving for air. At first, he thinks his foot is caught in a tangle of root. He kicks to get free, tries to stand – but something is pinning him down.

'Stand up, Jon.'

Hands close around his shoulders, hauling him into the air. The fingertips are cold, and he dangles there, unable to twist free. Then, with a jolt, the hands release him and he drops to the ground. His first thought is to bolt – but, too late, the hands are around him again, wrenching him so that he faces the way he has come.

At last, he sees a face. Judah Reed looks at him. By his shoulder, like a second head, there stands another of the men in black. Perhaps it is the man from George's dorm, but Jon cannot be sure.

'We've been here before, haven't we, Jon?'

His hands still on Jon's shoulders, Judah Reed crouches. The same height as Jon, he still seems monstrously large. There is a patch of dried spittle in the corner of his lips.

'Where did you think you were going to run to, Jon?' He seems almost sad. 'Don't you know how hard we have all worked?'

And now Judah Reed is holding him, hugging him, and his

touch is gentle and firm. It is the silliest thing, but Jon suddenly remembers being five or six years old, watching as the fathers came back to the terrace, seeing the little girl next door enter her daddy's very first embrace.

'Jon Heather,' he says. 'Look at me.'

Jon squirms back, just enough so that Judah Reed is no longer touching his face.

'Look at me,' Judah Reed repeats. 'You can't just leave the Mission, Jon. It isn't why you're here. What kind of parents would it make us, if we just let you wander off, into the big wild world?'

Words froth in Jon's throat. 'There were others,' he says. 'Boys who ran . . .'

If he hears at all, Judah Reed does not seem to care.

'It's going to be the very last time, Jon.' Jon can taste his breath, dewy and warm and smelling of today's mutton. 'Once, we can understand. Twice, we can even correct. But three times, Jon, and we start to get worried. We brought you with us so that we could rescue you, help you make something of your worthless little life, not so that you might bring everybody else to their knees.' Judah Reed takes hold of his chin, angles his face so that Jon can't help but peer into his own. 'Bad boys,' he says, 'can be the ruin, not of themselves, but of everybody around them. Bad boys,' he goes on, 'must take their medicine.'

Peter goes to the window, pulls back the blind. The evening redness is already fading to grey. Cormac Tate was supposed to be back here an hour ago. If there's one thing he's certain of, it's that that old engine would have taken him to the moon and back, without stalling once. Peter fixed it himself, and he'd stake his life on it.

There are voices downstairs. Peter listens at the door, resisting the urge to go down and tell them Cormac's in trouble. He opens the door just a crack, to hear if there's news of some accident out on the highway, and Dog seizes the advantage, wriggling through. After a quick cuddle against Peter's legs, he too rushes to the window, scrabbling to the ledge with his forepaws to keep watch.

Peter is about to slump onto the bed, when Dog lets out a shrill yap. He rushes to the window, shoving Dog out of the way. Below them, a ute draws into the yard.

'Dog,' he says. 'You deserve a bastard big bone!'

Dog looks at him, confused, but nonetheless pleased.

In the yard, the ute stops. Peter sees, for the first time, that there are two people in the cab. That must be why Cormac's late; he's picked up some hitchhiker or roustabout, as he's prone to doing.

In the yard, a man in black steps out of the cab. The station foreman emerges and greets him with a wary handshake. They chatter for seconds that last interminably long – and then, together, look up and scan the farmhouse windows. Peter drops back – but he knows he's been seen. He kicks Dog out of the way and tightens the straps on his tucker bag.

Peter rushes to the door, but there he stalls. Without Cormac Tate, there's nowhere to go. Perhaps it's nothing. Perhaps it's just one of the routine visits the Children's Crusade have always promised, some simpering man in black here to check that his transformation into loyal Australian boy is almost complete.

He hurries back to the window, peers through the blind. The ute is still there, but the man in black and foreman are nowhere to be seen.

Downstairs, the front door slams.

'Oh, Jon . . .' Judah Reed slumps against a red boulder, kneading at his brow. 'You don't know how much I hate this.' He averts his eyes. 'We promised you boys the world. You can have it all. It's here, waiting for you.' He pauses. 'But I've seen hundreds of boys come through this Mission, and there is always one, Jon Heather, who needs to be taught what's good for him.'

Jon tenses. His ankles are roped together, tied to a tree ten yards in front; his wrists, bound behind his back, are tied to a tree ten yards behind. He could move – but only to topple over backwards, giving slack to the cords.

'Sir, shouldn't we?'

It is the younger man in black.

Judah Reed stands, obviously wearied. 'You know this is for your own good, don't you, Jon?' he whispers brokenly. 'You need to start liking it here. You need to start seeing what life has to offer. If you don't, we've all failed. We might as well have left you in those terraces that the Lord abandoned, and gone on our way.' He opens his palms, a gesture of openness and honesty. 'Some boys start thinking differently after reading a book. For others, it's a song.'

Once, a jolly swagman camped near a billabong.

'But, for some, the lesson has to be more sudden. More permanent.' He walks past Jon. Jon sees him go, a blur of black through his drying tears. 'It can work, Jon. You'll come out of this stronger, prouder. You'll know what you have to do, if you're going to grow up. I've seen it work before.'

Because it happened to *you*, Jon thinks. Because you were a little boy whose father never came back, who got put on a ship and sent to the ends of the earth, who cried so fiercely to go home that they beat him and starved him and shackled him up.

The voices grow faint.

'We will be back for you, Jon. The Children's Crusade never abandons its own.'

There are footsteps, there is silence – and, too late, he realizes they have gone.

He bawls out. They can't leave him here. He's more alone than he ever was, that night he ran. He's more alone than he's ever been, slaving in the Mission or cringing in a dormitory bed. Though he knows it is futile, he strains until he feels his skin starting to tear. He screams out what he thinks are unintelligible curses, every vile thing he can think of – but a moment of utter clarity passes through him, and he realizes he has, in fact, been begging, saying sorry over and over again: sorry that he ever betrayed the Children's Crusade; sorry that he never worked hard enough; sorry that he doesn't have what it takes to be a good Australian boy.

His sobbing peters into silence – and then there is nothing in the world, only the whispers of the scrub and the desert to keep him company through the long, lonesome night.

He has no way of gauging time. He tries to keep his eyes on the horizon, but there are long hours until dawn comes and, already, his feet are tired. He wonders if he might kick forward with his feet, push backwards with his chest and, in that way, somehow lie down. But he hears things skittering – spiders or scorpions, lizards or snakes. He sniffles again, bleats out. For a second, the skittering is still, as every creature keeping this midnight watch with him freezes in uncertainty. Then, the night begins all over again.

'George!' he yells. 'George, help!'

He wonders if his voice can be heard, down in the Mission. He wonders if George is lying in bed, little ones gathered around, burying his head in his pillow so that he does not have to hear. Suddenly, he knows it is true; all across the compound, in every dormitory shack, they can hear him. It was, he remembers, that way once before. Luca's story loops and turns in his thoughts: a little boy, bleating in the night, and gone the next morning.

As soon as he has recalled the story, it will not leave him. Now, he knows, he cannot cry out. It is not only Mission boys who will hear. It is men in black. It is honoured guests. It is whoever watches these woodlands to take little boys away, the sort of men who might pay Judah Reed to take a little one away, the sort who might pretend to rescue a boy and lead him off to some darker prison.

Sometimes, the childsnatcher really does come in the dead of night.

He stifles his crying and tries to clear his thoughts. Once his breathing is under control, he blinks the tears out of his eyes and lifts his hands to inspect the knots. If he strains, taking up tension in his legs, he might be able to gnaw his way free. That, he knows, is what a proper wild boy would do. He puts the rope to his teeth. It is cold and hard and he can hardly grip it at all. Still, strand by strand, tweak by tweak, perhaps he can fight his way free.

Suddenly, there is a different sound in the darkness, a tread that is certainly not spiders or scorpions or lizards or snakes. He tenses. The spiders and snakes are fleeing, because this is a man in black, and even the scuttling creatures of the scrubland would run from Judah Reed.

'Mr Reed,' he says. 'I'm . . . sorry.'

He realizes he is only hoping that this is Judah Reed. Worse things happen to a boy alone in the woods than being staked out like some miserable animal. He thrashes from side to side, but he cannot see. He wants to know: is it Judah Reed, or is it somebody else?

'I promise,' he says. 'I've learnt my lesson.' He stops. 'I've had my medicine.'

It is true. If Judah Reed stepped out of the shadows now, he would follow him back to the Mission. He would drop his own trousers and climb on his knee and take as many rounds with a belt as the old man cared to give. He would do it gladly, not to be here when honoured guests descend on the woodland to spirit him away. If there are worse places than the Mission, he does not want to know them. He would not follow them there. Not for anyone. Not for Luca. Not for Peter and George. Not for his mother and sisters, who sent him here, deep into the woods.

He knows, now, what lengths the Crusade will go to make you a good, dependable boy. It isn't just hazings and beatings with sticks. They'll crush you inside if they have to. They'll sell you if they fail.

The footsteps grow louder, somewhere on his right-hand side. He twists, can just about make out a shape, a different texture in the darkness.

'Please,' he breathes. 'I won't do it again.' And then, for a reason he doesn't quite know, 'I won't tell anyone. I swear I won't.'

'Shut up, Jon,' comes a whispered voice. 'Oh, damn it, Jon Heather. I knew it would be you. It's been coming for a whole fucking year.'

That voice – it's Tommy . . . Tommy Crowe! Desperate to know for sure, Jon thrashes to his right, but the rope snaps taut and the pain whips all the way through his body.

The shadow moves, slowly coming into view. Jon's eyes, alive to the darkness, pick out his features. It's Tommy Crowe, all right – but he stands at a distance, drops onto a jagged rock, running both hands viciously through his hair.

'I watched them coming out. There was five of them, all fanning out in different directions. Knew it couldn't be anything else. Had to be a runner. Tried to ignore it, but here you are, just bleating away like any old little boy. What in hell's got into you? I thought you was one of the clever ones. I thought you were like me. Like you could make something out of . . . *this* . . .'

Make something out of this? Like a boy could just roll over and take what's given to him and be proud of it, when it wasn't even his to begin with?

'Tommy,' he croaks. 'Tommy, please . . .' He flicks his body, gestures with the ropes as best he can.

'You don't get it, do you, Jack the lad? If I untie you, they'll know you've been untied. Then they come looking. I've never taken a beating from them, Jon . . . and I don't think I want to take it just because of you . . .'

It isn't just because of me, Jon thinks. It's because of Luca. It's because of every boy in that Mission. It's because of *you*, Tommy Crowe.

'Why did you even come out here, if you're not going to help me?'

Tommy Crowe is cornered. Softly, he says, 'I didn't want it to be you, Jon Heather. Should have been any one of those stupid boys in there, thick as sheep shit, just knuckling on until they can be out there laying railroads or shearing sheep or . . .' He pauses, comes closer. 'You can't run, Jon.'

'I'm not running!' Jon screams. 'I ran before, Tommy. I ran and I came back.'

Tommy Crowe hesitates, one foot in the air. 'When?'

'When George got his beating,' he writhes. 'I came back for George.'

Tommy barely remembers. It could be any of a hundred beatings the boys have received in the last twelve months.

'They won't come back for you until morning. Then they'll bring some of the baddest boys, and they'll help carry you back.'

Tommy steps forward, bends down, muttering incessantly.

Before his fingers touch the knot, he stops. 'You've got to be back here before morning. And you've got to tie yourself up, best as you can, 'cause otherwise, they're coming looking for Tommy Crowe. You got it?'

The rope slackens around Jon's ankles. There is a rush of feeling, and for a moment he thinks he might faint.

'I got it, Tommy,' he breathes.

Tommy Crowe stands up, fiddles with the ropes behind Jon's back until, at last, they come free. 'I don't care where you sleep tonight, Jon. Bunk with McAllister's goats for all I care. But, if you're not here at sun-up, acting like you stood the whole night through, sobbing how sorry you are for ever betraying the Children's Crusade, I'll tie you up myself.'

With that, Tommy Crowe is gone, just another scuttling in the scrub.

Jon remains for a moment, gathering breath, making certain he can stand. One hour, two hours, three hours, four – however long he has been here, it might already be too late.

Peter careens around the landing, taking the stairs three at a time. He has gone only halfway when the foreman appears at the foot of the hall and starts to climb up. It's too late to stop now. Peter ducks right, evading the foreman's meaty grasp, and slides along the banister, landing in a heap of arms and legs below. By the time the foreman has swung around, he is back on his feet.

His only thought is – Cormac Tate taught me how to drive, and the foreman doesn't know it. Surprise, Peter. You can use that surprise – but first you'll need keys. He darts past the room where the men are dining, bursting out of the ranch at the rear. From the fence, the horses he only recently shod eye him suspiciously.

He freezes. He is looking straight into the eyes of the man in black.

'Peter,' he begins, a measured, fey voice. 'We must speak about this.'

Peter hurtles to the right, beating a path down the side of the station, scrub chickens squawking manically as he passes.

'You can't help little boys run away!' the man in black calls. 'You're older than them, Peter. You have responsibilities.'

He pounds into the front yards. One of these utes has to have the keys still sticking out of the ignition.

There are three in a row, a fourth jacked up. Peter races to the first, cups a hand and peers through the window. No keys. He slides over the bonnet to reach the second – but still no keys. By the time he has reached the third, the foreman thunders at him from the veranda.

Peter freezes. At the side of the station, the man in black appears again. He lifts a placatory hand at the foreman, but still the stupid bastard advances.

'I asked you a question,' he barks. 'Did Cormac Tate put you up to this?'

Peter hurtles to the other end of the ute, skirts around its engine. 'I don't know what you're talking about,' he cries. 'I don't even know where in hell Cormac Tate is.'

'You're going to come inside and talk about this, like a man.'

Peter shakes his head. 'I've been shovelling your shit for a year,' he says. 'You treat me like a man, and maybe I'll talk to you like one . . .'

He rushes at the third ute, climbs inside and slams the door. The foreman is almost upon him when he remembers to reach out and click the lock.

He shunts into the driver's seat, feels for keys in the ignition – but there is nothing there. Through the windshield, he sees the foreman rounding the cab. Quickly, he kicks the driver's door open, slamming it into the bastard's chest. When he reels backwards, Peter jumps out.

He isn't going to drive out of here. His eyes dart in every direction.

Maybe he could ride.

He has rarely ridden a horse, but if old Cormac can do it, it can't be that hard. He is about to take off when a hand clamps around his shoulder. He turns and sees the foreman bearing down.

'I didn't do a damn thing!'

'Well then, you can talk to the priest like a good little lad.'

He fights it, but the foreman is stronger. Legs kicking, he is dragged back across the yard.

They are rising to the veranda when a thick voice bellows

from the side of the building. Peter knows those tones well, though the words still sound impenetrable. With a sudden flourish, he rips his way out of the foreman's grasp, takes a shoulder to the man in black and belts back towards the utes.

At the edge of the station house, Booty draws his horse around. Wildly, he gesticulates, screaming at them in a language none understand.

Between the utes, Peter looks back. Booty's eyes fix on him, big and white – and, in that instant, he knows what he is saying. Run, boy, run! Fly, you fool!

Peter vaults a low railing and thunders onto the dirt track, snagging his tucker bag on a post. When it rips open, all the little things he has collected go flying. He claws them back but picks up only one of them: the picture of Cormac Tate and Judah Reed, little boys of the Children's Crusade.

A hundred yards on, and he sees lights. He stops, dazzled. Another wagon is approaching, swinging from the main road to follow the station track. He hears footsteps behind him, Booty bellowing out – a flash of yellow in the corner of his eye.

The approaching ute skids to a stop, slewing in the loose dust. The door flies open and light spills out.

'Get in, kid!' yells Cormac Tate.

Before Peter can move, the engine revs, the ute backs sharply and pulls around. Dirt kicks up, swallowing Peter whole.

He hurtles forward, dives into the cab. Grappling out to close the door, he feels something thudding into the back of the wagon. Looking back, he can see the foreman thundering down the track, with Booty somewhere behind. A face looms in the glass. He rears back, smashes his head into the windscreen – but it is only Dog.

Cormac pounds his foot to the ground and the wagon takes off.

'You OK, kid?'

'What in hell's going on?' Peter snaps. 'Where in hell were you?'

'They sent one of their clerks to meet me,' Cormac returns. His face flushed, he takes his eyes off the road and the wagon starts to veer. Peter thrusts a hand across and rights the wheel. 'In those black robes, just like when we were mites. There was a copper with him. Your lad's found out, Peter!' he cries. 'And he ratted us out. Told them we were helping him run off.'

It doesn't sound like Jon Heather. Jon Heather wouldn't lie.

'He told them what they wanted to hear, Pete.'

Peter shakes his head. 'We've got to go get him. Him and George.'

'Are you listening to me, Pete?' Cormac says. Something must be funny, because he lets out a deep, belly laugh. 'We go poking around their little playschool, and do you know what happens to me? They got me numbered as a dirty old man, tempting kiddies away from their parents with bags of toffee . . .'

'Then what?' Peter cries. 'Just leave him? He's waiting for me! What if he knows about Rebekkah?'

Cormac takes his foot from the accelerator, grinds the wagon to a slow rumble. 'He's found out, Pete. He isn't waiting for anything. Only a strap across his bare backside.' Cormac guides the wagon on. 'He's on his own, Pete. Same as you and me.'

Jon Heather bursts into the camp, eyes blurring. Luca's swag is strewn everywhere, like a ransacked house. Jon bites back the scream that comes to his throat; surely, the men in black haven't been here too.

Jon prowls the edge of the camp, kicking at the stray titbits he has brought Luca over the past weeks and months. He is about to send his foot flying at a heap between two skeletal scrubs, when he sees the bare feet sticking out of the bottom. He drops to his knees and drags back the ragged canvas. He shakes and shakes and, when he is so tired he thinks he can shake no more, Luca opens his eyes.

'Luca,' Jon breathes. 'It's time . . .'

'Jonny, Jonny . . .' Luca begins. Rolling eyes. The ghost of a smile. 'I waited, just like you said. Are they coming for me?'

He means Cormac Tate and his wagon, but Jon hears it differently. 'They came for *me*, Luca. Judah Reed and men in black. So we've got to run.'

'I can't run, Jonny Jonny *Jonny* . . .'

Jon is on his knees. 'I know,' he says, forcing his hands under the wild boy's shoulders.

It takes him an age to force Luca to stand. When, at last, he is draped over Jon's shoulder, he turns, tries to gauge the direction and distance by familiar sights in the scrub. But even in the bright light of day, he wouldn't be certain which way to go.

There is only one way he can know how to reach the rendezvous. He fixes himself on the Mission, and starts to walk.

He plods. He dares not lie Luca down, nor take any rest, for he pictures Peter and Cormac Tate waiting at the rendezvous, the world paling to dawn all around them. When he is weary, he swallows his weariness. When his shoulder burns, he does not let it burn. An interminable time later, he sees the thick scrub that runs around the Mission, turns to follow it around, until he hits the shadow wood that hides the dairy and the untilled fields. The vaults above are still the deepest black of night, but he has watched the sun rising countless times, and knows how suddenly dawn comes. He pushes on.

Along the way, Luca lolls on his shoulder. Jon asks him questions, the same ones over and over again, anything to keep the boy talking. He starts stories – *We Didn't Mean to Go to Sea,* the *Mystery at Witchend* – and leaves them hanging, so that Luca might parrot them back.

At last, they stumble onto the bend in the track. He slumps

down, careful to ease Luca to the ground. 'They'll be here,' he promises. 'Did you hear me?' he asks. 'I said they'll be here!'

Jon pats his face. It is clammy and cold.

'All I ever wanted was to go home, Jonny Jonny *Jonny* . . . But these men, these men you've brought to get me, they won't take me home, will they?'

The question fells Jon. 'They'll take you to a doctor . . .'

Even as he says the words, he falters. The question glimmers in Luca's eyes: what then? If a doctor's even any use, what happens to me after that?

'I used to think I could run and run. I'd leave footprints behind me, but footprints the trackers couldn't follow, things not even the bush men could see – because only little boys and girls could follow. Like breadcrumbs, Jonny . . . And there'd be a big damn procession, just like that picture in Judah Reed's office.' He stops. He wears that strange, bewitching smile again, and his head rolls. 'Have you been in Judah Reed's office, Jonny?'

Jon nods. Of course he's been there. He isn't clever enough not to.

'If I carry on running, Jonny, they'll all follow me, every boy and girl, no matter how old or horrid they've grown . . . And everyone can go home. *That's* the real Children's Crusade. Everyone to follow me and grow up, big and strong, in England and Malta and London and Leeds, the boys they're meant to be. I'm right, aren't I?' Jon nods, vigorously. 'Everyone to be the boy they want to be, and not a single boy left behind . . .'

He sits there, stars wheeling – and he knows, for certain now, that Peter and Cormac Tate have been here already, given him up for lost and gone, and disappeared.

At his side, Luca's eyes are closed.

'Luca,' he says, striking the boy's face with as much ferocity as he dares. 'Luca, wake up!'

He bellows it as loudly as he can – but still Luca sleeps, his breath rattling.

Jon stands up. Teetering, he looks once at the dirt road, and then at the stars. He puts an arm in the crook of Luca's knees, tests his weight. He won't be able to carry him far – but the Mission has made him stronger than he used to be. He'll get there somehow.

'I'm sorry, Luca,' he whispers. 'Don't hate me.' He turns around. There, over the low scrub, lies the shadow wood.

One yard, and then another. That is the way they came from England. Little steps can get you anywhere, even the worst places your mind can dredge up – so he takes the first one.

Long past the midnight hour, George lies awake.

Outside the window, there are footsteps. It is too late for boys to be visiting the latrines, so it can mean only one thing: a mess has been made. George studies the ceiling with more concentration. He doesn't want to know.

A hand reaches out, shakes him as if attempting to wake him up, but George keeps staring straight ahead.

'I don't care, Martin,' he whispers. 'Clean yourself up.'

'It isn't *that*, George!' the little one snaps, most affronted. 'Something's happened.'

Against his better judgement, George puffs his way out of bed. The rest of the boys are already awake. In the cloakroom, stinking of harsh white powder, they open the door a crack and peek out. Across the Mission, other doors are opening. Cottage mothers stand on verandas; boys press faces to windows; brave ones come out of their dormitories and stare.

A boy is walking through the compound, brazen as if it was day. In his arms, another boy is folded, long and angular, wild hair hanging down. The boy walks tall, but each step is an enormous effort.

'It's that boy Jon Heather!' says Martin.

George is crying, but for the first time in his life he cries without sound. It is, indeed, Jon Heather. Jon Heather is, indeed, a very bad boy.

He tries to wriggle back inside the dormitory, but the horde of little ones at his back won't allow him. He stares. He wants to shout out. He wants a mother and a father and lots of brothers and sisters who'll play with him every day and never once get cross.

At first, it looks as if Jon Heather is heading for his own dormitory – but then he turns. The lights flare in the sandstone building where the men in black sleep. Jon sets his eyes on it and walks.

When he is almost at the door, men in black appear from side entrances. Among them, George sees the man in black who looks over the bedwetters' dormitory, plays them his guitar and brings them Coca-Cola. He shuffles behind the little ones, refusing to watch.

At the door, Jon stops. His knees seem to buckle, as if he can go no further. He crouches and lays the boy he is carrying at his feet. Then, he reaches out with a fist and raps his knuckles on the door.

The lights have been on for some time. He does not have to wait. Indeed, it is almost as if somebody on the other side has himself been doing the waiting.

The door opens and Judah Reed stands there, framed in the light. Below him, Jon shakes.

'Mr Reed,' he says. 'I need your help.'

Judah Reed looks up, over Jon's head, at the faces watching him from every corner of the darkness.

'Very well, Jon,' he says, and welcomes him and Luca inside.

There is a hole where bad boys are sent – and in that hole they must sit and ponder why they are so rotten, why they are so different to all the good, dependable boys who work so hard as part of the Children's Crusade. There is no light. There are no books or toys or games to play, nothing with which they might while away the hours. There is only the thinking.

Jon Heather is in that hole, a sandstone abode with no windows and only a small porthole of a door, for three days and three nights. There is bread and there is broth, but there is nothing else. And, in that darkness, he does not think about his badness. He does not think about the apologies he will have to tender to Judah Reed, to his cottage mother, to every other boy in the Children's Crusade. He thinks only: I am good and I am right and my mother loves me, even if she had to send me away. And if, in this upside-down world, rightness can be punished, then I'll be punished again and again. I'll make my apologies, but I'll know that I'm lying. I'll make believe and pretend, but I won't let it change me.

Because they do want to change him, to make him believe he's bad – so rotten he needs their help to become a proud Australian boy. This place changes little boys and girls so much that their mothers might never recognize them. All you have to do is look at George. In here, George has friends. They worship him. He smiles and sings. He isn't the same boy Jon found back at the Home. And Tommy Crowe – surely he isn't the same Tommy Crowe who first came here. But Jon . . .

Jon stops. It doesn't have to be that way. He's got his rules. He can build more. All of these other boys, they'll change, for better or worse – and if their mothers should ever see them again, they'll look down and wonder: is this really my little boy? Did I really hold him when he was a baby? But if Jon works hard, obeys his rules, learns new ones, perhaps he can stay the same as ever he was. Then, one day, he might meet his mother again, and find that she still loves him.

On the day that he is released, he is taken to Judah Reed's office and given six of the best with the end of a stock whip, for his impertinence in escaping from his ropes. After it is done, he shakes Judah Reed's hand, and is told that he is also to be rewarded for his good deed in bringing Luca back to the Mission. The Children's Crusade, it seems, is nothing if not fair. He is awarded a new smock, a glass bottle of something called Sarsaparilla, and two days' rest from work.

Outside – a good, cleansed boy – he swaps his clean smock for some boy's old one and gives the bottle of Sarsaparilla to the nearest little one he can find. Fortune is a strange thing, and the boy who gratefully takes the fizzing drink is Ernest. Jon tells him never to go for walks in the wood, and slopes past. Ernest nods. He might even understand. Even looking at something as dangerous as a world without fences can land you in trouble.

He finds Laura in the laundry rooms, where once she would help hide George's midnight upsets. He does not need to talk to her for long, because it is a simple thing: he tells her he cannot be her friend anymore. If he is her friend, one day they will be good friends, and then the men in black will see them, and then Jon will be punished again. And, if Jon is punished again, a little piece of him won't be the same any more, and his mother might not recognize him when, finally, they find each other.

Laura looks at him, puzzled, but she says nothing more. She goes back to beating the sheets – but this time she beats more fiercely.

In the dairy, Tommy Crowe is milking the goats. Jon takes a pail but doesn't sit down – it would hurt too much.

He nods at Tommy.

'It's OK, Jack the lad. I'd do it again.'

They sit in silence for the longest time.

'Tommy,' he says. 'What happened to the . . .' He wants to say *wild boy*, but it wouldn't sound right. '. . . boy I brought in?'

Tommy squeezes his last teat with a flourish. 'They took him away, Jon.'

'To a hospital? A doctor?'

'I hope so.'

Jon Heather does not ask anything further. He knows where else Luca might have been sent. The Crusade home in New South Wales. Any of the other Missions in any of the other four corners of the Earth. A hole six feet under the ground. The only place he knows he won't have been sent is home.

Jon nods, slowly, and turns to leave.

'It's a good thing you didn't listen to me, Jon Heather,' Tommy whispers, so quietly he can barely be heard. 'Knowing how not to get in trouble . . . it's not the most important thing, is it?'

Jon pauses on the threshold – and then he is gone.

Outside the bedwetters', the boys are taking a break from filling one latrine and excavating another. Jon stands at a distance. The younger man in black is among them, but he is not dressed in black. Instead, he wears brown overalls and big thick gloves. The boys, it seems, have found a nest of bees. There were once hives kept just outside the compound, hardy things that roamed far and wide for desert flowers. Perhaps that time is coming again.

Jon finds George among the little ones, sitting cross-legged with a tin cup full of water.

As Jon approaches, George scrambles to his feet. It is almost as if he is going to flee. A gang of little ones spring up with him, as if they're his infantry, ready to repel the intruder.

'Jon,' George stammers, 'Jon, you're all right!'

Jon nods. He wades among the little ones. Over George's shoulder, the man in black has seen him, but only nods and smiles. Jon thinks deeply, and returns the gesture.

'Jon,' George whispers. 'Come here . . .'

They leave the gathering of little ones, but cannot drift far. At the edge of the dormitory shack, George starts ferreting in the folds of his clothes – and Jon notices, for the first time, that he is wearing leather shoes, too big but tied up tightly.

George sees Jon looking. He flinches, like a rabbit under a hawk.

'It's only because I'm doing the bee-keeping,' he begins. 'We've got a hive and I'm . . . I'm learning it, Jon. So we can have honey.'

Jon realizes, with a pang, that he is not jealous of George's boots. The very idea seems ridiculous to him. Boys with boots stand out.

George produces a sheet of paper, once crumpled but straightened out and folded neatly away. One side of it is shiny and coloured: the waxy wrapper from a packet of biscuits. On the other side, there is writing.

George's lips twitch, as if he is thinking about smiling.

Jon takes the wrapper. At the bottom, Peter's name is scored in with the nib of a pen running out of ink.

'I didn't see him,' George begins, bouncing up and down. 'He must have sneaked in through the wood. One of the little ones brought it. Peter gave him a biscuit.'

Most likely he came looking for news of Rebekkah, Jon thinks. I broke my promise on that too – but I'll break a thousand more promises before I get back home.

'He says . . .' Jon reads the words. He can even hear Peter's voice welling up inside him. He realizes he isn't going to hear that voice for a very long time. 'They've run away,' he begins. 'Him and Cormac Tate. But . . .' And this is just like Peter, exasperated at the lodestones around his neck, but refusing to have it any other way. 'He's going to wait for us. He's going to be there, when we're bigger boys, when we get out.' He has scrawled down the name of a roadhouse that Cormac Tate knows, and Peter promises to be there on a certain date, in the deep dark summer of December, in the year of 1956. 'He remembered my birthday,' Jon breathes. God damn you, Peter. You really are a friend.

'It's my birthday too,' whispers George, eager to join in. 'Remember?'

Jon is silent. He feels, suddenly, a dozen pairs of eyes boring into his back. 'You didn't ask me,' he begins. 'About Judah Reed and the wild boy and what happened out there.'

This time, the flinching is too obvious to disguise as a shrug or a simple tic. George throws a look to his left, a look to his right. His face scrunches up. Jon has seen this before – he saw it before he even knew George's name, hidden behind the chantry at the Home in Leeds – but, a year and more later, George is learning to control it. He has almost swallowed it – but he's still not good enough. At last, his tears break and his face flushes a disgusting scarlet red.

'I'm sorry, Jon,' he sobs. He reaches out, fat arms desperate to be cuddled. 'Jon Heather, I'm sorry. I just didn't want you to run away. I didn't want to be on my own. And . . . please say something, Jon. Jon Heather, I'm sorry . . .'

Jon backs away. Looks at George. His new boots are polished. His teeth are clean. Over his shoulder, the man in black is waiting, carrying two bee-keepers' veils.

'You told on me . . .' he breathes.

'Jon, please . . .'

'George, please tell me you didn't tell . . .'

'I thought you were going. Like Peter. I thought you were leaving. Just because I'm a bedwetter, Jon, and I thought . . .'

George barrels forward. If he gets there fast enough, he thinks, Jon won't be able to say no; he'll have to hold him, and that will make it all better.

Jon Heather steps back; George crashes down, all blubber and bone.

Jon turns and begins to walk away. Three steps later, he turns back. 'I would never have gone,' he says. 'Not without taking you with me.'

'I thought . . .'

'I didn't even haze you,' Jon whispers. 'They hazed me for it, but I wouldn't even *pretend* to hit you, George.'

Jon wants nothing more than to walk over, take those boots, tell this boy he's mollycoddled that now he's on his own. There he is, already lying on the floor. All he'd have to do is stride over, put his foot into his ribs. 'I gave you my mother. You wrote her a letter . . .'

George stands and stares. 'Jon, please?'

Jon reels back through the year he has spent here. It can't change you, he tells himself. You swore it. You're going to go home, the same little boy who got snatched away. What, he asks himself, would that little boy have done?

'It's OK, George,' he says finally. The fat boy's arms are stretched out and, mechanically, he steps into them. 'Five years, Georgie boy. We can do five years, can't we?'

The words are flat, without emotion, but if George understands, he doesn't let on.

He sniffles against Jon's smock. 'I'm sorry, Jon. I didn't want to do it.'

Jon hisses, softly, into George's ear. 'If you don't stop saying sorry, I'm going to stop believing it . . .'

George pulls back, nods urgently and dries his eyes. A thick globule hangs out of his nose. It might be the most hateful thing Jon's ever seen.

'Watch out for those bees, Georgie boy,' Jon says, a perfect imitation of the way things used to be. 'They'll want to sting you, every last one.'

Throwing a vague wave over his shoulder, he turns and walks away.

X

In the middle month of summer, in the year of 1956, a lone figure hitches along the Mullewa back road. He doesn't seem much of a threat to the shearer who picks him up – but, although the boy's invited to ride up-front, he prefers to sit in the back of the ute, huddled under a canvas with his cardboard suitcase tucked under his legs. It's how he was brought into this world, he says, so it may as well be the way he rides out.

The boy leaves the shearer outside the little township of Black Rock, a rabble of a town where shearers and station blacks come to waste their time. Somebody said there was gold here once, but that somebody was lying. He tramps the three miles into town from the junction alone and, when he's sure he's found the right place, pitches a stone at the upstairs window.

Three rocks later, a white-whiskered face peers out.

'You made it!' he grins. 'Our boy Pete's been rabbiting about it for weeks. Some of the hands bet against it, but Pete always put a lot of truck in you. Just in time for Christmas as well!

Wait . . .' He pauses. 'Is something wrong down there?' He retreats inside the window. 'I'll wake him up.'

Jon does not have to wait long. Lights flare in the downstairs hall and Cormac Tate, still only half-dressed, steps into the night. Behind him, a dark-skinned lady in a bathing robe nods, surly, at him. Jon gets the impression this is her house, that she brooks his midnight intrusion only because of Cormac Tate.

'Pete's in the top left,' Cormac says. 'Just getting his gear on.' He stops. 'Well, go on! Damn lad's been waiting on you best part of five years!'

Jon walks up a creaking stair, sees a door ajar and spilling lantern light onto the landing. Gently, he pushes through. At the bed, a wiry man with dirty red hair is hobbling into his jeans. A girl, long and blonde, lies in the sheets beyond.

Peter has filled out since Jon last saw him. His skin, still red, no longer seems burned, and he wears an untamed beard.

'Jon Heather!' he beams. 'As I live and breathe!'

He flings his arms absurdly wide to receive Jon – but, as he does so, his jeans fall back to his ankles and riding boots. He hangs there, ridiculous, until Jon submits to the hug.

'This here,' says Peter to the girl in bed, 'is my old pal, Jon Heather. Not *the* oldest, but damn near. A fellow refugee from sunny Blighty.' The girl nods, vaguely unimpressed. 'Come on, Jon, let's give a lady some privacy. She needs her beauty sleep.'

Together, they step into the hallway. Cormac Tate blinks up the stairs and shakes his head.

'Get some clothes on, Pete! The rest of my life is gonna be an anticlimax . . .'

He disappears, muttering something about beer and tea.

'Who's that, Peter?' Jon asks, gesturing at the bedroom door.

'That's Orla. She's my girl.'

'For how long?'

Peter checks a clock hanging against the wall. 'About another two hours,' he says. When he sees Jon's face puzzling, he claps him on the back. 'It's a joke, Jon Heather. I known her about a year. We see each other when me and Cormac pass through.'

'Look, Peter, there's something I . . .'

'So?' Peter begins. 'We all set? Little George waiting downstairs, is he? Not so little anymore, I shouldn't think. Shit, look at you, Jon Heather! You growed up on me! Didn't anybody ever teach you to cut your hair? George lose that gut of his yet?'

Jon hesitates. He has rehearsed this next part time and time again, but even in his head he's never got it right. But, just like those letters he once wrote to his mother, letters that never received reply, these words have got to be perfect. Anything less, and the world will surely come crashing down.

'Peter, that's the thing,' he says. 'Peter, George isn't coming.'

Cormac Tate drives. He and Peter bought the wagon together, fixed her up from scrap, but tonight Cormac won't let Peter near the wheel. He's surly and he's silent, and that means he doesn't care what he's doing. Knowing their luck, he'd run into a roving 'roo, and then the adventure would end only minutes after it was supposed to begin.

They drive through the night. It is still dark when they round the old farmhouse where Peter and Cormac once worked, still dark when they pass the Mission track with its legend hanging above. Cormac brings the wagon around, as if he might skirt the Mission and stop outside that patch of scrubland Jon Heather has always called the shadow wood, but Jon reaches out and puts a hand on his shoulder. He guides the wagon to a stop.

'You're right, boy,' Cormac Tate begins. 'We don't have to go sneaking about anymore. They're not going to go snatching you back now.'

Peter clambers out of the ute, slams the door before Jon Heather can follow. 'You coming, Cormac?' he snaps, craning back through the window.

Cormac looks dead ahead. 'Not me, Pete.'

'Snow on the Nullarbor, right?'

'Something like that.'

Peter is already under the sign when Jon catches him up. The scrub parts, and in front there stand wooden shacks, each shouldering a little sandstone abode. Further on, where the dormitories part, an oblong sandstone building stretches back. There are fields, hemmed in by scrub, and cauldrons of fire stirred at the edges, like this is a camp for soldiers forced to winter away from home.

'This way,' Jon says.

He leads Peter around the dormitory that he lived in for six long years. Dawn is almost upon them, and there are boys shifting inside. A cottage mother drinks from a dainty china cup outside one of the buildings. Jon guides Peter out of her sight – and there, at the very ends of the Mission, stands a sandstone house newer and bigger than all the rest. Of all the places in the Mission, it is the only one with two storeys, the only one with a grand wooden veranda, a swing in which a man in black might rest from the baking sun. There is a big wooden door, whose every contour Jon Heather knows, because he whittled it himself. There is even glass in the windows, and a steep pitched roof with attic space and a balcony sitting below.

They linger in the shadows between two dormitories and watch.

The door opens, and shadows move beyond: the men in black, preparing for morning prayers. One by one, they emerge into dawn's eerie light.

Peter flinches. Jon reaches out, steadies him with a hand.

'What happened here, Jon Heather? What did you do?'

This much, Jon has been expecting for a long time. Nothing has ever been George's fault. 'I guess I didn't do a thing,' he replies.

In the doorway, next to the man in black who has always tended the bedwetters' dormitory, George stands, wearing his own robes of black. He is thinner than Peter remembers, his features more defined. Nobody would ever call George handsome, but his cheekbones are pronounced now, and he has a certain bearing that Peter does not recognise. It might be because he is smiling.

A gang of little ones, led by a seven-year-old who has already been among them three years, rush past, entrusted with collecting kindling before the breakfast bell rings. Two of the youngest stop and chatter at George as they pass. George crouches, ruffles the smallest one's hair. The elder stamps his foot down, refuses to run on until his hair, too, is ruffled.

'He was good with them,' Jon begins. 'He was, ever since we came. They liked him. And, Peter, he liked them too. You don't know what it's like in here . . . It's a good thing to be liked.'

'He's coming with us . . .'

Peter is about to step out, but Jon holds him back. Peter only *thinks* he knows George. He doesn't know a thing about that night with the wild boy. He wouldn't understand Coca-Cola and jolly swagmen and leather boots for keeping bees.

From the shadows behind George, Judah Reed emerges. He puts an arm around George and the man beside him, and then a young girl, twelve or thirteen, turns up to offer them tea and juice from china cups.

'I thought they beat him . . .'

Jon can't answer that. There are things even he doesn't understand. 'In the end, they were nice to him. They trusted him. He started keeping bees, making honey for the whole Mission. Do you know how long it had been since any of us had had sweets? Well, George started making sweets. Then all the boys liked him. He stopped wetting the bed, Peter. And he didn't even tell me, not at first – because he had other people to tell. He was making friends . . .'

'*You* were meant to be his friend, Jon.'

Jon promised himself, long ago, that he wouldn't tell Peter about that night when George ratted on him.

'I wasn't a ship to carry George home, Peter.' Jon moves away. 'They might be sending him back,' he says. 'He'll go down to the Mission in New South Wales, work with the little ones there, help them settle in, so they can start treating the Mission like home. If he's good enough at it, they'll put him on a boat. He'll be in England, helping to tell boys what promises wait over here . . .'

Something relents. Peter's shoulders sag. Perhaps this is easier to stomach, Jon thinks. George put on black robes because George can go home. A pact like that, maybe Peter can understand.

'When did he tell you?' he asks.

'Oh, he didn't tell me,' Jon admits. 'But I found out.'

Peter stares after his old friend. He wants to ride a horse through here, whip George up onto its back like a damsel in distress, and ride on out. He wants to march in there and smash the toadying little bastard's face into a different shape. He's waited five years. He made a promise.

Jon is at his shoulder. 'Let's get out of here, Peter.'

Peter stands, Jon's fist closed around his arm, until George's eyes seem to drift his way. For a moment, it is as if their gazes meet, each looking into the darkness on the other side of the expanse. George's face drops; Peter's hardens.

Then, the enchantment shattered, George nods at the man in black on his left and takes off, chirping out for some little ones to follow.

'To hell with him,' Peter says. 'England or not, he can go to hell.'

At the ute, Cormac Tate is waiting, the engine still ticking over. He does not say a word as Peter and Jon squeeze into the cab. He guides the wagon out onto the track, and from there onto the main highway.

It is a new day in the new world, and together they set out.

BOOK TWO

THE STOLEN GENERATION

XI

If your mother calls for you, the little girl knows, you must always go – but sometimes, if she is screaming and crying your name, you must run as far as your little legs will carry you. Do you remember the dead tree by the dead river? You must run there and beyond, until you're up in the bush and away. Watch out for snakes, Dolly, and watch out for spiders – but, no matter how much crying you hear, do not come back. For there is something worse than spiders and snakes – and, one day, the childsnatcher will come for you, just like he came for your sisters.

She lives outside a cattle station high in the old country. Her daddy is a stockman, but she has never seen him. He is a different daddy to the daddies of her sisters. Mother talks about him like an old legend, but sometimes she has a wicked smile when she tells the story, and the little girl does not know why. One day, your father came riding in, and brought your mother treasures. Then he went – but he left behind the greatest treasure of them all – and that, Dolly, is where little girls come from.

Though she has never seen her father, she thinks of him often. She plays a game that her father is coming for her one day, bringing her the same treasures he brought her mother. The game raises titters from her mother and the other women, but Dolly plays it all the same. Late at night, her mother warns her: when the man comes riding in, it will not be a game and it will not be your father. He might be dressed up like your daddy once was. He might come on a horse or in a wagon with wheels and a clicking engine. But if you do not believe me and do not run, your mother will be left alone to cry for seven long years.

The others think she doesn't remember the day her sisters disappeared, but she remembers it well. It comes in her dreaming. She is too young to play with the other girls, and that, she has learned, is why she was not on the childsnatcher's list. On that day, she was watching from the deadwoods as her sisters bathed. When they saw her watching, they teased her with names, and she ran into the scrub, to watch from a place nobody knew.

There came the sound of engines. The engines were loud as monsters, and the women clucked and ran so that Dolly knew something was wrong. Her sisters, lazing too long in those cool, cool waters, refused to be alarmed. As these girls knew, the worries of mothers since time immemorial have always been unfounded, and instead of running, they chattered at each other, splashing in water and singing songs.

When the man marched in – tall and white, just like Dolly's father! – the girls froze. In the undergrowth, Dolly chewed on her dress. It was a lacy thing, one that Dolly remembers even to this day. The man smiled, like he was happy to simply say hello. But Dolly saw those teeth for what they were – the gnashers of a monster.

In Dolly's memory, he has her sisters' names on his paper, and he calls them out, one by one. Then he crouches, picks up the girls' dresses and tells them to put them on. I'm your daddy now, he smiles.

We have daddies! the girls cry out – though Dolly's certain they've never met their daddies either.

It's on my paper, the man insists. Nothing to be done if it's on my paper. I'm your father and I've always been your father. It doesn't matter who planted you inside your mother. It says so right here.

The girls cannot run, because now they see other men, in smart shirts and ties, lurking around the waterhole. Instead, they fight. They kick and scream and bite – but nobody comes. The men wade into the pool to take them. They are angry now, and they thrust the girls onto the bank. It does not do to ruin a good shirt.

The girls are marched, sodden in their dresses, to the waiting wagon. On a piece of paper, a cross is marked next to each name. In the scrub tonight, the women will wail. They will take stones and scratch at their eyes. They will not notice the little girl still left, hiding in the deadwoods, wondering who came and took her sisters away.

So, listen, Dolly. If your mother calls for you, you must go to her. But if she screams and cries, if you ever hear her telling a stranger that she has no daughters, you must make straight for the deadwoods by the dead river. Because the childsnatcher does not come in the dead of night. He comes in a police car, in the brazen bright of day – and if your name is on his list, you'll never be your mother's daughter ever again.

XII

In the north country, the seashores are white as salt, the inland sands the colour of rust.

By the side of the northern highway, where the road rides the coastline so closely that a lazy driver, bewitched by light playing on the water, might suddenly find himself submerged, a fire is burning. It smoulders below a tin pan, with a billy hanging above. The sea is at low tide, its waters azure where the waves break, and inky blue, further out, where the reef grows large.

A tall man, with sun-burnished skin and dark hair he has never been able to train, scurries, bow-legged, from a tide pool to the fire, hands clasped tightly around something that would happily snap off each of his fingers. Juggling it, he manages to knock the pan's lid off and toss the prize inside. The thing rears up and spits, but already it is too late. The brown-haired man grins and his bounty is trapped. He was once told that you could plunge your hands into any tide pool along this coast and bring them out holding enough slippery fish to last a man for weeks on end without ever setting out again. If that is truly so, he must be a most inept fisherman. All the same, they will eat well this afternoon.

A burly dog rises and shoves his snout, inquisitively, into the dish. The brown-haired man pushes him back, scolding him but grinning, nonetheless, at his transgression. The dog will get his share, just like the men. One for all, and all for one.

The brown-haired man looks up. On the bank above the beach, his companion is grunting under the hood of their ute. The old girl has carried them far and wide – but today she is guttering again. His companion rises out of the engine, red hair plastered to his brow. When there is no more water in his canteen, he tosses it down onto the beach. He skids down the bank soon after, sniffing – in his best imitation of a fine city diner – at the smells curling from the pot.

'She's done for,' he says, wiping his hands.

'She's never done for.'

'She'll take us through the night, but after that . . .' He slaps his hands together. 'One more angel in heaven.' He drops, just like the dog, and shoves his nose ridiculously in the pot. 'What is it?'

'It's a bastard big crab,' the brown-haired man answers, aping one of his friend's favourite expressions.

'We had crab last night. And the night before.'

'What can I say, *dear*? It's my speciality.'

They sit to eat as the midday heat starts to fade. There are dampers, too, and they wash them down with billy tea, laced with so much honey – donated by a grateful beekeeper whose fences they fixed somewhere down the coast – that the dog turns his snout up at his share.

After they are done, and the dog is cleaning out the still-scalding pan, they throw their gear in the back of the ute and turn their gazes north.

The brown-haired man drifts to the wagon door, patting the roof for good luck. 'I'm driving,' he says, teasing his fingers.

The other tightens his fingers, joyfully, around the keys. 'The hell you are. Who taught you how to drive?'

Reluctantly: 'You did.'

'Then it stands to reason, I'm the better driver.'

'Just because you're older?'

The red-haired man nods. 'I'll always be older.'

A deep breath – and then the second man throws himself, dramatically, into the passenger seat. 'You can't keep using that!'

The first man slides into the driver's seat, kicks up the ignition. 'I reckon I got a few years yet.' The engine complains bitterly, but she is as good a friend as any and she lets him push her back onto the road. 'Come on, Jon Heather, you know I drive faster. And he isn't going to be there forever . . .'

The wind whips through the window, a chill for which both of them are thankful.

'Don't you believe it, Peter. He'd stick around for you until there's snow all over the Nullarbor Plain.'

The red-haired man flicks his head back and beams. 'True enough,' he says.

It is the first day of December in the year of 1960 and, in the north country, an old friend awaits.

They reach the town of Broome long after nightfall. The highway plunges them straight into a town of wide, unsealed avenues, stretched out so that they might be in the centre of town and not know it, for the red ridges and scrub that abounds. They coax the battered ute in circles, until they stall on the banks of a bay, thick with mangroves and the choral sounds of night. At last, they see lights: Chinese lanterns hanging, gaudily, over one of the broad thoroughfares.

Leaving the ute by a jetty that extends over the mud flats, they head out. Dog stays behind to guard the truck – but there are a thousand new smells to chase down tonight, and Jon doubts he'll still be there when they get back.

'You hungry?' asks Pete, idling in a window where some sort of duck, glistening, is strung up by its feet.

'We ate this afternoon, remember?'

'You never know when you're going to eat next, Jon Heather. Maybe we should fill up.'

'I'm not a snake, Peter. We'll eat when we're hungry.'

A man emerges from what might be the entrance to another den and, with a bow, invites them in. Pete is almost through the doors, haggling a price, when Jon Heather claws him back.

'Later, OK?' he says. 'I thought we came here for a reason?'

The buildings around them tower, rickety and ill-kept. Walls of corrugated iron have been patched in stone, wide verandas sprawling out front. Each building sits alone, not like the crowded terraces of their childhoods. Trees line the avenues, boughs laden with blossoms to sweeten the night.

A mere amble further on, and the town stops dead: an oval of grass and dirt is before them. On the other side, the town simply begins again, as if nobody has noticed the hole.

'You reckon this is it?'

Pete looks up. The building is as rough and cobbled together as those on either side. If it is on a grander scale, it only emphasizes the bulging upper storey, the sloping boardwalk and uneven gables. A sign protruding over the veranda reads, in flaking paint, the *Old Arabia*. A crude camel train, carved into the wood, can be seen below.

'Why would Arabia be in the middle of Shanghai?' Pete asks, looking back along the thoroughfare.

'But this is the place, right?'

Pete pats his pockets, searching for the telegram – but it must be back in the ute. Probably Dog has eaten it.

'Let's find out.'

Through the doors, the Old Arabia's reception is empty.

Beyond a broad archway to the right, a scattering of guests sit in a saloon bar, drinking to the static sounds of a waltz. At the head of the hall, a staircase climbs to a wide balcony, from which a multitude of doors look down.

It has an air of opulence, but self-consciously worn; whoever owns this place must certainly have a sense of humour. A big canvas shows a camel train, heading across a desert; below that, a painting of a steam train is making the same journey. Pete tips his chin at it, bewildered; there isn't even a railway in this part of the world. Above the empty reception counter, photographs show old Chinamen in heavy metal armour, grinning as they show off, in cupped hands, piles of pearls.

Pete struts forward, slamming his hand on the counter. When no patron instantly materializes, he rolls his eyes at Jon Heather and slaps his palm down again.

Jon reaches over, lifts a dainty bell, and tinkles it.

'Always using your head, Jon Heather,' Pete mutters, half in admonishment.

Still, nobody comes.

They wander, kicking their heels, into the bar-room. They should probably be wearing shoes in a place like this, but nobody seems to notice; Jon Heather does wear boots when he has to, if he's mustering cattle or working some fence, but it never feels right. Pete clomps forward. The clientele of the Old Arabia are a mixed bunch: in one corner, men just like Pete and Jon, drifting through town before heading back to the road; in another, a cabal of men in smart suits and ties, city types who have drifted too far from their secretaries and typewriters.

At the bar, a grey-haired man polishes glasses while a barmaid, his daughter, rebuffs the good-natured invitations of one of their guests. Jon sidles over, but she has them in her sights before they reach the bar. Nobody has told this girl that the patrons here just want to be watered and fed, straight up with no fussing, because she puts on quite a show. Her brown hair is tied back and she wears a long dress, of the type widows were growing tired of at the turn of the century. Somehow it suits her.

'You boys looking for lodgings? Or is it food and drink and on your way?'

Pete leaps onto a bar-stool, props his elbows on the counter, and promptly starts chewing on the tree nuts somebody has left in a bowl there.

'We're meeting an old friend,' Jon begins. Pete chomps his agreement. 'He ought to have sorted rooms for us . . .'

'This old friend have a name?'

'He doesn't ordinarily use it. Any case, he's about six feet tall, big white hair . . .'

'Sometimes has whiskers.'

Jon nods. 'He does sometimes have whiskers,' he affirms.

'About like that old man waving at you over there, then,' the girl replies.

Pete and Jon turn. At the far end of the bar, a white-whiskered man sits before a table laden with plates of steak and veggies, his tucker bag splayed open at his feet. Already, he is laughing uproariously. He lifts a meaty hand and clobbers it back and forth.

Jon and Pete hurry over, sending a plate spinning on a table as they pass.

'It's bastard good to see you, Cormac,' Pete says, clasping the old man's hand.

'And you, Pete.' He looks over Pete's shoulder. 'Jon Heather,' he nods.

Jon suppresses the smile for as long as he can. 'Bastard good,' he says.

'That's my boy!'

Nobody has ever praised the food at the Old Arabia hotel – but for Pete and Jon, eating steak with Cormac Tate is a treat, no matter how tough the cut. Cormac stops short of chopping up their steaks for them, but he does insist on ordering tankards of the weak swill they call beer in this part of the world, and paying for every last drop.

'I brought you some things . . .'

Pete and Jon share a look. Of course, he's brought them some things. He's been bringing them presents every time they've met, ever since they stopped rolling together.

Cormac Tate produces two parcels, each wrapped in brown paper and tied with string.

'You shouldn't have,' they both say in unison.

'Get on with you and open them. I haven't got all day.'

Jon carefully unfolds the paper, while Peter tears his apart. In the package is a clothbound book. The title is stitched, in red thread, into the spine: *Saucers Over the Moor*.

It is one of the books Jon doesn't have. Most of his collection are, of course, presents from Cormac Tate, *Peter Duck* and *Strangers at Snowfell* and *Valley of Adventure*, but that doesn't make this one any less precious. He's certain they'd all have lined his shelves in England if he hadn't been shipped away, and Cormac must have gone to great lengths to find them.

Pete strains until the string finally snaps. Most times, Cormac brings him new editions of those stupid *Black Chaparral* comics he reads. This time, there are no comics inside the package, no new adventure with which the hotchpotch family who own the homestead might wrestle. Instead, there is a single piece of paper, wrapped up so well that Pete thinks he might be playing a children's party game. He lays it on the table, where it promptly starts soaking up grease.

Five Rivers Road, Kununurra

'Cormac,' he breathes. 'You did it . . .'

'What the hell's Kununurra?' Jon Heather interjects.

'Kununurra new town. Pete's sister's husband's up there, working on the new dam. Thing is . . .' And here, Cormac Tate leans over the table, as if to savour the reaction. '. . . it's not far, Pete. It would be a long day's drive, but we could do it.'

Pete marvels at the piece of paper. He has been hunting for these four words for what feels like an eternity, ever since Cormac Tate told him about the different Missions in all the corners of the world. Back then, he had thought it would be an easy thing to make the dream come true. The Children's Crusade had to have records, he remembers thinking. And you, Jon Heather, you can steal them for me, tell me where my sister has gone.

He has never spoken with Jon about that night. There doesn't seem to be anything either of them could say. Later, he did investigations of his own, wrote to the Crusade itself, demanded information – but when they would not write back, he had thought it was over. Of all the people pouring into Australia, how could anybody hope to find a single person?

'Wait a minute . . .' he breathes, eyes darting at Cormac Tate. 'You said *husband*?'

Cormac Tate has organized a room for them. It has two beds – which can, Cormac notes, be pushed together, should the occupants so wish – and a view of the old town. The windows are netted, but the room still buzzes with mosquitoes.

'Can we sleep with the lights off?' Pete asks, finger itching at the electric light. 'Them damn mosquitoes will get everywhere if we don't.'

Jon nods, though he'd like it otherwise. 'Lights out!' he mutters, with a hint of something Pete still doesn't understand.

Long after Pete is merrily snoring, Jon Heather prowls up and down, reading *Saucers Over the Moor* by the light of a little electric torch he carries. He'll be damned if anybody, friend or not, is going to tell him when to go to bed ever again.

Dog knows they are coming before they have even rounded the corner. He leaps out of the truck, careening along the street to the muttered disapproval of locals walking by.

When Cormac Tate rounds the corner, Dog bowls him over. Smothered in the beautiful fish stink of Dog's saliva, he wrestles his way back upright, steadying himself on Pete's arm. Dog barks and scrambles up.

It's been a while.

In the back of the ute, Pete finds the mangled remains of some sort of tern. Feathers litter the flatbed. With a guilty look into the mangroves, he sees that the terns are plentiful and heaves the carcass back.

'You're right,' says Cormac, his head in the engine. 'Shot to hell and back. I thought I told you never to take her over sixty?'

'We wouldn't have got here 'til 1974,' Pete answers.

'I could have waited.'

Pete kicks the bumper. 'How are we gonna get there?'

Cormac Tate thinks long and hard, finally ending with his familiar sanguine shrug. 'How'd you think I got *here*? Road coach. Hitching. Horses, if we have to. The *old* ways.'

'Here's me thinking we was moving *up* in the world.'

'Moving on, but not moving up, Pete. You remember how it is.' At once, Cormac quietens. Lifting his hat from his head, he presses it to his chest. 'Listen, Pete. I heard from Booty. He's been working down Moora way again. Says that holding's still just sitting there, stagnant, waiting to be sold.'

Pete makes eyes, as if they're talking about a bank heist and might be overheard.

'I just had to say it, Pete.'

'And I just had to hear it. I been thinking about it a lot. But if Jon Heather hears us talking like that, well, he's about certain to throw a fit. You know how tetchy he gets. He thinks we're plotting, it'll be 1958 all over. Maybe we won't see him *ever* again.'

Cormac nods. He presses his forehead to Dog's muzzle. 'You won't tell him, will you, boy?'

'Don't you bet on it. That dog's about Jon Heather's very best friend. Do you know, the two of us aside, I don't think there's a single person in the world Jon Heather might call a friend.'

Cormac swats a mosquito out of his eye. 'What do you reckon he's doing now?'

Pete thinks of Jon, in the Old Arabia, and the girl behind the counter. 'I can tell you what he's not doing,' he grins.

Jon Heather does not rise until he is sure Pete is already gone, off to show Cormac Tate what a ruin they've made of the ute. Nine years pounding the roads from one ocean to the next, following rumours of work and even vaguer rumours of riches, were always going to take their toll – but Cormac and Pete won't see it like that. They'll see it as dereliction of duty.

Jon is almost at the end of *Saucers Over the Moor* and, though he wants to push through and turn that final page, he knows he should savour it. He opens his suitcase to put it in with all the other books – he has never found another copy of *We Didn't Mean to Go to Sea*, and isn't sure he would want to – but, before he does, he ferrets down, and lifts out the bundle of banknotes hidden there. It has taken so long to get this far, but he judges he might only be a few months of hard work away. Australia is a strange kind of vortex: it can cost an Englishman ten pounds to sail over, but it takes a lifetime to save enough to escape.

He sneaks a guilty look at Pete's haversack. Pete spends far too freely – the bloke needs three square meals a day, for God's sake! – to have saved anything near as much as Jon. Still, he resists the urge to go ferreting; if Pete is as much of a pauper as Jon thinks, he doesn't want to know.

Downstairs, the hall is desolate, all but for the city men eating breakfast. The girl from the counter deposits a jug of water at their table and, crossing back over, notices Jon. For the first time, Jon looks at her: she has green eyes and, this morning, her thick brown hair falls around her shoulders. She is, perhaps, taller than Jon, as tall as Pete.

'Your mates went out bright and early,' she calls. 'Prone to leaving you behind, are they?'

Jon nods. As Pete would testify, it's Jon who is prone to leaving *them* behind, but the girl doesn't need to know that story.

He orders breakfast and takes a seat at the counter, where he can keep a sidelong eye on the city men hunkered around their table. Breakfast is a plate of steak and eggs, and he eats it slowly, methodically.

'Who are they?' he asks, between tiny mouthfuls.

'We don't get many city men up here,' she says, as if acknowledging some unspoken jest between them. 'But it's good trade for my dad when they do come through. They're Protection Officers.' She leans, her elbows on the bar. Jon can smell the flowery scent of her perfume. 'There, at the head of the table, that's Mr Cook. He used to come, sometimes, to carry his master's cases.' She says it with a grin, as if carrying cases isn't something anybody ought to do for anybody else. 'Seems he must have got a promotion.'

He might only be Pete's age, twenty-four or twenty-five. He has blond hair, trimmed in a military fuzz, and his cuffs are clipped with what look like silver brooches. Definitely a city boy. The men with him might once have worked on stations and fences; they have the look – sun-burnished skin and forearms tougher than they ought to be.

He realizes the girl has been watching him, waiting for him to reply. He stutters over a piece of steak.

'What's your name?' she asks.

It is an inoffensive enough question, so Jon will answer.

'I had an uncle Jon,' she muses. 'Worked on the highway.' Apparently, this is an endorsement that Jon Heather, too, must be all right. 'What do you boys do?'

Jon couldn't formulate an answer, even if he wanted. He and Pete, and at one time Cormac Tate, have ridden the roads and coasts all over this continent. It is more vast even than he had imagined in those first months when he was shipwrecked here. They brought him, he knows now, to a port called Geraldton in the west, and from there inland to the farm school of the Children's Crusade. He remembers those vast emptinesses of his youth now with a hint of irony – for, if he had known where to look, he would have found wheat farms and, further inland, more cattle stations of the sort Pete was tossed into. Begrudgingly, he will admit that the Children's Crusade performed their mission well; if he is not yet a farmer, with his own smallholding, he does at least know how to butcher a goat and harvest a field. In the first months, they found work along a vast fence being constructed up and down the western coast, following its lengths for days on end so that they might patch holes and fill ditches. There is nothing, Jon has decided, that Australia loves more than an enormous fence or wall: only, instead of keeping out marauding Picts and barbarians, as an Englishman might have done, here they marshal all their resources against dingoes, emus and rabbits.

'We came looking for Peter's sister,' he says, because the silence has to be filled. 'Peter always thought she might have been out here . . .' He says 'out here' like it might mean something to her; she thinks he means the Kimberley, somewhere bush, anywhere that isn't Perth. '. . . but we were never certain. Sort of just a gut instinct, I suppose. But Cormac – that's our old mate – he had this daughter, Maya, see. He hadn't seen her for years, but it turns out she worked in a registry, down in Perth. So, after he started seeing his family again, he started talking about Peter and me, and she reckoned she could help. She was searching for a Rebekkah Slade for months, no luck at all – until one morning, it just hits Cormac, like a bolt from the blue. What if she got married? So they start on marriage licences – and then, well, Peter and I, we got our summons . . .'

It has always been like that with Cormac Tate, ever since Pete heard the full story of Cormac's lost family and persuaded him to head back to Fremantle and find his daughters. One day, a telegram will arrive or a message will find you: Cormac is going to be in Jurien Bay, or Cormac is going to be in Narrogin, and off Pete and Jon will go.

'So your friend Pete, he's . . .'

'*Peter*,' interjects Jon, stressing the last syllable.

'. . . just going to walk in there and say hello?'

Jon does not understand the question. They're brother and sister; of course, he'll just walk in and say hello. 'I suppose he might knock first.'

The girl breaks into a smile. 'You're making fun of me,' she says.

He really isn't. Still, she just stands there, regarding him like an exhibit in a museum of natural oddities.

Jon is probably supposed to say something, ask her about her background, where she grew up, whether she'll always be in Broome, does she have brothers, sisters; where is her mother, if she even has a mother? That, Jon Heather has observed, is a rule of conversation. You have to bat the questions back. Another day, he might even indulge it. There is no better way of not having to talk about yourself than making somebody else fill the conversation with stories of their own. In that way, Jon's proved time and again, you can get through months of knowing somebody, have learnt everything there is to know about them, without having said more than a few words about yourself.

Once, somebody saw through this. Lying in bed, she said: 'I don't know anything about you.'

It pleased him. He said: 'That's because there isn't anything to tell.'

He realizes, suddenly, that the girl is no longer standing there. His plate, too, has mysteriously vanished. 'Hey,' he calls, when she has almost disappeared through kitchen doors. 'What do they. . . protect?' he asks, eyes lingering on Mr Cook and his posse of starched shirts.

'The black fellas,' she replies, as if he ought to have known. 'You know, out on the stations. They're here to look after their kiddies and . . .' As if a sudden idea has occurred to her, she delves into the kitchens and re-emerges with an extra cup of coffee, which she slides down the counter. 'I'm Megan, by the way,' she says, as if by way of reproach, and turns to disappear.

Pete and Cormac spend the morning scouring the old town in search of anybody who might have an old wagon to trade. They don't ask for a lot: if anybody has an engine good enough to get us to Kununurra, and wants to part with it for the princely sum of an old hat and pair of sandals – oh, and if you're really adamant, I suppose we could throw in this stupid crossbred mutt as well – we've got a deal. Though they wander the red roads from creek to port and back again, they have little luck.

In a grim little place, somewhere off the mangrove flats, they order piles of rice and beer. Pete makes this a banquet for a king, relying on the generosity of Cormac Tate's back pocket.

'I got . . . *some* set aside,' says Pete, a hailstorm of rice flying from his lips. 'Not much. Won't buy us into a new truck – but I know for a fact that Jon Heather has *plenty*.'

He can say it as confidently as he likes, but the fact remains, Jon Heather isn't giving those savings up just for a new ute.

'But,' says Pete, 'couldn't we tell him it'd be an *investment*? Without a ute, we'll end up washing dishes in a stink hole like this . . .'

The patron of this fine establishment glowers. He obviously has good English.

'. . . but with a ute, we could be back out there, making hay. Sure, it'd be a little setback – but, in the long run, we'd be better off.'

'Jon Heather won't see it like that. Got to keep moving forward.'

Pete flings his chopsticks down, and a fountain of shredded duck erupts. Damn that boy's logic. His thinking's as straight as the highway they followed into town.

Cormac produces the photographs of the smallholding he keeps jabbering about. 'We could keep sheep, cattle, an emu or two . . .' He says the last with a twinkle in his eye; Booty once showed them how to cook an emu chick whole, and Pete talked about it for weeks. 'Mostly, it'd just be wheat,' he says. 'But do you know what the market's like for an ear of wheat?'

'It's so precious, they're selling it by the single stalk now, are they?'

Cormac Tate raises his eyebrows. 'It's hardly about the riches, Pete. It's about . . . You know, I never had a place of my own.'

Once, Pete knows, he had the house in Fremantle, a gift from his wife's grandfather. Once, he had two daughters and a yard and probably a dog as well. The Cormac Tate-that-was walked away from all that. He disappeared on walkabouts for weeks, then months on end, traipsing back in with presents and stories, and a hunger for liquor that wouldn't go away. Then, one day, he just didn't go back at all.

But what Cormac Tate means is: since I fucked up everything in the whole wild world, I haven't had a place. Most times these days he is living in a lodging house in Fremantle, working on fishing boats and maybe skimming a little off the side.

'It would be a place,' he says. '*Our* place. One nobody gifted at you or made you fit into. Pete, it would be a place for my girls to come visit. You think they come visit their old dad and his bitching landlady? I meet them in cafés, Pete. In parks. They buy me *cake* . . .'

'You can do it, Cormac. I'm not stopping you. I could come visit too.'

'It ain't about your money, Pete. I can borrow the money.'

He has photographs of his family, too. Pete would never tell old Cormac Tate, but he likes looking at pictures of his daughters. It isn't anything untoward; there's just something about looking at a pair of sisters that makes him feel good.

Jon Heather says he had twin sisters, once.

Cormac hands the pictures over, talks about them out on his little farm, him showing them the wheat fields, his pet donkey; a proper home for Dog.

'You're welcome to him,' Pete says. 'All he ever does is moon on Jon Heather.'

Maya is twenty-three and Susanna nineteen. Cormac might have missed out on the long years of their childhood, but he is adamant he won't miss out on any more.

The whole of life, Cormac Tate says, is about leaving one family behind and finding another – and filling those years in the middle as best you can. For boys like he once was – like Jon Heather and Pete are now – that gulf is wide and deep as the ocean. Not for them the easy glide from mother's bosom to girl-next-door and wedding day. You cannot be wrenched from one family and be expected to land, sure-footed, in another. His daughters say they understand, though perhaps that is just a kindness for their wandering father. That they are glad he is back, he is certain; that they have forgiven him going, he will never be sure. He was never as good to them as he is to Pete and Jon Heather – that much everybody knows but nobody says.

'I know you'd never leave Jon Heather,' Cormac says. 'But, look, I'd miss the hell out of you if you ever made it back to England.'

Pete considers it for the longest time. 'We're not going anywhere fast,' he finally says. 'Those savings of mine I mentioned – Cormac, between you and me, they wouldn't even pay for this dinner.'

Jon Heather has known a host of aboriginal stockmen and shearers, and he hasn't once known any of them needing protection. Jon once saw Booty splint a wounded stockman's leg and ride, without stopping, eighteen hours to bring back help. Up here, it's those city boys who most likely need looking after.

He stops where the road bends around the bay, watches Mr Cook duck into the doorway of a corrugated office and come out again, with a sheaf of papers under one arm. Somewhere south of Chinatown and the Old Arabia hotel, he pauses outside a place that proclaims to be a hospital, its low buildings looking out over the bay's turquoise water. Jon has never been inside a hospital. He fractured ribs once, taking a tumble from a horse – but the foreman's wife strapped him up and told him he would be ready to ride again in a matter of days. He supposes hospitals are places where good things happen – but, all the same, he shudders at the thought of walking inside.

Mr Cook is inside for half an hour, probably more. When he emerges, he is not alone. At his side, there stands a man in uniform: not a doctor, nor a soldier. Possibly a policeman, though Jon hasn't had cause to cross their paths since he left the Mission. Soon, a nurse joins them. Holding each of her hands, there are two little children. Jon judges them to be eight and nine years old. They are both girls, with pale black skin and features softer than Jon might have expected. They wear the same clothes: grey dresses and long white stockings, ill-fitting and obviously uncomfortable.

Jon does not register at first that they are cowering, because they are children and children are always cowering.

Mr Cook drops to one knee. He is slightly shorter than the elder girl, and slightly taller than the younger. He smiles a benevolent smile.

Underneath the blossoms where he lingers, Jon Heather stops himself from crying out. He knows that sort of smile. It is the smile that tells you – bad boys must take their medicine.

Mr Cook thanks the nurse, takes the girls' hands and, with the policeman beside him, escorts them across the yard to a police ute that is waiting there. It is much like the wagon Jon and Pete have been scouring the continent in, but with four seats up front instead of two. Were it not for the cage that covers the flatbed, Jon might have thought them the same model.

The girls are instructed to climb inside. They have obviously done this before, for they go without complaint. It was ever thus, Jon remembers: you cry and nothing happens; you scratch and bite and nothing happens; at last, you are still and silent and as obedient as they demand.

Mr Cook climbs in the cab and the engine rumbles. Quickly, Jon crosses the dusty road, skittering in front of a fisherman's wagon to a blaring of horns. When he reaches the opposite track, he is close enough to see the girls' faces through the wire. The older has her head tucked into the points of her knees, but the younger one throws her head around, snapping at every movement in the corner of her eye.

Their eyes do not meet Jon's as the police ute pulls away. He only imagines that they do. It is what he will tell Pete. Their eyes met mine and, damn it Peter, they *knew*.

He turns and slopes across the yards into the hospital. The place has a foul smell, like the cloakroom to a dormitory full of bedwetters. Somebody mistakes him for a patient. Somebody else barks out: in here, you have to wear boots. He ignores them both, because he has seen exactly who he wanted.

'Excuse me,' he says. He remembers how his mother once taught him manners, and summons it all up. 'I'm terribly sorry. I was looking for Mr Cook, but I think I might be too late.'

The nurse has a nonplussed look. 'He just left,' she finally says. 'You might catch him at the lock-up. I don't think he's going anywhere for a few days.'

She has a nice tone, mothering almost.

'And . . . the little girls?'

'Scared,' she says. 'But the poor darlings always are. They'll be good as new once they're settled.'

Probably Jon should not ask anything else. Yet sometimes you just want to pick at the scab and see what is bubbling underneath. 'Settled where?'

'I think . . .' She hesitates, uncertain if she is betraying a trust. When she looks at Jon, though, she is certain he could not mean anybody any harm; nobody with such boyish eyes could hurt a flea. 'They have a Home for them, somewhere in the south. I wouldn't know myself, but Mr Cook says it's an excellent place, where they can get *instruction*. By the time they're finished, by all accounts, you wouldn't know they were from the bush at all. Just the thing for those sort of girls.'

She must have said something wrong, because Jon's brow creases.

'You must think me awfully stupid, but . . . what sort of girls *are* they?'

Now the nurse understands. He is playing a game with her. She will tell her sister about this strange boy tonight. 'Bush girls,' she explains. 'You can't just leave them out there, not when there's so much more they could have. They have to be *rescued*. Just to think of them out there, rolling in the dirt . . .' She lifts a hand to her breast. 'It breaks the heart.'

Jon thinks of Booty, the other blacks with whom he's worked. 'What about their mothers?' he asks.

'Oh,' the nurse says, vaguely disinterested. 'I'm sure they want what's best.'

Moments later, Jon Heather stands on the hospital steps, watching the town slope sluggishly by. Black faces. White faces. Chinamen and Japanese. It is a good thing that he came to this town. Sometimes, you follow the work – but sometimes there's a job to be done and the work finds you.

Pete and Cormac Tate have been back in the Old Arabia hotel for two hours, bitching about the flies and the heat, when Jon Heather shows himself. For some reason, Dog is trotting at his heel, head bouncing proudly and tail erect. Though Pete calls out to him, Jon does not look around; Dog gives him a cursory glance and follows Jon up the stairs.

At the counter, Megan calls over: 'Dad doesn't like dogs in here, you know.'

'That's all right,' answers Pete. 'Dog's barely half a dog in any case. He's most of a dingo.'

'Then why do you call him Dog?'

'Got to be one thing or another. That's what old Cormac says.'

Jon reappears only minutes later, heralded by a bark from his faithful retainer. Passing them again, he heads straight for the counter, where he calls Megan over. Pete watches them closely and rolls his eyes at Cormac Tate – but Cormac pretends not to notice. Jon Heather has had women, but mostly, Pete likes to say, they've had him. There is a story Pete loves to tell of a landlady they had for a month when they were digging the pit in Kalgoorlie. She was Russian, old enough to be Jon Heather's mother, and she'd coddled him as such; Jon didn't pay his rent for a single night that month, proud to be adding the funds to the roll at the bottom of his packs.

Pete sees Jon Heather reach into his back pocket and hand a note to Megan. The girl takes it, tentatively, and asks him a question. Jon looks back at Cormac Tate, then tells her: I'm paying; this is my thing now.

Once the girl has gone, Jon turns and strides towards them. Like a boy whose foreman is fast approaching, Pete instinctively sits upright, smoothing the creases in his two-week-old shirt.

Jon pulls a wad of notes out of his back pocket, flings it on the table.

Pete's eyes are agog. Jon Heather has always known how to save his earnings – but he has never seen as much money in his life.

Jon sits, taking Dog's head in his lap and teases his ears. 'We're going to be sticking around a few days,' he says. 'And Peter – we're going to need a new ute . . .'

XIII

On the first day of January in the year of 1958, Pete wakes to a hell of a hangover, in a campsite with a dozen other men. They have been laying a pipeline that will take water north – but, on a job like this, it is only to be expected that you cut yourself free once in a while.

It takes him a little time to notice Jon Heather is missing – longer still to notice that the ute is also gone. In his pack, he finds a note: '*Only to the highway, Peter*'. It is a two-hour slog, under a malicious sun – and, by the time he gets there, he is dehydrated and cursing the day he ever met Jon Heather. Still, true to the idiot's word, the ute is waiting there. To Pete's surprise, Dog stands sentry, with a tin bowl beside him. He looks about as forlorn as Pete has ever seen him.

Jon Heather has left the ute in the scorching sun, and Pete has to leave the doors open for an age before he can bear to sit down or take the steering wheel. Thoughtful boy that he is, he has at least left behind a canteen full of tea, and a stack of dampers wrapped in old newspaper. Pete crouches in the shade and shares them with Dog. 'Breakfast of kings,' he mutters. 'What do you think of your old pal Jon Heather now?'

He sees a corner of paper folded under the windscreen wiper. Lifting it out, he reads the message to the attentive Dog: '*Only a year, Peter. I promise.*'

Probably it is because of money. They have bickered about money, like an old husband and wife. Pete spends too much. He supposes this makes him the woman.

True to his word, on the first day of January in the year of 1959, Jon Heather walks into the plantation where Pete is picking fruit, takes up a basket, and – to Dog's ecstasy – joins in. Pete doesn't ask him where he has been, nor how he found him again.

He hasn't asked him to this day.

*

'You two,' Megan says, with that same hint of reproach that is fast becoming her mark, 'are like a pair of little boys.'

She has her hands in Pete's suitcase; Jon's is lying open on the bed alongside.

'Who ever heard of a grown man reading comic stories? And . . .' Her eyes flash sideways. '. . . I wouldn't even begin to know where these came from . . .'

She lifts up the *Mystery at Witchend* and reads the first sentences. 'Didn't your mothers ever tell you it was time to grow up?'

That is enough for Jon. Cormac Tate knows it, and suddenly raises his glass. 'To our boy Jon Heather!' he declares.

They drink together, the best swill that not-so-much money can provide.

It is the twelfth of December in the year of 1960, and Jon Heather is twenty years old.

There is work in Broome, if you know where to find it. The pearl farms won't take you and the diving's all dried up – but beds always need changing and toilets always need scrubbing. Jon takes to helping about the Old Arabia, while Pete and Cormac make themselves busy at the port. Mostly, they harangue old fishermen for work, try it on for size and quit the next day. For them, the real work is about spending, not earning money: somewhere in this town, the perfect ute is waiting to be bought.

Jon has not celebrated a birthday properly since before the Children's Crusade. Games of stones around the back of a dormitory with a boy you used to call your friend don't really count. Since he took to the road with Pete, birthdays have been a guarded thing, always with a new group of people, always in a new town or station. All a birthday really means is you've spent one more year trying to be some place you're not.

This year, he feels that weight especially heavily. He was nearly ten years old when his mother said goodbye; that is ten years gone. He has been in Australia half of his life, and now every day he is here is another day upsetting the balance.

None of this Megan knows. She has taken quite an interest in Jon Heather since he waltzed into the Old Arabia and instructed his companions they were going to stay. He is like an overgrown child, wandering around with a constantly bemused expression on his face, as if to say: this does not make sense, and this should not be here. If he started asking questions about why the sky is blue, or where little babies come from, Megan wouldn't be surprised.

For his birthday, she wanted to get him boots, but her father wouldn't allow it. In their quarters at night, he said: you can't buy boots for every vagabond who tramps through here; he'll only sell them for petrol money. Instead, she has her arm hooked through his and walks him north of the Old Arabia, into the dusty Chinese avenues. The air is cloying, and smells of rain tantalizingly near. Tonight, at Sun Pictures, they are showing *Swallows and Amazons,* the 1949 cut. She knew she had seen the name before, when she glimpsed into Jon's suitcase, and resolved, then, that she would drag him here, even if he declared it would make it the worst birthday of his life.

They reach the theatre, great sheets of tin around a paddock of deck chairs open to the air. There are people here already, and Megan urges Jon through. She is aware she has talked almost all of the way here – though at least Jon Heather seems content to listen. He moves to sit at the back, but she has to hurry him on.

'It's for the Filipinos, silly,' she says. There is a single Filipino family sitting there, a pair of aboriginal girls just behind.

Jon wonders where the English people sit, but Megan seems to be reading his thoughts. 'We're down there,' she says. 'Jon Heather, come on!'

She used to love coming here as a girl, she says. Her mother said they once did silent pictures, that the place went to the dogs as soon as the talkies came in, but for Megan it was always magical. It is what she remembers most about her mother. Often, you can barely hear the film for the wind or the rain or the chattering of bats, but *that* is hardly the point. The point is the sickly sugar drops they sell. The ice cream.

'It's going to rain,' she says, sniffing the air. 'Let's take a higher seat.'

Jon gives her a look.

'It gets like that old song if it rains too hard: daddy, get the baby, the river's rising . . .'

When the picture begins, Megan is busy telling Jon what it was like when she was a girl, how she used to hide under the staircase at the Old Arabia with her mother and father at night. On the night Broome was bombed, she was only four years old. Probably she remembers other people telling tales of it more than she does the night itself, but it seems like she was there: a little girl, huddled on the jetty to watch the waters of the bay on fire.

Though she quietens when the pictures start flickering, suddenly Jon is not interested in Swallows or Amazons anymore. He remembers, too, those nights huddled under the stairs.

'They killed my father,' he says. 'The Germans.'

She narrows her eyes, as if he has said another of those infuriating things designed to vex her. She just can't tell, with Jon Heather, where the joke lies.

'I'm talking about the *Japanese*, you roustabout,' she says, aware that she has probably taken the bait for some joke she'll never understand.

Up on the screen, England crackles. A coracle spins on a river and the camera draws back to show open fens. Into the frame, a young boy gallops, cups his hands to his mouth and makes a hooting sound, somewhat like an owl.

It is the England of all Jon's books, the England of Witchend and Grey Walls and Snowfell and more. Yet, looking at it now, he realizes for the very first time that it is an England he has never seen. Not for Jon Heather a childhood gambolling in the woods, tracking down smugglers to their coves or uncovering wartime secrets high in the dales. Jon Heather's England was red chimneystacks and grey slates, his whole world bordered by the roll of the endless terrace from which his mother never took him – until the day she signed her name on the pages of the Children's Crusade.

All the same, nostalgia burns in him. He looks away, peeking back in increments as the story unfolds. Is it possible, he wonders, to be nostalgic for something you never had?

Before the hour is out, the rain starts to fall. It comes suddenly and heavily, like a faucet being ripped from the wall. Megan must know it is coming before Jon, because she cringes upwards. Then, the deluge begins.

Megan drags him upright by a sodden sleeve, but the higher seats have already been crammed. 'Show's over,' she says.

Jon doesn't mind. He was beginning to think it didn't really look like England at all. 'We should be getting back,' he says.

'Not on your life, Jon. It's your birthday! Don't you want a drink?'

Ordinarily, he doesn't touch a drop – not because he's a prude, but because drinks cost money, and that money could be put to better use. One tin of beer is equivalent to a tenth of a nautical mile.

'Your treat,' he says. He's already thrown all of his money into a new ute, in any case.

The canteen on Carnarvon Street is an empty little shack with a dour Malay attendant. Megan orders for Jon, dictating to him the things he will like.

She has been speaking about herself all night, but now she begins to probe him. He is obviously not Australian, but she cannot pinpoint his accent. Probably they are Poms, but they don't sound like any of the other Englishmen who, over the years, have come looking for riches in Broome. Jon shrugs it off. He is indeed English, he says.

He thinks she might stop there, but she goes on. She wants to ask about his family, skirts around it until, like a carrion crow circling roadkill, she swoops in. Jon has been asked about his family a hundred times before, and he always has the same stock answer: Family? he replies. Who needs family!? Out on the stations and fences, a grin would erupt on the other man's face. They wouldn't be the men they were, Jon knew, if they needed families.

Yet, he cannot bring himself to say it to Megan. She has a father she loves; a mother who loved her; a home that has sheltered generations of her family. He does not want to lie, but he does not want to tell the truth. He tells her how he grew up far away. Then, before she might pry, he reels out a list of places they have worked and bunked. Most of these places, she admits, she has never heard of. They are as far away and foreign as England and France.

'So you three,' she says, 'must have seen more of Australia then us sorry sorts born here.'

Jon supposes she is right, but it is not an idea he can warm to.

'And you don't like it?'

It is such a very odd question that he can hardly believe she is asking it.

'I see why so many people are coming, Megan. I've worked with them. English and Irish and Jewish and Hungarian. Two years ago, I was . . .' He does not want to say where he was; that is like admitting to himself that he went there at all. It was only one moment at the beginning of that awful year, but it seems to haunt him. 'I was working on a big project,' he says, thinking of another story. 'A water project. And there can't have been a single Australian on it. I struck up with a man from Hungary. Took me three months, digging ditches with him, before he told me he was a doctor. A doctor, and he gave it all up, so he could come here!' There were others: lawyers and teachers and bureaucrats, all of them working out their two years until Australia would welcome them to whatever profession they desired. 'All those people, they've come here looking for a new beginning. But I never got to begin in the first place . . . It was *them* . . .' The word might mean anybody; it might mean the Children's Crusade; it might mean everybody in the whole wretched world. '. . . who decided we needed to start again. So it isn't that I don't like it here. It's just that – it isn't mine.'

They finish their drinks and step back into the heavy night. Seconds later, the rain returns.

'Happy birthday, you strange boy,' Megan says, shrinking from the deluge.

Jon is about to reply when a thought strikes him: this isn't just *my* birthday.

He forces the thought away and trudges on into warm, vertical rain. He is at the end of the road by the time he realizes her arm is not hooked through his – she has taken his hand.

Pete has been holding the receiver for ten minutes before he dials the first number. It is an old phone, and he has to tremble each finger around a ring, listening to the click and whirr, before it registers. He has dialled only four digits when he is startled by somebody going up the stairs and hangs up.

Damn, but he has never been this nervous before.

Probably he should go back into the bar and drink with Cormac Tate – but a strange thing happened today while they were spending Jon Heather's hard-saved money on a new wagon to toll them to Kununurra and back: Cormac went to buy them breakfast, and Pete felt *guilty*. It must be something to do with this smallholding. Pete has never thought there was a bargain being made in accepting hand-outs from Cormac Tate before, but the thought occurred to him today.

He steadies himself. He begins to dial again. This time, he has only dialled three numbers when the doors open and in walks a drenched Jon Heather, with that girl Megan close behind.

Happily, he slams the receiver down and spins around. 'Jon Heather!' he cries. 'You're a sight for sore eyes. Do you want to know what Cormac Tate and your pal Pete did today?'

Megan is finding a towel for Jon, and throwing down newspapers so that he doesn't trample dirty red water into her father's mat.

'We got ourselves a ute, Jon. A big bastard ute . . .'

'Good,' says Jon. He spies, through the bar-room doors, that Mr Cook and his entourage are holding yet another evening council. 'I don't know how long we'll need to stay.'

As Pete turns to contemplate the telephone yet again, he sees them heading through the bar towards Megan's family quarters. Probably, he decides, this is the reason they've been lingering in Broome so long, forgetting all about his sister. He picks up the phone and slams it back down.

The staff quarters are up a side staircase, beyond the bar. There are photographs along the walls, not of old pearlers and divers from the first days of Broome, but of a family through the generations, the young Megan and her mother in the very last shot.

'Come in,' she says. 'There's something I want to show you.'

It is a dangerous game, going into Megan's quarters. She opens the door and he has to steel himself before going through. Even in the years he has spent since the Mission, working with Pete, he has been careful not to go into a family home. Sometimes they were even invited – into farms or station houses, for meals with eager daughters or farmers' wives. Pete was always ready to indulge himself on such occasions, but Jon Heather was made of sterner stuff.

This time, curiosity gets the better of his valour.

The quarters are not large. A small lounge room opens onto a kitchenette and, beyond that, a hall, where the bedrooms sit side by side, one for Megan, and one for her father. Megan begins to walk that way and, when Jon Heather follows, trying not to take note of the family photos on the walls, she gives a knowing look over her shoulder.

'You stay here,' she says, with a smile that is half tease and half genuinely bemused. 'I won't be a second.'

She is longer than that. While he waits, Jon Heather begins to feel like an intruder, a thief poring through the drawers of the houses that he burgles. On a shelf, he sees a photograph of a little girl and her mother, both of them beaming into the camera. It is a long stretch of beach, sand the colour of oyster shells, the little girl burnt the colour of a crab.

He is lost in the photograph when Megan reappears, holding a tiny tea chest, only a quarter the size of Jon Heather's suitcase.

'My mother,' she says, joining Jon at the photo. 'She was beautiful.'

A hundred questions he wants to ask: how old were you when she died? Do you remember her voice? Her smell? Do you wonder how it would have been, if she was still here?

'Here, see,' says Megan. She sets the tea chest down, sits on the arm of a chair and opens the clasp. When she gestures for Jon Heather to join her, he finds himself shaking his head.

'I'd rather stand.'

She gives him a look.

'My leg . . .' he lies. 'It still twinges from when me and Pete . . .'

Fortunately, lost in the chest, Megan is not interested. Inside, there are piled beautiful rare shells and brooches, a simple silver wedding band, a necklace of perfect pearls. She lifts it out and marvels at it, showing it to Jon.

'My grandmother's,' she says, 'from when they still dived for pearls. My grandfather had it made the day she agreed to be his wife. That was the day he signed the deeds on the Old Arabia as well. It all started with this.'

She offers it for Jon to hold, but he dare not. Even so, she goes through each of the trinkets in turn, each an heirloom from somewhere in her history, the history of Broome, the history of this hotel.

A part of Jon asks: why aren't you disgusted? This should be like salt poured in a wound. But the greater part of him answers: I don't know. I think . . . because it's *her*.

'I'm boring you,' says Megan.

'You're really not.'

'They're things my mother wanted me to have. Things she'd want me to give, if I had a daughter.'

'Or a son.'

Megan gives a crumpled shrug. 'A certain sort of son, maybe.'

She snaps the box shut and hugs it close to her chest. 'Do you want to . . . stay for dinner? Dad will bring something back from the kitchens. I'm sure he'd like to hear about all of these places of yours too.'

'They're hardly *mine*,' Jon says. His eyes, for some reason, are still on the closed chest.

'Still,' she says, aware that this boy can find an insult in the most mundane of things, 'I'm sure he'd like to meet you. You know, since he's been changing your bed and making your meals for the last two weeks.'

He hesitates. When you were eleven years old, Jon Heather, you had a friend. She was called Laura and she loved to hear your stories of what you would do and who you would be when you got back to England. Perhaps she dreamed of being there with you. Yet, one day, you simply stopped talking to her, because to talk to her was to invite trouble, and trouble might mean you never got home unscathed. Some people might say you were defeated, because you gave the men in black exactly what they wanted; triumph would have been to carry on, and never get caught. But those people would be wrong. To deny yourself the very thing you want in the name of something bigger is the most important triumph there is. And you learnt a lesson there, Jon Heather, one that your pal Pete has forgotten in his dogged devotion to Cormac Tate: never get attached; attachment is cowardice; loneliness is brave – and you are nothing if not brave.

He leans in to hug her goodbye. 'I had a really great night, Megan.'

As he turns to leave, she stands and stares.

This has never happened before.

'You see?' says Jon, idling the new ute. Dog is stretched across his lap with his muzzle on Pete's knee.

Pete slams his fist against the door. 'Jon Heather, don't you dare tell me this is why we're still here instead of up and after my sister . . .'

At midday, every day, the old policeman takes the two pale aboriginal girls out of the lock-up and leads them on a walk around the big dirt oval. Along the way there is a little mound of tough grass, and they are permitted to sit in the shade of a boab tree, while the policeman doles out sandwiches. Then they are permitted to go down to the mud flats, instructed to throw their leftover bread to the birds – this being the sort of thing that children like – and taken back.

'I asked Megan. They come through five, six times a year, that man Cook and others like him. They get sent notes of where there's girls out there. They rustle them, Peter, like any old sheep. They're after anyone who's got a white daddy, but . . .'

'Do you know something?' Pete interjects. 'Me and Cormac Tate, we'd got it into our heads you wanted to stay because of the girl. *That* I could understand, Jon. Damn it, *that* would be something worth waiting for.'

'I would have thought . . .'

'You don't think for shit,' Pete replies. 'This has got you all riled up, hasn't it?'

Jon turns. 'It hasn't you?'

Pete breathes, itching to jump out of the ute and be away. He was going to go out fishing with Cormac Tate today – but instead he's sitting in the blistering sun, watching this.

'That place is a jail, Peter. They've barely closed it down. Used to lock up blacks in it.'

'Might be they deserved it,' Pete protests.

'Might be they did,' Jon says. 'But *they* didn't.' The old policeman rounds the corner again, bringing the girls back after their daily jaunt. 'I've been down here at night, Peter. I've heard them crying.'

Dog lifts his muzzle, sensing something is wrong.

'You come down here to listen to children cry? Jon, you're . . .'

He knocks his finger against the side of his skull. 'You don't even know why they're there. Might be they're orphans . . .'

'*I'm* not an orphan.'

'. . . or might be they did something bad.'

'It isn't that at all,' Jon breathes. His eyes are not on Pete, but on the girls instead. The policeman ushers them inside, dressed up as if, but for their skin colour, they might be his daughters. 'They're Protection Officers. Megan says they're in charge of making sure there aren't problems, looking after the blacks in the bush and out on the stations, but all it really is . . . they ship those kids to places down south, near where . . .'

Finally, Pete understands. 'It isn't the same thing, Jon,' he says levelly.

'It's exactly the same fucking thing,' Jon returns, 'and you'd know it, if they'd put you in that Mission with me.'

Back to this, thinks Pete. Every time Jon might lose an argument, he summons it up: you weren't there, Peter. As if it's Pete's fault the men in black threw him onto a station instead of sending him back to school.

'Put your foot down, Jon. We've been loitering too long.'

They cruise up to the rickety Streeter's Jetty, to meet Cormac Tate. The silence in the cab is heavy. Dog looks, miserably, between his two best friends. Then he stands up, walks over Pete's lap and sticks his head out of the window. Probably this is his way of resolving matters between them: he is showing both Pete and Jon his gaping backside.

'I mean, Jon, what do you think you can do?' He grins and needles at Jon's arm with the tip of a finger. 'You haven't got a jailbreak on your mind, Jon Heather?'

'It's Cook,' says Jon. 'He's still here. Megan says he keeps extending his stay at the hotel, day after day.'

'So?'

Jon looks at Pete. He might be his only real friend in the world. They haven't once let each other down, not like that friend they used to have. 'So,' he says, 'it means he hasn't taken those girls to their Home yet.' A cry goes up; Cormac Tate is just stepping onto the jetty, a pair of big snappers slung over his shoulder. 'It means,' says Jon, 'that he hasn't finished what he came here to do.'

There is no work to be found in the following week – so, at last, Jon relents and drives Megan to the long stretches of Cable Beach, where they can walk for miles and not see another human being. At the Old Arabia, Pete and Cormac Tate watch them go. Pete tries to bundle Dog into the ute alongside them, but Megan will not be persuaded. Jon Heather looks back through the window grille as he leaves, giving a plaintive shrug.

'Well, what do you make of that?' Pete grins, slapping Dog around the scruff to stop his howling. 'Jon Heather going off with a girl and leaving his mutt behind?'

'I've seen stranger things,' says Cormac Tate, lifting a can of coffee to his lips.

'Yeah?'

'Indeed,' he slurps. 'But I've always been asleep.'

When they get there, Cable Beach is empty, white sands fringed with a belt of rust where lizards scuttle in the scrub. Jon guides the ute down an incline of hard-packed red and rolls along the glistening sands. At a headland in the distance, where the rocks reach out to sea, there stands a tall tower of iron girders with what appears to be a white nest sitting on top. This, Megan tells him, is a lighthouse. She laughs when Jon's face crumples. 'Are lighthouses different in England?'

Jon has only ever seen them in books but he nods all the same.

'I used to come here when I was a girl. It was my mother's favourite place.'

'How old were you when she . . .'

Megan looks at him sideways. 'How old do you think I am?'

'I'm playing a dangerous game, aren't I?'

'Didn't anyone ever teach you not to ask a girl her age?'

'That they did not,' Jon says, trying to grin. 'They taught me about crop rotation, if that counts?'

'It counts.'

'You shouldn't plant the same thing in the same field for more than a couple of seasons. It kills whatever's in the ground.'

They drift towards the breakers, but the tide is out and they seem to walk forever. Seabirds wheel in strange, mismatched flocks.

'So tell me . . . what is it with you and Pete? You squabble like brothers.'

'I suppose we're a bit like brothers.'

'But brothers who make jokes about being . . .' The smile is deliberate. '. . . more than brothers.'

'Yes,' says Jon, suddenly chagrined. 'That joke probably ought to stop.'

They walk in the sea spray – 'this, Jon Heather, must be the reason you never wear boots' – but even after an hour has gone, they have not yet reached the headland. Over his shoulder, Jon can still see the ute, barely any smaller than it was the last time he looked.

'You're tired, aren't you?'

Jon shrugs. 'I could walk all day.'

'You don't get it, do you? When I say *you're* tired, what I really mean is, *I'm* tired. Let's take a rest . . . Jon Heather, you need too much tutoring!'

'Really,' he says. 'How old are you?'

She throws him a disparaging look and marches out of the spray.

They rest at the foot of the fiery red cliffs before taking off again. There is no shade and suddenly the sun is directly overhead. Jon has walked through deserts before, but today is the first time it has dizzied him. Even when he looks over the ocean he cannot see a horizon.

At last, they reach the headland. It looks unscalable, but Megan knows the proper paths and leaps up. On the first ledge, she reaches back to offer Jon her hand. Only after he has taken it does he realize what he has done.

They climb to the peak, Megan blazing the way and taking delight in the way Jon Heather keeps stopping to make sure of his footing.

'Here it is,' she says, offering to haul him up the last scrabble of rock.

In the rocks on the other side, there is a great crater, a perfect circle in which warm, clear waters ripple. Megan sits above and peers into it so that she can see her reflection blinking back. She looks at Jon Heather's reflection. His face is furrowed, puzzled as to why she might bring him here.

'The lighthouse keeper carved it. He had a wife, Anastasia. She was crippled, Jon, could hardly move . . . But the waters are warm, and every morning he would carry her down so she could sit in the water. She didn't hurt when she was in the water. It took him every hour he had, but he built it for her. I always wonder if my dad loved Mum like that.'

'Is it just a story?'

'Does it matter?'

'I don't suppose it does.'

They skid down the sharp red rocks and crouch by the pool. When Jon dips his hand in, it is, indeed, warm. The waves crash beneath them but the spray does not reach beyond the rocks.

They find a place to sit, where they can gaze out over the ocean again. From the sun in the sky, Jon judges that it is the small of the afternoon. He finds the place where the sea meets the sky, tries to judge which way England might lie. To do so he must look back along the curve of the beach, but the red rocks rise all around them and he is not certain how far they have come. It is useless; England might be in any one of a dozen directions. It is, he realizes, the very first time he has lost track of it. Pete and Cormac Tate would clap him on the back and say: bastard good, Jon Heather!

'You've got that look again . . .'

Jon looks round; Megan's eyes are boring into him.

'What look?'

Megan shakes her head. 'Never mind.' They sit, warm wind flurrying behind them. Then, when the silence has lasted so long that Jon dare not break it, she asks, 'Is it like this . . . in England?'

'Like what?'

'Beautiful.'

Jon Heather says: 'I really don't know.'

'What do you think you'll do? When you get back?'

Jon picks up a piece of red rock and lifts his arm back to pitch it high. 'Megan, please . . .'

She shifts back, rises onto her haunches as if she might stand. 'Jon, we can go, if that's what you . . .'

He lets the rock fly. 'No,' he says through gritted teeth. 'It isn't that.'

'Then what?'

'It's . . .' To say it would be stupid, and he doesn't want her to think any bad thing about him – and, as soon as he realizes that, he knows it is already too late. 'Let's not talk about England, OK?'

'I'd like to see it one day. That's all.'

'Megan . . .'

She sits back down, inches closer this time. 'What do you want to talk about then?'

Jon takes his eyes from the horizon and looks at her. He reaches out and takes hold of her hand. He closes his eyes and draws her into him, finds the corner of her lips. Something softens, the pair relaxing, and they kiss, almost without moving.

Sometimes, you don't want to talk at all.

By the time evening approaches, Cormac Tate and Pete are out on the great dirt oval in front of the Old Arabia, deeply entrenched in a contest of cards with the bush blacks who gather there. Pete's eyes, heavy with drink, are fixed on his hand – he has not noticed for six rounds that he is holding the Queen of Hearts back to front – when Cormac Tate drives an elbow into his ribs. Yelping, he looks up to see the ute gliding back over the rise of red. Suddenly, Dog hurtles from the hotel's veranda, and launches himself onto the flatbed while the truck is still running.

Jon and Megan step out of the ute.

'Jon Heather!' Pete bawls, showering the deck of cards. He turns, oblivious to the invective hurled at him from the crowd. 'Jon Heather, get yourself a beer!'

Pete tosses him a tin, hot as if it has been roasting in an oven. With a sideways look at Megan, Jon cracks it open. Instantly, she snatches it and takes the first pull.

'Get in on this, Jon Heather. They've taken just about every penny I got. And I got *them* from Cormac Tate.' Pete spins, sloshing beer into the lap of the man sitting next to him. 'Listen up, you rabble! There's a new game on. It's called . . .' He looks, wildly, back at Jon. 'Stones!' he declares. 'And this is how it works!'

The beer hits Jon, hard and fast. He looks at Pete's eager eyes, as wide and lovelorn as Dog's. There is little a man can do when his friends look at him like that.

'You don't have to stay,' he says, looking at Megan.

'I wouldn't miss *this* for the world . . .'

The circle parts and Jon and Megan take their places. As Jon ferrets in the grass for stones, Pete needles at Megan's arm.

'You two been out all day,' he slurs.

'We have indeed,' she replies.

Over her head, he catches Cormac Tate's eye. Both of them nod sharply, like men might do at a job well done, and then return to the party.

On the tenth day before Christmas, Jon sees Mr Cook going into the lock-up with an old aboriginal man, much darker than the girls he is going to see. Sitting in the ute on the edge of the dirt oval, Jon begins to fantasize that the man is the girls' grandfather, come to barter for their release.

Half an hour later, Cook and the black man emerge. Cook chatters like he is the old man's friend; that the old man does not chatter back only lends weight to Jon's theory: the childsnatcher is selling back the children he has taken. When, at last, they part, they shake hands. The deal is complete.

He decides to follow the black man for a while. The trail does not go far, only to a canteen on the bay, where he sits alone to eat, throwing coins onto a counter. Jon orders food to take out, his back to the black man at all times.

Back at the ute, he gives half of his food to Dog and looks at the problem sideways. He thinks how his own grandfather might have looked, had he ever known him, walking up to the Mission to make a pact with Judah Reed. In his mind, the old man rages. Surely, that is how it should be done. But Jon thinks: once upon a time, that is what I would have done too. Now, though, I have rules; everything else is buried inside – and perhaps I, too, could serenely shake hands with the childsnatcher if, in the end, I got what I wanted.

Seen like that, Jon can even convince himself that the black man is indeed the girl's grandfather – because the only alternative is too terrible to imagine: the childsnatcher has the girls' people on his side.

At the Old Arabia, he tells Megan what he has seen. There are few guests in the hotel this week, and they sit together in the shade at the back of the grounds, listening to the sea.

Megan listens but he wonders if she understands. She does not, after all, know about childsnatchers and men in black. He wonders: what would she say if I was to tell her?

'Jon . . .' Her fingers dance on his arm. At his feet, Dog looks up, considers if he ought to let this go on, and then slumps back down, too hot and exhausted to care.

'How many times has he come here before?' he demands.

Her fingers chase his. 'The Protectors have been coming here since I can remember, Jon. Since I was a little girl.'

'Just like the men in black came for us,' Jon says. He finds that his fingers have stopped retreating. He turns his palm to take her hand. 'They came for Cormac Tate and they came for boys long before that too, boys who'd have been dead before I was born. And they're still coming, Megan. Every year the ships set sail.'

The silence demands to be filled. Once, there was a time when Jon Heather could have sat through a year of silence, could have driven a thousand miles with Pete and Cormac Tate and not breathed a word. Now, when he looks at Megan, he isn't certain how long he can last.

So he tells her, every last thing. He used to imagine telling his mother this story, but he has not pictured that in so long that it feels strange – dangerous even – to be telling the truth. All the same, he spills it all: the Home, the snows, the letter, the sea; the scrub and the Mission, Tommy Crowe and . . . he checks himself; he does not tell her how he sold the wild boy back to Judah Reed.

For a long time, she only strokes his hand. Then, she goes to him and his lips brush hers. That is all. She lies back in her seat.

'How long would it take?' she asks. When Jon does not answer, she says, 'To save the money and get back home.'

Another aeon, thinks Jon, now that we have the new ute.

'I could ask my father – when trade's right, we take on help. We could find a use for you, I'm sure. I was barely walking the last time this place got a lick of paint. And . . .' She runs her hand up and down his forearm. 'You wouldn't have to pay, Jon. You could lodge here. And then . . .'

Jon rolls to his side, facing her.

'I don't know,' she smiles, 'but I've got used to seeing you moping around.'

He can picture it: long days out on some fishing boat; long nights painting and fixing and cleaning the hotel. In every frame, he sees Megan. He sees them lying together at the end of a heavy, hot day, drinking sour lemonade and ice; climbing, again, to that secret place on Cable Beach and bathing in the deep tidal pools; stolen moments between shifts.

Tonight he is weary. Perhaps, if he was not so tired, he would stop there – but, instead, he allows his imagination to reel on. He pictures going through the doors into the family quarters, Megan's father long gone, and waking there every morning, Megan at his side.

Megan's eyes drop and Jon realizes how long he has been silent. He squeezes her hand to draw her eyes back to him.

'It will be over soon, Jon,' she says, as if such a thing might soothe him. 'Cook and his colleagues, they're checking out tomorrow. They paid up in full tonight.'

Jon's hand tightens in hers. 'Leaving?'

'Back south,' she says. Suddenly she knows she should not have said a thing – but Jon's eyes compel her to go on. The moment is already gone, like an apparition seen in the corner of your eye; as soon as you focus on it, it vanishes. 'They have a boat readied in the harbour.'

'A boat?'

'They'll sail it down the coast. I think . . .' She pauses. 'Gerladton . . . and Perth.'

Jon twists so that their arms are no longer interlocked. He swings his legs from the chair. 'They have some place for them there, don't they? All the little black bush girls . . .'

'Jon,' Megan says, 'I don't know . . .'

It does not matter – because Jon does. He stalks back through the hotel, watching over the dining room. In one corner, Pete and Cormac Tate, deep into another night's drinking; in the other, Cook and his officers, conspiring like a coven.

A close, sticky night: Dog at the foot of his bed, chest heaving, feet scrabbling as he mauls some tern in his sleep; Pete whinnying like a mule in the bed alongside.

Jon Heather, lying awake, images moving across the backs of his eyes: what if, on the day Judah Reed took me to sea, some pirate had sailed out, boarded the HMS *Othello*, and taken me back?

The childsnatcher does not come in the dead of night.

Pete wakes to a firm hand on his shoulder. Pawing out, he sees Jon Heather's face coming into focus.

'They're getting a wagon ready. The black man's with them.'

It is just senseless words. 'What?'

'He isn't their grandfather. I think he's showing them where . . .'

'Where what?'

'Where Cook can finish up his business.'

By the time Pete has fully woken up – with a helpful shove from Dog's wet snout – Jon is at the door, pulling on the boots from his pack. Boots can mean only one thing: Jon is serious.

Pete pushes Dog away, but Dog leaps back onto his bed and starts digging in the sheets.

'You're not leaving me alone on this,' Jon says. 'This concerns you too.'

'Sleep concerns me. Finding my sister concerns me.'

Jon slams the door.

Downstairs, Megan's father is attending to some guests checking out. Jon hurries through and emerges, blinking, onto the street. Dawn has barely come, but the sun already seems high; only a mad Englishman and Dog might go out today.

Dog appears on his heels, scenting adventure – but Pete does not trail behind.

In the yard alongside the Old Arabia, Mr Cook climbs into the same police ute that Jon saw the girls trapped inside; at the wheel, the old policeman sits with his face set in stone. On the flatbed at the back, hunched under the arcs of wire as if he is himself their prisoner, the aboriginal man crouches on his haunches. Jon sees, not without horror, that he has a shotgun in his hands, the barrels broken back.

Don't let yourself be seen, Jon Heather. He repeats it to himself as he slopes along the side of the building, in shadow until he reaches the new ute.

He is just clambering in when a figure, still hauling up his shorts, careens around the side of the building, shirt splayed open to reveal a chest covered in coarse red hair.

Better late than never, Jon supposes.

'I'm driving,' Pete says.

'The hell you are,' says Jon.

'I'm older than you, remember!'

A split-second thought. 'It's my ute,' Jon says, and turns the ignition.

Cook and his companions round the dirt oval and take the highway out of Broome, swinging back south as they follow the coast. It is the same road that first brought Jon and Pete into town. On the flatbed, Dog sniffs the rushing air.

Few cars tread this highway, but the road is straight for hundreds of miles, so Jon is content to hang back, letting them roll on until they are nearly at the horizon. Only when the road banks to follow the swelling coast does he push his foot to the floor: he cannot miss the moment they leave the highway to follow one of the dirt tracks east. Out there, lies the Great Sandy Desert – all of Australia has the names Jon might have used, as a boy, to draw an imaginary world: the Snowy Mountains, Skeleton Bay, Kangaroo Island – but they will not push that far. There are stations between here and there; this, Jon Heather decides, is where they are bound.

Two hours south of the bay, Jon sees the police ute starting to slow, pushing forward in fits and starts as if its occupants were bickering about where the turn-off lies. Careful as Jon is not to mirror their flow exactly, the gap between them grows and shrinks like a tide.

'You know you're out of your head, don't you?' Pete says. He has said the same thing every few minutes since they set out, but Jon hasn't once replied. 'Jon, you don't want to see this . . . If Cormac Tate was here, he'd box your ears.'

Jon gives Pete a look like a serrated dagger. 'Cormac Tate isn't my father. And he isn't yours either.'

Up ahead, the police ute banks left, along a red dirt road. Jon brakes hard, approaches the turn-off at a crawl, wary that the police ute might be just beyond. The road, lined in broken fences, disappears into scrub and pitted pastures.

'How far do you reckon?'

In reply, nothing but stony silence.

'Peter!' Jon barks. At his side, Pete rears up. 'How far?'

Pete shrugs. 'Fences this close to the highway?' he says. 'Shouldn't be far, Jon Heather . . .'

The scrub thins. This is certainly grazing land, but there are no cattle to be seen. Grass grows in full colour, drinking greedily of the recent rains. There are no stock routes over the desert, but Jon knows that old routes, pioneered by other English boys cut adrift here, skirt it to the east and south.

'You see that?' says Jon.

Pete resists for as long as he is able. 'I see it,' he says.

Somewhere south of the trail, there is smoke. There are barns in one of the fields, but no station house that either of them can see. If drovers come here at all, perhaps they sleep with their animals like the shepherds of old. Further on, Jon sees other tracks going into the scrub, two rises of land, not quite hills, and a causeway of undergrowth between.

At the side of the road, there sits the police ute. At first, Jon brakes. Then, he rolls slowly past. There is nobody in the cab, no one imprisoned in the caged flatbed. He thinks, I could let down its tyres. I could smash up its windows, drain out its gas.

His eyes drift to the causeway between the rises. Where there is smoke in the Wet, there will be people. That is the way they will have gone.

Jon noses the ute off the track and into scrub where it might not be seen, unless somebody was already upon it. When he steps out, the heat hits him like a furnace.

They move slowly back to where the police ute is parked. All around them is still; only the buzzing of insects and the alarm of rainbow birds disrupts them. Jon peers into the cab, sees a sheaf of papers bound in leather, a little memo book in which orders might be made in triplicate: take the children; take the children; *take the children*.

He takes hold of the wire cage, tests it for strength. It is bolted fast onto the flatbed, built for thugs and drunkards.

'You bring the tools?'

Pete shrugs. 'I've got them in my back pocket,' he mutters.

Jon stands at the apex of the trail. They could be anywhere out there. If it is blacks working the cattle, they might have camps all around.

'We'll wait,' he says.

They bring the ute to a spot where they might see Cook and the policeman coming back, without themselves being seen. In the blistering heat, they loiter. Morning becomes noon, noon becomes high noon; the sun cuts its arc above.

'Merry Christmas, Jon Heather.'

‘Shut up,’ Jon breathes. ‘Someone’s coming . . .’

There are no shadows at this hour, so it must just be a feeling Jon gets. They sit in rigid silence, the glass steaming around them – until, at last, they turn to one another. There are voices: not one, or two, but a whole host.

Mr Cook is the first to appear. His fair complexion is already bull red, his scalp screaming with sunburn under his short hair.

Next comes the aboriginal man they brought from Broome. He is carrying his shotgun, but using it like a walking cane, a simple stage prop.

Next, a tiny girl, three or four years old.

Jon pitches forward, hands gripping a red-hot steering wheel. Pete snatches at his shoulder, but is quickly thrust off.

‘Easy, Jon,’ he says. ‘We didn’t come here looking for a fight.’

Something is wrong. The little girl should be crying. Instead, she is holding somebody’s hand, gazing up, perplexed at those around her. For a second, she smiles.

There are two women behind, darker than the girl: her mother? Her aunt? They bustle along like they are taking her to a market, careful that she should not stray too far from their sight.

Lastly comes the old policeman. He opens the ute, allows Cook to climb in, and then ushers the girl and the two adults around. If they are perturbed to see the cage at all, they do not show it. The policeman opens the back seat of the ute, and shows them where they are to sit. They slide in without complaint. The policeman takes his place behind the wheel – and it is left to the old aboriginal, one passenger too many, to slide into the cage.

‘Jon Heather, you dumb shit. They’re not capturing anybody. They’re taking them to see those other girls. Probably they were found wandering, didn’t know how to get home.’ Pete lets out a braying laugh. ‘Look at you! It’s like somebody stamped on your favourite toy . . .’

Jon waits until the ute has pulled away, hiding itself under clouds of dust. His hands loosen on the steering wheel.

'Come on, Jon. I'll drive back.'

Jon ignores him and starts up the engine. He remembers something he has not thought about in ten long years, that last night in the Home in Leeds, when a certain red-haired boy looked at him and said: I'm not happy Jon, and I'm not sad. This place or some other place – it just doesn't matter to me.

He looks sideways at the man lounging in the passenger seat, head slumped as if they are on yet another mindless jaunt to some station or fence. He thinks: how I hate him for his ease; how I hate him for the way he can scoff; how I hate him for being him.

'Jon Heather, stop!' Pete lunges forward, driving his right foot down as if it is him with the pedals underneath. Instinctively, Jon does the same. The ute skids in the dust, bouncing Dog around violently in the back.

Through curling dust, Jon sees the two aboriginal women standing in the middle of the trail. That they did not run from the skidding ute is madness enough – but Jon sees that they have rocks in their hands. Their eyes are wide and they glisten with tears.

The little girl is nowhere to be seen.

Jon leaps out of the cab, but the women start screaming at him. One lets fly with a rock. He goes to them, hands raised, but every step he takes only ignites their ire.

'Peter!' he bellows. *'Pete!'* he repeats.

Pete comes between Jon and the two women. He is better at this. Jon has never had the ear for it; when they worked with black stockmen in the year of 1957, Pete could talk with them for hours, ease his way in and chatter about endless nothings.

'They threw them out of the ute,' says Pete.

Jon could have surmised that himself. He tears back towards their own ute, bellowing for Dog.

'They've still got the girl.'

'Tell them to get in back,' Jon says.

Pete turns, tries to explain. They look at him dumbly: you two, you're with the childsnatchers.

'Tell them to shut their mouths and do it now! If Cook gets to the highway, that little girl's gone.'

Jon kicks the engine into gear, thrusts the ute forward, throwing open the passenger seat for Pete to slide in.

'Now!' he roars.

He keeps the ute rolling while the women climb up the back. Then he pounds his foot to the floor.

One mile; two miles; three miles; four. They pass the station's trail markers with terrifying regularity: the highway cannot be far.

Up ahead: rising dust. Jon kneads the accelerator, releasing his foot only when he feels the ground soften beneath them; he cannot afford to slide into a skid now. The police ute does not know it is being followed, but still it keeps its speed up. When you are in the business of childsnatching, Jon notes, you do not want to stay in the same place long.

He closes the gap, until he is certain they have been seen. One hand off the wheel, he hammers on the glass behind them, and the women crouch low. One of them holds onto Dog, muttering petitions.

'Jon,' Pete finally whispers.

'Can you see the girl?'

She isn't under the caged flatbed; she must be riding up front, like a good little darling, bouncing on Daddy's knee.

'Jon Heather, please . . .'

It takes achingly long until they are close enough that he can see the girl, sitting in the black man's lap, on the back seat. His hand hovers over the horn. He leaves it there for a second, if only to be a reasonable man.

Rule one: when you are angry at them, don't let them know you are angry.

New rule: to hell with rule one.

Jon hits the accelerator hard and smashes into the back of the wagon.

The police ute was built for harder things than this, harder than their own vehicle – but that doesn't matter; Jon has surprise on his side. Pete flails out, as if he might grasp the wheel himself and push them into the scrub, but Jon thrusts an elbow sideways and batters him off. Up ahead, they know that something is wrong. If the shunt did not give them a clue, they must certainly hear the screaming. Jon tries to blot it out: that little girl is screaming too; she'll be screaming for days and nights to come, if he loses his bottle now.

He forces the ute to the left, rides up and smashes the police ute again, this time catching it in the corner and forcing her into a sharp turn. In front, the old copper wrestles with the wheel, manages to right her. Jon sees the little girl turn round. Her face is pressed to dusty glass. Her mouth is wide.

There is enough space now that, if he rides the scrub, he can draw alongside. While they are still casting around, clawing to understand what is going on, he lurches forward, until they are almost level. Then, blotting out Pete's muttered invective, he pushes hard to the right. The police ute resists, but its driver is not quick enough; Jon Heather rams them off the road.

The ute spins with them, cutting a full circle in a tempest of dust. When the brakes grip and they skid to a stop, Jon can see, through the parting red veil, that the police ute has dived, nose first, down a bank where the scrub grows thick. It will not stay there for long. You have not destroyed it beyond repair, Jon. A moment to gather their composure, to rub bruised joints, and they will drive out of here as happily as they drove in.

'Stay here,' says Jon.

'Jon, you . . .'

'I've been doing what you told me for ten years, Peter. Do what I want once, and you can have another ten: just stay where you fucking are.'

Jon jumps out of the ute, runs across the dust to reach the police wagon. In the front seat, he can see the policeman slumped with his head against the wheel. Beside him, Cook too seems to be reeling.

He reaches for the door to the back of the wagon, but before he can grasp it, it flies open, catching Jon full in the chest. The blow winds him, and he staggers back.

The aboriginal man rises. If he was injured in the crash at all, Jon cannot tell. He barks out, and Jon bites back. Then, he sees him lifting something: the shotgun he was carrying when they rode out.

Throw a punch, Jon Heather. Not a simpering thump as if you are hazing your best friend. Do it properly. Do it now.

The black man's head snaps back. Instinctively, he lets go of the shotgun. Jon kicks it underneath the ute, brings his fist back, piles it again into the man's jaw. He does not drop like a sack of potatoes. He reels back, dizzied. It is enough that Jon can kick him down and push past. In the back seat, the little girl is huddled, head buried in her knees, against the far door. He reaches in to take her.

'Jon, watch out!'

Jon whirls around.

Mr Cook is out of the front of the wagon. He rests, an arm outstretched on the wagon's roof, and looks Jon up and down. 'Who are you?' he breathes, gulping back air.

He seems to think Jon is a robber, some common old highwayman. Once, a jolly swagman camped near a billabong.

'I might ask you the same question,' Jon replies.

Pete can hold them back no longer. Over Cook's shoulder, the women leap from the back of the ute and tear over the track. Past Jon they scramble, over the aboriginal man nursing his jaw, grappling to take the girl out of the back seat.

At last, Cook understands.

'She's a ward of the state.' He stops, wipes his bloody lip. 'I have an authority.'

'Whose authority?'

'The authority of the State of Western Australia,' he returns, as if there might even be magic in the words. 'We are here to *protect* these children.'

Jon is still, remembering one of his rules: if you don't have to, don't breathe a word; you'll never be able to say exactly what you think. He steps to the side, is about to shoulder past when Cook puts his hand out.

'You don't know what you've done,' he says. 'Look at you, you stupid station boy, and you don't know what you've done . . .'

Jon knows exactly what he's done, and he knows exactly what he'll do. The second Cook's hand touches him, something blossoms inside him, black and beautiful and no longer in thrall to every rule he's ever made up.

He swings out, catches Cook on the chin. When that does not fell him, he brings his other fist back, cuts up. Cook sprawls onto the crashed bonnet, but Jon hauls him upright. At first, it might be that he wants Cook to fight back – but, in truth, he couldn't care. He thrusts a foot around the back of the man's knee, throws another punch – and watches with glee as Cook falls into an eruption of red dirt.

Now Jon is on top of him. He straddles him like a lover and begins to pound: first left, then right, switching fists as ably as a man in black might switch the hand in which he holds his half hockey stick. Soon, Cook no longer protests. His legs stop thrashing and his body stops bucking. His eyes swell as Jon watches, his whole face purpling under each blow.

Jon feels arms clawing underneath his own. Too bent on watching Cook's face shine, he does not fight back as somebody hauls him off. His own face must be purpling, because suddenly he feels an incredible heat. He is faint. All of the world is very far away.

In the corner of his eye, he sees the red-haired man standing, ashen-faced. 'I thought,' he says, 'I told you to stay where you are?'

Pete stands over Cook's inert body. 'You've killed him,' he says. 'Jon Heather, you've killed him . . .'

Before Pete can fall to his knees, Cook's chest heaves. Jon is about to swing round with his boot, but Pete stands between them. After everything, he still does not want to hurt Pete.

Pete forces Jon back. If he is certain that Jon will not hit him, he still flinches every time he has to push Jon in the chest.

Pete rushes round, skids down the bank and pops open the hood of the police ute. It is all familiar enough. Reaching in, he comes back with a fist full of wires. 'Let's get out of here.'

He rushes back to their own ute, forcing Jon to follow. The bonnet wears a dent where Jon rode the other off the trail, but it will not take long to hammer out. Pete lets out a whistle, and Dog bounds over to them.

Along the track, the two women hold the child between them. Pete bawls at them to run and harries a distant Jon into the passenger seat. 'I'm driving,' he snaps, and reaches for the keys.

They hit the highway at speed, slewing wildly as they bank north. The road is empty; that much they can count as a blessing.

'Where to?' Pete says.

It takes a moment for Jon to register the sound. 'It's you who normally makes the decisions, isn't it?'

'Did I make *that* decision, Jon Heather? Did I tell you to do *that*?'

They pass a marker: Broome, a hundred miles north.

'You didn't think, Jon Heather. You never think!'

'No, I didn't,' he concedes. 'If I'd been thinking properly, we'd have bided our time. We wouldn't have jumped them until they were shipping all three girls south.' He pictures, dreamily, the lock-up in Broome, the girls peering grimly through their window at the big boab tree outside. 'Now they'll have to stay there . . .'

Pete slams his hands on the wheel. 'If we head back into town, we have to get straight out. Find Cormac, and get to the road . . .'

Trust Pete to instantly start swooning over Cormac Tate. All the same, Jon nods. Megan is there. He should not have let her take him to the picture house, should not have followed her up the rocks at Cable Beach and kissed her there. He should have kept away.

'We can be in and out in two hours,' he says.

'What?'

'Just drive, Peter.'

The redness rushes past.

Broome shimmers under a heat haze as they plough back onto its ochre roads. Trucks move sluggishly under the sun, a pair of Malays kick their heels in the path of the traffic, but the air is mysteriously still. They reach the dirt oval and skid to a stop in the shadow of the old hotel.

Pete is the first out of the ute. He lets his foot fly, uselessly kicking the ute's crumpled bonnet.

'Well?' says Jon, leaping out. 'Are we going in, or not?'

Pete doesn't say a word. He turns away and vaults onto the Old Arabia's veranda.

'Stay here, Dog,' says Jon, fussing him. 'Don't go wandering. I'm not leaving you behind.'

In the Old Arabia, Cormac Tate is waiting. When Jon and Pete barrel into the dining room, he is hunched over a newspaper. Head down, Jon marches past, making for the stairs. It wouldn't do for Megan to see him now, not when he's got work to do. If he sees her, he might have to tell her what he did to that man Cook, and even though he knows it was right, he isn't sure he could stand the condemnation in her eyes.

By the time he is at the other side of the room, he knows that Pete has not followed. He does not look back but, all the same, he sees a reflection in the glass as he flies through the door: Pete and Cormac Tate, huddled together, just the same as it's always been. He flings the door behind him and barrels up the stair.

In their room, his suitcase is open, his books piled high. If there is one thing he won't rush, it's packing these books – but, as he begins to slot them inside, he finds that he can't stomach the sight of them. He sits back on the bed, his head in his hands. Something seems to be rushing out of him, like shit the morning after some rancid desert meal. The books are splayed all around: stupid Witchend and childish Gary Hogg. Suddenly, he realizes that his vision is blurred; there are – he cannot believe it – real tears in his eyes.

He is sitting there, kneading some sense back into himself, when the door slams behind him. Thinking it some policeman, some Protection Officer, come to corner him, he wheels around, fists raised. In the doorway, it is only Cormac Tate.

The look on Cormac's face is enough for Jon. He's been here before. It felt exactly like this on the day George told tales.

'Oh, I see,' Jon says. 'He ratted on me, did he? Peter couldn't stand it so he ran off and told Cormac Tate . . .'

Cormac Tate folds his hands, like a penitent. Jon knows it is not a prayer; it is only to stop himself from thrashing out. Rule one: if you're angry at them, don't let them know you're angry at them.

'Jon Heather, of all the stupid, sorry things to have done . . .'

'Make yourself useful,' says Jon, refusing to catch Cormac Tate's eye. 'We don't got long. You can help me pack.'

'You know who those Protection Officers are, don't you, Jon? You know who they work for?'

'Australia,' says Jon. 'They work for Australia.'

'And what? You thought you could just knock out the whole of Australia?'

He begins to pack the books, one by one.

'You want to know the most pathetic thing in all of this? You haven't even saved anybody! That boy Cook'll just patch hisself, get back in his ute, and go and find that girl again. Might be you bought her a few more months with her mother and sisters. But that's all, Jon. A few more months . . .'

Jon's eyes lift. They are heavy with tears. '*I* would have wanted a few more months, Cormac. Wouldn't you?'

Cormac says nothing.

'You old bastard, you don't even remember. You let them *turn* you. You can't even remember what your mother looked like, can you? You didn't even stay in touch with your brothers. Well . . .' Jon pauses. He knows he is holding a dagger. It is time to twist. '. . . you're no better than Judah Reed, at the end of it, Cormac. You're no better than that fat bastard George. If you wouldn't have done the same thing I did, well, I can't even look at you, Cormac. I can't even look at you without seeing a man in black.'

Cormac's face darkens. His hands, already clasping each other, seem to strain and tear, like a monster in one of Pete's comic books. When, at last, they release, he lets out a breath. He turns, but has to snatch at the door handle three times before, in his rage, he can take it.

In the hallway, Pete is still standing, like a naughty schoolboy with his ear up against the wall.

As Cormac forces his way past, he pauses. 'You listen to me, and you listen good.' His voice falls to a low whisper. 'I'll be waiting. I'll be sitting there at that station, ready to make it *ours*. Me and you and Booty can make a go of that place.' He puts a hand on Pete's shoulder, and it seems to be the only thing stopping him from shaking. 'But you spend too long with Jon Heather, Pete, and he'll fuck you just like he's fucking himself. I mean it. He's been holding you back too long already, with those sorry notions of his. Home. England. Still being a little lost boy. You find your sister – but then you come and find me. Don't end up like Jon Heather. I've done it, Pete. I know how he's pinned.' Cormac lifts his head, but Jon only sees in the edges of his vision; he will not listen, and he will not see. 'Just another one of the desperate ones, drifting, pretending there's still a home to go back to, pretending *this* isn't home, everywhere, all around . . .'

Cormac's hand lingers a moment longer on Pete's shoulder. Then, his face paling, he disappears along the corridor, a gentle shoulder barge instead of goodbye.

Jon closes his suitcase. Perched on the end of the bed, he takes a moment to compose himself. When he looks up, Pete is still standing there.

'You're still here,' says Jon. There is, to Pete's astonishment, trembling in his voice, as if Jon cannot quite believe it.

Pete looks along the corridor, after Cormac Tate.

'Peter?'

'He's right, you know. You don't have anything, Jon. You spent all your money on the ute . . .'

'We can find more work. We've never been short of work.' Jon stands, heaving his suitcase to the door.

'But . . .' Pete stops. Perhaps Jon did not hear Cormac's talk of the smallholding. 'Jon . . .'

'We've got to go, Peter. Or . . .'

'You're right,' Pete admits, his voice softening. 'We can't be here when word gets out.'

'Peter, look . . . I'm sorry.'

Pete rolls his eyes, frustration and forgiveness all rolled up in one. 'You'd better be.'

Downstairs, Cormac Tate is nowhere to be seen. They clatter across the dining hall, and out into reception. Jon kicks open the front doors, looks out over the dirt oval, shimmering in the heat. An aboriginal man squints up at him from where he has been sleeping.

Dog is already on the flatbed of the ute, as if knowing that this is going to be a quick getaway. When Jon flings his suitcase up back with Peter's bag, the mutt takes up his station on top of it, the proud guardian of a childhood Jon Heather never really lived.

Without daring a joke, Pete takes the driver's seat, but Jon does not complain. He swings into the seat alongside and then Pete pushes the ute onto the road.

On the other side of the dirt oval, the highway broadens, leading inland. That is the road they will have to take.

As they glide around the oval, Jon quietly asks, 'What about Cormac Tate?'

Pete shakes his head but does not look up from the wheel. 'I don't think you ought to be asking about Cormac Tate.'

They are banking around the far side of the oval, where the road merges with the highway, when Jon sees Pete's eyes linger in the mirror. The ute slows, though there is no traffic to slow it, and Pete remains transfixed.

'What?' Jon breathes. 'What is it?'

He reaches to angle the mirror so that he too can see, refusing to risk a look backwards in case they are, even now, being pursued. Before his hand gets there, Pete grapples it, tries to push him away. For a moment, that is all it is: they are holding hands. Then, when Pete finally gives in, Jon twists the mirror and peers into it.

On the other side of the dirt oval, the doors of the Old Arabia are open. On the veranda, there stands Megan, watching them leave.

'She probably thinks we didn't pay up,' Jon says.

'You know it's not that.'

They are both frozen. Behind them, Dog seems to know something is wrong. He climbs to his feet, turning in a circle. It is only when he begins to bark that Jon realizes Megan has crossed the road, is already striding over the red dirt and hard grass.

'Jon,' Pete says. 'What do you want to do?'

Jon cannot look in the mirror any longer. He turns it back to Pete, buries his head. 'Drive, Peter.'

'Jon?'

'I said just drive . . .'

The ute slides forward again, banking right around the edge of the oval. There is only one other truck on the road. It blasts past them at high speed.

Pete's eyes are still in the mirror. 'She's still running, Jon.'

'I know.'

'Well?'

'Well . . .' Jon looks the other way. 'It wasn't for ever, was it, Peter? There's been girls before. For both of us. Only, you always know it's not forever.'

'Forever's one thing, Jon Heather. But here and now's another.'

'Forever can't start until we get back home.'

'Are you sure?'

Jon Heather rears. 'I said I was sure, didn't I? Drive, Peter. Please just drive.'

With a sigh, Pete pushes the ute out onto the highway. For a hundred yards they track along the edge of the dirt oval, running parallel to the Old Arabia.

Something tugs Jon's eyes back to the mirror. She is still coming, pounding across the earth now, kicking up red sand from her heels. The air ripples between them, so that it seems she is on the other side of a veil. Then, when she is only a stone's throw away, the heat haze seems to die. Megan, it seems, has stepped out of that other world, right into Jon's.

'Stop,' he says. 'Peter, stop . . .'

The ute jolts to a halt. Without a word, Jon Heather kicks open the door, jumping down onto the highway. In the middle of the road he shuffles along, until he can look over the flatbed.

On the other side, Megan is still. 'Jon,' she says. 'What's going on? I saw Cormac storming away . . .'

Jon grips the edge of the flatbed. 'I can't tell you, Megan. I haven't got time. I've got to . . .'

Her face changes, almost imperceptibly. 'You're . . . leaving . . .'

'I didn't want to.' He thought it would sound hollow, but it does not. With something approaching horror, he realizes that it was what he said to Peter that was hollow, not this. *It wasn't forever, was it, Peter? You always know it's not forever.* 'Megan, I don't have the time . . .'

'Where will you go?'

'We're . . . going to find Peter's sister. But, Megan, you can't tell anybody. Not which road we're taking. Not which . . .'

He pauses. He keeps telling himself to climb back in the cab, to bury his head, to tell Pete to plough on. That is what he has been teaching himself all his life, ever since Luca, ever since Judah Reed. One foot in front of another: that is how you get back to England.

'Come,' he whispers.

'What?'

'Megan, come with us. Come with *me*. It's what you said you wanted. Like everybody else. Up and out of Broome. Up and out of the Old Arabia.'

'Jon, I can't . . .' All the same, she has started moving again, lurching down the banks of the dirt oval. Now there is only the ute separating them, Dog lying indolently in between. 'I can't leave my father. Not just like that. I've got . . . ties. I've got . . .'

'Well, I don't, Megan. I don't got nothing but this truck and this stupid mutt. And . . .' He seems to have to wrestle each word out of his throat, like dragging a rabbit from its warren by its hind feet. '. . . you,' he says. 'I've got you, haven't I? A truck, a mutt, and you.'

She is silent.

'Megan . . .' Jon's eyes dart at the highway. 'I haven't got time. It's been ticking, ticking, ticking ever since I was a little boy. Now it's all running out.'

Megan nods. It is a tiny thing, almost unseen. She lifts a leg, about to climb onto the flatbed.

'I don't know what I'm doing, Jon Heather.'

Jon nods. If Megan doesn't know what she's doing, well, neither does he. One foot in front of another: that has always been his mantra. Don't touch them and they can't touch you.

Rules, he is finding out today, are there to be broken.

He slides back into the cab, heart thundering, pale as the southern sands.

Pete looks at him and nods.

'Snow on the Nullarbor,' Jon says, shivering. He breathes out long and hard, erupting halfway into a strange, high pitched laugh. 'Just like snow on the Nullarbor Plain!'

XIV

It is the youngest man in black who sees England first. He must have been looking out for it ever since they sailed out of the Suez Canal, but now, at last, it is here. He is certain it is England and not some silly rock sticking out of the sea, because it is raining: thin, grey drizzle, of a sort he has not known in more than a decade.

He is nineteen years old – but don't tell Judah Reed; Judah Reed and the others think he is already twenty – and finally he is coming home.

They come to port in Liverpool, the same port from which he once set out. He has sea legs and he staggers along the docks, carrying a suitcase of crocodile skin at his side. He feels silly as a little boy, and is thankful when Judah Reed takes charge and leads him away.

They spend one night in lodgings at a Home in the city. It is not a Home of the Children's Crusade, but perhaps they share something: a poster on the wall shows Australia in all its sandy glory, and pictures of little boys traipsing to school in smart bush hats. He is given a room to himself, a godsend after his bunk on board ship, and he spends the evening writing up his journal and filing away, in precise order, the sketches that he made during the voyage. He likes order and he likes neatness.

In the morning, he wakes early, though the train is not scheduled until after noon. He writes again in his journal, detailing everything he can remember, everything he has dreamed, about the place they are going to. He finds space also, to write about companions who have fallen along the way, boys who might never get as close as he is now.

They reach Leeds. He had planned on walking from the railway station so that he might breathe in some of the old city – but, to his persisting bewilderment, he finds that he has absolutely no idea which way he should go. Judah Reed will laugh if he tells him; it will be a pleasant, fatherly laugh, but nevertheless he does not want to hear it. He lingers around the railway station, watching people on their daily trudge and giving thanks that, today, he has not had to wear his black clothes. He is wearing a pair of slacks and an overcoat, and for that he is still as much out of place as he ever wants to be.

The Chapeltown Boys' Home of the Children's Crusade is being rebuilt when the taxicab drops him at its gates. There are builders in a yard full of bricks, and boys watching keenly. Snow ices the slag heaps where the digging works have stalled – and the newly felled trees that were once a fortress of thorns, keeping boys in and mothers and fathers out, are roped together in pyramids, ready to be taken away.

He walks underneath the iron arch and follows the path. When you are a child, the blanket with its nose sticking out from under the bed is a serpent that will devour you as soon as you fall asleep; when you are an adult, it is only a blanket you should probably pick up. All the same, he stops at intervals, terrible shivers running through him: here was the place your first ever friend used to play hide-and-seek; here is the place he picked you up when you fell and told you not to be a baby, ruffling your hair gently all the while.

A little boy, eight years old with a nose caked in grime, looks up at you and cocks his head. You're new, he says. I'm really not, you reply, and reach down to ruffle his hair. When he recoils, you are suddenly filled with a guilt you have never known before. You wish you were yourself that little boy, and that your first ever friend, all red hair, buck teeth and freckles, might be here to punch you on the shoulder and tell you not to be such a big girl.

Watched by a dozen boys, the man approaches the door that was once so much taller and lifts its monstrous knocker. The face that appears does not leer at him, nor conjure a grin to hide its malice. It is only an old man, who reaches out and pats him on the shoulder.

Surely it is not that man's fault that he himself recoils.

'Michael Andrews,' the man says. 'I'm the caretaker.'

'George Slade,' the man in black replies.

Jon Heather's birthday and Peter's surname. For as long as you can remember, George, you have been a composite of the people you used to call friends: this year perhaps, back in the old town, you might discover who you really are.

In February, it is supposed to snow – and snow it does. He wakes up in his quarters behind the chantry, and is delighted to feel the cold in his bones. He takes some time to splash water onto his face before putting on his black trousers and shirt and peering out. At the end of the short corridor, Judah Reed is already in his office. He might have been up for hours; the little boys probably think he never goes to bed.

Martin is already in the office. He has been here for three months already, working with the boys and telling them of the adventures they might expect on the other side of the world. Martin is the only other boy George knows who joined the Crusade like he did. He left at sixteen like all the others, but he came back two years later, wondering if there was work he might do. George was glad to see him. It made him feel less dirty, somehow – less ashamed of how happy he had become while he was looking the other way.

George takes a seat. Today, there is a list of chores he must perform. There is story time in the chantry for the little ones; there is a walk to the playing fields and back, with time for the boys to play tag. These were things that did not happen in the Home when George was a lad, but he is glad to see them now. Only a little piece of him twinges, but it can't mean a thing; surely, it isn't possible to be jealous of some six-year-old orphans?

'George,' Judah Reed begins, after Martin has been excused. 'You might stay behind.'

There is a new boy, Judah Reed explains. His name is Charlie. He is six years old and has only just come to the Children's Crusade. Once, he was fostered with a family in Harehills, but it has been eighteen months since the boy had any semblance of a real family. He is an anxious sort of boy, and he has not yet been told that he will be going to Australia to make a better life for himself. It will fall to George and Judah Reed to sit with the boy and break the news: your mother, little boy, has passed away. You are to come with us now, on a quest for something greater.

'In the meantime, perhaps you, George, might spend some time with the boy? We will ease him into the news. Some boys need it that way.'

George nods. Judah Reed and the other men in black have always admired George's way with boys who tend towards anxiety. It is said that boys who cry themselves to sleep might spend a few days in George's company, listening to stories and playing games, and then cry no longer. He tells them strange tales: a story called *We Went To Sea But We Didn't Mean It*; another about a family who live at a place called Witchend, which is surrounded by Grey Walls at the head of Snow Fell. The other men in black have no idea where George might have got these stories; he has, they say, a 'versatile' imagination. They have watched him teaching little ones the rules of a game called 'stones' and wondered how he could come up with such simple things to enrapture the little children.

George expects there to be some papers about Charlie: a birth certificate or a surname at least. There is, Judah Reed says, a single family photograph: Charlie and his mother, on a sunny day up on Woodhouse Moor, with bothersome students from the colleges basking around. He will keep it on file here, but it would do no good to give it over to Charlie's possession; such things can upset a fragile little mind.

George finds Charlie in a playroom. He sits on the edge of a circle of boys, casting marbles. He has a single dragon's eye in his own hand, but he holds onto it tightly. If he casts it, he might lose it to some boy more talented than him.

The boys ignore George, but gradually they leave the game to go and find some other sporting ground, outside in the snow.

'Charlie?' George begins.

The little boy freezes. Most likely, he thinks he is in trouble. He is the sort of boy, George would wager, who will always be there when trouble starts, but who doesn't think to run away before somebody comes to deal out a punishment.

'Here,' says George. 'I want to show you something.'

There are four boys left. They sit in a circle with George at its head, the oldest ten, the youngest six. On the floor, nine marbles are left. Nine is nothing; George can do nineteen. With one hand, you must toss them up. In the other, you must catch them in the crooks of your knuckles. If one slides out, you must pay a forfeit: stand on your head, or sit on your hands until they go numb.

'The trick,' says George, tossing a trio up and catching them between index finger and thumb, 'is to keep your fingers splayed, just *so* . . .'

'You've got a funny voice,' one of the boys says.

George looks up. 'I suppose I have,' he replies.

When he casts the next round, the boys are all eager to learn.

At night, you wander the streets you might once have called your own. It is snowing, and though you are not used to the cold, you go out with only shirtsleeves and a scarf.

The snow is like icing on red bricks and slates. The terraces are still, but you ghost through them, trying to remember if these were the streets in which you played before they sent you to the Home. Somebody mumbles a hello as he passes, his face half-hidden beneath a hood; when you do not reply, he lets fly with all sorts of invective, like you have dirtied his virgin sister. You hurry on, up ledges where somebody has neglected to take down their Christmas lights, along a broad, empty road where warehouses loom.

You have been walking for hours, wondering if this might have been the house you would have ended up buying, if this might have been the corner shop you stopped at every morning to buy a newspaper and milk, when you realize you have no idea how to get back. The city that might have been yours has been working to ensnare you; it has led you in merry circles, its avenues and lanes contorting behind you. You are a miserable fly trapped in its web, and now you must perish.

You have no friends to ask what you might do, so instead you knock on the first door where you see light. A middle-aged woman answers, her head haloed by cigarette smoke. Obviously, she thinks you are her daughter's guest, for she turns and bawls a name up the stairs, and a girl who is probably your age descends. She is as bewildered as you are, but you manage to get across your meaning. She is pretty, unlike her mother, and as you leave, another thought strikes you: if I had grown up here, might I have had the guts to ask a girl out for an afternoon stroll?

When you reach the Children's Crusade, you must sneak in, so that Judah Reed is not cross. Crossing the hall, you see a dim figure scurrying out of the laundry. His eyes are alight, like a kangaroo frozen in the glow of a ute's headlamp, but you steal past, pretending not to notice. Then you lie awake for long hours, writing a story you will never commit to paper: a little boy whose mother did not die, who has a dull job filing papers in an office, but a lovely home to come back to each night. He never meets a girl, he never marries and has children of his own, but lives instead with his mother until the end of his days.

In the hour before dawn, you wake. You are chilled to your bones. At first, you roll over, thinking, this is England – this is what I have always wanted. Then you feel the dampness that has already soaked through the sheets and deep into the mattress. You breathe in a familiar smell. It is not fair that such a horrible feeling brings such a rush of pleasing nostalgia.

'There's a big farm, where all the boys live, and where it's summer all year round. We'd get up bright and early to go and milk the cows . . .' He says cows, though they'll find only goats; Judah Reed has told him, from past experience, that milking a cow is more appealing to little boys than touching up a grumpy old goat. '. . . and then it would be time for breakfast. And, because it's summer all year round, there'd be mangoes and apricots, and fruits I'd never even heard of – but all big and ripe and juicy. You'll like kiwi fruits.' He leans in, as if he is sharing an illicit secret. 'They're not really Australian, but it's close enough.' He catches sight of Judah Reed in the corner of his eye. He is nodding, so he must be pleased. George is suddenly shame-faced about last night; it has been a long time since he kept a secret like that from Judah Reed. 'All the boys live together in big cottages, with cottage mothers to look after them. Oh, there are lessons, but not horrible, stinky lessons like you have in schools here.' He makes a disgruntled spittley sound. 'You'll learn how to grow plants and look after animals. You'll learn how to go fishing. For the girls, there's cooking and baking, but . . .' Here's the special part, he thinks. Here's how you reel them in and turn a frightened boy into an awestruck one. '. . . for the boys, there's *hunting*.'

The assembled boys' eyes widen. He can see them nudging each other.

'We used to hunt rabbits.' It is a lie, but only a little one; you're allowed to tell little lies. 'They don't like rabbits in Australia. All those big open spaces are perfect for rabbits, and they run everywhere. So we'd hunt them, and then we'd skin them and pop them on a fire – and, like magic, that's your dinner! Now,' he says, beaming, 'that's better than soggy cabbage and gristly stew in this old Home, isn't it?'

'Can you catch a kangaroo?' somebody pipes up.

They have looked at pictures of kangaroos and wombats. He has even shown them a Tasmanian devil, but told them not to fear – they're frightened of oranges, and all you have to do to drive a devil back is scatter some orange peel on the ground. Judah Reed has brought with him an embalmed platypus, but the boys do not believe such a thing can really exist. They are, they know, being made sport of. There are dragons in Australia, and dinosaurs still in the desert.

'Kangaroos are brave and intelligent,' George declares, standing tall and lifting his fists like a boxing 'roo. 'You don't pick a fight with a kangaroo!'

Afterwards, the boys are permitted to look at a big book full of pictures and postcards. In one of the photographs, George sees Jon Heather, lined up with all the other boys in his dormitory. Jon Heather always got on better with the boys in the dorm after George was gone; George has always known that he held him back. If Jon was here now, he would say: thank you, Jon. But Jon Heather wouldn't want to know.

Martin marvels at the photographs too. He finds himself, at thirteen years old, showing the little ones how best to go about the village muster.

'When was the last time you saw Jon Heather?' he asks. 'The day he left the Crusade?'

'No,' says George, lost in the picture. 'There was one more time. It was . . .' He can hardly think about it; it is the same way he sometimes thinks about his mother, as if he might hold her hand one final time. '. . . 1958,' he whispers.

The boys file back to the dormitories, there to chatter and think about what they have been told: we are going on a grand adventure, like the heroes of old. In the chantry, Judah Reed pats George mechanically on the shoulder – he might act like a father, but he has never had a father's touch – and tells him he has done well.

They stand at frosted windows and look out. In the snow, the boys who will not be joining the voyage have been playing. There are two black boys out there, but black boys will never be sent to Australia. Charlie plays with them, but he is not on either side; he does not know where to throw his snowballs, so he just stockpiles them in a big mound by his feet.

'I want you to tell him tonight,' says Judah Reed.

George nods. 'Do you remember . . .'

'What is it, George?'

'I was just thinking,' he says. 'Do you remember when you told me *my* mother was dead?'

Judah Reed holds his eye. 'I'm afraid not, George,' he says. 'I've broken the news to so many boys.'

‘We were here, in this very room. I don’t think I cried. Not at first.’

Actually, he bawled. Peter had to tell him to stop. Then, when he met Jon Heather, he started crying again, just so that somebody might ask for his name.

‘I think it will be that way with Charlie too. Tell him . . .’ Judah Reed pauses, as if to contemplate a tactic of battle. ‘. . . that she loved him very dearly, and wishes for him all the best things in the world. Tell him . . . she asked us to provide.’

It is the very thing George’s own mother said about him, before she passed on. Mothers the whole world over, George reflects, must be made of the same things.

He sits with Charlie that night, reading a book from the library shelf. In the book, there is a castle and an enemy pilot has crash-landed, taking refuge in the keep. He is befriended by a group of local children, who swear not to betray his presence to their mothers, even though he speaks in a nasty, guttural accent: probably he is a German who came to kill them all, but he shows them how to make bows and arrows and to ford a river – and, when one of the boys tumbles into an abandoned mine shaft, it is he who makes the pulley to hoist him out and sets his broken leg with a splint. This is the sort of story Jon Heather would have loved.

By the time they have come to the end of the second chapter, Charlie is so enthralled that George cannot bring himself to break the bad news. Instead, he ploughs straight into the third chapter – and, after that, the fourth. By then, it is too late to bring a boy to tears. George packs him off to bed, with the promise of more story tomorrow.

So that he might not have to face Judah Reed and admit to his cowardice, he decides to wander out again. Out there, in the builders’ yards, he might even find a latrine at which he can relieve himself before retiring to bed.

He retraces, as best as he can, the route he took the night before. When he stops thinking about the terrace, though, a most strange thing happens: his feet seem to find a different path. Blindly, he follows. Can your body remember things your mind cannot? Might that be the reason that he flinches every time Judah Reed swings around, even though it is Judah Reed who has nurtured him, taught him, brought him back to England?

His feet take him north; he knows, somehow, it is north, though the stars are not the ones he learnt the names for with the Children's Crusade. He imagines, suddenly, an old man, weathered face and breath like gravy, telling him: the Pole star shines the brightest, and she shines due north. He imagines a tumbledown run of terrace, where bombs have carved big craters, and a lollipop that tastes like mint. The men in black have always said he has a versatile imagination – though, in truth, George knows full well where he gets the stories he tells. There is no such thing as imagination; you just cannibalize things you have heard or seen or done.

George stops. Every thought is a road that leads back to Jon Heather or Peter. Yet, you're the one back in England, he tells himself. For the first time in your life, *you're* the one leading the way. Can't you let yourself be proud?

His feet have brought him far, to the banks of a glowering heath. He imagines a little fat boy cavorting here at the height of summer, wearing only a striped shirt, tumbling on a bedspread used as a picnic blanket. Too late, he recognizes it as the tract of land in the photograph of Charlie with his mother. That mother is dead now; so, too, is the fat little boy he sees in his mind's eye.

He wants to go back. Night has hardened, and the banks seem to deepen as the frost encases them in hard shells. Yet, while he has no will to press on, his feet push him further. Over a rise between towering oaks he goes; past air raid shelters bricked up and covered in ice. Down a steep hill there is a taproom, but he does not go in. His feet lead him, instead, to the door of a nondescript terrace, where a blue lantern is suspended over a door.

Vividly, he imagines a little boy holding an old police commander's hand and going through those doors. The little boy, round as a barrel, has a face flushed with tears, but the old policeman speaks gently to him and gives him a sweet that tastes of nothing he has ever tasted: it is called liquorice and it tastes of *black*. The little boy is led through the doors and waits in a windowless room, until a nice lady brings him sugary tea and biscuits. He sleeps in the same room that night, the policeman sitting near, with a crocheted blanket on his lap. The next morning, he is taken to the Chapeltown Boys' Home of the Children's Crusade.

Yes, he realizes, there really is no such thing as imagination; you just cannibalize the things you have heard and seen and done.

He rises long before dawn and heads back to the police station. This time, both his feet and his head know the way. The city bursts forth in torrents of memory. Streets come alive. He remembers a terrace where boys kicked a ball and he would sit on the kerb to watch. He sees a house charred black and abandoned, nestled between two lovely gardens where flowers grow and washing hangs to dry in the factory smoke, and thinks: the witch woman lived there; you could only see her at night, if there were no stars; she used to have children, but she magicked them all into mice.

At the police station, a lady with a bob of thin black hair sits behind a counter. She has tea and toast, and she splutters as George walks nervously in.

'Can I help you?'

He must look as if he has been a victim of some horrible

assault, because then she moves to comfort him. In truth, it is only another attack of memory: I was a little boy, sitting in that corner, watching big ogres of men come and go and talk about me.

'I'm not sure,' he says. 'I do hope so. I've a rather odd question, actually. I wonder – is there still an old captain here, a big stocky man, sombre-looking . . . He had rather sad eyes, I think. And . . .' George doesn't know whether to say it. '. . . a big old nose, almost as big as his whole face.'

'I think you must mean Captain Matthews. He doesn't work very much anymore. He keeps trying to retire, but keeps coming back.' She tilts her head. There is something about this boy, dressed up like a man but still wearing a little boy's puppy fat, that can mean no harm. 'You might find him at the tearoom on the corner of the moor. He potters around there most mornings.'

Somehow, George's feet know the way there too.

The tearoom is a drab little affair, a counter and scattered tables and chairs. There, at the table nearest the back, sits an old man, sixty or seventy years old, with a newspaper spread out before him and a pot of coffee at his side. On the old man's lap, there sits a boy. He is, perhaps, three years old; his face is smeared in jam deeper than on the old man's toast. A woman emerges from a back bathroom and swoops the little boy up.

George hovers at the door for an unnaturally long time, and then pushes in. Thinking himself too ridiculous to approach the man straight away, he takes a neighbouring table and orders toast. Too late, he realizes he has no money with which to pay.

'I'll help you out, son,' the old policeman begins. 'You look like you need a good feed.'

It is not true; George did not look as if he needed a good feed even when he was at the Mission, starving on breakfast slop and hunks of billy-goat meat.

On hearing the voice, the memories start rampaging. His

body must remember how it felt the last time he heard that voice too, because suddenly he wants to cry.

'Son,' the policeman replies. 'Are you OK?'

'Are you Captain Matthews?'

'Is everything all right, boy? Has something happened?' He stops, as if he too is being assailed by memories only a shred of him can recall. 'You're Bethan's boy . . . Bethan Stone?' He says it as if he is bewildered, but he cannot be as bewildered as George.

He merely mouths the words: am I?

'Here, drink up, son. You look like somebody's bled you dry.'

The policeman pours coffee and presses it into George's hands. 'Now, son,' he begins. 'Why don't you tell me what it is? Whatever it is, we can get it sorted . . .'

'I haven't been back for a long time,' he begins.

'I can tell that, boy,' the captain says, risking a grin. 'You sound as if you're from the moon.'

'I've been away.'

The boy might be an imbecile, but the old man has dealt with imbeciles before. He nods, considering.

George twists around, as if some unseen hand is forcing him from his seat. 'I was wondering,' he begins, the words slurring in their rush to get out. 'Could you tell me what it was like, that night . . .' He is about to say: that night you took me away. '. . . that night I had to leave my mother?'

The old captain kneads his brow. He makes eyes at a waitress, who brings him fresh coffee and bread thick with butter.

'It's a hell of a time ago,' he says.

'I can hardly remember.'

'You and your mother were our neighbours. That was back before we moved house: too many memories in my old place, you see. But I used to know your father, before he went off fighting. Got himself killed somewhere in Africa, didn't he?'

George nods, though in truth he has no idea.

'Your mother had a hard time of it after he didn't come back. She was slaving almost everywhere she could to make it work, but that meant leaving you with neighbours and friends and . . . I suppose, when she got sick, she thought she couldn't stop working, or else the pair of you would starve. That's probably what did for her, in the end.' The captain shakes his head dolefully. 'She loved the hell out of you, and it put her in the infirmary. She had them call me right from there. Well, I hadn't heard from her in the best part of three years, but off I went . . . You were with one of the neighbours. They had a little boy, too, much younger than you, but you liked to play with him. You might have been brothers.'

'You took me to the police house, down in Burley . . .'

The captain nods. 'Fifty years old, and there I was, creaking in a chair, my legs seizing up – and you slept, sound as pup, on a blanket on the floor.'

'You had liquorice.'

The captain leans in, conspiratorially. 'Son, I've *always* got liquorice.' He fumbles a short black stick from his pocket onto the table. 'Your mother had made provisions, of course. She knew she wasn't well. And she'd leant on her neighbours too much already . . .'

Now he stands up, tossing some coins on the counter, and shuffles to the door. When he is almost gone, he looks back. 'Strange, I'd have thought your mother might have told you all that. You being all grown up. How is your old mother doing, any road?'

George stops. Coffee scalds his lips. 'Sorry?'

'London was never a place for me. I spent some time in Southwark once, but couldn't wait to get out. Too much . . .' He shrugs, as if there isn't a word for it. '. . . weighing down on you. Still, you go where the money is.' He puts on a cap and opens the door. Winter, that desperate marauder, steals quickly in. 'Look after yourself, son,' he says, and bows his head to the snow.

George sits until his coffee gets cold, and a waitress asks if he would like her to boil it up. For the first time, he doesn't even feel like crying.

George lifts his fist and raps, three times, at Judah Reed's door.

A voice calls out that he may enter. As if it proves a point, George waits a beat before pushing through.

'We missed you at the assembly this morning,' Judah Reed begins.

'I'm sorry,' George replies. 'I lost track of time.'

'And?'

He asks it pointedly, as if it is to be assumed that Judah Reed knows exactly what he has been doing, out there in the terraces.

'I have a question,' George says. 'If I may?'

Judah Reed nods, but he would ask it anyway; in his head, he can hear Jon Heather and Peter saying that he must.

'How did Charlie's mother die?'

'I don't have the details, George. She had been ill for some time.'

'But you have her death notice, don't you?' When Judah Reed looks up, George is staring straight into him. 'I think Charlie would like it, when he's older. When he understands.'

Judah Reed pauses, as if he must consider this. He stands and makes certain that the door is closed.

'George,' he says. 'Why don't you tell me what's bothering you?'

It is on the tip of his tongue to say it: you lied to me; my mother isn't dead. And yet – he is silent a moment too long. An insidious thought has ensnared him, throttling him back into silence: if your mother still lives, why, then, did she never send for you?

Jon Heather stood up to you once, Judah Reed, and he was hardly ten years old. Surely, I can do it now?

'Charlie's mother isn't dead, is she?'

Judah Reed returns to his desk, lifts a file from a deep drawer. He removes a letter and sets it down. The page is a typewritten form, with two spaces where names might be filled out: in the first one, Charlie's own; at the bottom, his mother's signature. Steeling himself, George reads it over and commits the name to memory.

'If she is not dead,' Judah Reed begins, 'she is surely dead to him now. Do you understand, George?'

'She told you to tell him she was dead, did she?'

Judah Reed has never heard George raise his voice. It is almost comical; it breaks like a boy bewildered by his own pubescence.

'She affords us the right to do what we feel is best for the boy. If that means we offer him the chance of forging a new life for himself, in a new country, without anything holding him back, then that is for us to decide. We are, in effect, the boy's parents now, George. We want what is best for our sons.' Judah Reed hesitates. 'Or perhaps you think he would be better left to rot here, in this sorry town, wasting his life at some lathe until he can pump out little boys of his own? This place is a warren, George. You escaped it. Why shouldn't he?'

George trembles. 'You didn't answer my question. Does she know about Australia? Does she know he'll think she's dead? What if . . . what if a mother came back, wanted their boy again? It's happened, hasn't it? God help us, we spent every night here waiting for it to happen . . . Didn't you?'

'It isn't every boy, George. But sometimes a boy needs help in . . . readjustment. Charlie is a nervous sort. I have seen it a hundred times, George, and you will see it a hundred more: it is better for them to believe.'

It is only a little lie, George thinks. You're allowed to tell little lies.

'Do you remember when you were little, and you were ill, and you had to take a horrible brew to make you well again? It's a little like that for Charlie.' Judah Reed's face pales. 'He has to take his medicine.' He stops. A thought, it seems, has occurred. 'Have you told him yet, George?'

George breathes, soft and steady. He has to think – but, fuck them, they never let you think. They haven't let you think since you were eight years old, without a birthday or even a name to call your own.

He takes his time. Judah Reed can wait.

When you were a little boy, he thinks, your best friend ran away. You woke in the night and you had soaked the sheets with your own piss, like the pathetic little bastard you were. Later that day, when someone ratted you out, you took a beating for it. But, when you thought your best friend was running away again, God help you, you had an idea. You tugged on a man in black's sleeve: Jon Heather is leaving the Mission, you said. He's got a friend at a station, and he's leaving tonight; he's leaving right now!

There are things in life for which you will be sorry forever. You cannot take them back and you cannot make them right. It is like the piece of grit lodged under your flesh: it doesn't hurt, but you feel it still. This, George decides, will not be one of those times.

'He was silent at first. Then he cried and cried. I stayed up with him until he'd cried himself out.'

Judah Reed might even be pleased. 'And Australia?'

'Frightened,' George lies, 'but he'll come around. It's the best thing for him, in the end, isn't it?'

'We wouldn't do it for them, if it wasn't,' he says. 'We are not a society of monsters.'

In the corridor outside, George freezes. At the very end of

the passage, Charlie is waiting, his back pressed against the wall.

'Mr Slade,' he says, nervously. 'I thought you'd forgotten. You said we could do more . . .'

'Of course,' George answers. 'The story awaits!' He puts his arm around the boy and guides him from the corridor. 'But you must do me a favour, Charlie. One favour, and then all the stories in the world!'

'Yes, Mr Slade?'

George crouches and ruffles the boy's hair. 'Never call me Mr Slade again, Charlie. My name is Mr Stone.' He stops. 'Or you could always just call me George.'

They climb the stairs to the playroom above, passing dormitories where boys lounge and make mischiefs of their own. In two months, a ship sails from Liverpool harbour, and all of these boys will be gone.

The old wisdom is right: the childsnatcher does not have to come in the dead of night; he is, George reflects, already here.

XV

Pete stands on a bank of red dirt and grass, on the edge of the highway. Behind him, sweet smells rise like mist from the waters of a marsh hidden by walls of thick reeds. Finches, scarlet red and tiny as his thumb, flutter through the air. He looks nervously along the highway, as if he can't bear the thought of taking another step. Where the road banks left, a great mound of red rock rises like a slag heap. All the way to its zenith, scrub huddles and clings.

He has come this far. He can't back out now.

It is a new house whose steps he shuffles towards, a timber frame and whitewashed walls, with a trellis where nothing is growing, and piles of dirt where the excavations have yet to be smoothed over.

He slides back a screen door and knocks. There – it is done. He takes a step back, finds himself praying that nobody is in; one more day, and he might be ready. They could make a camp outside town. There must be fish thronging the river.

The door draws back and, standing there, is a girl, no more than five years old. When the sun catches her brown hair, it shines the colour of rust.

She squints at him.

'What's your name?' he asks.

'Elizabeth,' she says, kicking from one foot to another.

'I wonder, Elizabeth – is your mother home?'

The girl nods, shyly.

'Could you fetch her for me?' The girl turns to slip back into the house. 'You can tell her . . .' he whispers. 'You can tell her it's your Uncle Pete.'

In the ute, Jon Heather picks at his nails with the end of a blade.

Kununurra is a small town, with a handful of houses still under construction. Further along the river, where a makeshift jetty has been erected, there are canvas shacks, permanent bivouacs for the men who are coming to build the dam. It is work that might suit Jon Heather – long hours and good pay – a place to be anonymous and win back some of the money he so uselessly poured into this ute.

Suddenly he slips, digging the blade of the knife deep into the flesh around his thumb nail. Consciously, he zones back in on what Megan is saying.

'. . . I suppose I did always want a sister. When I was a girl, I'd ask Mum about it, over and over. Dad had to shut me up. If Mum had lived, I think they would have wanted to give me a sister . . .'

Jon Heather imagines what it will be like, when he sees his own sisters again. They will be ten years and more older, they will probably have children, just the same as Rebekkah, but they will still be his sisters.

All of this reminds him how little he has. There has been precious little work in the weeks since they left Broome, just enough to tide them over while they kept out of sight. Megan found work waiting tables in a road station, while Pete and Jon dammed a stream with some locals – but that was barely enough to feed them. Every day, Pete talked about what it would be like to find his sister, so much so that it might almost have been as if they had been spending the last years saving to get here, not slaving to get back home. Now, every night, Jon has to tell himself – you will get back to England, you *will* get back to England. Every reassurance, though, just magnifies the doubt.

Jon has not heard from Cormac Tate since Broome, though Pete has kept up his practice of secret phone calls, whenever the opportunity arises. Jon is sure they have exchanged letters. For his own part, he does not care if he ever sees Cormac Tate's face again. The old man would have seen him strung up for what happened in Broome – as if any of that, the Protection Officers, childsnatchers, the whole damn thing – was Jon Heather's doing.

The screen door slides open again, and Pete's ugly mug appears on the veranda. He gestures wildly at the ute. 'You can get your backsides inside now,' he says, unable to wipe the grin off his face. 'It's a dinner. A bastard family dinner – and you two are both invited . . .'

Rebekkah stands in a porch where little shoes are lined up in perfect rows, and an axe handle is propped against the wall. She is taller than Pete but, other than that, it might be as if Jon's best friend has simply gone into the house and donned a wig.

Pete marches ahead of Jon, turns on the spot like a soldier, so that he is standing abreast of Rebekkah. She looks askance at him, admonishing as a mother, and he launches into a sweeping introduction: this, Rebekkah – my *sister* Rebekkah – is my brother-in-arms, Jon Heather; this, Rebekkah – my *sister* Rebekkah – is Megan, Jon's girl who's come along for the ride. And *this* – he bounces to his haunches – is my goddamn niece.

Rebekkah's eyes flare: you'll teach her bad language.

The little girl, Elizabeth, hides behind her mother's legs.

'You coming on out?' Pete grins. For some reason, he is on his hands and knees, like a dog. 'I've got a sweet for you.' He cranes his neck around. 'Megan, have we got any sweets?'

Megan shakes her head.

'We'll get you one,' Pete says. 'God damn Rebekkah, it's good to see you . . .'

Rebekkah swoops Elizabeth into her arms and invites them all through. As they go, she begins whispering to Pete out of the side of her mouth. Jon Heather hangs back. It is, he understands, exactly as if the fourteen years they have been parted mean nothing. The knowledge steels him, even if he has to fight back a horrible envy: if it can be this way for someone who has changed as much as Pete, it can be even better for him.

Rebekkah sets them down in an open living room, at the back of which a stove and counter top make up the entire kitchen. It is not like any living room Jon would have, too wide and light, as if the whole world might be able to peer in. There are family photographs on the wall, but they are not the perfectly poised ones his mother used to have taken, just snaps somebody has taken of Rebekkah, Elizabeth and a slight, balding man in the back of a ute. There is no hearth, nor an old chest full of books; no lovably ancient armchair or coat draped over the banister rail. It is, Jon Heather decides, hardly a home at all.

Rebekkah is pouring tea – not real tea; it smells of lemons – when suddenly she freezes. Jon is aware that something is wrong, but still he says nothing. Pete, too, is silent. At last, it is left to the little girl, wandering bewildered through these new faces, to venture over. She tugs at her mother's dress.

Slim and statuesque, Rebekkah turns around. She has not shed a tear, but it has been an epic ordeal to keep them in. 'How on earth did you find me, Peter Slade?'

'It was my old mate Cormac Tate. He's been looking out for me ever since I crash-landed here. You'd like him, Rebekkah.

Well, it was him figured it, in the end. We knew you was in Kununurra,' says Pete, 'but we . . . got a little waylaid . . .'

They spend the afternoon lost in conversations – and, though Jon Heather and Megan barely say a word, it is enough to watch it unfold, breathing in the things brother has never known about sister and sister has never known about brother. It is a joy, too, to watch Pete lovingly belittled in the same way he has always treated Jon, the way he once treated a boy named George. She calls him a big girl, needles him with the point of her finger, recalls every time he fell over and cried or banged his head and threw a tantrum. She could list, all day, the times he made a fool of himself, and Pete would drink it in.

In the early afternoon, Rebekkah's husband arrives home. His name is James. He is older than her, scrawny and balding, with a great hook for a nose that suggests some sort of buzzard. If there is any handsomeness in him, it is in his soft, ovoid eyes, blue as the western oceans Pete and Jon have coasted up and down. Wearied from his day's work at the construction site, he begins kicking his boots off in the porch. Elizabeth wriggles out of her mother's lap and hurtles over, screaming out for him.

James scoops Elizabeth up like a dirty pup, tosses her in the air to shrill cries of delight. On the third throw, he catches her and hangs her, like a bundle of kindling, under his shoulder. He looks up – and sees two strange men, scruffy and stinking to high heaven, staring at him.

Standing on the cusp of the kitchen, Rebekkah gives a tiny shrug, as if to say: there's something I have to tell you.

'It'll be you three's dog that's tearing up my yard, will it?' he grins.

At the dinner table, Pete tells Jon that they have been invited to stay. There isn't much room, he says, but Rebekkah and James won't take no for an answer: Elizabeth will sleep with her parents, and Pete will sleep in her crib. There's a spare room, filled with boxes, but if Megan and Jon don't mind bedrolls, they're welcome to it. Better than the yard, Pete winks – James says they found a crocodile just basking there the day after they started building the place.

'How long?' Jon whispers. Around him, the table is set with foods he has never eaten: strange white sausages and sweet potatoes, a huge fish, its eyeball turned hard.

Pete shrugs. 'A few days,' he reckons. 'James says there might even be work, up at his construction site. They've been damming the river . . .'

Before Jon can reply, James proposes a toast. Glasses are raised in honour of absent friends, and blood being thicker than water. Jon isn't sure he follows either sentiment, but he drinks all the same. On the opposite side of the table, Elizabeth holds a tumbler as tiny as a thimble, filled with the same drink.

Jon throws it back, splutters as it burns his throat. Looking at him reproachfully, Elizabeth sips hers daintily and smacks her lips.

'It must have gone down the wrong way,' mutters Jon, and turns to the big family fare he has never tasted before.

After dinner, James brings in a cask of some dark liquor he has been brewing, and he and Pete drink, to the determined fussing of Rebekkah. She is, James insists, only complaining because, since Elizabeth, one of them has to remain sober. There was a time – and on this account he is enormously proud – when Rebekkah could drink him under the table. In fact, it was this very thing, in a roadhouse motel at the Victoria River crossing, which first threw them together. There isn't many a man who would be proud that their wife might match him, drink for drink, and still be able to carry him home – but James is one of the gallant few, and Rebekkah one of the north's real Australian heroes.

At some ungodly hour, Megan, her eyes heavy, digs her elbow into Jon Heather's shoulder. 'Jon?'

'Yeah?'

'We should leave them, Jon.'

She is right, but he doesn't like that she's right. All the same, he nods.

Jon takes her hand and allows himself to be hauled upright. As always with these vicious home brews, his legs are drunker than the rest of his body. He reels against Megan, she reels against him – and, in that way, they manage not to collapse in a crumpled heap.

'Goodnight all,' Megan says, leading Jon by the hand. 'It's so good of you to let us stay.'

If they hear at all, they do not reply. As the family huddle together, Jon and Megan beat a stumbling retreat, half-falling and half-clambering their way up the stairs.

In a backroom, where boxes are piled haphazardly against the walls, two bedrolls have been laid out, side by side. As Megan kicks off her boots, Jon Heather plunges onto the first one. He sits where he lands, not spreadeagled, but curled in a crooked ball.

Through eyes heavy and tired, he watches Megan disrobe.

'Tomorrow, Jon,' she whispers, kissing him so that their lips only just brush, 'I have to do it. I have to call my father.'

She has timed her words well. Jon gives her that. He is suddenly kissing her back.

'Please,' he says, unbuttoning his shirt, 'not yet. I just need a little more time. Something has to happen. As soon as I'm working again.'

'He'll be out of his mind. I've never done this kind of thing before.'

Jon flops back, onto the bulge in the bedroll. Megan follows, as if to kiss him again. She has tried to contact her father before, only a day after they fled Broome, but her fingers were as useless as that day Pete tried to call his sister.

'What difference does it make, a few more days, a week, two . . .'

'You don't know how he worries. I'm his only daughter.'

A different look, something other than drunkenness, ghosts over Jon's face. Momentarily, Megan draws back.

'You're right,' Jon says. 'You *are* right.' Even so, suddenly Jon is pulling away from Megan, sitting up, scrabbling back into his shirt. He puts an arm around her, manoeuvres so that he is wrapped around her, instead of she around him. He whispers into her ear, 'You can't tell him, Megan. Tell him you're OK, but don't tell him where you are. Don't tell him who you're with.'

'He knows who I'm with.'

'He doesn't,' says Jon, lips brushing the back of her neck. 'He thinks he does but . . .'

A sudden thought hits him: you had a best friend once, Jon Heather, and that best friend, thinking you might leave him for good, had a terrible idea.

'You wouldn't tell him where we were, would you, Megan?'

Their legs are entwined, their bodies pressed together, but Megan pulls herself free, pushing away from Jon so hard that the bedrolls separate and a gulf of empty floorboards opens between them.

'What do you think of me, Jon? Would I have climbed into that ute if I was just going to turn you in?'

There is nothing like knowing you are wrong, when you have been right all of your life, to make you feel guilty. Jon reaches out.

'I'm sorry,' he says. 'Megan?'

After a second, she gives in, takes his hand. The bedrolls draw back together, like two ships colliding at sea.

'I just don't want them knowing where we're going.'

He feels Megan tense against him. She has stopped breathing. When she exhales, it is with a question that she must have had to steel herself to ask.

'Where *are* we going, Jon?'

'What do you mean?'

'Well,' she says, 'we were coming *here*. And now we're going *there*. But you haven't told me where *there* is.'

It is England, in the end. 'Wherever there's work, Megan.'

'There could have been work in Broome, if . . .'

Jon shushes her. He does not want to hear it. Not because of Cook, nor those girls, nor the thing he did that still makes his knuckles sore. There is, he has already decided, no earthly reason why bringing Megan along was better than staying with her in Broome, and working in the old hotel like she once offered. Back then, the thought had made him sick, that he might find himself staying for days and weeks and months in the Old Arabia, just because it was the easy, comfortable thing to do. Being with Megan now is all of those things and more. She changes things. She lights him up. She fills the long desert silences, when he and Pete can't bear to talk. When he wakes every morning and she is there, it makes him think a day is worth it, even if there isn't any work. This, he knows, is weakness: but it is glorious, beautiful weakness, sweeter than any victory he has yet to taste.

They lie in silence, on a reef of alcohol and exhaustion.

'Do you think she's like Peter,' Jon says. 'His sister?'

'I'll tell you what I think. It's the little girl – Elizabeth. She's more like Pete than that sister of his. The way she squirms and wriggles, always on the move. The way there's always a joke. She'll grow up just like him.'

'That,' says Jon, with an air of defeat, 'is exactly what I think.'

Jon hardly sleeps that night. He listens to the cheering downstairs. Then he listens to the crying. He is not happy but he is not sad.

On the second day, they ride into the sandstone hills, following a trail to look down on the fledgling town. Jon has never seen Dog so demented. Another yellow shape watches them from on high, and he sets up a bark that Jon has never heard before.

Strange whoops return from the crevices above. Elizabeth is proud to show Pete a campsite that they have used before. She tells the story as pedantically as Jon might one of his own: her daddy brings her out here to spot birds. She can name every last one of them that live in these miniature mountains, and Pete, she is certain, won't be able to name a single one.

In the afternoon, Rebekkah's husband has time off from the construction site, and takes Pete out onto the river, in a rowboat he has fitted with an outboard motor. Although Elizabeth begs to go, James insists she must stay behind, and a tantrum of epic proportions ensues. Jon watches her face turn scarlet in exactly the same way as Pete's; then, the way her silence descends like thick, impenetrable mist.

Though they cajole him to come along, Jon watches them leave from the veranda and plods back inside. It is time that Megan made her telephone call, and there isn't a chance he won't be around to overhear.

In the lounge room, Megan looks up from the rug, where Elizabeth has her dolls lined up, playing a parade.

'It's time,' says Jon.

'Are you sure?'

Jon nods.

'Thank you,' Megan mouths, and gets to her feet.

The little girl watches as Megan goes to Jon's side, squeezes his hand, and proceeds to the telephone that stands in an alcove. Dropping onto a stool at the telephone's side, she begins to dial. First, there will be an operator; then another, and another, as she is relayed through countless layers of exchange. Yet, even before she has reached the first operator, she has stalled.

'I can't do it,' she says.

Jon thinks: this is it. My chance. Say the right thing now, Jon Heather, and she need not speak to her father at all.

Even so, Jon puts his hand over hers. 'Do you want me to dial?'

Perhaps it is Jon's touch, or perhaps just the thought that, in the end, he really would help her – but Megan shakes her head and, with new strength, finishes the number.

'Yes,' she begins. 'I'd like to go to the Broome exchange.'

Jon stands and watches her until, feeling too awkward, he drifts away to listen in from the other side of the room. Making a show of playing with Elizabeth, he drops onto the rug where she has her dolls arranged, and picks the first one up.

Sometimes it is in the most unexpected moments that memories attack you: the touch of one of those dolls, and he is suddenly fifteen years and nine thousand miles away. He is a little boy, brought up by his sisters, playing with a dolls' house and wooden horse.

'Yes,' Megan says. 'The Old Arabia. It's a hotel. I have the number . . .'

Back in the present, Jon looks up to see Elizabeth pondering him curiously. Her eyes are aglow with deep suspicion; her new Uncle Pete she can stomach – but this Jon Heather is an unwelcome intruder.

'Do you want to play?' Jon asks.

She puts her arms out, draws the dolls close, and shakes her head. Then, thumb in mouth, she scrabbles to her feet, and out into the open kitchen. As Jon watches her go, Megan's voice comes back to him; her words have whirred along countless lines, through countless exchanges, and now at last she is speaking with her father.

'It's me,' she breathes. 'Dad, it's Megan.'

Jon strains to hear more, but she is suddenly speaking more quietly, as if ashamed of what she is saying, or else terrified to hear the reply.

'I tried, Dad. It wasn't about you. It was just something I . . .'

In the corner of his vision, Elizabeth reappears, staring at him accusingly. Clumsily, he teeters towards her. He is closer to Megan now, but she is not saying anything. The telephone receiver buzzes, as if her father is bawling into it from six hundred miles away.

Rebekkah appears, dressed in an apron splattered with food. The little girl stays close, but it is not as if she is seeking protection; it is as if she is the one who must protect her mother.

'I'm sorry,' says Jon, with an attempt at a lopsided smile. 'I didn't mean to scare her.'

'You mustn't worry,' says Rebekkah. 'We're not used to visitors out here.'

One ear still on Megan, Jon nods.

'I don't know. Soon, I hope. Dad – I wouldn't have left if I wasn't sure . . .' Her voice fades. 'You don't have to have planned it to be sure. Wasn't it like that when you fell in love with Mum?' Then she falls silent.

In the kitchen, a pot steams on the stove. Where the lid rattles, great reefs of flavour billow out, suffocating even the smell of wildflowers that comes in through the window.

Jon Heather breathes in the scent. The steam envelops him, forming condensation on his face and neck – and, just like holding that doll, he is suddenly in a different time and place.

'Are you OK, Jon?'

Elizabeth stands on tip-toes, trying to steal a look in the pot. 'It's my favourite,' she says. When she sees the way his face has crumpled, she gives him another scolding look. 'Don't you like mutton?'

Rebekkah seems to be looking directly into him. They might have shared a whole conversation, and yet no words have been spoken.

'You still make this?' he asks.

Rebekkah lifts the lid to stir the pot and flavours erupt. 'I suppose . . .' She pauses. 'I got good at making it. I've adapted it since then. We have herbs and . . . It's kind of our Sunday roast. You might even like it.'

Jon does not say as much, but he knows he will go hungry

tonight. All it would take is a single spoonful of this muck and he would be a little boy again, shovelling it into his face just so he doesn't feel the cramps at night.

'There was a girl at the Mission, a year or two older than me. She got good at making it too. You could tell when it had been her in the kitchens.'

'Chop into fist-sized pieces and throw in a pot. That's about as much as they ever taught us.' She is trying to laugh, but reining it in each time she suspects Jon will not join in. 'How long were you there, Jon?'

Jon shrugs, as if he cannot remember every blasted second. 'I was ten.'

'I was only there two years,' Rebekkah begins, almost as if tendering an apology. 'Some of us my age, they sent straight off to keep house. On board ship, I thought I was going to a place in Perth. But I suppose things changed.' She has not once looked at Jon; she stirs the pot instead. 'They wanted me to stay. One of us went down to New South Wales to be a cottage mother. But me, well, I wanted something different . . .'

'Home,' breathes Jon.

This time, Rebekkah looks right into him. Jon thinks it is as if a seal has been broken. Then, her face creases, confused. She shakes her head. 'I remember the boys used to talk about it a lot. They were going to be like pirates – steal a galleon to get them home and plunder for treasure along the way.'

Jon thinks it a fine idea, can almost imagine himself hoisting the black flag as he retreads the route of the HMS *Othello* – but he hears Rebekkah laughing.

'We didn't talk the same way,' she goes on. 'I suppose you could say – it wasn't home we wanted, it was just *a* home.' She bends low to give a spoonful of the simmering stew to her daughter.

'You got yours, in the end,' says Jon, looking around.

Rebekkah nods.

'Peter . . .' She checks herself, shakes her head. 'I'm sorry – *Pete* says you had sisters back in Leeds.'

'Two of them,' Jon utters through tight lips. He will not forgive her for using the past tense. 'Twins.'

'Maybe it would have been different, if we'd have had those things.' She puts the lid back on the pot, granting Jon momentary respite from the terrible smell. 'I suppose Pete must have told you about our mother . . . but, when there's nothing to go back to, you don't really think about it. I've got everything I ever wanted here. I suppose that's why Pete's got his eye on that smallholding with your friend Mr Tate . . .'

Rebekkah quietens. She sees the look on Jon Heather's face. 'What is it, Jon?'

He breathes deep. There is mutton stew in his nostrils. The little girl is on her tip-toes, eager for more. She wouldn't be eager for that filth if she knew where it came from. Somebody should tell her. Somebody should make her take her medicine.

'What holding?' he demands.

Rebekkah lets go of the spoon. It clatters to the floor and, as if a much bigger thing has crashed down, Elizabeth starts. At first, she wants to run from the kitchen – but the big bad ogre, Jon Heather, is standing in the way.

'Jon,' Rebekkah begins, her freckled face turning red, 'I thought you knew. I didn't . . .'

Jon steps forward, deeper into the mist of mutton and steam. 'You didn't answer my question. What holding, Rebekkah?'

'The one he's looking at with your friend Cormac.'

From the other room, Jon hears the telephone slamming down. A stool is pushed back, there are footsteps, and then – through racks of pots and pans – Jon sees Megan crossing the lounge.

'And you?' he says, whipping around as soon as she approaches. 'You knew this too?'

Jon hardly sees that she has been crying.

'Jon, what happened?'

He cannot bear her to touch him, but he does not want to step back, lest he has to touch Rebekkah and Elizabeth too. Shaking Megan free, he pushes past, finally breathing air that is not thick with mutton and herbs.

Megan's eyes dart between Rebekkah and Jon.

'I didn't know,' Rebekkah breathes. Behind her Elizabeth sets up a squall.

'Tell her to shut up,' says Jon.

Megan snatches at his wrist. 'Jon!'

'I can't listen to spoilt little girls crying. Not when they've got nothing to cry about. When they took to us with hockey sticks, *we* weren't allowed to cry. You remember that, Rebekkah?'

The question hardens something in Rebekkah. She is not sorry anymore. 'I want you to leave my house.'

Jon tramps across the living room, making for the door. On the threshold, he hears the crash of footsteps behind him, but still he ploughs on out, over the road, to where the ute is waiting, deep in the grass.

'Jon!'

Jon swings into the driver's seat, scrabbles for the keys under the dash. He has not yet kicked the engine to life when Megan forces open the passenger door. He claws out so that she cannot climb in.

'Jon, you've got to believe me. I didn't know . . .'

In spite of himself, he really does believe her. 'You'd like to see me there, though, wouldn't you? Getting up every morning to feed a coop full of chooks. Collecting eggs. Shearing sheep.' The engine comes alive. He drops his head against the wheel. 'You'd like that, wouldn't you? The two of us living on Peter Slade's station. Some little cottage at the edge of the grounds. Taking the ute up into town on a Saturday night. Baking in the sun on a Sunday afternoon. Day trips to the coast and visits with Cormac Tate and . . .'

His voice has mellowed.

'Jon,' she says. 'I hadn't thought of it. I hadn't thought much further ahead than tomorrow . . .'

He lifts his head. 'It's me, isn't it? *I* want it. I keep thinking about it, Megan. Ever since Broome. Since Cable Beach and . . .' She knows what he means: the time they first kissed. 'You put it in my head, Megan. You didn't mean to, but you put it in my head, and now I can't get it out.'

Jon reaches to close the passenger door.

'Where are you going?'

'I can't believe he'd give up on me. I can't believe he'd give up on himself.'

She whips open the passenger door, flings herself into the cab. When she has slammed the door back shut, her eyes pierce Jon's. 'Don't run away, Jon Heather.'

It is an instruction. Jon kills the engine. 'I thought I was strong enough to do this, Megan, take you with me, be with you for just a little while . . .'

He leaps out of the cab and rushes around the back while Megan is still trapped inside. Out of the flatbed, he heaves his suitcase of books.

'And that's it?' Megan demands, tumbling out to follow him. 'Damn it, Jon, but you can't just run away. You're not a little boy. It was *you* who asked me to get in that truck. *You* who kissed me . . .'

Some way along the grass bank, Jon stops and turns around. 'I'm a whisker away from it, Megan. I feel like a breeze could push me over. One wrong foot, now, and I'll never see my mother and sisters again.' He does not mean it to, but his voice rises in a crescendo, like a boy in the throes of becoming a man. 'Don't you get it? If I gave in, like Peter and Cormac Tate, it would all be your fault. You – for keeping me here. How could I ever love somebody like that?'

She approaches slowly, tries to take his hand.

He thinks, if I say it, I can't take it back – and, God help me, but I'll have to take it back.

'I love you, Megan. I do.' It is the first time he has said it, but it seems more like a terrible confession than a wild, unbidden declaration. 'But if I do love you, well, love can go to hell . . .' He looks up, into her eyes. 'Love,' he says, 'just isn't what I want.'

When Pete walks through the door, he knows from Rebekkah's face that something is wrong. Night is beginning to fall, one of those pale northern darknesses, and he has three huge river trout strung over his shoulder.

'Pete,' Megan says, rising from the settee. 'It's Jon Heather.'

'What happened? Is he OK?'

The look on Rebekkah's face changes. 'I didn't mean to, Pete. I thought he knew. I thought you were taking him with you.'

Pete traps one foot in the closing door. 'Where did he go?'

'Anywhere,' Rebekkah interjects. 'Anywhere but here . . .'

He listens to her story, Elizabeth sitting with a look of quelled panic at her feet. Then, he shoulders back past James, dumping the fish as he goes.

'How will you know which way he went?' Megan calls.

'Only two ways to go on a road like this,' Pete says. 'Forward and back. I know where my money is, don't you?'

He reaches the ute at a run, twists the ignition. When he pushes onto the highway, he sees Dog, harrying more birds at the edge of the marsh. If he is not careful, a crocodile will leap out and end an ignoble career. He slows down, tells the bedraggled mutt to jump up back, but Dog is more interested in trying to taste these new birds than he is in a ride. He presses his foot to the floor, and the ute takes off.

The night is deepening, shadows spreading until they hide completely the hollows and crags through which Pete drives. He has gone scant miles when he sees a figure loping into the darkness, a single suitcase at his side.

Leaving the ute upended on a tall red bank, he scrambles out. 'Jon Heather!' he barks. 'Jon Heather, you better turn round! I'm not about to hit a man who isn't looking me in the eye . . .'

This is not the greatest incentive for a man to turn around, but Jon does it all the same. Pete bears down upon him like a rampaging bull. At last, only a few feet away, he rises to his tip-toes, struggling not to launch forward.

'You're yelling at my sister, Jon Heather? With that little girl in there, wondering what in hell's going on? What this damn stranger's doing in her house, just hollering hell at her mummy?'

'You're just as much a stranger to that little girl, Peter . . .'

'She's my goddamn niece, and she doesn't need *you* yelling like that.'

'Well?' Jon Heather says. 'Is it true?'

'Her daddy's about ready to come out here and teach you a lesson. Megan's had to calm him down.' Pete rocks back, like he might throw a punch. Instead, he hurls his hands up, runs them through his hair. 'Jon, you can't just walk into my sister's house and . . .'

'We all know it, Peter. She's your sister. Well done.'

'I don't even know you anymore, Jon Heather. I mean – what's going on in there? It's like that brain of yours is just rocketing around your skull. You don't got no control.'

Control is all he has ever had, ever since he was a boy. Rule one: if you're angry at them, don't let them know that you're angry. But – Pete is right. It wasn't just Mr Cook. It wasn't just Rebekkah. He feels coiled, like a spring he's been crushing down for ten years – only now the spring is fighting back; it's been coiled too long.

'What is all this, Peter? You and Cormac Tate, sloping about some smallholding . . . behind my back?'

Pete's shoulders slouch. At last, the fight drains from him. 'There wasn't supposed to be any secret in it. Cormac heard about it the last time he saw Booty. It was just some old man, selling off his little plot before he's run out of time to go see his grandkids . . . A few fields, some wheat, probably some chooks . . .'

'And you bought it.'

'I didn't buy a thing!'

'Cormac Tate bought it for you. Told you to ditch me and shack up with . . .'

'It wasn't like that,' Pete admits, his voice wearying. 'Cormac's been hammering on about it for months, a year even. He's there right now, but I'd have followed you to the end, Jon – I'd have followed you all the way to England, if it hadn't have been for . . .'

Jon does not need him to complete that sentence. If it hadn't been for coming here. If it hadn't been for seeing what my sister's got, what I might have one day: the only thing that matters in the whole of this world.

'Peter, please. You've got to listen to me. Don't let them turn you. Own a farm? That's exactly what the Children's Crusade wanted for us! They've got you, and you weren't even in the Mission . . .'

'It isn't about winning and losing, Jon. If the Children's Crusade want me in Australia, and I want to be in Australia too, it doesn't have to mean they won. You can't let your whole life be about the Children's Crusade.'

'If you go to that holding, Peter, it's *you* who's letting your whole life be about what those bastards did.'

'Jon, I can't leave. I could never leave . . .' Pete's voice quavers. Not since he was eight years old has he told anybody he loved them, but the thought comes to his lips now. 'I've been thinking about it so long, Jon, but I can't leave Cormac Tate. Damn it, Jon. I thought I could, but I just can't.'

'Cormac would be all right. He'd have his station. He'd have his daughters . . .'

'Jon, for shit's sake.' Pete looks away. 'It isn't about if Cormac Tate would be all right. It's me, Jon. It's like I couldn't carry on, the same as I am, not without him. It would eat me up inside, not to see him again.' He hesitates. 'I can't remember what my dad was like, Jon, but . . .'

A shape moves on a sandstone ridge high above them, and they fix on it, in case they are its prey.

'Your mind's made up, isn't it?'

Pete's head snaps suddenly, so that he faces Jon. 'But I want you to come.'

'Oh, Peter . . .'

The silence returns. This time, there is nothing to puncture it.

'There's this thing Cormac Tate used to say to me, when we were out on the road. He'd say – there comes a time when you have to make a choice. And it's your choice to make, Jon Heather. There isn't any Children's Crusade telling you what to think. But . . .' He offers a canteen of water to Jon; when Jon does not want it, he takes a long draught. '. . . either you'll settle down for the long haul loneliness, or you'll start to chip away, make a fist of what you've got. That's all George was doing, in the end. I hated him for it, same as you hated him for it – but that's all he was doing. That's even how it was for Judah Reed, once upon a time. You get older, and it doesn't have to be perfect anymore.'

He's wrong, Jon thinks. It isn't just one choice. It's a hundred different choices, tiny choices, things you don't even notice, like Pete starts saying 'fair dinkum'; like George starts singing bush songs with a man in black.

'I'm tired of it, Jon.' His voice trembles, as if contemplating something too terrible to acknowledge. 'I don't want to end up like Cormac Tate. He held out so long. He lost his wife, lost his daughters . . . All because it still burned somewhere, deep inside him, this idea he wasn't where he was meant to be . . .'

'I don't see it's such a bad thing, a little loneliness. Not if it means never giving up hope. People live with a crooked leg, a crippled back. It's all just a little bit of pain.'

'Loneliness isn't like a crooked leg. It gets worse, Jon.' He stops. 'But what you're thinking of is a great loneliness – one that makes you bigger, better than the rest of us. Better than me and George . . .'

'I'd be lonely forever,' Jon says, 'if it means not giving in.'

Pete hesitates. He doesn't want to say it, but he feels like a man unhanded by a superior swordsmen, fumbling for whatever weapon he can find. 'What about Megan? What about her, Jon Heather?'

'What about her?'

'You could have something with . . .'

'Don't talk about her like that, Peter. I know what it is.'

'I haven't seen you like it, ever since I've known you. That day we left Broome, when you told her to get in the truck. You said it was like . . .'

Jon remembers. 'Snow on the Nullarbor,' he says, voice breaking into a laugh.

'Like a miracle,' Pete says. 'You, Jon Heather, English even after more than half your life . . . Jon Heather, who doesn't make friends and doesn't think about anything but going home – asking her to come along, even though you knew what it could mean.'

'I never acted like that before.'

'You did some fucked-up things that day.'

'Peter, I've got to tell you something. Something I did in 1958. That time I just disappeared . . .'

'It doesn't matter,' says Pete. 'Wherever you went, why ever you had to go, I don't care.'

Whatever it is he was about to say, Jon swallows it back down. He extends his hand, holds it out until Pete is ready to shake it.

'Don't do this, Jon.'

'You'll look after Dog?'

'He's going to have a hell of a time, chasing chickens, rounding up sheep.'

'He doesn't have it in him to round up any sheep.'

Neither one of them has broken the handshake, but slowly their fingers untwine.

'Peter . . .' Jon can hardly force out the words. 'Peter, I'm glad you found your sister. You deserved that.'

Pete whispers, 'I don't want to do this without you, Jon. I don't want to grow old not knowing where you are, what happened to my old mate . . .'

Even so, Jon breaks away, wanders a few paces.

'Where will you go?'

Jon turns around. The night is growing thick around them, blinding Pete so that he can hardly see more than a few feet. Jon Heather, it seems, is already gone. 'Wherever the work is,' he says. 'Peter . . . *Pete* . . . Thank you . . . For when I was little and, well, for everything after.' He turns onto the road. 'I had a hell of a time, Peter. I'd love it down there with you and Cormac Tate. With Megan. But that – that's why I got to go.'

One footstep, and then another: that is how you cross the world. He throws his arm up in goodbye and, gulping on air to hold in the tears, he leaves his friend forever.

*

The sea rolls and the ship rolls, and though George too rolls, his stomach seems to stay still. He has retched everything out of his body; probably, he would heave his heart out, but he feels as if he's done that already.

He is aware of another sudden rolling, and the door of his cabin swings open. Boys are filing past. They seem to be pushing each other, clattering against the walls, but it is only the way the ship casts them. One after another, they make their way to the deck.

George stands up. He has no clean shirts, so he finds the one least dirtied and straightens it out. By the time he reaches the deck and the dining halls, the sea seems to have stilled. They must be in the eye of something, but George doesn't care; he is glad of any respite.

Judah Reed stands at the door of the main hall, watching the boys scurry through. He acknowledges each of them by name. It is a trick he has been trying to impress on George, and now George knows why: when the childsnatcher calls you by name, you never see home again. He begins to walk that way, but a voice calls after him.

Charlie breaks off from the procession and gallops over. 'Mr Stone!'

At the door, Judah Reed's eyes flash up.

George puts his arm on Charlie's shoulder, angles him so that Judah Reed cannot see his face. 'What is it, Charlie?' He feels suddenly sick again. Please, he thinks, don't let me retch on the boy.

'I remembered something else,' he whispers.

George nods. 'And what did you do?'

Charlie cups his hand to his mouth. 'I wrote it in the note-book, just like you told me, just like everything else. But I don't think I spelled everything right.'

It is a game they have been playing, one much more important than marbles or stones. The rules are simple: everything you remember, you write it down. That way, you'll remember it still in two, three, four years' time. If you remember the name of your neighbours, you write it down. If you remember the birthday of your brother, you write it down. If you remember there was a slate missing from a house three houses along the terrace, you write it down and make yourself a drawing. In the end, you'll have a treasure map of your life. X marks the spot where, one day, you'll find the golden trove – your old existence.

'What did you remember?' George asks.

'My neighbour's dog. It was called Maisie . . . but it was a boy dog.'

'That's a girlie name for a boy dog.'

Charlie sniggers. 'That's what I always say.'

They walk into dinner together, George nodding an amiable hello at Judah Reed. Though they must sit at different tables, Charlie catches his eye twice during the meal. He sits among other boys his age. Once, he even laughs. If the boy has friends, thinks George, it must surely be a good thing – but something in the thought makes him sick to his stomach.

The sea is still, but he excuses himself to go and retch into the ocean.

At night, he walks on deck. They are still somewhere south of Colombo, weeks into their voyage but with weeks yet to come, and the air does him good. He props himself at the balustrade, as dead centre as he can find, and lets the spray whip his face. He was petrified of sea spray when he first made this voyage; sometimes, it takes his breath away, but now he knows not to be frightened. You are an adult, he tells himself, and you can choose when to be frightened and when not.

George feels a sudden stirring in his gut – but, when he goes to retch, nothing will come. He stands up again, sees Judah Reed at the rails only twenty yards further towards the prow. He is gazing into the east, as if he can already spy Australia. The stars above them have changed; they must be nearer Australia than home.

A thought strikes him. All he would have to do is creep twenty yards to the prow, make one motion, and Judah Reed would topple into the black water below. You would have to be decisive about it, he tells himself. If you faltered for even a second, he would know what you were doing and fight you off. You are still a fat weakling in body, George, but you are made of sterner stuff in the head. Go on, he wills himself, march over and do it! Judah Reed would be twenty leagues under the sea by the time anybody noticed.

He slopes back from the railings – but, by the time he has advanced ten yards, murder now a delicious thought, he feels his stomach convulse again. This time, he does not reach the balustrade before he throws up. Yellow bile dribbles down his chin.

Roused by the noise, Judah Reed approaches. He brings a handkerchief from a pocket and begins to dab at the mess on George's face.

'George,' he says. 'You should take to your bed. You haven't been right, ever since England.'

George nods. For once, Judah Reed speaks the truth. He hasn't been right in more than ten years.

He wakes in his cabin to a cold sweat and eyes boring into him. Judah Reed sits by the edge of his bed, as if he might have been there for endless hours.

'George,' he says. 'How are you feeling?'

'Better,' he begins. 'How long have I . . .'

'We need to talk, George.'

George sits up, catching his reflection in a mirror on his cabin door. It is difficult for a man with as round a face as George to look gaunt, but that is how he looks. His skin has acquired a curious complexion: white as a wraith, yet still burnt by sun.

'I spent some time with the boys this morning. We had a lesson in history.'

George knows not to interrupt. He busies himself tidying his shirt in the mirror.

'I happened to hear Charlie, talking to his friends. He was telling them how, one day, he is going to go home and see his mother.'

George freezes. When he looks up, Judah Reed's reflection hovers above his own. In the glass, their eyes meet.

'He must be . . . confused,' he begins. 'Denying it's true.' He turns; he cannot contemplate seeing Judah Reed behind him any further. 'It's a fantasy. But we all have our fantasies, don't we? I remember . . .' He does not need to lie now. 'I used to play a game where my mother was coming to pick me up from the Mission. And she died before we even left England, didn't she?' He pauses, cannot tell whether he has won Judah Reed over or not. 'It's just taking some time. He has to get used to the idea.'

For a second there is silence. Then Judah Reed produces from a pocket a little notebook. It is a scrappy thing, the sort a boy might buy with salvaged pennies from a corner shop. On the front, it says: 'Memo'. There is space for a little pencil to be slipped into the spine. 'This sort of thing won't help him adjust though, will it?'

He casts it, derisively, onto George's bed. George doesn't have to open the cover to know what is inside. Here is every memory Charlie has of his home, written in childish script: his old address, his mother's name, the name of a boy who picked on him and then was his friend and then picked on him again. On the reverse of the inside cover is a drawing he has made from memory: Charlie and his mother up on the heights of Woodhouse Moor. It is the same as the photograph Judah Reed has filed away, never to be seen again.

George keeps a blank look. His mind races. Has Charlie told Judah Reed who instructed him to keep this notebook? His mind reels even further back, and he understands: yes, Charlie betrayed everything I said to him. He is a little boy and he is frightened and he would have seen a way out, back into the affections of the monster who is making him.

'He's afraid,' says George. 'He's alone. His mother's dead and, in his heart, he knows it. I'm sure he does.' He takes the memo book and rips it in half. Then, he rips it into quarters and eighths, sprinkling the floor with confetti. 'I thought it would help,' he says. 'I got comfort from it, when I was a kid. Making up stories about Mum and Dad. But . . .' And here he must steel himself, for if you are going to walk into the monster's lair, you must make certain that he thinks you, too, are growing a thick hide and scales. '. . . you've helped boys for longer than I've been alive. If you think he has to . . .' He makes as if he is fumbling for the phrase, but in truth he can barely bring himself to utter it. '. . . take his medicine . . . then, I understand. I'm sorry.'

Judah Reed gathers together a fist of the confetti and nods.

'I know it's hard, George. But . . . these boys need Australia, quite as much as Australia needs them.'

Only after Judah Reed has gone does George allow himself to breathe out. He wants to plunge back onto the bed, but he refuses to let himself.

This is not over. To give up over a little thing like this would be a bigger failure than ratting on your best friend. He pictures Judah Reed, the relieved look that came over him when George performed his genuflection, and thinks: you had me when I was little, but you don't have me now.

I can't murder you. I can't fight or stand up to you. I'm not Jon Heather. I'm not the wild boy Luca. But I don't have to be like them. I can do it my own way, quietly and studiously, so that nobody even sees. I'll have my hour. Just wait and see. You won't see it coming. You won't guess it's me – because you think I'm something I'm not. You don't even know my name.

He reaches under his pillow and takes out another little notebook, identical to the last. In these pages, he has copied down everything Charlie ever told him – just in case. He takes a pencil and writes a new note: my neighbour's dog was called Maisie, even though he was a boy.

Oh yes, Judah Reed, you can steal memories and families

and loves from little boys, but you can never touch a man who knows who he is.

And I'm George Stone.

He writes it down, big bold letters, lines scored on top of each other until the paper tears.

I'm George Stone. My name is George Stone.

*

That night, when Pete returns to his sister's home, he walks like an old man. It hurts to take each step. Defeated, he lingers on the veranda, looking back the way he has come. Dog, knowing something is wrong, twists between his legs, desperate to be petted. When Pete obliges, he rolls over, exposing a belly matted with red earth and shit. Pete does not mind; he pats him all the same.

Though it is late, the lights are still on in the house. In the lounge room, Megan sits alone.

They stare at each other. Pete can only shake his head.

'Did he even mention me?'

'He mentioned you.'

Megan sees the webbed patterns that tears have stained all down his cheeks. She goes over to him, but he is as intractable as Jon Heather; he will not be consoled.

'I tried,' he says.

He turns onto the staircase, every step a new torture.

'What now?' asks Megan.

'Now?' whispers Pete, lumbering away. 'Now everybody just lives their lives.'

Alone, Megan listens to Pete prowling in the bedroom above. She goes to the door, opens it a crack and looks out into the different textures of night. It is as far as she has ever been from home, the Old Arabia, the empty halls and stale rooms and occasional guests. She came this far for Jon Heather. He would tell her: you did not come so very far at all, not nearly so far as the rest of us. But he would be wrong. In her own way, she too has crossed the world. That she came at all was for Jon; that she is left here, now, in the company of strangers, well, that's for Jon too. It has been about him from the moment they met: what *he* wanted, when *he* wanted it, how much of every little thing *he* can stand. She wonders: why does she even care? She ought to hate him now. If she was seeing straight, she would find a way of getting back to Broome and slide back into her old life, forget she ever crossed paths with that boy who pretends he comes from nowhere at all.

She drifts outside. Behind her, the door falls shut.

He cannot have gone far.

She starts walking. Pete was right. There is only one road Jon Heather would take: the road deeper in, the road further north. At first it is familiar, because it is the very same road they took in the morning, when they went out into the sandstone hills. There are stars to light the way, but the road between the crags leaves only a ribbon of stars shining down. In fits and starts she runs, then walks, then runs again. Jon Heather is hours ahead of her; if road trains have passed this way and taken pity on him, he might yet be so far away she will never catch up.

She has been walking, running, walking for more than an hour when she hears a dull vibration, some truck coming out of Kununurra. It is five minutes before the headlights appear. Throwing herself onto the bank at the side of the road, she begins to wave her arms, like a drunken man making semaphore. When she thinks it is too late, blinded by the headlamps, the truck slews to a stop and a voice barks out.

'It's late to be out alone . . .'

'I don't need to go far,' she says, hoping it is true.

'You want to get in?'

Her eyes, now accustomed to the light, can see into the cab, piled high with newspapers and cans.

'I'll hop up back.'

The man seems to be disgruntled, but all the same he waits until Megan has clambered onto his flatbed before he takes off again.

As dark shapes thunder past, she sinks into herself and, for the first time, holds herself tight: there is, she knows, no going back. It is exactly the way Jon Heather lives his life.

And there it is – the thing she has been looking for, the dull outline of a man sloping along the road, pressed to a rockface high up on the bank.

Megan reaches round, hammers at the glass separating her from the cab. 'Stop!'

A hundred yards on, the driver understands. When Megan leaps from the flatbed, he calls out to her, but she is already running. The cab sits there for a time; then the driver climbs back into his cab, the headlamps illuminate the sandstone, and off he goes.

Megan flails, her feet finding scant purchase on the stone. As she flies, mosquitoes smear her face. She squints, sees the dim outline on the road ahead. He has stopped moving. He knows what is coming.

Twenty yards from where he stands, Megan stops. A stitch burns in her side. 'I thought I could let you go,' she says. 'If it's really what you want, I will. I'll find a way back to Broome. I won't breathe a word of what happened here. But Jon, I have to know what happens to you . . .'

Jon Heather drops his suitcase, his swag. 'Megan . . .'

'Don't, Jon. Don't fill me with your stories. I don't care. I don't care about who you are or where you're from or . . . I only care about where you're going.'

'England,' he whispers, a petition, a prayer.

Jon comes to her, in fits and starts, just the same way as she was running. Megan, still taming her breath, stands still – until, at last, his arms are around her. Then, he is kissing her face.

'I want you to say it to me. I want you to tell me to go, to disappear. Say it, and I'll never see you again.'

Even in the black of night, he can see the greenness of her eyes. Imperceptibly, Jon gives a shake of his head.

Slowly, Megan releases her grip. Though she is still holding his face, now she is stroking him, drawing a finger along the line of his jaw.

'It's useless anyway,' says Jon Heather. 'Peter was right. I'm as far away as ever I was. Just about all of the money I saved, I poured into that ute.'

'All for the sake of that little girl . . .'

Uncertain, Jon tenses. 'I wouldn't take it back,' he utters.

'I know,' Megan says, breath escaping in a ridiculous laugh. 'You wouldn't give anything up, would you, Jon? Except, perhaps, for me . . .'

He wants to tell her that isn't fair, but this girl can see through it every time he tells a lie.

'It doesn't mean I don't want it. It never meant that. It's only . . . What do you do if you want two opposite things?'

Megan looks down. Jon Heather's suitcase has opened where he dropped it at his feet. The books are haphazardly piled within; between them, a single roll of banknotes, barely enough to find a bed for the night.

'You make it so you can take both.'

Jon lifts his eyes.

'How much,' she says, 'would you need?'

'It took us years to get that stake. That's with Pete eating away at it, of course. Out there, it was always two steps forward, one step back. I think . . . A year, and I could do it, Megan. If the work was right.'

Gently, she lifts each book and slides it back into place. *Strangers at Snowfell* and *Seven White Gates* and *The Sign of the Alpine Rose.* After she is done, she lifts the roll of banknotes and tosses it in her palm.

'What if there was a way you could go tomorrow?' she breathes.

'We weren't that close, even before we came to Broome.'

'What if I said I could get you . . . could get *us* a stake? Enough for a passage to England.' She hesitates. 'For both of us, Jon.'

Somewhere above, a bird breaks, in a frenzied cacophony, from where it has been roosting, hurtling, unseeing, into the dark.

'Do you remember what I showed you, back in Broome? The things my mother left for me. Her necklaces. Her wedding ring. My grandmother's pearls . . .'

'Megan . . .'

'It would be enough, Jon. It wouldn't be luxury, but if I pawned them, it would get us there.'

It would, Jon Heather decides, be the bitterest kind of trade: Megan's mother, in exchange for his own.

'I can't . . .'

'Can't, or won't?'

Jon Heather steps back. 'I can't ask it.'

'You didn't ask. I gave. But . . .' She takes hold of him. 'If you want this, if you really want it, more than anything else, more than never having come here, more than never having seen the Children's Crusade or the Mission or met Pete and George and Cormac Tate, more than that filthy dingo you cart around . . . If that's what you want, you have to promise me.' She kisses him. All else is gone; he kisses her back. 'Promise me you'll never leave me again, Jon Heather. Wherever you go, wherever you end up, England or Australia or anywhere in between . . . Don't you ever walk out on me again.'

XVI

When you are hitchhiking, Jon Heather discovers, it is better to be a pretty girl than it is to be an unkempt down-and-out with no boots on his feet.

They have a ruse and it hasn't failed yet: Megan stands at the edge of the road, a hopeful smile on her face, while Jon Heather hides himself and his swag in the scrub above the road. Only when a truck has stopped and Megan has engaged the driver in some banter, tempting him with the promise of more to come, does Jon emerge to climb, without waiting for permission, into the cab. In this way, they have covered five hundred miles.

Tonight, even though the truck would plunge them straight into the heart of Broome, they ask the driver to leave them on the side of the road. Megan, who has been sitting in the cab, dances a hand on his shoulder as she says goodbye. Probably that is payment enough. Meanwhile, Jon Heather crashes out of the flatbed, only just managing to snatch his suitcase and swag before the wagon lumbers away.

This year the Wet has lasted too long. Though it should be fading, the sky is still swollen, and Jon knows it will not be long before it returns. Being cold and wet is nothing to Jon Heather, but he would rather not see Megan sitting out in it.

'How far do you reckon?'

She ought to know this road better than him, but she is uncertain. Broome might be a mile away and there would still be no sign. This terrain can swallow towns whole.

'We should find you a place to camp, Jon. Somewhere warm.'

That will not be so difficult.

'Somewhere dry,' she adds.

Jon shakes his head. 'Let's settle for somewhere I won't drown.'

The road here is banked by steep rises of rock. The scrub that clings to them is verdant, the trees in full leaf. Somewhere off the road, Jon finds a depression in the land and sets his suitcase down.

'How will I know where to find you?'

Jon scrabbles in coarse grass, and picks up a piece of crumbling red stone.

'X marks the spot,' he says. 'I'll mark it on the road.'

She plants an ungainly kiss on his cheek.

'It's going to be all right.'

Rather than risk taking Jon Heather into town, he will remain here, while Megan returns to the Old Arabia to rescue her tea chest. If she is lucky, she might be in and out in only a few hours. After that – England awaits. They will hitch a ride south, find a pawnbroker in Perth and head for the docks.

Jon is not true to his word. Something inside him, the same thing that made him give George his birthday, wants to know that she is safe. So, as Megan drops back to the road to wait for a ride, he finds a vantage point and watches.

The roads are empty. When trucks pass at all, they come out of Broome, heading out on runs to Katherine and Darwin beyond. One slows, winds its window down, seems to be asking Megan endless questions, and then stutters off again. Megan finds a rock to prop herself against and, patiently, she waits.

Pete used to tell Jon that they had to be patient, that things would come good in the end. Patience, Cormac Tate would decree, is a virtue. How wrong those two were. Patience is what caught them out in the end. It turned them into Australians, much more so than any Mission or Children's Crusade. Keeping watch from his nest up in the scrub, Jon Heather knows now that the only real virtues are impatience, restlessness and resentment.

A truck appears on the horizon. From where he is perched, Jon sees it long before Megan. A plume of red dust is coming this way. He thinks about calling out for her, but it will not change anything, so he settles in to watch.

Once she is gone, there is nothing to do but wait.

He settles down for the long haul. He takes a book from his suitcase and tries to get lost in its pages, but it is not the same; his eyes can hardly follow the lines. He tries another book, but it happens just the same. Intermittently, another truck passes on the road below, utility trucks on their way to some station; once, a police ute patrols up the highway, and then back into Broome. The sun rises and the sun sinks.

She should have been back.

Before night, the rain starts to fall. It is thin at first, a mizzen mist, but steadily grows worse. Jon Heather sinks into the depression in the rock. Here, at least, there is some shelter.

Headlamps illuminate the road below. Down there, a ute has stopped. He gets to his haunches, pushes forward into the rain and peers down. A figure has emerged from the truck and is peering into the scrub, but it is certainly not Megan. He watches, carefully, until the man climbs back into the ute and drives away. Sometime later, Jon cannot say how long, the same ute retreads its path, disappearing back into Broome.

He has an ache in his belly, so he fills it with the biscuits he has left in his swag. He collects rainwater in a tin cup and drinks it. Snatches of sleep, and still she does not come. He tells himself: she said that she loves you – but that does not help. He tells himself: she has nothing to gain by ratting you out; this, at least, brings him a little comfort.

All the same, when she has not arrived in the dead of night, he drops out of the scrub, and begins to follow the road.

It is not, in the end, such a very long way into Broome. The highway plunges into the heart of town, and he feels a peculiar rush of warmth. Too late, he realizes that this is how it must feel to come home. The town is achingly familiar. Rain patters on roofs of corrugated tin, seabirds shriek in the bay; the night is close and hot as hell.

In these rain-swept streets not a soul is abroad. He limps on, in a dream, following the line of the mud flats, and sees the big boab tree outside the old lock-up. He means to walk past, but curiosity is a terrible thing. There are no lights inside the lock-up tonight, nor the cries of any captured children. He wonders: might this be the perfect place to sit out the storm?

Somebody has evidently had the same idea, for there is sudden movement in the darkness. A man's eyes glimmer at him, hunched under a raincoat. He is propped against the corner of the lock-up, where scrub has been left to grow wild.

'There's room for two. You don't have to go.'

The man is genuine, lonely. Still, he turns around. There has to be a better place to spend the night.

He finds his way along the ocean road, to the dirt oval. There are few lights on in the Old Arabia hotel, but there are eaves out back where he might find shelter. He walks to the veranda, climbs the stairs, tries the handle. Under his fist, it turns. Even so, he knows he cannot go in. There are no guarantees that Megan is even behind that door. If he came across some night porter, he might not be a free man for long. Knowing that, though, does not stop him from *wanting* to go through. It would be warm in there. Dry as well. It would smell of varnish and old paint. He could slope up to the room he shared with Pete, meet Megan for dinner, help around the old hotel . . .

A gust of hot wind pushes a curtain of rain quickly into his face, making him gulp for air. It came, he knows, at just the right moment; another, and he might have convinced himself to go through those doors.

He is halfway back along the street, when the cone of a torch sweeps across him and traps him where he stands. All of his body tells him to run, that this is some policeman who remembers the last time he was in Broome, but his head tells him different, so he turns around.

Megan skitters down the steps of the Old Arabia, a black raincoat held high over her head.

'Jon Heather,' she whispers, half in scold, 'I knew it was you . . .'

Jon turns. Where they stand, the rain comes from all directions, drawing a veil that shields them from prying eyes. As it gets stronger, Jon can hardly see the Old Arabia, except as a rippling collage of timber and stone.

Megan squirms out of her raincoat and envelops Jon.

'You said you'd be back. I thought . . .' That you might be ratting me out? That somebody changed your mind? These are things he cannot say. They are like daggers, waiting to be drawn.

'It's my father,' says Megan. 'When he saw me . . .'

Jon understands. It is, after all, the way he wants it to be with his mother, when he finally gets home. Megan has been gone from her father for only a few weeks; imagine what it will be like for Jon, with the mother he has not seen in more than half his life.

'He asked after me, didn't he?'

Megan nods, jerking her head to avoid another surge of rain. 'But I told him it was you who made me come back. You who made me see sense.' She pauses. Jon Heather seems to be drawing away.

'They know, don't they? What I did . . .'

'Everybody knows.'

This time, he nods. It was always going to be the same.

'You'd better come in, Jon, before anybody sees . . .'

She urges him back across the dirt oval, up and into the hotel lobby. The place is deathly still, not even a night porter wandering up and down. It is an easy thing to cross the barren dining hall, along the bottom hallway, and to a room right at the end. At first, Jon thinks she is taking him to their private quarters – he has a horrible feeling that, this time, he would want to stay cocooned in there forever – but it is only a guest-room, empty and ordinary.

'You'll be safe in here,' she says, flicking on a buzzing electric light. 'It hasn't had a sleeper in six months.'

Once she has closed the door, she breathes out, as if she has been delivered from a terrible nightmare. Jon drops his suitcase onto the bed.

'I'd have come back for you, you know. I'd have been there in the morning.'

Jon nods.

'You don't believe it, do you?'

'It's got me on edge. Being here . . .'

She thinks he means Broome, but it is more than that; it is the Old Arabia, these four walls, the corridors she ran down when she was a little girl, the hallway along which they carried her dead mother. The place stinks of her, stinks of memory, and he loves breathing it in.

'Why don't we go?' he asks, suddenly chill. 'Get your mother's things and just . . .'

She moves to him, starts unpicking the buttons of his sodden shirt. Draping it on the back of a chair, she produces a towel from a trunk. When she starts to dry him, his shoulders sag.

It is a terrible thing, but he seems to have submitted. To what, Megan is not sure. She dabs his breast, his shoulders, and an archipelago of clean skin begins to reveal itself. Jon watches in a mirror as she makes a strange atlas on his body, like the map of the world Peter tore from a book on board the HMS *Othello*. Here, he thinks, be monsters. Under here lies Jon Heather.

'I can't leave in the morning, Jon,' she whispers. 'I need another day. For my father.'

'You can't do it, can you? Leave him behind . . . I wouldn't hate you for it. If you said you had to stay, I wouldn't . . .'

From the look on her face, Jon understands he is dealing her an insult. He did not mean it; he meant only to offer her – to offer *himself* – a way out.

'I said I could,' she begins, towelling his hair more viciously, 'and I will. He'll have to understand.'

She wraps the towel around him, and makes as if to leave.

'Stay,' he says. He does not know until after, but he is begging her, like a frightened little boy pleading for his mother to leave a lantern on at night.

'I can't. He'll know something's wrong.'

She kisses him, tells him she will be back before long. Even though she leaves him alone for only ten minutes, it is enough for Jon to feel suddenly spooked. The walls are bearing down on him, like the cabin of a ship taking him to another world.

When she returns, she is carrying her grandmother's tea chest. This time, when she sets it down, it is Jon who opens it. The treasures are lying inside, carefully placed between sheets of thin baking paper. He makes eyes at Megan, asking her permission, and lifts the first: the string of pearls.

He asks, 'How could you just . . . give it away?'

Megan does not want to reply. She lifts a small brooch, the shape of a peacock, and pins it to the collar of the raincoat she still wears. The two make a mismatched couple.

'You never wore them?'

'They're not the sort of things you wear. They're the sort of things you . . . have.'

Each of them, she tells him, has a story. The peacock brooch was a gift to her mother on her fifth birthday; before that, a gift to her grandmother from a dear friend, on the day they set sail for the new world. The silver pendant was the only thing a great-aunt had left from the husband who sailed away with the Anzacs in 1915 and never returned.

'My grandfather,' she says, 'used to say he dived for every one of these pearls himself. He used to sit me down and tell me how deep he went, what he found down there, monsters and mermaids and serpents . . . all so he could make a necklace for my grandmother.' She pauses. 'He was lying, of course.'

'Really?' Jon Heather gasps, as if he cannot quite believe it.

Megan sees herself in the mirror. She starts. 'Jon, I have to . . .'

'I know,' he nods.

'And you too, as soon as morning comes. Before anyone wakes.'

After she has gone, he does not sleep, but sits up for long hours instead, lifting each trinket out of the miniature tea chest, recalling her stories. When he cannot remember them correctly, he changes and embellishes them, just the same as he used to do with bedtime stories for George. At some point they become, not stories about Megan's family, but stories about his own, things his father left behind for his mother, things that were meant to be for Jon and his wife. He imagines what it would be like: his wedding day, back in Leeds, sliding this simple silver band onto her finger, looking up to see a peacock brooch fastened to her dress.

In his head, the girl is English, some local girl from the terrace. She is dressed in Megan's finery, but she is not really Megan at all.

Now he cannot sleep. He packs away the trinkets, lies down, stands up, prowls the room like a stolen aboriginal girl in her cage.

He opens the box a final time. Peering into it, he sees the things she would sell for him, her past in exchange for his own. You let your guard down, Jon Heather. She got a foot in the door, and somehow squeezed her way through.

He flops onto the bed.

But, God, it feels good.

He wakes later than he meant, to the sound of footsteps in the passageway and a trolley wheeling past. Rushing to the door, he shoves Megan's tea chest into his swag, forcing his arms into the sleeves of a shirt still soaking from the night before, and peers into the corridor.

When there is nobody to see, he scuttles along the hall, sticking close to the wall. Doors flutter back and forth, revealing the dining hall by inches at a time. Somebody walks past, eclipsing his view, and it is only after they are gone that he knows it is Megan, her familiar scent rushing through the gap in the doors.

There are men in the dining hall. At one table, a group of them eat breakfast, dressed in brown suits, with small cases for papers at their feet. Jon Heather cannot see any of their faces, but at least that means they cannot see his. Behind the counter, Megan's father, squat and stern, is poring through a newspaper with some other guest. For an instant, Jon thinks it Cormac Tate – they have the same grizzled look, the same habit of taking their mouths to their food instead of the other way around – but at a second glance, it is just some bastard Australian roustabout.

He is retreating along the corridor when he hears the footsteps behind him.

'Jon, you promised . . .'

'I know,' he says, turning to see Megan hustle him back towards the room. 'There has to be a back way . . .'

'My father would know.'

'If you distracted him, I could just go, straight through the dining room and . . .'

'No, Jon.' Her voice peters out, so that Jon knows something is wrong.

'What is it?'

'Promise me you won't go into the dining room.'

He remembers: men in brown suits with small cases for their papers at their feet.

'The Protection Office?' he breathes.

She is trying to force him back into the bedroom, but he stands fast. 'I tried to tell you before, Jon. It's where they work. You thought it was just one little girl, well, it . . .'

'I want to see.'

Her eyes drop to the swag in his hand. She can make out the corner of her grandmother's tea chest sitting ungainly within, giving shape to the fabric.

'I want you to promise me, Jon. Not this time.'

'They already did their work, didn't they?'

In spite of herself she shakes her head, watching as Jon Heather shrinks.

'Think,' she says, reaching for his swag. 'Jon Heather, think. We can leave here tomorrow. You and me.' She says it again, as if to hammer the idea into him. 'You and me, Jon . . .'

'I could have left the last time I was here. I was so close. A few more months, a few more jobs, and Peter and I could have . . .' It feels as if somebody has their hands around him, holding him underwater. 'I'm sorry, Megan.'

He is marching back to the room now, but even though he is not marching towards the Protection Officers, there seems to be new vigour in his stride. Megan hurries after him.

She slams the door, locking them both inside. 'Do you want to go home or not?'

'Stay out of this, Megan.'

'In my hotel? In my home? When your hands are full of the things *I'm* selling to take you away?'

Each question feels like a slap.

He sits down, wants to bawl out. 'Listen to me when I say this,' he says. 'Those men out there, they're going to destroy those little girls. The same way they did to me and George and Peter. To Judah Reed and Cormac Tate! They're going to grow up in some Home somewhere, or on some station, or on some farm, and . . . it's not going to be *them*. They're going to make them what they're not. They're going to hate it. They're going to hate themselves . . .'

'Jon, how can you possibly know what . . .'

He stands. 'Because *I* hate myself, Megan. I hate waking up in the morning. I hate going to bed at night. I hate hearing my voice with this stupid fucking drawl. I hate knowing how to mend fences and butcher goats and play stones.' He opens his suitcase, snatches up the first book that comes to hand and hurls it so that she must either catch it or take a blow to the face. 'I hate reading these bastard books, over and over and over again, as if they might keep me English. I hate the boys who came through it with me. Just because they remind me. And . . .'

'Go on,' says Megan, fingers grasping the pages: *Strangers At Snowfell*, with its dainty picture on the front of children stranded on a train.

'When we were last here, Peter didn't want me to go after them. He said I was losing all my senses. But I had to – I had to see for myself. And, when I saw, how could I just look the other way? I wouldn't let him stop me, and he was my best friend. So tell me . . .' His eyes, roaming the room, stop suddenly and hit hers. '. . . why should I listen to *you*?'

Her back against the wall, Megan utters, 'Because I'm *me*.' She hurls the book back at him. 'Jon, please. All you need is a few more hours, another deep breath . . . and I promise you, you're going back home.'

Her shoulders sag, she turns her back and inches open the door. 'You'll be safe in here until dark. Hit the highway south. I'll find you in Perth. There's a place . . .' She takes a pencil from the dresser and, when she cannot find a scrap of paper, snatches the book back from Jon and scribbles on the inside cover. 'It's the place we stayed when I was a girl, where my mother came from. I'll find you there.'

Jon snaps the book shut, the frayed picture of the children and the train staring back. 'You're not . . .'

'Not without saying goodbye. My father doesn't deserve that . . . again. But you – you can't stay here, Jon, not with . . .' She has in her hand a key, and she slides it into the lock. 'Do I need to do this?' she asks.

Silently, Jon shakes his head.

She seems to think twice, but then drops the key in a pocket. 'Jon,' she says slowly, as if she is still thinking about not saying it. 'If you won't do it for yourself, do it for me. If you love me at all, if you really want to go home, please . . .' Jon realizes, for the first time, the way her voice is fracturing, the way she must concentrate to rein it in. 'Just look the other way.'

After she has gone, Jon throws himself down, buries his head in a pillow. When finally he looks up, the copy of *Strangers at Snowfell* has fallen open at his side, the address that Megan has scrawled looking up at him. Underneath the address she has written, in clearer type, a simple word – *Please.*

He gets up, takes hold of the dresser and hauls it against the door, so that no man could get in – and no man get out. All the while, he is saying the same thing to himself: please, Jon; please, Jon Heather; just a few more hours, another deep breath . . . and you're going back home.

Never has he waited so long.

In the small of the afternoon Megan brings him food. Jon has no appetite, but he eats what he can, not knowing where and when he might get his next meal. He packs his swag, his books, over and over again.

He wonders, for the first time, where Pete and Cormac are now. He spends an hour picturing them on their smallholding, raising fences and harrowing patches of land while Dog careens about, massacring nests of baby rabbits. He has been dreaming of it for what feels like an age, when something hauls him viciously back to the present. It feels like he has gone ten rounds with a bare-knuckle boxer. There is no earthly reason, Jon Heather, why you should daydream of a life on the land, not when you are this close to home.

Night comes. He knows because he hears the evening meals served. Probably the Protection Officers are dining out there. If they are still here, Jon reasons, it means that today was not the day. Perhaps they went into the bush, spent long hours spying – but, if they are still here, their work is not yet done.

He goes to the door, pulls back the dresser he is using to imprison himself and creeps into the corridor. Where the doors open to the dining hall, he presses himself against the wall. He can hear snatches of conversation, idle, boring things, from the other side, but it is not enough. He steels himself, thrusts out a foot, pins the doors ajar, and looks through.

There they are: two men who could only be Protection Officers, one much older than the other, dining with the very same policeman who took them out the last time. Jon can see no sign of the aboriginal guide, but, he supposes, a man like that is not welcome in a dining hall like this.

He is still standing there, watching them eat, their smiles, the funny furrowing of their eyebrows as they share some joke, when he sees Megan waltz across the hall, bringing them beer. She does not linger with them long, but the easy way she has with them, the tipped head as the policeman raises his glass in thanks, makes Jon want to stride out.

It is then that he sees the book in his hand. He did not know he had brought it, cannot say why, but he brings it up and fingers the inside cover. There, the pencil lines now smudged, is Megan's hand: *Please*, she implores him, all over again. The word makes him pause. He sags against the wall, drawing back his foot, and the dining hall disappears from view.

There is no rain tonight. Indeed, the skies are clear for as far as he can see, all those familiar, alien stars and constellations. Once the dining hall is empty, he gathers up his suitcase and swag and, head buried in Megan's raincoat, strides through. He does not pause on the veranda, but ploughs across the road, straight onto the dirt oval. There is, he decides, only one stop he will make. Even with Megan's scrawled word emblazoned on the backs of his eyelids, he will afford himself this.

He walks the ocean road until he reaches the lock-up, where the big boab tree sits out front. There are no lights inside – and that, at least, bodes well. In the scrub out front a police ute is parked, but there is no sign of the policeman, nor of any Protection Officer. He creeps closer.

There are holes in the wall, with window grilles but no windows. He peers into the first and sees nothing peering out. It is difficult to scrabble around the back, for here the scrub grows wilder, but he forces himself as far as he can go, until, at least, he can peer into one other cell. Here, again, there is nothing. Nobody.

Back on the ocean road, he looks in the direction of the Old Arabia.

They are still there, he says to himself.

Pete's voice: this has got you all riled up, hasn't it?

Megan's hand: *Please* . . .

He shoulders his swag, swings his suitcase and hurries off.

The highway once plunged him straight into town; now it will take him far away. It is never a good thing to beg for a lift so close to a town, so he lopes across the dirt oval and starts to march. He goes at a quick pace for an hour before he takes a rest. By that time it must be midnight, and he marches again.

In the starlight he sees a hollow at the edge of the road. He fell asleep in a hollow once before, waking up in the back of some farmhand's ute, but he will not let it happen again.

Some time later, headlights appear in front of him. Whoever it is, they are heading back into Broome. The highway is so straight and true that it is an age before the wagon draws past, forcing Jon Heather off the road. A horn blasts. He imagines it is the driver wishing him farewell.

When he can go no further, he finds a bank where the scrub is thin and he can check easily for snakes, and makes a cushion out of his swag. He dares not sleep, for then he might miss his lift south, so he begins to play a game: he finds sixteen small stones, lines them up, and prepares to toss them with one hand and catch them on the back of the other. He will not play this game when he is back in England, but tonight he will play until he beats his old record.

He is relearning old tricks, knowing how to shuffle stones from one knuckle to the next, when he sees headlights, some wagon coming south out of town. Quickly, he casts the stones into the scrub, and skids back down to the road. He need not have hurried; the headlights, pinpricks in the distance, take another age until they are near enough to spot him.

The wagon draws down. Its headlights, still full-beam, dazzle Jon Heather so that all he can see are shreds of a silhouette. A door flies open, changing, for an instant, the quality of the light. Then he hears footsteps.

'You all right, boy?'

Jon hunches down as if to get under the glow. 'How far are you going?' he asks.

'Only as far as Thangoo Station.'

It is still an hour further south.

'Hop up front, boy.'

As ever, Jon Heather would rather lie in the back, where he doesn't have to breathe a word in polite conversation – but, in the blinding light, he can see the dark mounds of the man's cargo piled up on the flatbed. He scurries around the side of the cab and sinks into the passenger seat. Amorphous pools of colour swim across his field of vision, blotting out the road.

The door beside him slams and the driver eases the engine off again.

'Thank you,' he breathes, closing his eyes so that his sight might come back more quickly. 'I was afraid I'd be out there all night.'

Jon opens his eyes. The pools of colour have dwindled to tiny points floating across the dashboard. He shifts, tries to make room to set his suitcase down at his feet, and looks up. In the mirror hanging over the windscreen, he sees the driver's eyes.

The policeman glowers back. 'Steady now, boy,' he utters. 'We're going at sixty klicks. There's neither of us coming out of this pretty if you start up again . . .'

Jon throws a look behind him. Through the glass, he sees now what the mound of cargo is: nothing but an empty wire frame, arcing over the back of the ute. His hand fumbles, instinctively, for the door, opening it a crack. Hot wind rushes past, a swarm of grains of burning sand.

'We heard a rumour that you were kicking about town. That you were gone bush,' the policeman says. He has one hand on the steering wheel and one hand hovering just off, as if expecting Jon Heather to pounce. 'Really, boy, to wander into town like that, to wander into the hotel . . . What did you think, that us country types just *forget*?' The door whips open just a little wider, and desert wind rampages within. The driver watches from the corner of his eye. 'You know what the ground would do to you at this speed?'

As he says it, he presses his foot firmly to the floor. The ute lurches forward, snapping the door shut.

'How long have you been here, sloping about under my nose, Mr Heather?'

'How do you know my name?'

'We made it our business to know your name.'

There was no record at the Old Arabia. Of that, he is certain: he only ever stayed there in rooms Cormac Tate had booked. It must have been Megan's father – or some other guest.

'You don't know what you're doing,' Jon insists. 'I'm out of here. I'm getting out of Australia . . .'

'Don't you know what you did that day?'

'I got that little girl away from you, didn't I? Didn't I, you bastards?' Jon swings out with his fist. In the confines of the cab, he cannot cut a proper arc, and makes only a loose connection. The policeman is bigger than Cook ever was, and wears the blow well. When Jon tries to pummel him again, he brings his own fist up, hammers Jon back into the door. The latch catches, the door swings wide open – and suddenly Jon Heather is flailing about in the whirling desert air.

He feels a meaty fist close around his wrist and haul him back in. The door still flaps wide.

'You sent her back to the bush,' he says. 'A goddamn little girl. She might have grown up proper, had an education . . . And, because of you, she'll just grow up wild, pump out a hundred more like her. We're trying to stop that. We're trying to *help* her. Don't you know what happens to girls from the bush? She'll end up selling herself to some stockman somewhere, and you could have stopped it.'

'I saw her mother,' says Jon Heather. 'I saw them sobbing in the scrub. You put them in your car, tricked them. You threw them out.'

The policeman's voice seems to pale. 'I know what you're saying, son. But you can't pick right or wrong. You got to pick best or worse. And you ruined that little girl's life.'

The road widens where a dirt track cuts east, and the policeman slows so that he might bring the ute around. When he begins the turn, Jon Heather senses his chance. He has his hand tight around his swag, but the suitcase of books is at his feet. It will, he decides, have to be left behind – those books have been tormenting him for too long already.

The driver locks the steering wheel into as tight a turn as he is able – and Jon Heather thrusts the passenger door wide open. He hits the road at a roll. Though he tries to cushion his fall with his swag, his shoulder hits the dirt and he bawls out in pain. He lies there for an instant, determined to gulp it back down, and hears the ute skid to a stop. The driver's door flies open and the policeman barrels out.

There is still time. Pull yourself together, Jon Heather, pull yourself up. He lifts himself, first onto his knees and then onto his haunches. The policeman is still on the other side of the ute. He will not outrun him along the highway – but there is always the bush.

Too late, Jon realizes that the swag, with all of Megan's treasures, is still at his feet. He bends to grab it, but his fingers will not do his bidding; his arm, he knows, is definitely broken. Quickly, he snatches out with his other hand, rips the swag onto his shoulder and starts to run. The policeman thunders for him to stop – he is already under arrest, he is making it worse, he'll be put away forever – but Jon is deaf to it. He scrambles up the sandbank and takes off into spinifex and stone.

He stumbles on, oblivious to the heat pounding in his arm. Before he has gone ten yards the road has disappeared. All is silence and scrub. It was like this once before: a world without fences, as he fled from the Mission. Like then, he has no idea where he is going. He stumbles. He falls. He gets up and runs.

A light arcs across him and he turns, realizing that he has been following the same dirt trail whose jaws the policeman was using to turn the ute. On his right, the wagon is gaining fast. He turns to flee it, but finds he is pointing directly at Broome. He needs to be on the other side of that track.

Throwing himself into the scrub, he lets the wagon roar past. Once it has gone, he bolts over the trail, leaping through low mounds of red. He hears the wagon skid to a stop, its engine screaming as the policeman kicks it into reverse and prepares to sail around. Its headlights swoop high and then low – and fix on Jon Heather. He launches himself forward, as if the light itself propels him – but there is no good in hiding; he has already been seen.

The ute pounds through the scrub, bucking like a wild brumby who will never be broken. Already it is on top of him. He darts to the left, deeper into the desert, but the ute banks that way too.

Think, Jon Heather, you useless Pommie bastard – just think!

To his left, he sees an outburst of scrub taller and denser than all the rest: a shadow wood. The ute will not follow in there.

He hurtles towards it. He does not have to look around to know that the ute is rapidly closing, for the headlights grow in intensity. At last, he reaches the line of the trees. He claws his way inside, listens to the skidding of tyres as the ute slews to avoid a crash.

Now there are footsteps – big, heavy footsteps – gaining on him. He is a lost little boy, running from the childsnatchers again. Yet, this time, it is different. This time he knows where he is running. He has the means to get back to England. He has treasure in his swag. A few more weeks, another voyage at sea, and he'll be there. Twelve years too late, but he'll be there still . . .

A hand swipes at his shoulder, and lightning bursts along his broken arm. Pain drives him to a halt. The hand comes up and clamps around his chest, pinning him in place. He drops the swag and, as it falls, it flies open. Starlight spills through the sweet-smelling canopy, illuminating all the treasures Megan gave him.

'Take it!' Jon cries. 'Take it all, just please . . . don't take me in . . .'

The policeman drops him, deliberately, onto his broken arm. The world explodes in a myriad of colours. He can feel nothing – no agony, no pounding, not even the texture of the earth where he has landed.

'I don't think you understand,' the policeman says. 'You ran me off the road. You beat my mate to within an inch of his life. And you snatched a little girl from us, her rightful guardians. You don't make the decisions here, Mr Heather.' He crouches, picking up a string of pearls and peering at them in the starlight. 'You're in a lot of trouble, Jon.'

Before the world fades to blackness, Jon hears the policeman's words over and again: you snatched a little girl, Jon Heather, from her rightful guardians: the government of Western Australia.

You can't run away from the childsnatcher, Jon. He's already here. For now and ever more, he will be everywhere you turn. All you'll have to do is look in the mirror.

BOOK THREE

THE THREE CHILDSNATCHERS

XVII

They are met at the gates of the home, and a prim white woman, whose perfectly poised accent does not suit her meaty demeanour, tells them how glad she is that they could come. It is Pete who shakes her hand, while Cormac Tate lingers behind.

'I reckon I might stay with the truck, Pete,' he mutters.

The red-haired man nods gruffly. He has been expecting as much, ever since the letter first landed at their station. They pored over it together for long hours – hours in which nothing much was said, but no less vital for that – before deciding to make the trip. The ute, now four or even five years old, has seen better days, but at least it got them this far. Perhaps Cormac can tinker with it further while Pete is inside.

He follows the woman through the gates. On a plaque against the black grille a legend is spelt out. Even though the woman is chattering on, Pete stops so that he might take it in:

Mogumber Native Settlement
A home for the homeless, the forgotten in our midst, the desperate ones who deserve a new world

Down the hill, Pete sees wooden shacks, sitting on stilts, arranged in a horseshoe around a clump of low, sprawling trees. There is a wooden lattice table close to the gates, and at it an aboriginal man is sitting, smoking a dark cigarette.

'We're so glad you could come. You'll see, for certain, that our girls are well prepared for life on a holding like yours.' She pauses, halfway down the hill. On one side, separate from the rest, there is a bigger building, with three utes lined up outside; on the other, a patch of scrub has been harrowed, with poles put up for growing beans. The plants look straggly and untended. 'What was your station called, again?'

'Black Chaparral,' Pete says, absentmindedly. 'It used to be East Hermitage.'

They seem to be ignoring the shacks built in the horseshoe, and head towards the broader building instead. There are faces in the doors of all the huts they leave behind, some of them as young as five or six. An ancient memory stirs in him, and he remembers sneaking through a place Jon Heather called the shadow wood. He has, he thinks, slipped back in time – only here there is not an English boy in sight; all of the faces are black.

The building, it turns out, is a hospital of sorts. A nurse scurries from partition to partition. For all her work, Pete does not see any patients, only a pale-looking aboriginal girl with a thermometer stuck in her mouth and yellow crust around her eyes.

'This way,' the woman says.

The office is a simple thing, a desk and a cabinet and nothing else. The woman takes a ledger from the desk, opens it, and runs her finger down lines of dates and names.

'Our girls deserve the brightest start in life, Mr Slade. They are studious and willing to learn. They're *eager* to leave behind the degradations of the past. We work hard here to give these girls the skills they need.' She throws him a smile. 'We have a chaplain, now, who has been no end of help in delivering moral lessons. Morality, you see, is not something that comes easily to these girls.'

'Why's that?'

She doesn't seem to hear.

'In the end, you know, their rehabilitation is a long, slow process. So we must look to members of the community to complete their training, to give them roles that might best service the society they've joined.' She pauses. Perhaps she senses something in Pete, because she begins to steer him back outside. 'Perhaps you'd like to meet some of our girls?'

Out in the sunshine, Pete stops. He is, he thinks, beginning to understand why Cormac Tate would not come through the gates.

'Where do these girls come from?' he asks.

'They are rescued, Mr Slade.'

'Rescued?'

The woman nods. 'I shudder to think where these girls might have ended up, if it hadn't been for good works like this.'

'Where from?'

'All over, Mr Slade. It used to be we'd just take girls from the south, but some of them here, they're from the Kimberley, the Pilbara.'

'Way up north.'

She nods.

'North of Broome.'

She rolls her eyes. 'The ends of the earth!'

He is taken into one of the shacks in the horseshoe. It is, he sees, a dormitory, though not like the dormitories of the boys' home, nor the ones Jon Heather used to describe. This one has been scrubbed clean. The beds all have pillows and the blankets are freshly laundered. It is not, Pete decides, a dormitory for the girls living here; it is a dormitory set up especially for him.

'I'll be back shortly.'

Left alone, Pete wanders to the airy window. From here, he can see the neighbouring hut, a trellised building with a ditch of deep slush at its feet. It is a moment before he realizes what is wrong; on this hut's windows, there are bars.

'Mr Slade . . .'

He turns to see the woman has come back, shovelling before her two pale aboriginal girls. The elder, perhaps fourteen, has an arm on the younger's shoulder. They stand silently, dressed in demure little frocks, with no shoes upon their feet.

'Say hello, girls.'

The younger buries her head; the elder speaks, but it is not any language Pete can understand.

'Dolly,' the woman whispers, 'you heard what I said. You mustn't speak black fella language to Mr Slade. He's here to give you great things.'

It is not something he has thought about in more than four years, but suddenly Pete can feel the sting of swirling red dirt against him and he is watching, with horror, as Jon Heather pounds his fist into the face of the man named Cook, a little black girl huddled up in the back of the ute behind.

'I'm sorry,' he says, 'you'll have to excuse me.' He brushes between the girls, past the woman, stumbling at the door. 'Sorry Dolly,' he says. 'I'm . . .'

Up at the ute, Cormac Tate is drinking coffee from a flask. When he sees Pete lope back through the gates, he spits out the grounds. 'What is it, Pete?'

'It's like you said it would be. You want to say it?'

'Say what?'

'You're always right, Cormac, my old mate!' he beams. 'You've always got one up on me!'

By the time he is in the driver's seat, ready to wheel the ute away, his smile has disappeared.

'It doesn't do no good, though, does it?' He kneads the steering wheel. 'Storming out of there's just as bad as Jon Heather putting his fists in that bastard's face. Well,' he demands, 'ain't it?'

'What else would you do, Pete?'

It is no good. Pete kills the engine, climbs back out of the ute.

'I'm sorry, Cormac,' he says. 'I just got to.'

Endless hours later, Pete re-emerges from the settlement. Tramping up the hill behind him come two pale aboriginal girls.

At their sides, each of them carries a little suitcase made out of card.

In the middle month of winter, in the year of 1961, a new signpost could be seen along the inland roadway leading from Northam to Mullewa. It was a crude thing, letters scored by knife into the back of a chair – but even passers-by might have noted with what care the letters had been carved. Now, years later, it has been replaced by a simple, stencilled design: *Black Chaparral Station*. At the end of the trail, there is neither a real cattle station, nor any chaparral, but little things like that don't mean a thing to the men who own it. For them, the words are a joke, a secret code, a pair of crooked fingers raised joyfully at the country that keeps them. They say, we can make what we want of this world – it's all up to us.

It is a long ride from Mogumber, though not nearly so long as the roads Pete and Cormac Tate used to ride. On the way they make frequent stops, fussing over the girls on the flatbed and the sullen, elderly Dog that guards them. For their part, the girls do not seem distressed. This, Pete surmises, is because they have been here before, forced into the back of a ute and told they are going somewhere to live better, healthier lives. So has he, and Cormac Tate; at least, now that he is driving, he knows he is telling the truth.

They reach home just as the daylight is starting to pale. There are no other trucks on the road and they glide through fields of gold – the neighbouring farms – and fields of dirty yellow – their own – before taking a track through the bloodwoods, towards home. This is not the natural country for bloodwoods, but it is not – or so an old friend would say – the natural country for Pete and Cormac Tate either. Over the years, they have both found something to laugh at in the idea.

The first building they come to was once the ruin of a barn. Now it is Cormac Tate's own lodge, a place to rest his weary bones at night, prop his feet upon the grumbling Dog, and – soon enough – tell stories to the grandchildren with which Pete and his daughter Maya are obediently providing him. At the gate, Pete brings the ute to a crawl, but Cormac motions him to go on, climbing the road until they reach the farmhouse proper. There, Cormac will help the new girls settle, and indulge himself in a long game of cards with Booty and the rest of the blacks.

At the head of the trail, there sits the farmhouse. In the yard, one of the foremen is deep in the engine of the only tractor they could afford, while the housekeeper, one of Booty's daughters, is beating out a mat against the wall. Black Chaparral will never be like the great wheat farms that surround them, but it doesn't have to be: it will keep them, and one day it will keep their families. They have a pig and a goat. There are wild rabbits for roasting and chooks in a coop out back. A fox in a pen, just for the sheer hell of it. It is, indeed, a bastard sort of family.

Booty emerges from an outhouse as they approach, trudges down to receive them at the gate. While they are still a distance away, his face seems to crumple, as he considers the two unexpected passengers up back. Climbing out of the cab, Cormac tells him to stop his staring.

'We'll have to make up a couple of bed rolls,' he says, reaching out to help the girls down. When the elder sister shakes her head, he steps back, lets them help each other to the ground instead. 'There's a spare room out back, girls. *Your* room. Booty here'll show you, get you settled down. Then, I hope you'll join us for dinner.' He looks over his shoulder. 'That's right, isn't it, Pete?'

'Got to get some grub in them,' he says. 'They'll have been wasting a . . .' Pete stops, for Booty is still rolling his eyes. 'What is it?'

'You better come, boss,' says Booty. 'They's a man.'

'A man?'

'I tell him he can wait.'

'He didn't want to wait inside?'

'Some fella don't like inside.'

Pete follows Booty's eyes along the edge of the yard, where straggly ears of wheat ripple in the evening breeze. Out back, the land is still opening up. Some of it was scrub when they came to Black Chaparral, but every season another stretch gets harrowed, and every season there is more to till and harvest.

The evening redness in the west is setting his bedraggled fields to a burst of life but, though his eyes are drawn that way, he cannot stop from seeing the fat man bent over the railings, watching the sunset just the same.

Pete coughs, flamboyantly loud.

Up ahead, the fat man startles, turns around, his cheeks flushing at the embarrassment of being sneaked up on. 'Peter . . .' he begins. He is not wearing black today. He is wearing jeans and a checked shirt – it does not suit him – and has a little case at his side. His face, plump and ruddy, is hidden behind a boyish fringe. 'It's me,' the fat man whispers, 'George.'

Pete idles to the fence. He sets one foot on the rail and gazes out over the fields he has worked, the scrub he has reclaimed: the years of his life.

There are only a dozen yards between them. The last time they met, it too was across a field of upturned earth; there were a dozen yards between them back then as well, but George flew across them so urgently he felt as if he might take off. Now, nobody moves.

'George Stone,' he repeats.

Pete tilts his head, and for the first time George can look into him. He is stronger, fuller. Even so, he is shorter than George has always imagined; as grown men, George is the taller of the two. It is wrong that he should ever be able to look down on Peter Slade.

'I recognize you, George.' His voice is different, too; it does not chip and dive as once it did. 'I never knew that was your name.'

Though they stand beside each other, they are not really together.

'It's a *place* you've got here, Peter. Black Chaparral . . .' He ventures a smile, careful not to let it grow too big. 'I remember those comics.'

'I remember reading them to you.'

In the backdoor of the farmhouse, a woman with cropped blonde hair appears. Her dungarees are stained and she looks exhausted. Pete makes eyes at her, and she turns back into the farmhouse.

'That your . . . wife?'

Silence – long and sticky.

'That your baby crying up there?'

Something in the question seems to smart with Pete, as if it is something George should not have asked. For the first time, he turns to face the fat little boy. 'We came to get you, you know. Jon Heather rode out and told me what you were doing, and I made old Cormac Tate drive right back to that Mission so I could see for myself. I just wouldn't believe it, George. But we kicked up dust all night – and there you were, just drinking coffee with Judah Reed.'

George lets the silence stretch out, unsure if he should go on. 'Peter . . .'

'Actually, it's *Pete*.' He kicks back against the fence, jumping forward only when a goat emerges out of the wheat to investigate his backside. 'George,' he says, 'it's been hellish good to see you, but if you don't mind I've got a whole heap of shit to be . . .'

He is striding across the yard, towards the open door of the farmhouse, thinking of those girls, when George calls out.

'Peter . . . *Pete* . . . It's . . .' Words seem to be failing him – but, then again, they always did. 'It's about . . . Jon Heather.'

Another second, and Pete would have gone up the steps, walked in to find his mismatched family waiting, and not looked back.

'I wonder,' says George – and, here, Pete knows, is the real reason he has come to Black Chaparral – 'when was the last time you heard anything of Jon?'

'Sooner than you, I shouldn't wonder.'

It was not meant to be a challenge. George hurries after him. Quickly, he is out of breath. 'I've only seen him once since . . .'

That George has seen him at all is both a comfort and a barb to Pete. He stops so that he can kick his boots off – Maya always screams blue murder when he tramples dirt where the baby might crawl – and waits for George to finish.

'When?'

'It was January 1958.'

The words pile into Pete with the power of a road train. '1958?'

George can only nod; the year must have some significance for Pete.

'Jon left me,' says Pete. 'Just woke up one morning, and he was gone . . .'

'I was back at the Mission . . .' George strings each word out, uncertain whether Pete wants to hear the story. 'I'd been in New South Wales, at the farm school there, but . . . I'd been back three months when Jon Heather turned up.'

'Just turned up,' Pete repeats. 'Why don't you tell me what you're really doing here, George *Stone*?'

So, like a bigger boy who has entrusted himself with looking over a pathetic bedwetter five years his junior, George spins the story:

In the middle month of summer, in the year of 1958, the man who calls himself George Slade wanders to the shadow wood to look over the little ones out on village muster – and there he sees a vagrant, sleeping in a swag under the shelf of red where boys sometimes stake out rabbits.

At first, George is afraid. His instinct is to turn tail and tell Judah Reed, but Judah has lectured him on the need for spiritual strength – so, instead, he strides across the field, through the wheat the boys have sown. He is about to admonish this trespasser when the wild man turns.

Jon Heather looks at him from beneath a mop of brown hair. The conversation is strained between them. Neither asks how the other one is. George cannot bring himself to ask Jon what he has been doing in the time they have been apart, for the answer might be too horrible to bear: I've been out there, being a man, working with Peter.

At last, Jon breaks cover. 'I need to ask you something, George. Call it a favour. For an old friend.'

George grapples at the chance, like a drowning man so desperate for air that he drags his brother down.

'It's the wild boy,' says Jon Heather. 'I need you to help me with the wild boy.'

It is a question Jon asked George once before. Then, George failed. Now, he cannot. He will do anything to win back the light in Jon Heather's eyes. 'What is it, Jon?'

'I need you to find out . . .' breathes Jon, '. . . if Luca is still alive.'

Jon Heather's eyes shine. He was never a boy for crying in dormitories, but now you might think him one of those terrible bedwetters with whom George was cast down.

Because Jon Heather has never stopped thinking about the night he bore Luca back into the Mission and begged Judah Reed for his help. He can remember in intimate detail the things of which they spoke, how Luca had dreamed of leading another Children's Crusade: back to the promised lands, England and Malta and all the other places where lost boys belonged. Jon Heather, now, is a grown man, who rides fences and musters cattle – but all that he will ever do pales against the thoughts of that little boy.

'Judah Reed must know.' He stops; he is haggard as an old man, and only seventeen years old. 'And I have to know as well.'

George makes arrangements to meet Jon Heather again in three nights' time. Jon has a camp, somewhere sunrise of the compound, and he promises he will return.

Through those days, George sees Jon more than once. He drops out of the shadow wood to watch the boys at work and play. He brings some little ones hunks of chocolate from his own pack. Jon Heather – spending the money he has been so fastidious in saving so that little boys might have a taste of chocolate.

On the third night, George sneaks out to meet Jon. He is late in arriving – not because of any difficulty in getting away, but because he cannot bring himself to come. The wild boy Luca, George must relate, was sent to the farm school in New South Wales. Six months later, he was found cold in his dormitory.

Jon Heather cries, loud and long. Luca might have lasted

another six months in another farm school – but in his heart Jon knows that he died on the night he was delivered back to Judah Reed.

'I thought,' says George, 'that that would be the last I saw of Jon Heather. But he was there the next night, and the night after that. Pete, he could hardly tear himself away. The little ones started talking about him: the wild man in the woods. I caught them playing stones with him . . .' He stops. 'It's a game Jon made up. For me.'

'I know it,' says Pete. 'I seen Jon Heather teach it to some blacks.'

'Then, one night, he just calls me into the shadow wood. He looked so lonely, Pete. He asked me . . .'

George's voice wavers. When Pete looks up, he understands that this is the point of the story. It was never about that wild boy at all.

'He asked me if he might stay. If there was work he could do with the boys. Not be one of the Children's Crusade, but . . . like old Mr McAllister used to be, or one of the teachers who'd come in and show woodworking or shearing . . .'

Pete rears up. 'You're lying, George. I could always tell when you were lying. Your chins used to wobble.'

He is about to turn, but something stays him. 'So I went and asked Judah Reed. He could hardly remember Jon. Bit of a troublemaker, he said – but I convinced him he'd changed, that he'd grown up, wanted to help. Jon was always good with little ones. Better than me. The only way I got good at anything was by copying Jon Heather. In the end, I think he . . . hated me for it.' He pauses. 'But when I went back to tell Jon, he wasn't there. I searched and searched for his camp, had boys out with me . . . but I never saw him again.'

Pete picks up his boots and hits them, methodically, against the wall. This isn't any Jon Heather he knew. The Jon Heather who fought so hard to walk away from Megan, who turned his back on Black Chaparral, who denied himself even food and drink, could never have thought about giving in like that.

Pete slides into the kitchen. Maya is there, rocking the baby back and forth. She is, Pete knows, determined to linger and find out who this interloper is – but before she can ask, the baby sets up a squall and she disappears.

'Why are you telling me this, George? We all got our different lives now. You included, by the looks of you. Why do you want to rake up that past . . .'

'Perhaps it's because I went back home,' he begins, 'but home wasn't there. Perhaps it's because I know I was wrong – the Children's Crusade was lying to me all along, Peter, just to turn me into what they wanted. Or perhaps it's just that . . .' Each word is an effort; he wishes Pete could know just how much. '. . . I still remember when we were three little boys.'

Against his will, Pete sits, kicking out a chair so that George can do the same.

'Jon's in trouble, Peter. I want to help him. You want to help him too. Seems like we could work together on that.'

'Yeah,' says Pete, pushing a tin of coffee across the table. 'That seems like a thing we could do.'

George reaches into the cardboard suitcase and produces papers, copies of copies of typewritten forms.

'Jon Heather,' he says, 'has been in prison, largely in Fremantle, for the last four years. As far as I can tell, he is the only person in the history of that prison to have *requested* solitary confinement. He's been on his own, in a cell, for one thousand and three hundred nights, Pete – and, in five nights' time, they're setting him free.'

Pete's face is buried in the forms: an arrest report; minutes from a trial, reliving in intimate detail every blow that Jon threw that scorching summer morning.

He looks at George: fat, ugly George, whose piss he used to

wring out of the sheets, whose hair he used to ruffle as he read him comics.

'I haven't heard from him in all that time,' he says. 'Not since the day he and Megan ran out. He was so angry at me that day. So let down. I suppose I thought he'd got himself home.' The papers strain beneath his fingers. 'When I didn't hear from him, I thought that was it. That he'd forgotten it all, like he always wanted.'

'I think we should be there.'

Among the papers, there is a newspaper dated the 2nd of September in the year of 1961. In the picture, Jon is being led out of court with shackles around his wrists. He is concentrating on the ground, on putting one foot in front of the other; that, Pete remembers, is how you cross the world.

'I think we should too,' Pete whispers. Then he looks up. Into the kitchen doorway comes Cormac Tate and, behind him, still holding hands, the two aboriginal girls, plucked from the bush somewhere to wind up on Peter's farm. 'But, Georgie boy,' he says, 'I don't think he's going to like what he finds.'

*

On the morning of his release, Jon Heather sleeps in late. It is one of the pleasures of solitary confinement that you are not torn out of bed each morning and thrown into a mess hall with the rest. Today, however, he will have to have *conversations*. There is, he will admit, a little piece of him that would rather stay inside, so that he does not have to join the pantomime.

All the same, when the warden comes to collect him, he is sitting patiently, ready to go. In the end, there is no shaking of hands. He is given a ticket for a train that will take him to Perth, and the details of a halfway house at which a room has been assigned him. Then, doors are drawn back, and he walks out into the low sun.

He is kicking his heels along a street lined with market stalls, listening to the sound of sea birds, when his eye is drawn to a wagon parked up on the side of the road. He stops. Though he only rode in it for a few weeks of his life, he knows that wagon well.

A red-haired man steps out of the ute and nods his head. Jon wanders towards him. Yes, it is certainly Peter Slade – older, perhaps, with a fuzzy beard that does not suit him, but still Peter Slade.

'Jump in, Jon Heather,' he says. 'I haven't got all day!' The familiar tone sets pulses running along Jon's every sinew. 'We'll get you a good feed, shall we? Looks like you've been wasting away.'

If he wants to protest, Jon Heather cannot. Something rushes inside him, like a geyser. There is, he knows, only one other thing that could make him erupt like this.

A yellow snout appears, dozily, from the flatbed. It stands, shakes itself out of sleep, and stares.

Somebody might have presented him with a huge mammoth bone, and told him to start chewing. Though he has a pronounced limp, Dog turns in berserk circles, barking once each circuit. His rear half squats, as if he is about to take a delighted shit, and he falls, flat-footed, from the ute, waddling over to Jon and leaving a thick trail of urine behind him.

'You got old, boy,' whispers Jon, bending down to slap the hairless tummy.

With Dog trailing after them, Pete and Jon take off up the street.

It is three days before they make the long drive. Before then, there is Perth: the halfway house where Jon will prove he is a reformed Australian citizen; and an officer he must check in with. When the third day comes, they set off early, riding the inland highway that might take them to Geraldton and the Mission, and then following the signposts for Moora. From here, it is empty, endless road. They take it in turns to sit behind the wheel and, though there is much silence, they talk, too, about the days when they worked these wheat fields together: Pete and Jon and Cormac Tate, three adventurers on their quest.

Dusk is nigh when they leave the road and follow dirt trails east. This is uncharted country for Jon Heather, so Pete takes the wheel and Jon sits, kneading Dog's head in his lap. The old brute smells worse than ever; Pete takes grim delight in telling Jon the prognosis of their travelling veterinarian: all of his glands are rotting.

They reach Black Chaparral before darkness is absolute. Under the stars, Jon sees fields of wheat, horses in their stables. At the top of the trail there is a farmhouse. Lights blaze inside.

In the yard, they sit in the ute, neither making the move to get out.

'You know, Jon Heather, I never for the life of me thought I'd see you here.'

Pete's head rests against the wheel. He lifts it a fraction and smiles.

'I never planned on it,' Jon says.

'I thought you was home. That night Megan went after you and didn't come back, I thought that was it . . .' He bunches his fists around the steering column. 'I was happy for you, Jon Heather. Figured you'd seen sense at last, taken that girl with you.'

It is Jon's turn to bunch his fists. 'I almost did,' he whispers. 'She had a plan.' A smile erupts. 'That girl always had some sort of a plan. She wanted to . . .' At first Jon does not want to say it. '. . . sell her mother's things, buy us a berth we could share. But we had to pass through Broome.'

The rest can remain unsaid; Pete is not sure he wants to know about the night his old friend was hounded through spinifex and scrub.

'You ever hear from that girl, Jon Heather?'

Jon nods, but there is something ghostly about the way he moves. 'She even came to Fremantle once. She wrote me a letter, said she wanted to see me. She tried to bring me my books. But, Peter, I couldn't see her. She came three days and still I couldn't do it.'

'Why not?'

His voice fraying around the edges, Jon whispers, 'She changed what I wanted, Peter. All of my rules, all of my strictures, they were useless, up against someone like her. She was making it so I didn't want my mother and my sisters anymore.'

'Might be you should be making a trip north?'

Jon is silent.

'Jon, you know, *I* got married.'

'I figured it,' says Jon.

Pete arches an eyebrow. 'Oh yeah?'

'Yeah, I can see it all over you. You got soft.'

'I got a baby boy too.'

This time, there is a lurching in Jon's gut, like uncooked chicken announcing itself. 'What's he like?' he asks, a touch too eagerly.

'Oh, you know. He pretty much shits and sicks.'

The ute headlights die and, out back, Dog tumbles from the flatbed.

'Jon,' Pete says, his voice a hoarse whisper, 'it's bastard good to see you.'

He kicks open the door and plods towards the farmhouse door. Some distance behind, with Dog at his heel, Jon follows.

Through the door, Jon sees Cormac Tate standing in a broad kitchen. His face is etched with deeper lines than the last time they met, but at least his face is not purpling, and at least he is not stopping himself from lashing out. Jon has gone only three steps through the door when the old man barrels forward, smothers him in his arms. Rigid, Jon does not move. He feels the warmth of Cormac's tears against his shoulder.

'I'm glad you're back, son. Son, I'm sorry. For what I said. For what I . . .'

Jon is about to speak out, when someone gets there first. At their feet, Dog lifts his head and lets fly with barks so shrill that Cormac has to pull away and order the stupid mutt to sit.

'I wish you'd been here, Jon. All this while.' The old man rocks back against a kitchen cabinet and quakes.

From another door, two black faces appear. When they see the old man crying, the youngest – a girl with doleful eyes and hair of the deepest black – goes to him, tries to slip her tiny fingers in his giant hand.

Pete leads the way to a room next door. There, Jon sees a woman with short-cropped hair, holding a baby against her breast. Pete says hello to her first, dangling a finger about which the baby wraps its whole hand. Then, he steps aside. In the doorway, Jon Heather stalls. He has grown used to silence in the last years, and now he has nothing to say.

In front of him is a thing he has not seen since he was a real, live boy: Georgie boy, fat baby George, is here, with Peter Slade, to welcome him home.

There will be little sleep tonight. There will be talking. Before long, Maya takes the baby away – and, soon after, Cormac Tate himself trudges off. Then, only Pete, George and Jon Heather are left. Now, the talking comes less easily, so that, at last, George has to bring polished stones out of his suitcase and range them around, just so that they have something to do. Pete is useless at stones; George and Jon Heather devour him.

There are stories to be filled in: Pete is married to Cormac Tate's daughter; George might soon become headmaster at the farm school of the Children's Crusade. Jon himself has no story to tell; he never has done. He suspects they both know it, for neither ask him about prison, nor even about the night he was captured.

George tosses a twentieth stone in the air, slowly bringing his hand around, angling it so perfectly that the stone lands in the gap between his fore and index fingers. It is the first time that Jon has smiled so freely: George has beaten him, fair and square.

'Jon,' he says, 'there's something we've got to show you.'

It is not Jon's place to resist any longer, so he follows George and Pete up the stairs of the farmhouse. At the end of the landing there is a little box room, made up with a bedroll and blanket. Curled up, there lies a boy, ten or eleven years old. He sleeps soundly, but there is a Mission smock hanging on the back of a chair beside him.

Jon snaps a look at George. This, Pete thinks, is the real Jon Heather. He hasn't quite died yet.

'His name's Charlie,' George whispers.

'From the Mission?'

'Nearly five years. But I'm sending him back.'

They drift back downstairs, out onto the veranda. The night is warm, and bats chitter in the gutters.

George tells Jon everything: the first night at the port in Liverpool; tramping back to the Chapeltown Home and seeing the place being gutted. Then, how he sat with the policeman and listened to his own life's story filled in. My mother, he tells Jon Heather, never really died. I've written to her, and she has even written back. Once upon a time, she made a terrible decision: she gave me to the Children's Crusade. It was they who told me she had died, so that I might forget – all about England, all about my old life.

They think they've told Charlie as well – but I haven't let them.

For five years now, Charlie has written down every little thing he can remember about his life in Leeds. George produces a bundle of notebooks, some in his own hand, some in the trembling script of the boy sleeping upstairs. You can trust what is written in the first books, George says. Later, come interpretations and imaginings – but there are seeds of truth in those memories as well, so they are not to be altogether discounted. It amounts, George says, to a record of a boy's beginnings.

'There was enough in it,' George says, 'that, a year ago, I found his mother. I'm friends with that old policeman, and he did some nosing around for me. She's still in Leeds. She's one of those who'll never leave.'

Jon flicks through the pages: we went to the moor and sat in the sun; there was a garden with a tree called a monkey puzzle.

'Jon, my mother didn't know about Australia – but she signed the waivers, trusted the Children's Crusade to do what was best for me. If she told me she was coming back to get me, she never told that to Judah Reed and the rest. They knew the deal from the start.'

For a second, Jon is a little boy again, looking at his own mother's signature in Judah Reed's hand.

In the end, it is an encouraging look from Pete that drives George on. 'We were given to the Children's Crusade, Jon. For better or worse. But Charlie was taken.'

'When they knew where she lived,' Pete interjects, 'George helped Charlie write to her. Posted his letter in secret.'

'But we wrote to our mothers too . . .' Jon remembers.

George lifts a finger to excuse himself and returns to the farmhouse, emerging moments later with a cardboard suitcase, from which he produces an envelope. On the front, the writing is unmistakably Jon Heather's: bigger and less precise, but still his. It is a strange comfort to think that something as simple as his handwriting might have stayed the same.

He takes it in a quivering hand and removes the paper folded inside:

I'll be your best boy, if only you come and take me back. I'll get you anything you want – and, mother, if I haven't got it, why, I'll go for and get it.
I am your son who loves you,
Jon (Heather)

Jon crams it back in the envelope, unable to read anymore.

'They have them filed away in big boxes in the back of the Mission house,' says George. 'My own too. I remember,' he blanches, embarrassed, 'you let me write to your mother too.'

To his shame, Jon does not remember. The cabinets of your mind are like Charlie's memobooks, he thinks: perhaps some of it is genuine, but the rest is distorted. The Jon Heather of fifteen years ago – he is only an imaginary little boy. It is no wonder you could not preserve him with strictures and rules.

'Did his mother write back?' he asks.

George nods. 'She'd been writing for years, Jon. First to the Home in Chapeltown – then to the Mission out here. Charlie was supposed to be at the Home for six months. His mother was offered a job at an estate outside Edinburgh, the sort of money she couldn't turn down, not without a penny to live on back in Leeds. So she trusted the Children's Crusade to look after him while she was gone. Only, when she came back . . .'

'The Home was empty.'

'It took another six months, but the Crusade told her, in the end, where he was – and where he was going to stay.'

Jon feels Pete and George looking at him. 'What now?' he asks.

'The Children's Crusade used to believe in its mission,' George begins. 'I've seen all the archives, the boys abandoned and living wild in Leeds and Liverpool and London . . . They really did want to help. But now . . .'

It is as if, George says, the object and the means of the Children's Crusade, once so deeply entwined, have become inverted without anybody noticing. Once it was to rescue these boys and send them to Australia; then, it became: we need to send boys to Australia, so we must find some boys to rescue.

'Now they round up boys like Charlie. They spring nets and dig pits to catch them.' He pauses. 'Charlie's mother is waiting for him. But I can't send an eleven-year-old boy, no matter how far he's come already, across the world on his own.'

Jon Heather rocks back. 'You're not going?'

'You are,' breathes George.

Thoughts stampede through Jon's mind. 'I don't have the money,' he says. 'I almost did, but they . . .'

Pete steps forward, a gentle shoulder barge. 'You've got more than you think, Jon Heather.' He puts an arm around him, guides him along the fence, where the fields of Black Chaparral sleep under southern stars. 'Five years ago, you upped and left. You wouldn't come with us, you miserable bastard, but you did leave us something.'

'Dog,' mutters Jon.

'The ute,' Pete corrects. 'Though Dog has his uses too.' The ute sits in the yard, battered and rusty, but still running strong. 'It was another year before we could buy a second ute. All that year, we rode that old thing from one end of the farm to the other, fixing fences and digging ditches and taking our eggs off to flog to whoever would have them. We couldn't have done a thing without that ute. I reckon that's about enough of an investment that you own a third of this place.'

Jon pushes himself away. 'Peter, I couldn't . . .'

'It's too late, Jon. Me and Cormac Tate already bought you out. Gave you a terrible price, so you wouldn't feel too guilty. About the price of one flight home. We've bought Dog off you too, so you have a bit to tide yourself over until you find work.'

For the longest time, Jon does not breathe a word.

'Dog isn't worth nothing,' he finally says.

'Then you've robbed us blind.'

The three men stand at a distance to each other, but slowly, in the silence, they shuffle back together: first, Pete; then the barrel-shape of George; then Jon, scrawny and shaggy and still looking like a street urchin. Up against the fence, they make a curious portrait. An aged yellow snout appears between them, completing the vision.

'I couldn't go until they'll sign me off. I'm meant to check in, every month . . .'

'Well, Jon,' George says. 'It's not as if you'd ever be coming back, is it?'

XVIII

A boy sails to Australia, but a man flies home.

On the tenth day of September, in the year of 1965, Jon Heather sets foot on English soil for the first time since he was a ten-year-old boy. It is a nondescript stretch of tarmac in an airport outside London, a land as alien to him as Australia, but all the same he knows, in his head, he is home. Charlie hurries into the terminal building, but Jon Heather takes every step carefully, considering each one.

Neither one of them has baggage to pick up, so they are the first through the gates and out, into England. They catch a guttering train, through underground tunnels, to King's Cross station and spend the night on the concourse there. Beggars do not ask them for money, for they look more wretched and out of place than any.

In the morning, they board a train going north. In the carriage, they sit opposite each other. Jon has brought stones, but it is not the perfect game for a moving carriage – and, besides, both would rather gape out of the window, watching England rushing past.

When the sun is out, parts of the land can look exactly like Australia: fields of grain, tracks running off in between. It is one of the great disappointments of Jon's life. Yet, only an hour into their journey, the land has changed. Hills have risen and forests crept down to the tracks. They rattle through towns where redbrick terraces crowd together, and factories belch out smoke.

Jon puts down Charlie's memobooks and kneads his hands. He feels things firing inside him, each sparking the next, like a trail of dominoes toppling over. Once, his thoughts were slow and long, like a desert road; now, every thought erupts, vivid and violent – and, for a moment, he is out of his body, hurtling down the tracks, reaching home long before the train has even pulled into the station.

They arrive in Leeds before noon. It is ridiculous that England could be so small. Once, Jon remembers, there were giants here. They had a causeway that took them over the sea, and they could cross England in three simple strides.

It is Charlie who leads Jon from the platform. He remembers this station well, for he has written of it in his memobook: at Leeds station, there is a stand to buy a newspaper and another to buy sweets. It is raining, but the rain feels different. It is cold and it does not hang in the air.

Jon recognizes nothing, but that does not shock or sadden him, for he has never seen this part of the city. The road sweeps away through an empty square, with squat towers on one side and a grand hall, with broad white steps and statues of lions, on the other. Taxicabs are lined up and their drivers, Asian men, stand idly beneath the overhang of a bus shelter.

An old man approaches. He wears a long greatcoat and wellington boots. 'Jon Heather?' he begins.

Jon nods, guardedly.

'I believe we have a mutual friend, Mr Heather. George Stone.'
'You're Captain Matthews?'
The old man nods. 'You've come a long way, boys. Let's get out of this rain.' He turns his eyes to the greyness creeping sullenly over the city roofs. 'Come on, my car's round back.'
Captain Matthews' car is a Mini, with just enough space for Jon and Charlie to cram in the back. In scant minutes, they leave the city centre behind, cresting a motorway bridge with the city colleges hunched on either side. Leeds, Jon decides, is like England in miniature: its vastness compressed into an island of land smaller than Black Chaparral.
A sprawling heathland rises on their left, with trees that would dwarf the greatest heights of the shadow wood. They crawl through a labyrinth of narrow roads and houses without yards, and come to a stop outside a run of the terrace where the houses are newer, spread out with gardens in between. Captain Matthews parks the Mini and steps out onto the kerb. Though Jon follows, Charlie remains in the car.
Jon leans back in the window. 'Do you remember?' he asks.
Charlie shakes his head.
'Charlie's family used to live in a much older run, up by the old cricket ground,' the captain explains. 'They moved some years ago.'
Jon coaxes Charlie out of the car, but he will not go far. At last, Captain Matthews opens the garden gate and approaches the door.
When the door opens, Captain Matthews obscures the woman on the step – but, when he shuffles aside, they can both see her: Charlie's mother, wrapped in a cardigan, taking the faltering steps of a baby deer. Charlie has his chin down, and she calls his name four times, her voice rising, before he dares look up.
At his side, Jon trembles just as violently. He has seen this before. Then, it was fathers coming back from war to children they had never met. Now, it is the child who must return to a

parent they barely know. Something tells Jon to pick Charlie up, wrap his arms around him, cradle him until they reach the end of the street, the end of the town, the edge of the city. There might be a cave they can live in together, never speaking to another soul – a lost boy and a lost man.

But Charlie's mother takes his hand and together they walk up the steps. At the door, Charlie strains not to go through. He cranes a look back at Jon Heather, and then he is gone.

Jon spends that night with Captain Matthews. He is recently widowed and the house betrays a man of few needs and a weight of memories. He has a son and grandchildren – and, though their photographs line the wall, there is only one of his wife: somewhere in the Victorian quarter of town, standing with her husband, only two years gone.

In the morning, Jon has little idea what he should do. While Captain Matthews fusses with breakfast, he takes out an envelope from the folds of his jacket. Peter was given one like this from Cormac Tate – but this particular envelope bears George's writing on the front:

19 Mayville Place, Burley

Jon is careful to fold it precisely as he puts it away, as if destroying the address might eliminate the people who live there. With the letter hidden, he takes breakfast with Captain Matthews, staying long after to help the old man potter around the garden.

For some reason, he does not want to go out into the city.

The Captain would let Jon stay for as long as he wished, but on the next day he answers an advert in the local gazette and takes a bedsit off the Clarendon Road, hidden behind the University. Many students mill around here, and he likes the idea that he might have been one of them, if things had been different.

His landlord is a weasely man from outside Leeds, and he rents most of the rooms to immigrant men who work for the city. Most of them, he tells Jon, are Pakistani: he might do well to double-lock his door at night. There is a meter on the wall for electricity, and a handful of tokens stacked on the sill. Jon nods his thanks – and is, at last, left alone.

He has had his own room before, but only in prison. This cell is just as bare. He looks around, thrilling at flaking plaster walls and the cockroach in the corner. For the first time ever, he has a bookshelf on which he might line up his books – but those trinkets that he once carried around with him have long since disappeared. Once he has found work, he will take a trip into town and find a second-hand shop: he will read science fiction and then he will read classics. That, he decides, is the way things would have gone.

He takes the envelope from George and plants it on the mantelpiece above a fireplace that has long since been bricked up. When you want a life, you need to know where to start. There are three things a grown man needs: a roof over his head; a day of honest work; and a wife. One foot in front of the other; that is how you grow up.

There are adverts for work in the local gazette. Jon answers each of them, and by the end of the week he has found work unloading pallets at a warehouse along the canal. It is a long walk from where he lives, but it lets him take in the city. As a boy, he knew none of these roads – but as a man he would have known them all. He attacks the problem systematically, allowing himself an extra hour each morning so that he can follow detours and investigate dead-ends, slowly filling in the blanks of a knowledge that should have been his.

At the weekends, he drinks with the boys from work. He has little he can talk to them about – he will not tell them about Australia – but, in any case, they talk about little other than their working week. Men from one side of the world to the other, Jon learns, all hate their foremen. On this, he bitches like the best of them. He cannot hold his beer and the men mock him for it – so he takes to buying a case each Wednesday night and sinking it in his bedsit alone, certain that, before two months are out, he will have caught up with his workmates and nobody will question, ever again, that he is only just learning how to drink.

Some of the boys have girls. The girls change, week on week, and it occurs to Jon: you thought too much about Megan; if you were a real man, not that fake human being you became in Australia, you would be able to take a girl, drop a girl, and take another one without caring. You could come down to a club like this and tell your mates and they would laugh, and then it would start over again.

He has a roof over his head, he has work, and now he needs a woman.

There is a bar he has heard of, in the basement of a shopping centre, where students sometimes go to dance. He goes there each evening for a week, decides that Friday evenings are the best, and makes a point of making it a regular haunt. The third girl he talks to agrees to go to the pictures with him.

Her name is Emma, or Emily, or something like that. He makes arrangements to meet her at a bus stop close to the shopping centre on a Friday night, and presents her with a garland of flowers he has picked up from a newsagent's further down the row. She squints at him curiously and accepts the flowers, but hardly moves when he goes to lock his arm with hers. Instead, a foot apart, they wander through the cold of the gathering night.

He has discovered a picture-house, nestled in the warren of

buildings underneath the parkland close to where he lives. There are three films showing. He tries to steer her towards the Western, thinking of the comics a boy named Peter once had, but she wants to go to something starring a man named Elvis Presley. He buys her pieces of hard rock candy and spends the next five minutes turning one over in his mouth, eager to spit it out.

In the cinema, the rows are filling up. Here, there are no places for the Malays and aborigines, though there are three Asian men sitting together up high. Jon is about to sit behind them, but Emma shoots him a look and wanders into the centre rows.

'Is it for them?' Jon asks.

Emma drops into her seat, looking up with an inscrutable gaze. 'What?'

'I didn't know there were different seats for different people.'

Emma says nothing, coldly turning to her box of rock candy instead. A moment later, she offers up the box. Jon can still feel the last piece in his teeth but takes one nevertheless. It is another five minutes before he is able to speak. By now, the ice-cream seller has gone and the projector has begun to whirr.

'You go to that place often then?'

She looks at him sideways.

'That place I found you.'

'I suppose,' she shrugs. 'I have a friend.'

'A friend?'

'She likes it there.'

'Do you like it there?'

'I suppose.'

It is still some time before the film will begin, so he fills the silence by asking her questions about her life. He has a list. He learns that she comes from a place called Guiseley, a place as foreign as any but only a few miles outside of Leeds. She is studying to be a secretary. She knows short-hand and typing and thinks her boss is contemptible. With this, at least, Jon can join in.

'Every foreman's the same,' he says, 'all the world over.'

'Every what?'

He catches himself, and shrugs off the question.

At last, something in her softens. She hasn't been to the pictures in weeks, she says, so this is a treat. She begins to ask him questions and, with each one, Jon feels his hackles rising. He had a system for this once: bat the questions back; ask them about their life, and you don't have to tell them about your own. It takes a little while to get the conversation back on track. By that time, he has concocted a past for himself, something to explain the strange vowel sounds she sometimes struggles to understand. He has, he says, just been working in London. That is probably as alien to this girl as Australia ought to be to Jon.

'Oh,' she says, seemingly disappointed. 'I thought you might have been an American.'

'No,' Jon mutters. 'Just boring old Leeds.'

She kicks her heels. 'Sometimes I wish everything wasn't just boring old Leeds.' She sits up straight, swivelling to face him. 'Do you know, one day I'd like to get away. Somewhere where it's sunny. Somewhere where there's . . . *wine*.'

'Wine?'

Such a thing is patently absurd.

'Somewhere they have *fun*. Anywhere but . . . here.'

Up on the screen, the pictures start flickering. Jon settles into his seat, grateful not to have to listen to her voice any longer, that asinine dreaming of hers: as if anything was better than being right here, right now, where they're both *supposed* to be.

In the film, a ridiculous man with a voice he can hardly understand plays a soldier and hillbilly both. Beside Jon, Emma laughs and hoots like all the other girls scattered across the picture house. A beat behind them every time, Jon joins in.

Come the end of the story, he can judge when to laugh and not laugh. The final scene is fading to black before he realizes he has not absorbed a single scene; he has been too busy watching the other patrons instead.

Outside, the rain has already begun. Jon cringes into it, walking close to Emma as if to protect her. They drift along the street. A motorbus rolls past, spraying up puddle water and sludge.

'Well,' she looks at him, 'I should be getting back.'

'Not on your life!' exclaims Jon. 'Don't you want a drink?'

She steps back. He is darkly aware of the way she is holding the flowers, loosely by the stem, their heads drooping down.

'I thought we'd get some food,' says Jon.

Emma trudges on. Three feet behind, Jon follows.

'We could find a canteen. I'd order for you.'

At this, she turns around. 'You'd order for me?'

Jon knows now he has said something wrong. 'What did I do?'

'The film was lovely,' she says, 'but you're a . . . strange boy.'

This, Jon has heard before. 'I'd drive you home,' he begins, 'but I haven't got a ute.'

'A what?'

'A car,' he stammers. 'I'd have driven you but . . .'

At least she laughs. 'I didn't expect a boy like you to have a car.'

'Well?'

'You can walk me to my bus stop if you like. You don't have to wait.'

At the bus stop, he kicks his heels for a few silent minutes. Then, he looks up to see he has kicked his way ten yards along the street. He looks back to say goodbye, but she is not looking in his direction. It seems easier just to walk away.

Jon does not want to go home. Instead, he finds a public house and empties his pockets of the money he was going to spend on the girl. When it is all gone, he sets off again – and, this time, his roaming leads him home.

At the bedsit, all he can hear is fucking through the wall. He sits and listens. This, he supposes, is how his own night should have ended. He closes his eyes, but the sounds only seem to intensify. He has had too much to drink – the men at work would say he has hardly touched a drop – and images cavort across the backs of his eyes. Some of them he thinks are memories, others contorted visions of things that might have been: a night in the shadow wood; taking the little boy Luca to a hospital; holding Megan's hand as they climb the red rocks at Cable Beach.

It is the last image that sobers him. He can taste salt, suddenly, on his lips – but it is not until he feels hot tears that he understands this is not merely a memory of spray from the sea.

Sitting on the end of the bed, he kneads his eyes dry like a little boy in his dormitory at night. If only that girl – Emma, Emily, whatever her fucking name was – might have come home with him. At least, then, he would have had something to hold onto tonight, something to beat back whatever is in his chest, straining to get out. He realizes he would give anything just to be ten years old again, with George huddling up to him at night and pissing all over him before morning.

Perhaps it is thoughts like these that make him go to the dresser and pull out the envelope that George pressed into his hands. *19 Mayville Place.* He hardly needs it; he will not forget the address.

He is holding the envelope when he goes to sleep at night, and holding it still when he wakes in the morning.

Mayville Place is a short walk from where he has been living. In England, one coast is a short walk from the next, with a multitude of kingdoms cluttering the hills in between. Another of the nondescript terraces, its houses have little yards where people have lined up terracotta pots for flowers. Number 19 has a tree overhanging the doorway. Jon Heather puts one foot in front of the other and knocks on the door.

When there is no reply, he beats a retreat around the block, following the thin alley behind and counting off the houses until he finds the right one. He knocks at the back door, but when there is no answer, he has no hesitation in trying the door handle. If anybody asks, he will tell them: it is a family home.

The door is not locked and opens into a small kitchen with crockery piled high. A pantry has stairs leading into a cellar, and a second door crosses a tiny hallway to the living room. In here, there is a television set and an upright piano.

Jon stands in the doorway, looking in like a man in a museum. The wallpaper has a floral pattern and bubbles where it has been inexpertly hung, and there are photographs in frames: a collage of scenes, two girls and their mother.

Jon recognizes his sisters at once. His mother, he finds, is harder somehow, as if her face has always been clouded in his mind. He stares into the photographs and thinks: it is before I was born. His sisters are younger than he was when he joined the Children's Crusade. He paws at the glass that separates him from them, leaving a sweaty smudge behind. These twins are not identical, yet he cannot tell them apart.

He closes his eyes. Concentrate, Jon Heather. You didn't go through all those years of waiting, of silence, for nothing. Your sisters are called Rachel and Samantha. Your sisters helped you groom a toy horse. Your sisters . . . He opens his eyes. They glimmer back at him from the photograph, but it is useless.

He turns away. On top of the upright piano, there is another photograph: his mother and father, on the day that they were married. He wanders over, lifts it up – but this man has light, sandy hair, not the dark mop his father had, and the woman is years older than the one who wished Jon goodbye outside the Home.

He whirls around. There has to be something, somewhere, to tell him what has happened, what has gone wrong. He opens a cabinet behind one of the settees, scrabbles there to pull out wads of papers, until he finds what he is searching for. It is a photograph album, one he has never forgotten.

His sisters – those strange girls up on the wall – once sat with him and showed him pictures of his true father: a man with wild black hair glowering into the camera. Those same girls are here, but there are no pictures of his father. He tears through the pages, a record of the girls growing up. They are eleven, and then they are thirteen, and then they are the sisters Jon Heather can remember: eighteen and nineteen and twenty years old. Now, at last, he can tell them apart. He rears up, victorious against himself – until a terrible thought dawns.

There is not a single picture of you, Jon Heather, in any of these albums.

His sisters, here, are of an age when they looked after him, put him to bed. Once, there were photographs of all of that, but not any longer. His mother, of whom he dreamed, every night, must have believed the very same thing as the Children's Crusade: if you are going to live in the present, you have to eradicate the past.

There is noise behind him: the clicking of a key in a lock, the shuffling of feet. He spins around, the photograph album still open in his hands. All around him paper is balled up and trailing out of the cabinet. He is like a dog whose master has come back to camp and found him with his snout in the tucker bag.

He stands up, showering the photographs everywhere – but then he reins himself in. He is Jon Heather. He has come thousands of miles. He has come, he thinks, thousands of years.

Every boy to grow up the boy they were supposed to be, said Luca, and not a single boy left behind.

The door opens and a tall man with sandy hair appears. He is looking down when he enters, so he does not see Jon at first. Instead, he sees scattered papers and a picture of himself looking up from the ground. His eyes rise. If Jon really was a cut-throat, he could have killed him where he stood.

'Who in hell are you?' the man demands. It amuses Jon to hear his voice thundering so, when every muscle in his body twitches and hauls him back.

'I'm Jon,' he says. 'I'm Jon Heather. Ask me again,' he insists. 'Ask me again who I am.'

At the man's side there is movement, another figure bustling him out of the way, until they stand, two abreast, in the doorway. She is older than Jon has imagined; her hair has turned grey, her jowls are starting to sag – but her eyes are the same vivid blue, her lips still the thin red lips that kissed him goodbye.

She is ugly, thinks Jon. She wears make-up, so she must think she's pretty, but she drips in ugliness like a fat Sunday roast, stewing in its own juices.

'Hello, Mother,' he breathes.

The doorway is hardly broad enough for them both to stand there: this stranger and her husband. Though the man is raging at him, Jon barely hears a word, barely even sees him. He is just an amorphous mess of colour on the edge of his vision, for he is looking only at his mother.

She is tiny, diminutive where she once was tall and statuesque. She has grown into a stoop, and her eyes refuse to meet his.

'You might say hello,' Jon says, his words swamped beneath the man's incessant questions.

'Jon . . .'

When she whispers the word, lifting a cupped hand to her

mouth as if to hold back more, her husband is suddenly hushed.

'Annie,' he says. 'What . . .'

She flings her arms up, to hold onto him. 'It's him.'

'You're certain?'

'Of course I'm certain . . .'

Jon might be watching a puppet show, for they are not addressing him. He takes a step, then another. He could cross the room with a third. This is England, and he is a giant.

He thinks he is going to hold her, yet before his foot has landed, he knows it is not true. She shrinks back, half behind her husband, into the doorway – but it is not only that that stops him. He realizes he does not know how. It would not be the same as holding Megan. It would not be the same as holding onto Dog, late at night. It would not even be the same as clapping Cormac Tate on the shoulder and beaming 'bastard good'. He does not know which arm to lift, whether he should hold her under her arms or above; whether her head should be buried in his shoulder or his in hers.

None of it matters, because she is saying 'No, no, no,' over and over. The words repel him more powerfully than any of the commands her husband utters – empty threats circling a thousand feet away.

'Jon . . . How long have you . . .?'

'Fifteen and a half years,' he whispers.

'I mean . . . in Leeds?'

'Weeks. A month. Two. I wanted to come before. I had it in mind. I got your address . . .' His voice cracks. He hates it. If they were going to cry, they should be in each other's arms. '. . . on a piece of paper. My friend found it. I left them behind and I came to . . .'

He holds George's envelope up, as if she might take it. It flutters to the ground on the carpet between them. 'I'm sorry,' he says. 'I wasn't thinking straight. I shouldn't have bothered.'

He turns side-on to shoulder between them, back through the door. Yet, he will not touch them. They stand, uncomfortably close. Jon can smell her perfume. It is heavy, and smells of being a scared little boy.

'Jon,' she says. 'It's not that . . . It's only – I wasn't expecting it, Jon.'

He manages to break past, out onto the doorstep. 'Ever?'

'What?'

'Were you *ever* expecting me, Mother?'

Her husband envelops her in his arms, but a shudder courses through her body and she casts him off.

'Jon,' she breathes. 'I just don't know what to say.'

'No?' Jon's laugh is full of spite. Of all the times he pictured this day, every time he shut his eyes at night to dream of it, not once did he think it would feel like this. It is, he decides, exactly the way he felt when he brought back his fists to pound Cook's face into the dirt. 'Well, I do.'

He reaches into his back pocket, pulls out a scrap of a letter that a little boy once wrote. He holds it up, puffs out his chest, clears his throat before he reads. 'I'll be your best boy,' he chokes, 'if only you come and take me back. I'll get you anything you want – and mother, if I haven't got it, why, I'll go for and get it.'

He pauses, but he does not mean to pause. There are too many words clogging his throat. 'I am your son who loves you,' he says. 'Jon Heather.'

It is late when he leaves. There have been tears and there has been silence; there has been storytelling, of a sort, and an invitation to return – but: fuck this, thinks Jon, I don't need an invitation.

He pounds the beat from Burley Park to Woodhouse Moor, cutting over its tamed heaths and reaching his bedsit before full dark has come. He does not go home, but prowls into the city instead, walking the length of the canal and back again.

He drinks beer in a public house where the men look at him askance, as if he has walked into some private room in which he does not belong. When the glass is half empty, he sets it down and prowls on, finding himself again at the doors of the basement bar in which he first met Emma.

Inside, he buys another beer – but his pockets are empty and, when he cannot produce any change, a lumbering man wearing a long black coat asks him to leave. Jon tells him, I'll just sit; I don't have to drink. Yet apparently this is not allowed. He stands, makes as if he is about to leave, but drops into another seat instead. Music is playing, deep and tinny, through speakers that rattle and gyrate.

'Look,' the ogre says, looming above, 'you think I like this job? You think I want to spend my nights here, pushing people around?'

Jon would take a draught of his drink if he had one, just to keep himself from lashing out. 'I wouldn't have thought you'd like it at all.'

'Then do me a favour, won't you, and get the . . .'

The man does not have the chance to go on, for suddenly somebody is at his side. At first the figure is obscured. Then Jon hears a familiar voice.

'I'll buy him a drink,' says Emma. 'He's not going to cause any trouble . . .'

The man steps back. In the cavernous light, Emma stands there, in a dress her mother has stitched, flowers tracing up and down her arms.

'It's your funeral, love.'

As the man knuckles away, Emma squints at Jon, her head angled slightly to one side. 'What are you doing here, Jon?'

Jon doesn't even have an answer. He stands. He does not want to push past her, but she gives him no other choice. He goes towards her with his shoulder; it will hurt less that way and, even now, he does not want to hurt her.

'It wasn't so bad, you know. I *could* get you a drink . . .'

'It wouldn't change a fucking thing.'

She laughs, off-key and nervous. 'It would for a couple of hours.'

'It would at that,' admits Jon – but he does not look at her as he tramps out of the door.

In the small of the next afternoon, he is busy burning the shreds of his passport in the bedsit sink, when somebody hammers at the door downstairs. In the basin, his face melts. George did well to obtain the documents to get him back home, but he cannot suffer to have his place of birth marked as Geraldton, Western Australia, for very long.

He stumbles out of the bedsit to find a postman standing irate on the step. The old man presses an envelope into his hand and then retreats, muttering invective.

It is the first letter Jon has ever received that was not written on the back of a biscuit wrapper. He retreats back to the bedsit and flings it onto the bed. There is no knowing what is written inside, but until he opens it, it could be anything. He circles it warily, like a cat waiting for its catch to try and escape. There is a stamp on the front that leaps out at him. He had hoped never to see that sort of stamp ever again.

Dear Jon,

I heard from Captain Matthews that you have found a home and got yourself into work! Pete and I are not surprised. You always worked so hard, Jon Heather, and you deserve it. We're proud as hell (Pete has made me promise I would write this).

It seems you are adjusting far better than I ever could have done, Jon Heather. England was a terrible shock to me. I sometimes think it was a worse shock than Australia. At least, then, I didn't think about it so much. Things seemed to just happen when we were boys. I think you will understand what I mean when I say – it's the thinking that can catch you out . . .

I am writing, Jon, not just because I miss you! (Pete says I am to tell you this also.) There is a girl in the Mission, named Martha Gray, who I have taken an interest in. She is five years old and came to the Crusade last year because her mother passed on – but she speaks freely about her grandmother, to whom she thought she was coming to stay. For a long while, I thought that her grandmother must have been somewhere in Australia, but I know, now, that I was wrong.

I wonder if you might help me in tracing the girl's grandmother? She has only been with us a year and I am of the hope that she might one day remember the Mission only like a distant dream.

I am forwarding, here, some of the details I have been able to glean from her – and do hope, Jon Heather, that you will want to help. I hope to be making a trip to England in the New Year and, should things progress, I will bring the girl with me. I do hope you're looking forward to a visit from your old world!

Your friend, as ever,

George Stone.

Jon Heather sits for the longest time, with the letter resting in his lap. He supposes he had always known he was not done with Crusades and Missions, but that world seems so absurd to him now, hemmed in by these four walls of flaking plaster, the little kettle whistling viciously on the hob.

When he is almost ready to shred the letter and burn it along with the fragments of his passport, a genuine smile erupts out of him, like vomit after a twelve-hour drunk.

Old friends, he thinks, wryly: they'll always be back.

Captain Matthews still has friends in the constabulary, and they are happy to look the other way while he and Jon Heather pore through records. The girl's family name is Gray, but her grandmother was always Granny White. It is a laborious day matching up certificates for weddings, births, deaths – but by nightfall they have managed to come up with three addresses. The girl, George writes, remembers an abbey with wildflowers and long grass, so they head, first, to the address closest to the ruins in Kirkstall.

The woman who answers the door is not nearly as old as Jon had expected, younger certainly than his own mother. At first, she is wary of letting them in. Only when Captain Matthews produces some identification, long since defunct, does she allow them through.

That night, Jon paces the bedsit and recalls the bewildered way the woman had looked when he showed her the memories George had been collecting. It would seem to be an absurd thing that a girl's whole life would be scribbled down in newsagent's notebooks – but Jon Heather looks at the brown paper bag lying open at his bedside, the stack of the pads he has bought lying inside, and thinks long and hard: like some cartographer of old, George has pieced together distant shores and contours, so that lost boys might make their way home. If George can do it, surely Jon Heather can do the same.

After lights out in the bedsit, Jon opens the first of his memobooks and begins to write: I remember keeping a vigil for my father, because I didn't know he was dead. I had a cap gun and mulled Christmas wine (was there alcohol in the wine?). I was eight years old, proud to be nearly nine, and I wasn't allowed beyond the end of my terrace.

It is hardly, Jon reasons, the essence of being an eight-year-old. He tears it out and begins again. If you cannot capture the way you were, he thinks, surely you can capture the way you are now.

I am lying in my very own room (the only other time in my life I had my very own room was when I was in prison) and I am not happy and I am not sad. Yesterday I met my mother. She is small and she has grey hair and her fingernails were bitten down to the quick.

After he has stared at it for some time, the novelty wears off, and it is just words on a piece of paper. It is like dropping ink into water; it bleeds and then it is gone.

He throws the memobooks down, and turns to try and sleep. Maybe it works for little boys and girls, but there isn't a thing that can be done for Jon Heather.

On the 12th of December in the year of 1965, Jon Heather is introduced to the sisters who attended him on the day of his birth. Rachel and Samantha do not bring their husbands, but Samantha does bring her son. He is called Benjamin, and he is ten years old. When she looks at Jon for the first time, she says she knows now how Benjamin will look when he is fully grown. She is, she says, very pleased. One after the other, his sisters embrace him; it is more than his mother did.

As they sit down for dinner, he thinks: I was sleeping on one of your floors on the night Mother gave me away, but I couldn't, for all the money in the world, tell you which one.

There are no tears this dinnertime. His mother's husband, whose name is Lewis, is keen to hear about Australia, and particularly eager to hear about bush blacks. He is of the opinion that England itself has a black problem. Benjamin, too, wants to hear about it: is Australia all criminals and kangaroos?

Jon does not want to regale them with stories of the bush, but he tells them what he can. He does not tell them about Peter and George, but he tells them about Dog. He makes up a story that he rescued Dog from a litter of wild dingoes, and that thrills Benjamin. His mother, he says, prodding at a parsnip, won't even entertain the *idea* of having a pet.

'They're dirty,' Samantha tells him.

'Your mother's right,' says Jon. 'They'll roll in their own shit if you let them . . .'

A fork clatters and a host of eyes scold him.

After dinner, the adults take drinks while Benjamin is sent off to play in the front room. At the kitchen table, Jon Heather pretends he likes sherry and listens to his sisters talk about their weeks. When they ask what kind of work Jon is doing, he tells them about the job loading pallets. Then they ask him what kind of work he would like to do. It is a question he does not understand until they repeat it a second time, and suddenly he feels ashamed. Then he is ashamed of himself for being ashamed – this way madness lies.

From the front room, there comes the sound of Benjamin hammering at the upright piano.

Samantha rolls her eyes. She is about to go after him, when Jon intervenes.

'I'll go,' he says.

At the piano, Benjamin spins around, as if expecting to be scolded, but Jon only slumps into one of the settees and sets his sherry down on the coffee table.

Benjamin drops down to take a sniff. 'I'd rather have orange,' he says.

'Me too,' grins Jon. 'Hey,' he says. 'Do you want to see a trick?'

He opens the front door, picks up a handful of pebbles and brings them back into the front room. With one hand, he tosses eight into the air. With the other, he catches all but one in the grooves between his fingers.

'Your turn,' he says.

In seconds, Benjamin is locked in concentration. Once he

has caught one stone on the back of his hand, he is more determined than ever. Two is straightforward, three a tricky prospect, and four impossible.

'A friend of mine can do twenty,' Jon says. 'Took him fourteen years to perfect it, but he can do it every time.'

'Is it an Australian game?' The very idea seems magical.

'I suppose it is,' says Jon.

'My dad says they have rabbits in Australia, but they kill them all with diseases.'

'There were plenty of rabbits in some of the places I was . . .' He shifts forward, cross-legged, and Benjamin mirrors the action. 'I remember one time, my friend Peter and I were making our way to a place called Carnarvon. They have a big banana plantation there, and we were going to do some work.'

'Would you get free bananas?'

'It's all we ate,' says Jon. 'But, on the way, we were getting hungry, and our ute . . .'

'What's a ute?'

'A wagon, like a motor car.'

Benjamin nods eagerly.

'Well, our old motor car kept breaking down, so one night we had to camp out on the side of the road, not a thing to eat and hardly any water. But our old friend Dog spotted a rabbit burrow at the side of the track. Well, it's too hot in the dead of day for the rabbits to come out, but as soon as dusk came around, there they were dozens of baby rabbits, just pouring out of those holes . . .'

Benjamin grimaces, half-delighted. 'Did you . . . eat them?'

'Oh yes,' says Jon.

'How do you eat a rabbit?'

'Well,' Jon begins. 'First, you have to catch them. But young rabbits, they catch easily, because . . .' He grins. '. . . they're not very bright. Once you have him, you dangle him and just slap him so he's stunned. Then, you can just chop him on the neck with your hand. It breaks his neck, so now he's ready for gutting. You get your knife, and slide it right into . . .'

Jon does not even hear the tears begin. By the time he realizes something is wrong, Benjamin is already on his feet, his face ruddy, flailing right past him to tumble through the kitchen doors.

Jon still sits, cross-legged, on the floor when his sister Samantha charges back through.

'Jon Heather,' she demands, 'what have you done?'

Jon kicks his heels on the doorstep, like a naughty boy. Soon, his mother comes to him. She doesn't say a thing, but offers him a cigarette instead.

'He's all right,' she says finally. 'He'll get over it.'

'It's nice you care so much,' says Jon. He is trapped, as if between a parted sea: the waves are rushing in at him from either side, but he doesn't know which tide he would rather do battle with. 'Do you know what I had to do the first week after we hit land?' he asks.

'Jon, you don't have to talk about . . .'

'I was put in the dairies,' he says. 'A boy called Tommy taught me how to butcher a goat. Here's how, Mother. You whisper to him, and he's scared but he calms down. Just like Samantha whispering to that boy in there. Then he trusts you. So you press on his rump and he rolls over, and you tickle his tummy – and then, one of you holds his legs, and the other just wrenches a knife across his throat. If you're canny, you can do it in one cut – but, Mum, it took me a couple of years to master that. I was younger than Samantha's son, and that's what I was doing. The boy can hear about how to gut a little bunny. He doesn't have to piss his bed at night for that.'

She slaps him, but he barely feels a thing.

'You've had a hard time, Jon. But I . . .' She labours over it. Just say it, Mother. Just spit it out. 'I had a hard time too.'

It is a remarkable thing, but words can change meaning as they twirl from a person's lips to the other's ears.

'Thank you for dinner, Mother.'

'You don't have to be like that. You don't know how much I wanted you back, Jon.'

'Yeah,' says Jon, 'but time heals all manner of wounds, if you let it, doesn't it? The difference is, Mother, I wouldn't let it. I loved you too much.'

'Jon, look at me.' She takes hold of his chin, angles it towards her. 'I love you. We all do. But . . .'

Let it be known: your mother does love you, Jon Heather; she just doesn't like you very much.

'Will we see you for Christmas?' she asks. 'We should be . . . together . . . for Christmas.'

Yes, Jon thinks as he returns to the terrace, families should be together for Christmas – and they should be together for birthdays as well.

It is the 12th of December in the year of 1965, and though nobody has said a word, Jon Heather has turned twenty-five years old.

XIX

On the fifth day before Christmas, Jon Heather wakes in the small of the afternoon to the sound of pebbles thrown against his window. Still half-dressed, he shoves his head out of the window.

Captain Matthews stands on the edge of the street, and Jon hurries down. Frost ices the hedges running the length of the road. Streetlights throb, hours before dark.

'It's Charlie,' says Captain Matthews. 'Is he with you?'

Jon shakes his head.

'His mother put in a missing persons report last night. He didn't come home from school.'

Jon throws a look at his bedsit window. Some part of him wishes Charlie really was up there.

'Why did nobody come to tell me?' he demands.

'I'm not here officially. His parents . . .'

Jon hawks up a torrent of phlegm. That is what he thinks of Charlie's parents. 'They should have told me,' he snaps. 'They checked everywhere?'

'Went door to door.'

Jon sees the captain's Mini sitting on the kerb. 'I'll drive,' he says.

The captain does not let Jon near the wheel, but follows his every direction. It is only a short drive, around the moor and through the warren of streets beyond, before they come to the corner where the Chapeltown Boys' Home sits. He makes the captain park at a distance and walks on alone.

Around the Home, the trees have been felled and a new road laid, but something of the old place remains, like an after-image on the back of the eye. He stops, and knows for certain he is in the same spot where his mother said goodbye.

He does not have to look for long. Charlie is sitting on a tree stump, wrapped in a duffel coat that is not his own, with a swag bag lying at his feet.

Jon wanders up to him. 'Where did you sleep last night, young man?'

'I can sleep out,' Charlie mumbles. 'It isn't a big problem, is it, Mr Heather? You don't *really* need a bed . . .'

Jon grins and sits down.

'I don't like it,' Charlie says. He shrugs his shoulders inside the enormous duffel, and Jon realizes it is the coat of which he is speaking. '*He* bought it for me. He says I'll grow into it. I only brought it because it's cold. I'm so cold, Mr Heather.'

'It's winter, young man.'

'I miss the *proper* winter.'

Clear nights and mild days, long enough that you can do your chores and still have time to play outside the dormitory. Yes, Jon misses the proper winter too.

'Who is *he*?' asks Jon.

Charlie looks up. He has not been crying, but he has long ago learnt how not to cry. 'Just my new dad. But I'm to call him Owen. They took me *shopping*.' The word drips with disgust. 'I don't like it here, Mr Heather. I don't have any friends.

And . . . I miss Mr Stone. He sent me a letter, but they didn't let me keep it. They said – they said I've got to forget . . .'

Yes, Jon thinks, you do have to forget: if you're going to live in the present, you have to eradicate the past.

When he catches himself thinking it, he has to gulp it back down. Can he really think the same as Judah Reed and his mother?

He shunts Charlie gently with his shoulder. This is a thing he learnt from Peter Slade. 'They're frightened,' he says. 'They wonder what you got up to, out there.'

'They don't like me playing in the garden. But I don't like staying inside. It's dull and it's dreary.'

'What about school?' Jon ventures. 'You've made new friends at school . . .'

Charlie fidgets; if he does not say anything, he does not have to tell a lie.

'You don't have to pretend.'

'I hate it, Mr Heather. They put me in remedials.'

'Remedials?'

'It means the stupid class. But it's not as if I can't read. It's not as if I couldn't write. I wrote all those notebooks, just like Mr Stone told me to. It's just . . .'

'School doesn't last forever, Charlie.'

'Put them boys in the Mission and they'd be the ones in remedials, wouldn't they, Mr Heather?' For the first time, Charlie beams. 'We didn't do much reading or writing in the Mission. But not one of those boys in school would know a thing about digging or woodwork or how to fix an engine or . . .'

'How to kill a goat,' remembers Jon.

'I'd like to see them try. I bet it'd take a hundred of those boys just to kill one silly goat!'

'Do you remember what your real father was like, Charlie?'

He nods. 'He used to work at the warehouses on the Meanwood Road. I asked Mum about it, but she said it isn't there anymore.'

'And?'

'And I have to forget about him too, don't I? I'm not allowed to think about Australia and I'm not allowed to think about before Australia either. So what am I allowed to think about, Mr Heather?'

Jon stands, reaches out a hand and is pleasantly surprised when Charlie takes it. Together, they meander up the street, away from the Home.

When they reach the Mini, Charlie strains. 'Do we have to?' he asks.

They drive up and out of Chapeltown, snaking through the terraces until they hit the Meanwood Road. The thoroughfare is still banked with broad empty yards where its buildings were carved apart and, as they come to a stretch where new warehouses loom, Jon helps Charlie out onto the kerb.

Jon finds, as they walk, that Charlie's hand is still in his. They venture deeper, scuttling through the darknesses to reach pools of orange spilling from the street lights. Men are still at work, and on occasion they see trucks wheeling from vast open doors, solitary workers throwing buckets of boiling water onto paths encrusted in ice.

'My father used to work in a place like this,' says Jon. 'Maybe he worked here as well.'

It is a lie; Jon's father laboured in warehouses and factories on the other side of the city. Yet – you're allowed to tell little lies.

'Do you remember him too . . .' Charlie asks, '. . . from before Australia?'

Jon Heather shakes his head.

'Do you remember anything?'

'Some things,' Jon admits.

Charlie's fingers tense and Jon realizes he is trying to extricate his hand. Without a word, he lets go. The boy drifts a few steps into darkness, but goes no further.

'I want to go . . .'

Charlie does not finish the sentence, but it doesn't matter; Jon already knows what is coming next.

'Really?'

Again: silence.

'Every second you were out there,' Jon breathes, 'weren't you thinking about this?' He opens his hands, taking in the warehouses, the red bricks, the slates, the snow. 'Weren't you thinking about your parents?'

Charlie nods.

'And if you could go back, but never saw your mother again . . .'

The boy's face twitches in an exact impersonation of a fat little boy Jon used to love.

'I know, Charlie,' says Jon, wrapping his arm, for the first time, around the boy.

He thinks: you want and you want and you want – and then, when you get back home, you keep on wanting.

'Do *you* want to . . .'

'Go back home?' asks Jon.

'I don't think I'd like it if you went back home, Mr Heather.'

'Charlie boy,' says Jon, 'we're in this mess together.'

They begin to wander back through the warehouses, over the rise, back to the kerb where they left the car.

'You've got to pick and choose, I suppose,' says Jon. 'Try and forget the nasty bits and remember the good. You don't have to forget your friends. You don't have to forget George. But Judah Reed and old McAllister and hazings and . . .' He stops. 'Well, it's OK to forget those.'

'That's a bit of a lie though, isn't it? Just picking and choosing?'

'But only a little lie. You're allowed to tell little lies.'

High on the kerb, they meet Captain Matthews by the Mini.

'We're here now, Charlie boy. We've got to make a good fist of what we've got in England.'

Captain Matthews opens the door – Charlie is to be allowed to ride up-front – and ruffles his hair.

'That's what they told us to do in Australia, Mr Heather,' Charlie says as he climbs in. 'Why was it so wrong in Australia but OK here?'

It is not right that such a childish question should be able to crush a grown man.

'I don't know,' says Jon, and slides into the back seat.

When they reach Charlie's street, Captain Matthews slows the car to a crawl, letting the boy chatter with Jon, listing the things they both know from that faraway world. If Jon were to tell his friends from work where he has been, they would screw up their eyes and look at him as if he is bereft of all sense: a man, they would say, should not enjoy the company of schoolboys; not a *real* man. But fuck it: Jon Heather knows he isn't a real man. He's got more in common with this lonesome little boy than he does with those men he goes drinking with, who talk about football and girls. This boy is more his family than his nephew or his sisters or even his own mother.

Before Charlie has clambered out of the car, a porch light flares, the door flies open, and a man barrels out. 'Inside!' he barks.

Charlie does not even have time to say goodbye before he is bustled through the gate of the yard to find his mother.

The man has his hands on the car door before Jon can spring out.

'I don't want any trouble,' Captain Matthews says. 'We found your boy . . .'

'Has he been with you all this time? His mother was worried sick . . .'

'He's fine,' says Jon, standing. 'He just wanted . . .'

'Look, we're grateful. We *thank you*. Is that what you want to hear? You saw him right out there, and you saw him right until he could get back to us. But that's *all*.' He stresses the last word like an oath. 'We don't want you coming round here. All you do is remind him. We want him to forget.'

Jon's eyes find the man's. He had wanted to stay silent, but he can't do it. 'He won't forget. The more you forbid him, the more he tries, the more it'll still be there. You can't stop it from having happened. He'll end up hating you for it.' Jon breathes out. 'He'll end up hating himself.'

The man's hand falls away. Perhaps it is only the rain driving him back, but Jon thinks something else has softened too.

'He's home now . . . Isn't that enough?' With a lingering look, Jon drops back into the car. 'You can never really go back home.'

'But . . . where does that leave us, Mr Heather?'

Jon slams the door shut, squints up through the window and driving rain. 'With a little boy to love,' he says, as if it were the most obvious thing on earth.

Past his stepfather, Jon sees Charlie on the doorstep. Headlights illuminate the boy, his mother's hand balanced delicately on his shoulder. Charlie wears an odd half-smile.

'And you, Mr Heather?' Charlie's stepfather asks. 'Where does that leave you?'

Jon Heather uncrumples the letter from George and spreads it out on the back of the seat in front. Rain trickles through the window to smudge the words: a little girl on her way back home. First there was one; then a second; perhaps it really can be as the wild boy once dreamed: the real Children's Crusade, leading children back to the place they belong.

'I think there's only one thing good enough for me,' he says, and the car rolls down the road.

*

Christmas, a little boy once knew, is a time of miracles and a time of family.

On Christmas morning, Jon Heather leaves the bedsit early, his swag bag packed with presents. The streets, half given over to students from the colleges, are empty and he walks alone.

He reaches his mother's street. Neighbours shriek their Christmas tidings to each other above his head, and by the time he reaches the door he has received a flurry of good wishes himself. When he thinks of Australia now, there is only one Christmas he remembers. Christmases with scrub turkey in the Mission, Christmases with Peter out in the bush, Christmases in prison with countless Aussie brawlers crooning 'Silent Night' – all of them are forgotten; he thinks only of Broome.

This time, he knocks. It is Benjamin who answers. He stands there, frozen, as if terrified Jon might be about to produce a Christmas rabbit and kill it on the doorstep. Then he scampers back inside, shouting for his mother. Samantha appears soon after, a glass in hand.

'Jon,' she says, 'we didn't know if you'd . . .'

She dangles an arm around his shoulder and whisks him through into the front-room, where a table has been set. There are three children here today, though who the other two are Jon Heather does not know. At the sink in the kitchen, his mother turns. She trembles, rips off rubber gloves, dumps them, without looking, into a tray of potatoes.

'Happy Christmas, Jon . . .'

Today they do not talk about Australia. Today nobody asks, are there bush blacks? Are there kangaroos? Are the stars different on that side of the world? Today there are presents.

At the tree, before dinner, Jon Heather empties out his swag. He has never bought presents before and admits, as the awkwardly wrapped packages cascade around, that he had absolutely no idea what he should buy. There are bottles of brandy, smelling salts, a picture frame without a picture.

When it comes to Benjamin's turn, there are only two packages left in the swag. The boy must have forgiven him for murdering all those helpless bunnies, because he inches forward on his knees, peering into the swag bag as if it is some bottomless well where treasures might be found.

'Can I?' he asks.

Jon hesitates before nodding. He had come here thinking that both presents were for the boy, but now he knows better; he lifts up the swag in such a way that Benjamin can reach only the first. Eagerly, he rips open the paper to find a model plane.

'Is it like the one that brought you from Australia?' he asks.

'No,' Jon laughs. 'It's like the ones that dropped bombs all over this city.'

Dinner is a round of crackers being pulled and carols being sung. Jon Heather does, at least, know Christmas carols, even if the tunes seem dull and pompous to his ears. He remembers Christmas pudding from being a boy and watches, incredulous, as everybody wolfs it back; he has never tasted a more disgusting thing in his life – and Jon Heather has eaten his fair share of uncooked kangaroo.

After dinner, the children play. Jon stands at the window and watches. In the street, wrapped up in mittens and scarves, Benjamin flies his model plane, even though it is still in its box. Jon looks at his feet, the open swag that's lying there, the unopened present within.

It has, he decides, been altogether better than the last time he came to this house. There has been no screaming. There have been no tears. And yet – that is all it has been.

'Mother,' he says, taking up the swag. 'It's been . . . a pleasure.'

His mother and sisters stop their chattering as he goes to the door. One after another, they leap up and cover him in kisses.

'You'll come again?' his mother asks.

Jon Heather nods, returning her hug. Yes, he'll come again. One day, he hopes, he'll even want to.

Once he has reached the end of the street, he begins to run. He kicks his legs wildly, skids in the slush, careens until he is running in the shadow of the moor. Soon his legs are heavy, but still he ploughs on. He is running, now, like a man who doesn't care: a drunkard who, summoning some hidden reserve of strength, wills himself home. Over the broad thoroughfares he goes, along terraces where Christmas lights are strung, round the curve of a green where patches of snow still glow across the grass.

At last, he slows. He counts the houses until he is certain he has the right one. Then he gazes up: there are lights hanging in the window and, through net curtains, a Christmas tree lit up with baubles. It has already been Christmas on the other side of the world, he remembers. For them, Christmas day has been and gone. He pictures them gathered at Black Chaparral, at Broome, at Rebekkah's home in Kununurra.

He thinks of the little boys at the Mission at Christmas: toys whittled out of wood and scrub turkey for dinner. He thinks of George, alone in the sandstone huts.

On the doorstep, Jon Heather opens his swag and produces the present. He knocks on the door, watches it pull back to reveal Charlie's beaming face. Without a word, he hands over the gift. In seconds, the boy has torn off the paper. And there, soft and springy in Charlie's hands, is a toy kangaroo, shiny black eyes, a curious joey peeking out of its pouch.

'Thank you, Mr Heather,' he beams. 'Did you . . .' He pauses. '. . . want to come in? I'm sure they wouldn't mind. Not after . . .'

Christmas, a little boy once knew, is a time of miracles and a time of family.

After all of these years, it turns out the little boy was right.

*

On the 20th of January in the year of 1966, Jon Heather makes the long march into Chapeltown, where the Home waits like a sleeping giant. On the step, two boys are rubbing sticks together but not making any fire. He sees Captain Matthews'

Mini parked beneath the overhang of the very same window he used to look out of at night.

'What are you doing here?' pipes up one of the boys.

'Looking for a friend,' Jon Heather replies.

He expects a familiar face when he knocks at the door, but not this one. The man introduces himself as Martin.

'It's been a long time, Jon Heather,' he says.

Jon nods – though, in truth, he cannot place the face or the name.

'George is here?'

'He got in last night.'

Martin takes him to the office where George is sorting out Judah Reed's cabinets and shelves. He expects memories to rampage at him as he walks that familiar hallway, but there is nothing. All the same, he walks the corridor with a horrible emptiness. It was easy when there was Judah Reed to hate. You could lie in bed and imagine him coming to lead you away for a beating. You could remember being tied up to a tree and told to take your medicine. It was easier, too, to imagine you were trapped in Australia, fighting the valiant fight to put right what they did wrong. That way, you had a story and you had to give it a happy ending – or else perish in the attempt. Now it is different: you've got your happy ending; all you have to do is find a way to live with it.

Jon stops at the open door, reaches out and knocks. He sees that the office is not nearly as big as he remembered it. Up on the wall, the tapestry of the Children's Crusade still hangs – but it seems a silly thing now, a stupid patchwork.

Paunchy George Stone is straining over a box when Jon appears, his sleeves rolled up and his cheeks ruddy red.

At first, they only mutter hellos. Then, propelled by some unseen hand, Jon launches forward and throws his arms around George, pulling back only when the fat man starts to splutter into his shoulder.

Embarrassed, George stares at his shoes.

'Where is she?' asks Jon.

'She's playing with some of the little ones,' George replies. 'Captain Matthews is with her.'

'And?' Jon holds out a scrap of paper for George to take.

'Is it far?' George asks, reading the address. 'I don't know Leeds very well, Jon . . .'

'Nowhere's very far in England, Georgie boy. Take a few short steps and you're off the end of the map.'

George stands. 'It's hellish good to see you, Jon Heather.'

'Hellish good? You've been seeing something of Peter, haven't you?'

George bounds to the desk, lifts up a little cardboard suitcase and ferrets inside. 'Here,' he says, 'I brought them for you . . .'

He hands over a stack of photographs: wheat farms and vivid blue skies; sand the colour of rust and beaches of untarnished white. In the first, Pete and Maya Slade stare into the camera, with their baby between them. It is somewhere at the back of Black Chaparral, the height of summer.

'I've got more,' George begins. 'I mean, if you want them . . .'

And there she stands: the girl from the Old Arabia. Pete and Maya Slade are with her, sitting together on the old dirt oval. Dog has his head resting in her lap.

Jon Heather's eyes glimmer oddly, so that George knows something is wrong. He has the photograph between forefinger and thumb and suddenly it starts to crease, as if he is holding on to it too tight. 'When was this?' he asks.

'This Christmas,' says George. 'It's a place called Broome. Peter had it in mind to visit, on the way up to see his sister. Said it was a place you went, back when you were . . .'

'She looks . . .' He wants to say she does not look real, but he thinks: she was the only thing I wanted to be real in the whole bastard country. Instead, he settles for 'older'.

George creeps around him, so that he can peer over Jon's shoulder, try and see exactly what Jon sees in the picture.

'Do you remember,' Jon whispers, 'when I came back to the Mission, when I was thinking . . . I could stay?'

George nods.

'She was like that, George. It felt the same with her. I could have stayed and been happy with her. I almost did.'

'Jon Heather, you're kidding yourself! You? Happy? Without coming back here?'

Jon takes the photograph, folds it to put it in his back pocket. He is about to hand the rest back when George stops him.

'Pete said you were to keep this one.'

Jon takes the second photograph. It is an ordinary thing, red rocks and azure water, and it takes him a moment to understand what he is looking at. It is Anastasia's Pool, the head of Cable Beach. Megan is not in the shot but she is surely the one holding the camera; Jon Heather can see a shadow, and he is certain it is her.

On the rocks at the pool's edge there sits an open suitcase. He has to squint, but now he is certain: that suitcase once belonged to him. Inside there are piled the books he dragged from one end of the country to the other. He can make few of them out – but, sitting on top of the pile, there peers out a torn dustjacket, children clambering off a train stranded in snow.

Jon turns the photograph over. On the back there is writing. It is made up like a postcard, a line drawn neatly down the middle with a stamp at the top – 'Australia, 13c', with a black and white seabird strutting across the frame – and, beneath that, a simple address: *Jon Heather, ENGLAND!!!* The last word is written in big bold letters and underlined. Somebody, it seems, was excited to write the word.

Jon knows it is Megan's hand. On the left side of the postcard she begins:

I read them, Jon. Every last one.

George sees a strange smile burst onto Jon Heather's face. 'What is it, Jon?'

'It's a telephone number.'

He turns the photograph back over, sees the books lying there: a little piece of England in the great vastness of Australia; a little piece of the real Jon Heather left behind in Broome.

'That's all?'

Jon Heather thinks: that's everything.

George rounds the table and leaves the office. Jon, still soaking in the image, committing the number to memory, is slow to follow.

The reception hall is cluttered with boxes, but they clamber over them and climb up the stairs. The dormitory where they once slept is empty but for two boys, one lying at either end. Jon pauses in the doorway and says hello. The closest boy has his head buried in a comic book, but he looks up when Jon appears, as if he is expecting somebody else.

He realizes he has been standing there too long; George is almost at the other end of the corridor.

'Georgie boy,' he calls out. 'Are they being sent over?'

'Some of them, Jon Heather. I'm trying my best. I'm making them all keep notebooks, just the same as Charlie. I'm keeping names and addresses like Judah Reed never did, every scrap of information I can find. But . . .'

'It's not easy, is it?'

George stops, shuffles awkwardly. 'Thank you, Jon Heather.'

'It's just something Peter said to me. You're older and it doesn't have to be perfect anymore . . .'

'I'll get some of them back home, Jon, I promise. But there'll be others . . .'

Jon nods, thinking suddenly of those aboriginal girls with

Pete and Cormac Tate. 'You make sure you stay in that Mission, Georgie. I wouldn't trust any other bastard to do it right.'

Through a door at the end of the corridor, a group of boys and a single little girl sit ranged around an old man who reads from a book of fables.

'Her grandmother thought she had been adopted,' Jon whispers, eyes finding the girl.

George breathes deeply. 'So did my mother,' he says.

'You've seen her?'

'She's in London. We've . . . spoken. I was afraid, Jon.' His eyes, jittery already, refuse to meet Jon's.

'Go to her,' says Jon. 'See her.'

'I might not like what I find.'

Jon says, 'You might not hate it either.'

'Not yet, Jon Heather. Not while there's work to do . . .' In the room, Captain Matthews looks upwards involuntarily. He nods at George and begins to close the storybook, battling off a chorus of cries. 'I've got to go back to the Mission, Jon. I can't leave them alone. I could use your help in England, but . . . You could have it all. If it's England you want, if it's Australia, it's yours.'

Jon shakes his head. 'I'm staying here, George.'

George moves as if he might pluck the photograph of Megan out of Jon's pocket. 'What about her?'

'Maybe I could go back to Broome,' he says. 'Or maybe I could work with Peter and Cormac out at Black Chaparral. Maybe that *is* home.' He pauses, thinks about Charlie, the girl in the room, all the other ones who might one day find their way back. 'But if I wasn't with them, I wouldn't be me. And damn it, George, but I'm going to be me.'

He thinks – in the end, the Children's Crusade really did win. You kicked and you fought and scratched and bit and every time they told you you were one thing, you thundered back that you were the other. But you couldn't stop them changing you, any more than you could step out of your own skin; without Judah Reed, without Tommy Crowe, without bedwetters and dormitories and McAllister and his goats, you wouldn't even be Jon Heather.

Then he thinks – but if you weren't Jon Heather, those boys and girls would be alone. If you weren't Jon Heather, you'd be useless. You're Jon Heather, and you're going to make a good fist of what you've got.

'Do you remember the wild boy, George?'

George nods.

'There's a thing he said to me. He was going to leave footprints, ones only little boys and girls could see, and we were all going to follow them, all the way back to London and Malta and Leeds, all the places we were taken from. Every boy to be the boy they want to be, and not a single boy left behind.' Jon trembles at the memory. He was eleven years old again, cradling his feral friend in the scrub. 'He was a little boy, and that's what he was dreaming. How could I be a grown man and dream of anything less?'

Storytime over, Captain Matthews takes Martha Gray by the hand and tells her it is time. She nods, matter-of-factly, and scuttles past George and Jon Heather to find her coat in the dormitory.

Slowly, George and Jon follow. As George hurries down the stairs, whisking Martha along, Jon remains at the top. Here is the banister from which he first spied Judah Reed; there is the door to the closet where he hid to read his book and, instead, found a best friend. Suddenly, he grins, wildly and without thought. His mother, his sisters, the house where he grew up – all of that is dust. This is where his real memories begin.

'Jon Heather!' George calls. 'This little girl hasn't got all day!'

Jon drops down the staircase and crosses the hall. Before he opens the door, he sees a big winter coat lying in a crumpled heap among piles of boxes. It is January, he thinks; it is winter.

He beats the dust from it and slips inside. To his surprise, it fits perfectly. Cold wind rips across him as he steps through the doors of the Home.

'Are you ready?'

George hops from foot to foot to ward off the cold, nodding sharply at Captain Matthews, who slides into the front seat of the car and coaxes the engine to life.

'What was it like,' George asks, 'when you took Charlie back?'

'It was,' Jon proclaims, 'a sorry mess.'

George nods, as if he expects nothing else. 'Then I'm ready.'

Together they hurry to the car. As George takes his seat up-front, Jon Heather slides in beside the girl, making certain that her coat is buttoned up tight.

Jon takes the photograph out of his back pocket and cannot but grin. There are two rooms, one at this end of the earth and one at the other, but the world is getting smaller; perhaps there can be a tunnel between the two. He wonders what she has been doing since that last night in Broome, how many wayfarers she has taken pity on, how many men she has accompanied on long walks along Cable Beach. He supposes he'll have to get a telephone now.

The engine sputters and the car wheels around, rising slowly through the skeleton trees to leave the Home behind.

'Are we all going home now?' the girl asks.

'Some of us,' says Jon Heather.

Once, there was a boy who ran away. He ran as far as he could run, and when he could run no more, he burrowed down into the baked red earth. There he stayed, perfectly preserved, not growing any bigger, not getting a single day older – until, one day, tired of being alone, he simply rose from the redness and started to live.

AUTHOR'S NOTE

In late 2010, I was travelling in Western Australia, researching the novel that would become *Little Exiles*. I had known of the story of forced child migration for many years, and had had my eyes opened to the policy's broader issues by Margaret Humphrey's heartbreaking memoir, *Empty Cradles*, and David Hill's honest account of his own experiences in *The Forgotten Children*. Yet, one incident – among a number of months researching in archives, speaking to child migrants, and exploring the landscapes in which the novel would be set – stays with me more than any other.

I had been staying in Perth and had been alerted to a school south of the city to which child migrants were sent. Soon to be turned into a function centre, the school nevertheless had archives of its time as a home for child migrants that might have been invaluable for my research. An appointment was made to look through the archives, and I made the three hour drive to visit the centre. Yet, upon my arrival, before I had finished introducing myself, the lady who had greeted me simply said: 'You should know that we didn't abuse a single child here.' She went on to tell me that there were many more interesting novels to be written, and in particular impressed upon me the urgent need for a novel chronicling the good works Catholic missionaries had undertaken with Australian aborigines in the north of the state. It was this moment, perhaps more than any other, that solidified my sense that this was a novel worth writing: there is something simmering beneath the surface of this history that provokes heated opinion, fierce criticism and defiance. On that day, there felt, to me, a sense of hostility – and, above all else, a questioning of why I wanted to rake up a past best left buried. History, for some, should remain history – but already I knew that there were others out there for whom that history was a living thing, never to be buried or forgotten.

Child migration as a policy has its roots in much earlier times than the story of *Little Exiles*. Our first record of the forcible shipping of orphaned children to Britain's old colonies is from 1618, with the transportation of more than a hundred vagrant children to the new colony of Virginia. In the nineteenth century, schemes were devised to send children to Australia, Canada and Rhodesia. Yet, for all the injustice of those periods, for me, the history of child migration reached its horrifying zenith in the years following the Second World War – when Britain's government, at the same time as proudly founding a 'welfare state', looked the other way as charitable organisations schemed to send children abroad, often by systematically telling them their parents were dead and that better lives awaited. If the argument, as members of the Children's Crusade in *Little Exiles* would express, was that the organisations schemed only in the service of a greater good, then there is still no accounting for the criminal lack of care, hardship, and abuses – psychological and physical, as well as sexual – that many of these children suffered on arrival in their new, better lives; nor can there be any doubt that, in many cases, these children carry scars, much deeper than those that Jon Heather wears, to this very day.

Little Exiles is an act of fiction, and the characters and institutions that it portrays – while based on historical fact – can only ever be recreations of a world that I, with my happy childhood, have never experienced. But I dedicate it to those who shared their stories with me and hope that it does justice to the experiences you all shared.